Tyce this is your book.
Thanks for being such a sweet boy. I love hanging out with you,
watching you play lacrosse, and listening to all the facts you know
about animals.
You'll always be my Tyce-Bear.

THE
Holiday
STAND -IN

KORTNEY KEISEL

First edition November 2023

Cover design by Melody Jeffries Design

www.kortneykeisel.com

one

SUMMER

NOEL.

Star.

Eve.

Belle.

Ivy.

Holly.

Or even Mary (if you're feeling religious) would've been more appropriate than what my parents named their December 24th baby.

Nothing says the holidays, snow, or Christmas magic like the name Summer.

Summer.

Seriously?

I blame my very non-Christmasy name for why my boyfriend hasn't fully grasped my obsession with Christmas. Okay, obsession might be too strong of a word. It's not like I keep decorations up year-round or sleep with a stuffed elf. I just like the season and *all* the events leading up to it. Plus, it's my birthday month, so this time of year is extra special to me.

So it's more like enthusiasm.

I am enthusiastic about Christmastime.

Who isn't?

But if my parents had named me something more festive, this revelation wouldn't be a revelation at all. It would just be common knowledge, something Justin would have anticipated and planned for. Nobody expects Summer Stanworth to be obsessed with Christmas and everything leading up to it. But if my name had been *Angel* Stanworth, well then, that's par for the course.

And it's not like Justin doesn't know I like Christmas. We've been dating for nine months. I've dropped hints here and there and plan to fully reveal my love for the holidays during the next few weeks. I'm not hiding anything. I'm easing him into it slowly, which is more than my brother-in-law Rick did when it came to his passion for hunting.

Juliet met Rick in December, married him by July, and BAM! By the end of August, he was gone hunting every single weekend. She had no clue. Completely in the dark about the fact that the man she married would be absent from mid-August through November, chasing after animals. Going on a family trip in the fall? Forget about it. Having an October baby? Only if Juliet wants me holding her hand at the birth instead of Rick. That, my friends, is why you date someone through all four seasons before you get engaged and marry them.

Christmas just happens to be the last season Justin and I have to go through, and if all goes well—assuming he can handle my holiday enthusiasm—an engagement is on the horizon. I mean, I'm *hoping* an engagement is on the horizon. Ever since I was a little girl, all I really wanted was to get married and start my own family. And I will. This will be my last holiday season as a single woman. I'm manifesting.

Do you know what else is on the horizon?

Thanksgiving.

Which kicks off the beginning of a month-long celebration full of family traditions, Christmas parties, and holiday events. Meaning, I can't hide my obsession any longer. It's about to slap us in the face. If I'm being honest, our *other* problems are about to slap us in the face as well because you can't tell your workaholic boyfriend about your calendar full of activities during his busiest time of year and have him be excited about it.

Can you?

Because if you *can*, I'd like to know exactly how you do it without starting World War Three.

"Summer?" Justin's voice cuts through my no-vacancy stare.

I knock myself out of my Christmas trance and blink back at him. I expect his light eyes to drill me, but his attention is on his computer. Maybe he didn't say my name...but I swear he did.

"Sorry." I don't know why I'm apologizing. Lately, that's become my MO. I stare at him, waiting for him to expound or look at me. "Justin, did you say my name?"

"Yeah." He finally looks up, nodding to the stack beside me. "Can you pass me that file over there?"

"Sure." I hand him the manila folder, hoping to catch his eye, but his gaze goes right back to his laptop. It's funny how someone can sit right next to you at a kitchen table yet feel so far away.

Where most couples spend Friday evenings eating takeout and binge-watching a show while cuddling on the couch, Justin and I work. It wasn't always this way. When we first started dating, we used to laugh and play and have so much fun I had a perma-smile on my face. We did normal stuff like going to movies, hiking in the mountains, and hanging out with friends. We were great together—the whole this-is-the-one complete fairytale. That honeymoon phase where you eat, breathe, and live for the other person were some of the best times of my dating life. Then we both got busy with work.

Justin has his blanket business, and I have property management.

Romantic, right?

My boss offloaded a bunch of responsibilities onto me. Justin went on *Shark Tank,* striking a deal with Lori, launching his All-Weather Blanket from obscurity into high demand, and that's when the craziness set in. Our relationship has been running on fumes for the last four months. But it's just temporary. 'A short-term problem for long-term stability'—Justin's favorite line.

I close my laptop and push it to the side, sitting up with a newfound energy. "Let's do something! We could binge-watch every *National Lampoon's Vacation* movie or at least watch through *Christmas Vacation* because that's the best one."

I stare at Justin, waiting for some kind of acknowledgment that he heard me. The soft glow from his computer screen does all sorts of good things for his handsome face. It brightens his light-blue eyes and illuminates the stubble on his usually smooth jaw. This is my favorite version of him, with his sleeves rolled up to his elbows, his styled brown hair falling out of its perfect place, and wrinkles creasing the front of his button-down.

"Or we could go to one of the fancy resorts and sneak into their hot tub." My eyes brighten. "Ooooh, let's do that!" My fingers tickle his arm in what I hope is a seductive way, not an itsy-bitsy-spider way. "I can wear that hot-pink bikini you like so much, and we can gaze up at the stars and watch our breath in the cold air."

His gaze moves from the sheet of numbers on the screen to me. "Huh?"

"Let's go hot tubbing," I repeat with the same enthusiastic smile that's gone unnoticed.

"What time is it?" He checks his Apple watch. "Eh, it's only ten twenty-five. I can't go hot tubbing. I still have a couple of hours here. But you can go without me."

My chin drops. "Sneak into a resort and go hot tubbing by myself?"

I hate being alone more than I hate spiders, snakes, nails on chalkboards, and creepy men in dark hallways. Mottos like 'it takes two' and the buddy system are what I live for. They are creeds I base my entire life around.

"It wouldn't be fun to sneak in by myself."

"Babe..." Justin glances over all the work in front of him and shrugs like he has no choice in the matter.

"That's okay. We'll do it another time." I stand, keeping my voice upbeat as I pack my things. "Work hard now so we can play even harder next week, right?" I'm inwardly congratulating myself on my passive—yet smooth—transition into the conversation I've been avoiding.

His eyes bounce from the screen to me. "What?"

"Well"—I drag my fingers through my hair, flipping half my blonde bob over past the middle part, creating a wave—"tomorrow marks the beginning of the holiday season."

"It's still November."

"Yeah, but tomorrow is the last Saturday in November, and that's when my family goes to Irvine Ranch to cut down a tree." Justin doesn't seem to remember, so I continue. "My dad built their barn, so now he's best buddies with Bob, the owner."

"Right." He nods in recollection. "Bob Irvine."

"We go early to get the first pick on the best Christmas trees before everyone else. Plus, this year, my dad thinks he has a great idea for how Bob should arrange the trees."

"Do you think Bob Irvine would want to sell the All-Weather Blanket at his ranch?" It's the first time Justin has looked excited during this whole conversation. "I bet people would go crazy for my blankets in his gift shop."

"Maybe." I give a hopeful shrug. "We can ask him tomorrow when we go to his ranch to pick out a tree with my family."

Justin's excited expression crumbles like a broken candy cane. "I can't go tomorrow. I have so much work to do. You'll have to ask Bob Irvine for me."

This is a negotiation. I can give him tree hunting in exchange for everything next week.

"Okay, well. What about next week? It's Thanksgiving." I casually place my hand on his shoulder and massage, as if I can relax him into being excited about the upcoming parties. "Wednesday night is our annual Turkey Stuff, then Thanksgiving dinner on Thursday, the Christmas light parade on Friday, and turkey flautas on Saturday."

And that's just the next seven days.

Justin's brows skyrocket. "There's an activity every night?"

"No, Sunday, Monday, and Tuesday are free." More sweet smiling with a tone that's an octave higher than my regular voice.

"That's still a lot."

I drop into my chair again, placing my hand on his forearm to ease the blow of what I'm about to say. "This is my favorite time of year."

"I know. You've told me that before."

"No, I don't think you do *know*." I scratch the back of my head, causing my wave of hair to slowly fall back into its parted place, piece by piece. "I've been sheltering you from the truth since we met." I suck in a deep breath for this next part. "I'm Summer Stanworth, and I'm addicted to Christmas."

Justin's lips quirk. "Yeah, I know. You always talk about Christmas, and you've been wearing festive earrings since September first."

"Don't be ridiculous. I always wait until after Labor Day to wear my holiday earrings." A self-conscious hand lightly touches the dangling peppermint hanging from my ear. "But you don't *really* get it. I've shown you a watered-down version of my love. I've been holding back so you don't think I'm crazy. But now the truth has to come out." The faster I talk, the more hand gestures I use. "I've been obsessed with Christmastime since I was a little girl. I think about it all year long. I begin calendaring holiday events in July. I buy presents for my family in August. Start wearing earrings in September. Decorate in October." I pause briefly to see if Justin has figured out that the overload of Christmas decorations is why we haven't gone to my apartment in the last month and a half. He seems unfazed by that piece of information, so I keep going. "And I start listening to Christmas music in November. But the celebration really begins the Saturday before Thanksgiving at Bob Irvine's ranch. From that moment until December twenty-sixth, I'm like a sponge, soaking in all the Christmas spirit I can. That means I go to every family party and town event that Telluride has to offer, and if I'm double-booked or miss something, I have debilitating FOMO and feel like my Christmas season is ruined. So there it is." I puff out a breath. "I'm a yulephile."

He squints as if he's processing my confession. "A yulephile?"

"Yes, a lover of Christmas."

The corner of his mouth lifts. "It's definitely better than a pedophile."

"This isn't funny." I slump back in my chair. "It's more than just an obsession with a holiday. This time of year holds the happiest moments of my life. Christmas is when you're with the ones you love. I literally take that to heart. The family together-ness is what I live for. The memories of this season keep me sane for the rest of the year. I love my family and being with them, and I'm looking for someone who loves all of that as much as I do and will be *with* me the entire time."

He grabs my hand, running his thumb over my knuckles. "I'm that guy."

"You are?" Why does my voice sound so surprised by that?

"Yeah, of course."

"Right. Of course you're that guy." Tension releases with my breath. "I guess I've just been stressed about telling you all this, because I know how busy you are. And my love for Christmas and family togetherness can be a lot for some people."

Justin laughs, drawing my eyes to his cute smile. "As long as you're not sleeping with an inflatable Frosty the Snowman instead of me, I think I can handle a little Christmas spirit. I don't know why you were so worried to tell me. I'm not the Grinch. I love the holidays too, and my family has traditions."

"I don't know why I was stressed either."

Maybe it's because, lately, I've been going stag to all my family parties before this.

I mute those thoughts, refusing to dwell on our past problems. "So we're on for all the Thanksgiving festivities next week?"

"Oh, no, I didn't say that." He nods at his computer. "This week is crazy. I have to prep for our Black Friday sale. I'm expecting thousands of orders the day after Thanksgiving. You know how perfect the blankets are for Christmas presents."

"I thought maybe you could take a break this week, find some time for *us*. Especially now that I explained how important being with my family is this time of year."

"Sum Sum, I just don't see how I can." I hate it when Justin calls me *Sum Sum*, but I hate it even more when he pairs it with disappointing me. "I'm sure I can duck out for a few hours to eat Thanksgiving dinner, but otherwise, I'll be swamped all week."

"But you missed my family Halloween party."

"Because we'd just aired the QVC infomercial."

"I know, but you promised to come to my next family party."

He squeezes my hand. "From the sound of things, there will be a family party every day leading up to Christmas. I'll go to something later in the month when things calm down."

"But what if they don't calm down? Later, you'll be busy filling orders from the Black Friday sale. And after that, it will be the rush to get blankets in the mail so they can arrive before Christmas."

"Then I'll come to a family event in January." He shrugs as if it's all so simple, and maybe it is *simple* to someone else—someone who doesn't love my family and Christmas like I do.

"But my sister, Erin, will be in town this week with my nieces, Cora and Berkley. I wanted you to meet them."

My family is not complete without Erin and Tommy and their girls. I mean, Erin is my steady sister. She just does life right. I've looked up to her since I was a little girl, and ever since she moved, I only get to see her a few times a year. We have to make the most of her visits.

"She's the one that lives in Denver, right?"

"Justin, we've been dating for nine months, and you barely know my family."

He pulls his hand away, rubbing it across his forehead. "I don't have time to fight about this right now." There's a tiredness behind his words that I relate to. It's exhausting having this same argument over and over or ignoring the argument because there's never a fair way to resolve it. Or because we're too busy to get to the bottom of it.

"I'm not trying to fight. I just..." My words dangle between us like the problem itself.

It's just temporary.

Things will get better when his business is more established.

His drive and ambition are what you love about him.

Being in a relationship is a give and take, and right now, it's your turn to give a little more.

We're great together, and we will be again when the dust settles.

Once he gets to know your family, he'll love them and vice versa.

I've repeated those words so many times over the last nine months that I don't think I'm even hearing them anymore.

"Listen"—he shifts his eyes back to me—"I'm not trying to disappoint you. I'm just really busy right now and need to focus on my business. I'm not saying that your traditions are stupid or that I don't want to get to know your family. I'm just saying I have to work to build a future so that, one day, I can provide for a family. Be patient with me while I do that."

My eyes drop. I'm usually pretty understanding of Justin's work schedule and everything he's putting into his business to make it successful. It's admirable, but that doesn't mean there's not an aching in my chest. It doesn't mean I don't hate the canyon in our relationship and that we're standing on opposite sides of the divide with no easy or fair way to meet in the middle or close off the gulf.

He hooks his finger under my chin, lifting my eyes to meet his. "What are you thinking?"

"Just how hard it is to be patient when I want you all to

myself this holiday season."

His thumb drifts across my cheek, and his lips hitch in a perfectly charming way. "Aren't I worth the wait?"

I begrudgingly smile while I roll my eyes. "Yes, you are."

He is. I know he is. That's what everyone else doesn't see— what an incredibly sweet, kind man he is.

"Then can you share me with work the next few weeks even though you love this time of year with your family more than anything else?"

My shoulders sink. I'm a toddler, pouting because my mom won't let me eat dessert before my string beans. I don't want to be this needy woman. I want to be the kind of girlfriend who supports my man no matter what, because Justin is a good guy— the best guy I've ever dated. Don't sacrifice what you want most in life for what you want right now, and a future with Justin is what I want most. So I can't screw up the best relationship I've ever been in because I'm not getting *all* the attention. Being patient this holiday season is key to making us last.

I just have to keep reminding myself that.

Every. Single. Day.

"You're right." I muster a smile. "You need to work. It's unfair of me to ask you to take so much time off right now. I mean, these are just silly holiday traditions that shouldn't mean so much to a twenty-six-year-old. I can go alone."

I'll hate every second of it, but I can do it.

"Your traditions aren't silly. I love that you care so much about them and your family and want me there." My smile lifts a little with his words. "Like you said, you love this. So I want you to go and enjoy yourself tomorrow at the tree farm. You don't need me there to have a good time. You'll have your sisters. Plus, it's better if I work so I can take more time off on Thanksgiving Day. Okay?"

Right. I'll have my sisters. So I won't be *alone* alone.

"Okay." I nod, pushing the smile on my face even wider.

But nothing about me feels okay.

SUMMER

"TAG! YOU'RE IT!" My nephew Jack touches my arm before running away. I'm left with no choice but to chase after him and my other nieces and nephews. They weave in and out of picnic tables, dodging my efforts. I'm surprisingly out of shape for someone who has an active gym membership, but maybe it's the slushy snow on the ground that's to blame. I have to work twice as hard for every step I take.

I wrap my arms around Max. "Got you! Max is it now. Aunt Summer's going to go take a break."

"Nooo!" Peter whines from across the parking lot.

"I'll play again. I just need to catch my breath first."

I walk to the table where my sisters and parents sit, drinking hot cocoa from the ranch gift shop.

"I told Bob that leaning the trees up against the barn will show them off more." My dad's opinions on how Bob Irvine should run his ranch go well beyond his place as a friend. He gestures to the row of fifteen pine trees that the ranch employees spent the last hour dragging over to the barn and lining up. "He'll see. This is how you sell Christmas trees."

My mom lifts her brows, hiking them way up on her forehead

—so high that they disappear under her silvery-blonde bangs. "Marty, Bob Irvine does not care about what you think."

"Well, he should. I've lived in Telluride for twenty-seven years." I smile at my dad, knowing how much his pride in Telluride means to him. He nods back at me in his cheery way, and I'm reminded once again how he'd make the perfect Santa Claus, minus the white hair and beard. He has the round belly and the twinkle in his eye, but I guess the similarities stop there.

"Bob Irvine has lived in Telluride his entire life," my sister Anna says as she glances at her boys. "Peter! Jack! Stop running around. You're going to break something." Her eyes dart to her husband, Jeff. He's sitting at the brother-in-law's table a few feet away, holding their baby, Lucy. "Can you gain control of the boys?"

"They're playing tag." Jeff shrugs, but after a pointed look from Anna, he changes his tune. "Boys, you heard your mother. Stop running around."

The kids ignore him, and Jeff goes back to his riveting conversation with Tommy and Brian.

"I dated Bob Irvine!" We all glance at my great-aunt, Carma. I thought she was asleep this whole time. It's hard to tell with the giant black sunglasses covering most of her face. "Good kisser." She says the entire thing without moving her body.

"It wasn't Bob." My mom leans into her. "It was his dad, Kenneth Irvine."

Aunt Carma whips her head to her. "Are you telling me I don't know who I kissed?"

My mom shakes her head like it's useless to try and talk some sense into her. Now that my grandma died, we're all my Aunt Carma has left. She moved in with my parents earlier this year, and now we've adopted her into our family full time.

"Dad, Justin was wondering if Bob Irvine could sell some of his All-Weather Blankets in his gift shop. Do you think I should ask him?"

"Ask your mother." My dad looks directly at my mom before

flipping his newspaper in front of his face. "She knows when it's okay to have an opinion on Bob Irvine's ranch."

"Oh, Marty!" Her eyes roll. "I did not say that."

"Where is Justin, anyway?" Hailey stirs her hot cocoa with a wooden stick. She's my only brunette sister. Actually, her hair matches the color of her hot chocolate, which is an odd realization that keeps me from immediately answering her question, but it's okay because my mom answers for me.

"Working."

I glance at my mom and then at Hailey. "He's prepping for Black Friday next week."

"But did you tell him how important picking out a Christmas tree with your family is?" Hailey asks.

"He knows," my mother snips again.

"I told him it was important," I say, ignoring my mom's dig. "And it made him feel even worse about missing the tree cutting today."

"He should feel bad!" My mother lifts her chin. If you cross one of her five daughters, it's hard to get her love back, and in her mind, Justin has crossed me time and time again by not coming to my family parties and dinners over the last nine months.

"He does feel bad." I look directly at her. "Nobody likes working on Saturdays."

"I don't think he loves you." Anna flips her long blonde hair behind her shoulder as she leans back into her chair. She's the oldest in the family and always the boldest with her claims.

"I don't either," my mom says under her breath but purposely still loud enough for me to hear.

"You guys, he's *working*, not cheating on me with a stripper."

"Who's a stripper?" Aunt Carma perks up.

"No one's a stripper." My mom waves her off. "Justin is cheating *with* a stripper."

I throw my arms up. "He's not cheating with a stripper!"

"We haven't confirmed that yet." That's my mother, always giving people the benefit of the doubt.

I turn to my dad. Despite the newspaper in front of his face, I know he's still listening to the conversation. "Please, talk some sense into them."

He folds down the corner. Reading glasses sit on the bridge of his nose, but he dips his chin to look at us over the rim. "Justin is working. Drop it." The paper flips up, and he continues reading as if his word is the final say.

"Listen, if Justin really cared about you, he'd find a way to show up for you when it mattered." Clearly, Anna has no intention of *dropping* the subject.

"Rick isn't here." I nod to the husbands at the other table. "How come Rick gets a hall pass from family activities?"

"Well, Rick is hunting. It's the last one of the year." Juliet bounces her baby in her lap, and it's like I'm looking at a carbon copy of myself. Juliet is only fifteen months older than me, but everyone assumes we're twins with our matching blonde bobs and our affinity for bright-red lipstick. Her innocent shrug makes it seem like she truly believes Rick's excuse is better than Justin's.

"Rick never shows up for you, but nobody questions whether or not he loves you."

"Because Rick comes around when he's not hunting, so we know him and therefore know he loves Juliet," my mother explains. "But Justin doesn't come around when he's not working, and we know nothing about him, including whether or not he loves you."

"Who's Justine?" Aunt Carma leans into Juliet, asking her on the side.

"It's *Justin*." A condescending pat on my aunt's shoulder accompanies Juliet's answer. "He's Summer's boyfriend."

Aunt Carma's head flips to Hailey. I can't see her expression because of the massive sunglasses, but I can imagine her pinched brows. "Summer has a boyfriend?"

"See." My mom gestures to her as if that one comment from my semi-delusional great-aunt proves everything.

"He would come around if he wasn't working," I defend.

"All-Weather Blankets just launched. He has to work day and night to keep up with the demand."

Erin frowns at me. "Is that really the kind of life you want? A husband that's a workaholic and never shows up?" That's a low blow coming from Erin since I've always looked up to her so much.

"Yeah," Anna agrees. "You hate to be alone. You'd never be able to handle life without a plus-one."

"That's not true."

My sisters eye each other before Hailey speaks up. "Uh, yes, it is. Ever since you got left at Greg Hiddleston's party in the seventh grade, you've made sure you always have someone with you. That's what's happening here."

"Are you saying that Summer is just keeping Justin around so she doesn't have to be alone during the holidays?" Juliet asks.

"Yes, but it's backfiring because he's a workaholic," Hailey says.

"I am not keeping Justin around so that I won't be alone during my favorite time of year. That's ridiculous. And he's not a workaholic. This is just a nose-to-the-grindstone kind of situation. It'll pass."

"You guys have been dating for a year and—"

"Nine months," I correct my mom.

"Fine. You've been dating *nine months*"—she looks directly at me as she overemphasizes the words—"and I've only met him twice. I know your mailman better than Justin."

"That's because Dale, the mailman, is very friendly."

"My butcher's name is Dale," Aunt Carma says from the cheap seats.

"And Justin isn't friendly." My mom folds her arms.

"He *is* friendly. You just haven't given him a chance."

"In the two times I've met him, I definitely gave him a chance."

"It's been more than two times."

Right?

15

Please tell me that Justin has met my parents more than two times.

"No, there was that time you stopped by the house to get a paddleboard, and we spoke for ten minutes. Then, when we accidentally ran into you at Tiki Taco."

Huh.

Two times.

And one of them was an accident.

Something about that doesn't sit well in my stomach.

"Well, don't worry. Justin will be at everything next week, and you'll have plenty of time to get to know him." Even as I say the words, I know I'm being *wayyy* too optimistic. Justin only confirmed attendance for Thanksgiving dinner, nothing else. But part of me hopes I can change his mind between now and then or that I can convince my family that he really is a good guy who loves me.

"I'll believe it when I see it," my mom huffs.

"Tell me about the blankets." Anna crosses one leg over the other, eyeing the All-Weather Blanket I currently have wrapped around me.

I glance down, gladly accepting the change of subject. "It's tarp material on the outside, so that snow and water can never get through, and then a plush blanket on the inside to keep you warm."

"Are you warm?" Juliet asks.

"Yeah."

"Is it heavy?" Hailey leans over, feeling the tarp fabric between her two fingers. "It looks heavy."

"A little."

"Well, they're ugly as sin," Aunt Carma grunts.

"But maybe that's good," Erin offers. "If the blankets are ugly, maybe the business will fail, and then Justin can spend time with you."

"I want to buy a blanket before he goes out of business."

Hailey looks at Anna. "They'd be great to take to a cold soccer game."

"I'm not buying one." My mom shakes her head. "I'm not supporting something that makes my baby girl sad."

"Fine!" Aunt Carma slaps the table, startling all of us. "I'll invest in the blankets. I want sixty percent of the business."

My dad lowers his paper. "Carma, quit giving away money you don't have." He lifts the paper back up, walling us out again.

"Justin is not going out of business. And I'm not sad."

Actually, maybe I am.

Or maybe I'm lonely.

It's either that or I'm premenstrual.

There must be some explanation for the half-pan of brownies I ate last night after I left Justin's house, or the fact that I didn't enjoy Christmas tree hunting today like I normally do.

But I can't tell my family I'm sad.

They'll never like Justin if I start sharing my real feelings and fears about our relationship. Because when Justin and I are good, we're *good*—the complete fairytale. I just need to buy some time until we can get back to that spot, and my family can learn for themselves how great he is. Once they do, I know they'll love him as much as I do.

Patience.

Apparently, it's a virtue.

Peter runs up, giving me a hug. "Summer, come play tag with us."

I smile back at him. "I will in one sec."

That answer is good enough for him, and he runs off again.

Aunt Carma leans forward, staring me down. I think she's staring me down, but it's hard to tell with her giant black sunglasses. "Summer, honey. He's way too young for you. I'll find you somebody more your age." She sits up straight, swiveling her head around.

Anna laughs. "Is she talking about Peter?"

"I think so." Erin presses her lips together, trying to suppress her laugh.

"Young man!" Carma snaps at one of Bob Irvine's grandchildren working on the ranch. He looks maybe eighteen. "Do you want a girl that's sweet with a little spice?"

His brows drop. "I'm just transferring firewood."

"Pfft!" Aunt Carma folds her arms, repositioning herself in her seat.

Miles screams as Peter and Jack push him into the first Christmas tree, leaning against the barn. A domino effect ensues as one tree knocks into the next until the last tree tips, landing on the hood of my dad's parked twelve-passenger van. The car alarm starts, and the boys all burst into tears.

"My van!" My dad jumps to his feet, headed toward the precious van that he only keeps for occasions when the entire family gets together.

All my sisters scatter as they try to round up their kids. I'm left sitting at the table with my Aunt Carma.

"You know who's a good kisser?" she says to me, completely unfazed by the chaos around her. "Bob Irvine. I'll set you up with him. Don't worry. Carma will take care of everything."

I smile as I glance around at my crazy family.

This is what the holidays and Christmas are about.

I'm not worried about being alone. I'm worried that I won't have anyone to share this with.

three

CALEB

THERE'S an open parking space on the street across from Justin's condo. It's probably a little tight for my Bronco, but being an exceptional parallel parker is something I'd list on my resumé—if I had one—so I swing my arm over the bench seat, glancing behind me as I back in.

"Still got it," I say when I've angled my car into the perfect spot.

The door slams, and I stay pressed against the Bronco until traffic passes and it's safe to cross.

Calling before you show up out of the blue is a good idea. Unfortunately, I didn't call first. But Justin is my twin brother. He has to let me stay at his place. That's just what you do when another human looks identical to you. Besides that, my parents are remodeling their house and turning my old bedroom into a storage closet, so he's my only option, unless I want to spend a fortune on a hotel with outrageous holiday pricing, which I do not.

My footprints on his driveway are the first tracks in the fresh snow, telling me Justin either hasn't left for work yet or never came home last night. I mentally flip through our text conversations, trying to remember whether or not he has a girlfriend. That feels like information I should know off the top of my head, but I'm coming up blank.

I knock on the cream-colored front door, shifting my gaze behind me to the view of the Telluride ski resort and San Juan mountains. Fresh powder calls my name. Even after my seventeen-hour flight from Thailand, I still want to hit the slopes. I'm thinking snowboarding today. Maybe skiing tomorrow.

The door swings open. Justin's eyes go wide.

"Surprise." I lift my hands.

"What the—?" He drags me into a hug. "I didn't know you were in town."

"I didn't know I was going to be." I pull back, keeping my hands on his shoulders. "Look at you. I'm afraid I'm going to wrinkle your fancy shirt." I flip his tie into his face, but he swats it away.

"I'm headed to work." He opens the door wider, letting me in. "What are you doing here?"

"Nice place." I glance around his mountain condo decorated in neutrals and dark wood with a stone fireplace. All he's missing is a deer head hanging above the mantel. But Justin would never display a stuffed animal carcass. He's too soft for something like that. "How long have you lived here?"

"About ten months." He stands close to the door with his hands on his hips, giving me the feeling that he's just biding his time until he can politely leave for work. "Actually, that's how I met my girlfriend. Her company does the property management for the entire complex."

I guess he does have a girlfriend I should know about.

"Right." I nod. "What's her name again?"

Justin laughs. "Don't worry. I haven't mentioned her before, and I don't expect you to know her name."

"Good, because I don't know it."

"Summer."

I nod again, committing her name to memory so Justin can't complain to our mom that I don't listen to him or take the time to get to know him—which seems to be his chief complaint since we became adults and drifted apart. But I'm here to change that, to work on our relationship, so I repeat in my mind his girlfriend's name one last time.

"You never answered my question. What are you doing in Telluride?"

"I'm taking time off from filming."

"Won't your bazillion YouTube followers protest?" There's an edge to his voice, a hint that he doesn't respect my job as a YouTuber.

"Eh, they'll be fine." I drop my canvas backpack on his couch.

He eyes it. "Oh, so you're staying?"

"I thought I'd spend the holidays with family, unless you have a roommate—or does your girlfriend live here?" I move my gaze around, looking for any sign of female existence.

"Summer and I aren't that serious." He reaches for his jacket hanging by the door. "Listen, I have a conference call I have to be on in thirty minutes. I'd change it around, but it's Monday morning, and with Thanksgiving—"

"You're fine. I don't want to mess you up with work."

"I'm sure Mom and Dad don't have room for you with the remodel, so you can stay here." The leather satchel on the table is the next thing he grabs before wrapping a magenta scarf around his neck. It's fascinating that there's a version of me that wears a scarf. I wouldn't have been able to picture it if it wasn't for Justin. "Can we catch up tonight when I get home?"

I force my eyes away from the pretty-boy scarf. "Yeah, go. I need to shower and sleep anyway."

"The spare bedroom is the first door on the left, and the bathroom across the hall maybe has soap. I don't even know. Steal whatever you need from my bathroom." Justin's hand is on the door handle, but he's trying to be a good host.

"Go." I wave him off. "I can figure it out."

"Okay, sorry." His steps pause. "It's good to see you."

"You too." I'm surprised by how much I mean the sentiment,

considering the last time I saw Justin, he told me I wasn't a grown adult and I didn't take life seriously enough. Kind of a douchey comment from someone I'm three minutes older than. But if we're being subjective, I can see how he came to that conclusion. I barely graduated high school. I didn't go to college. I don't have what some people consider a real job or even a real home. I spend my days traveling the world, filming myself doing daredevil tricks. To my straight-laced twin brother, my choices seem childish. But that's the theme of our existence. He's the smart, responsible twin, and I'm the reckless, athletic one. The yin and yang of our family.

"I guess I'll see you later tonight, then." Justin nods once, shutting the door behind him.

In the silence, my jetlag hits hard, and I have a headache, but once I'm speeding down the slopes, all of that will disappear.

SUMMER

IT'S ANNOYING when couples send each other funny texts or memes all day long when they should be working. We get it: you miss each other and are flirting via text. So cringy.

Okay.

It's not cringy.

It's cute.

So cute, in fact, that I check my messages at the next stoplight to see if Justin has texted. There's nothing new since the last time I looked two and a half minutes ago. I pull up my notifications just to be sure I haven't missed a call. All clear. Alexander Graham Bell is probably rolling in his grave. He invented an amazing way to communicate, and my boyfriend doesn't even take advantage of it.

Friday night was the last time I spoke to Justin. Does that seem odd? Because it does to me. Shouldn't there have been a Saturday-evening check-in, a *How did the tree search go with your family?* Or even a Sunday, *let's get brunch* convo. Honestly, I'm an easy gal to please. I would be satisfied with a simple, *Hey!* Because we all know Justin's freaking phone has been attached to his hip all weekend and all day today. There isn't a good excuse for why he hasn't answered my three—okay, *four*—phone calls and five text messages.

But I try one last time.

Summer: Just making sure you aren't dead. Are you dead?

I drop my phone into my lap and focus on the disappearing brake lights in front of me as the traffic slowly pulls forward through the intersection. Despite being only six p.m., it feels like midnight. Thank you, winter, for being the darkest time of the year and officially making me depressed.

No, that's all wrong. *Winter* isn't making me depressed. I love winter—usually—and all the things that come with this time of year. So I can't understand why I feel so sad and lonely. But I'm an adult now, and maybe part of being an adult is being depressed around the holidays, which has never happened to me before. I've always made sure I had plenty to do and someone to do it with.

Last year, my boyfriend's name was Gil—a terrible name, but he was in town for the winter as a ski instructor and made it to most of my Christmas events as my date. I knew the whole time that the relationship wasn't permanent. But it was better than being alone.

The Christmas before that, I spent the holidays with Bart. He graduated high school two years after me and then left for college but was home from USC for winter break. It was just enough time for me to feel like I had someone.

But this Christmas, I thought I had more than *someone*. I thought Justin and I would spend our first of many Christmases together.

My phone screen lights up, and I impatiently wait until the next stoplight to read the text.

Justin: Sorry I haven't called you back. The website crashed, and we've been working nonstop to get it up and running again. Can you forgive me? I miss you and want to make it up to you. Meet me at my place tonight for dinner?

And suddenly, I'm no longer depressed. I guess it wasn't seasonal depression. More like boyfriend-is-too-busy-for-me depression. But Justin misses me and wants to make it up to me, so basically, I'm all better. No judgment, please. I'm trying to make this relationship work.

Summer: I'm sorry about your website. I bet that was really stressful. You deserve a night off. Dinner sounds great. I'll pick up your favorite and meet you there in twenty minutes.

Justin: Okay, leaving soon. See you in a bit.

And just like that, the world is right again.

CALEB

I KNOW BETTER THAN THIS.

Going from sea level to a 12,000-foot elevation at the top of the ski lift in the span of twenty-four hours is bound to mess you up with altitude sickness.

And I'm messed up.

My head is pounding.

My stomach is weak.

I'm tired, dizzy, and lightheaded.

I can't even think straight.

I don't know how I made it off the mountain and back to

Justin's condo in one piece. But things have definitely worsened since I came home and laid down.

I hold my head as I walk down the hall to the kitchen, using my other hand to steady myself against the wall as I slowly put one foot in front of the other.

Everything is dark.

I like dark.

Dark doesn't hurt my pounding head.

I need medicine.

Medicine. That's a silly word.

"Medi-sinny," I say the word out loud, how it's spelled in my brain. "That doesn't sound right." I shake my head, even though it hurts.

A glow from outside stops me in the middle of Justin's family room.

"Thatsh pretty." I watch headlights dance through the window as cars pass by Justin's house. I reach my hand out, trying to grab the rays, but when I open my palm, there's nothing there. I squint at the window, and now everything looks like a laser show with colors and light rays shooting everywhere. Nope, *spinning* everywhere.

The room is spinning.

I shift my gaze to the kitchen, reminded of why I'm out of bed in the first place.

Maybe there's medi-sinny in the spinning kitchen. Medi-sinny, that's still not right.

I stumble forward, using my hands to feel my way around the bar like I'm in one of those fun houses where the floor tilts and you can't walk.

I fling open the refrigerator, and the blinding light hurts my head so much that I slam it closed again.

"It's here shumwhere." I open the dishwasher, then straighten, letting the door drop to the ground. In the back of my foggy brain, I'm aware that medicine would never be stored in the dishwasher, but I'm also so out of my mind confused that I can't stop myself from doing stupid things like opening the dishwasher to look for a bottle of Tylenol.

After the dishwasher, I start flinging open cupboards.

If I don't find it soon, I might just lie down on the tile floor and sleep until my body and mind feel a little better.

SUMMER

I MARCH UP JUSTIN'S FRONT STEPS, IMPRESSED THAT HE found the time to shovel the snow from last night's storm. For some reason, I can't picture Justin shoveling snow, as if the act is beneath him and his expensive leather shoes. But I guess you can't live in Colorado without being willing to dig yourself out occasionally.

Balancing the warm burritos in one hand, I turn the handle. It's unlocked. He must've gotten home just before me. I push his front door open. Everything is dark, but rustling in the kitchen lets me know he's home.

An idea flitters across my mind, pulling my lips into a smile. It hinges on absolute silence as I remove my coat and shoes and tiptoe to the kitchen. Rounding the corner, my stomach stirs at the sight of him. There's enough glow seeping through the windows to see Justin standing in his kitchen with his back to me. He's shirtless with dark joggers slung low on his hips. Lights from outside dance across his back, creating shadows that tease fleeting glimpses of his corded muscles. It's been so long since we've spent time together like this that I've forgotten just how good he looks without his shirt on. He looks more muscular than I even remember.

There's a different feel about tonight—the darkness, the fact that Justin is purposefully greeting me half-naked. My blood is pumping in a way that makes all of our problems momentarily disappear.

I crave the warmth of his skin, and I don't even think twice about closing my arms around his bare chest, wrapping him into a hug. His body startles and then stills as it relaxes against my touch.

I raise to my tiptoes, whispering in his ear, "Guess who."

"I'm dreaming. This is a dream." The deep, sexy texture behind his voice has my body humming with desire.

"Do you want it to be a dream?" I shift my hands, feeling his hard chest beneath my fingers. Justin's bench-pressing regimen has not taken a backseat to his busy work schedule in any way whatsoever. I skid my lips across his shoulder blade, kissing a trail up to his neck. He smells like his regular body wash but also like something different, a manliness that's driving me crazy. Just another sign of how starved of affection I've been.

"Uh..." His breaths are heavy. "I like this dream."

That's all the encouragement I need to draw his mouth to mine, forcing him to spin around and face me.

"Wa—"

Before he can even get the word out, my lips close over his. They say if you want something in life, go after it. Well, I want to remind my boyfriend that I'm better than work. This kiss is romance CPR, and I'm single-handedly bringing our physical relationship back from the dead to the beat of "Stayin' Alive" by the Bee Gees.

At first, Justin stands like a limp statue. I feel like I'm holding him up. His lips are stiff, and there's a tenseness to his body that should make me pause, but instead, it does the opposite. I'm a woman on a mission, and the game: weaken Justin's defenses until he is helpless against my touch. He's overworked, stressed out, and a man. It shouldn't take too long to break him down.

I press my body into his—a total vixen move. My determination knocks him back against the counter, awakening his senses and driving his hands to my waist. I drift my fingers along his bare back and move my lips over his, forcing pliability into the kiss. He tries to mumble something, but I smother his words by deepening the passion. It only takes a second before his arms fully wrap around my body, and he gives in to my efforts.

His hand travels into my hair as the kiss shifts from a one-sided game to a two-person showdown. We essentially went from solitaire to chess, and I couldn't be more invested in the process if I tried.

The kiss is full-body contact and excitement and newness—a nice change from the last few kisses we've shared. As Aunt Carma would say, it's Bob-Irvine good. It's so next-level that I get lost in it, not even trying to analyze *why* it's so amazing. I'm just enjoying the ride as my body fills with delicious butterflies that build in intensity with each passing second.

I've died and gone to heaven.

His lips part from mine, barely enough to speak. "Is thish real?"

I laugh against his mouth. "It feels pretty real to me."

"Summer?" The tone of his voice really accentuates the question behind the word.

I press my lips into him, mumbling over the kiss. "Yeah?"

That's when he pulls back, swearing under his breath.

Headlights slice through the front window, dancing across his face.

There are moments in life that are so horrific that you know they'll be ingrained in your mind and soul forever. They'll pop up at two a.m., when you can't sleep, and make you so embarrassed you feel like smothering yourself with your own pillow just to escape the humiliation of reliving it all over again.

This is one of those moments.

Because while my body thinks—*thought*—this man was Justin, my mind has been picking up on clues all along that it's not. Like the stubble on his face that's more than just a five o'clock shadow. Or how my tippy-toes still put me shorter-than-normal next to his frame. Or how his hair is longer with an unruly waviness that my fingers loved ruffling through. Or his bulging arms and well-defined back and chest. Or the final straw: the kiss was more explosive than anything else I've ever experienced. That probably should've been my first clue that the man I just kissed wasn't Justin Davidson but his twin brother, Caleb.

Whom I've never met.

The horrifying realization causes me to jump back, hitting my calves against what can only be the open dishwasher. Why did it have to be open and in my way at this exact moment? I wish the horror stopped there, but in true embarrassing-moment fashion, I fall backward into the dishwasher, landing on the open door and bottom rack. I yelp in pain as the plastic rods and dishes stab into my butt. The appliance jerks forward, sending the top rack slamming into the back of my head. All of this gracefulness is accompanied by a loud crashing noise as glass plates and cups bang into each other.

Caleb swears again, trying to chase after my fall with arms extended, but he somehow manages to trip on the open door and fall over me to the ground. I roll off the jagged prongs poking me and slide to the tile, lying on my back beside him.

My chest heaves up and down with an ache that's so tangible I should probably check myself into the ER.

What did I just do? And why did he let me do it?

I twist my head, looking at him. He's pressed to the floor on his stomach like pancake batter just poured on a hot grill. His brows lift, and his eyelids pull open slightly.

"Al..ti...tude."

"Huh?"

"Al..ti..tuuuude," he groans as his eyelids flop closed again.

My brows drop in confusion. "What?"

"I'm sick. Get medi-sinny," he groans again.

Then I know.

Caleb has acute mountain sickness from the high elevation.

And I just made out with him.

Now, I'm the one who feels sick.

SUMMER

"OKAY, HERE WE GO!" I grunt as I help Caleb to his feet. He drapes his arm around my shoulder, putting most of his weight on me.

Thirty seconds ago, when he was kissing me back, he could hold his own weight. But now? Now, he's so bad he needs me to drag him to the couch. It's like a man-cold on steroids. And everything is made a thousand times worse because he's shirtless. So I'm not just touching him. I'm *touching* him. What started as a blessing has now become my worst nightmare.

"Where's your shirt? It's like ten degrees outside. Are you homeless? Does Justin know you're here?"

"The room is spinning." His neck rotates in a circular motion like he's following the spin with his eyes. "Does it spin for you?"

"Nope." Once we're close enough to the couch, I lift his arm off my shoulder, pushing his body so he falls into the cushions.

He slumps back as if he's out of energy. I'll have to lift his feet onto the couch so he can lie down fully.

"Why not?" I say out loud to myself as I grab his ankles and swing them up onto the cushion at the opposite end. "We've already made out. Why don't I just tuck you in? I'm sure Justin won't mind."

Oh, my gosh! What if Justin had walked in while we were kissing? I can't even wrap my head around how bad that would've been.

Caleb scoots his body farther into the couch until he finds a comfortable position. He lifts one arm up to his head, using his thumb and index finger to rub his temples.

"Medi-sinny. Please."

"You want medicine?"

His other hand points at me. "That's it. Me-di-sinnnn."

I refrain from rolling my eyes, because he's sick, but I also want to roll my eyes because I'm annoyed that he's so sick that he didn't stop me from kissing him.

"Hold on," I say as I walk back to the kitchen, flipping on the lights.

"Bright light! Bright light!" His voice goes high and tiny like a Gremlin.

"Sorry." I shrug over my shoulder. "I can't find the medicine without the lights on."

Caleb doesn't react, just covers his eyes with the palm of his hand.

I take a moment and straighten up the kitchen from the dishwasher debacle. It's a Christmas miracle I'm still alive. Those plastic prongs could've stabbed me to death. I'll probably have tiny bruises all over my butt and back.

It only takes a second for me to find the medicine cupboard. I grab four pills and fill up a glass of water, taking it all back to Caleb.

"Here." I open his hand, placing the pills inside.

He throws them into his mouth and reaches for the water, downing the entire glass in one long gulp. He hands me the glass, then resumes his position with one hand rubbing his head.

I stand over him, trying to figure out how in the heck this whole mess happened. The light from the kitchen helps illuminate the problem.

Caleb Davidson is Bizarro Justin—the perfectly opposite

duplicate of my boyfriend. And when I say perfect, I mean *Purrr-fect* with a capital P. Everything about him is enhanced. His eyes are bluer. His hair is browner. His lips are fuller. His muscles are bigger. His six-pack is more defined. He's even three minutes older than Justin. It's like someone injected Justin with a whole lot of flawless.

In the world of twin brothers, that's just not fair.

But for me, Justin will always be the better twin.

Caleb gifts me a lazy smile, and good grief—even *that* is more charming than Justin's. Didn't I just say that Justin is the better twin? And oh, my gosh! This isn't a competition. There's no such thing as a *better* twin. I cover my face with my hands, horrified by this twin-brother compare snare I'm trapped in. And more importantly, I'm horrified by the fact that I just kissed Justin's brother.

"Are you crying?" His question is valid since my fingers are covering my face.

Aside from popping my head up and shouting, '*Peek-a-boo!*' I don't think this moment could get more embarrassing. I slowly lower my hands, meeting his half-awake gaze. "No, I was freaking out because I'm a cheater. Thanks for that, by the way. Thanks for turning me into a cheater."

"You're Summer," he says, closing his eyes again. "Justin's boyfriend."

"*Girl*friend," I correct, placing a pillow behind his head. "But after everything that just happened, I might not be that anymore."

"You're beautiful." His statement is just that—a statement. There's no smirky smile or glimmering eyes—his eyes are actually closed.

"Uh..." I straighten. "Thanks."

"And a good kisser." Another statement with no flirtation behind it, but that doesn't stop me from looking around the room at no one in particular because we're alone. But if there were actually people here, I'd make eye contact with them, sharing a knowing look that any sane human being wouldn't have said that comment out loud.

I think he's a good kisser too, but those words will never be uttered out loud.

I nervously run my fingers through my hair, flipping it to the side. "Well, just so we're clear, I didn't mean to kiss you."

"And I didn't mean to like it." That's good. We're on the same page.

Wait.

Did he like it?

I mean, I liked it, but I thought I was kissing Justin, so of course I liked it. But Caleb? This has to be the confusion from the altitude talking.

I place my hands on my hips. "How sick are you?"

"Sick." He shakes his head, closing his eyes. "My head hurts."

Oh, crap. He's like *sick* sick. Do I need to take him to the hospital or something?

"Okay, don't worry." This sounds like a situation for WebMD. I rush to the table where I left my phone, Googling acute mountain sickness as I walk back to the couch. I kneel beside Caleb, reading off the symptoms.

"Headache, nausea, fatigue, dizziness, lightheadedness..." I glance at him, catching his nods with each thing I list. "What about breathlessness, elevated body temperature, or coughing?"

"No."

"Okay, but all the dizziness and confusion could mean you have HACE, which is fluid accumulation in the brain." I gasp, looking at him with wide eyes. "It's deadly."

He shakes his head. "Water. More water."

I scramble to my feet, refilling his water and bringing it back as quickly as possible. I chew on my nail as I watch him gulp it down.

In addition to kissing Justin's brother, I'm going to fail to diagnose his life-threatening symptoms, and he'll die under my watch.

Then, no one will have to know about the kiss.

I tilt my head. Tempting...but no.

I decide to call Justin instead. He can be like a co-conspirator if Caleb ends up dying.

"Hey, babe!" He sounds breathless. "I know I'm not home yet. I was on my way out, and then Isaac—"

"Justin, I don't care," I snap. "I just got to your condo, and your brother—which, by the way, thanks for warning me he was here."

"Oh, yeah. I forgot to tell you Caleb is in town."

"Whatever." I shake that topic away, shelving it for later. "I think he has altitude sickness. He has a headache, and he's dizzy, *confused.*" I make sure to add that symptom, hoping it will come in handy later when I tell him about the accidental kiss.

"Really? Are you sure?"

"Pretty sure." My eyes drift over his shirtless body on the couch. "Do you think I need to take him to the hospital? Or drive him to lower elevation?"

"No, it's just altitude sickness. He'll be fine."

"Well, he's pretty confused. I Googled it, and in some cases, it can be really serious. Like when they're showing signs of delusion."

"Is he showing signs of delusion?"

"Uh, just a few." If you count kissing your brother's girlfriend a sign of delusion.

"Keep him hydrated. Fluids help with altitude sickness. You can take him in if he doesn't improve in the next half hour."

"Are you sure? His death will be on your hands."

"Make him drink some water, and I'll be home in a little bit."

"Okay." I grab the empty glass from Caleb's limp hand and rush back to the kitchen, filling it up again. "Hurry!"

"I will. See you soon."

I set my phone on the coffee table, kneeling in front of Caleb again.

"Hey," I whisper, forcing the glass into his fingers. "Drink some more water. It'll help you feel better."

I place my hand on his upper back, helping him lean forward. My other hand helps steer the cup to his mouth. My eyes drift while he gulps, noticing the perfect little crunch of muscles his position creates out of his six-pack. I jerk my eyes away.

Not the time to be noticing that. Geez, Summer!

And for the record, I didn't notice his abs in an appraising way. More like a factual way. It's factually true that Caleb has a six-pack. I could say the same thing about the steroid man at the gym who wears shorts that are a little too short in my opinion.

I wait until he's finished drinking before looking back. "I'll get you some more." I move to stand, but he grabs my arm.

"No, I need a break." His eyes close again.

I study Caleb in a very nurse-patient way. I'm on call, and Justin's brother isn't dying on my watch. Because of that, I don't feel like I can move from his side. I also don't feel like I can scroll Instagram while I wait the half-hour to see if he dies—doesn't seem ethical.

So I sit, resting my forehead in my arms as I listen to him breathe.

"Summer?" It's been about forty minutes since Caleb has moved.

"What do you need?" My head pops up. I'm on high alert. "Do you want more water?"

"I have to go to the bathroom."

"Oh." I sit up. "Okay, well." I look at his body, trying to figure out how I'm going to get him to the restroom. "Let's get you up."

I grab his hand, lifting him to his feet. He's a little unsteady until he slings his arm around my shoulder for support. I wrap my arm around his waist, telling myself the entire time that holding his bare hip is no big deal.

I'm in my nurse era—something I never thought I'd say.

We walk into the bathroom together, and I stand by his side, supporting his body. I turn my head, averting my eyes so he can take care of business.

"Are you planning on staying?"

I peek back at him, seeing the most amused smile I've ever seen on a sick man. I guess that's a good sign for his health. "Oh, no. Sorry!" I wiggle away from Caleb while turning fifty shades of red. I walk backward, shifting my eyes around the tiny bathroom so I don't have to look at his amused face. "Looks like you have everything under control here, so"—I point behind me—"I'll just be out in the family room if you need me." I pull the bathroom door shut as I exit, scurrying down the hall, cringing at how cringy I am.

I drop into a chair, letting my head fall into my hands.

On a scale of one to sucky, this night sucks.

And where the heck is Justin? I glance at the clock. It's been forty-five minutes since we spoke, and he's still not home. Not to mention the fact that my burrito is now cold. But at least my patient isn't dead. No, he's coherent enough to realize he doesn't want me standing beside him while he pees.

I hear the toilet flush and the sink turn on, but I stay put. I don't care if Caleb falls flat on his face from trying to walk back out here. I'm not entering that bathroom for anything.

The door opens, and slow footsteps creek down the hall. I turn my head, watching as he uses the furniture as support on his way back to the couch. I could help. I really could. But I keep my hands clasped together in my lap. The bathroom mishap was the end of my nurse era.

Caleb flops his body back on the couch, looking over at me.

"Hi." He smiles, and it's the kind of smile that makes me think he's a little more with it than he was before.

"Hi." I nervously glance around before swinging my eyes back to him.

"Sorry about all this."

"Oh, it's no problem." I swat the air in front of me.

"I'm Caleb, by the way."

"Yes, I believe we've met." When I was making out with his shoulder blade—an unfortunate turn of events.

"Yes, we have." He shoots me a loaded smile that's way too charming for somebody as sick as him.

"Stop that," I snap.

"What?" He smiles wider, shrugging his massive shoulders.

"Stop smiling at me like you're thinking about our kiss."

There's another lift of his shoulders. "What kiss? I don't remember anything. I was delusional and hallucinating."

"Yes!" I point at him. "Yes, you were."

My comment makes him smile even more. What's with all the handsome smiling? It's messing with my head. I loop through all the things I know about Caleb Davidson—things Justin has told me.

He's immature.

Shirks responsibility.

Doesn't take relationships seriously.

Reckless.

Has never held down a real job.

Goes through women faster than deodorant.

So, while Caleb has super-enhanced looks, Justin is the steady one. And it's not like Justin is ugly. Before this moment, I thought he was the most attractive man ever. Now I know he's the most attractive man *besides* his brother. They're identical twins, so dating Justin is like winning the consolation prize. But what am I even saying? Looks mean nothing. I *love* Justin. I'm just all screwed up right now because of the kiss. This will pass, like the acute mountain sickness.

"I'm guessing Justin didn't tell you I'd be here."

"We haven't talked in a few days." At that piece of information, his brows lift, and I feel like I should explain. "I was doing family stuff all weekend, and he was working, so we didn't connect."

Connect? I make it sound like our relationship is dial-up internet.

His eyes scan me in a who's-this-girl-dating-my-brother kind of way. I scratch my head under his scrutiny, hating that he knows me more intimately than any family member should. The slow spread of his smile as his stare finally returns to my face has me feeling fidgety, like maybe I need to adjust my bra strap so it fits perfectly over my shoulder or pull the hem of my shirt down even though it's already down. I settle on glancing longingly at the front door.

"Does Justin always work this late?"

"Yes, but he should've been here by now." I reach into my back pocket for my phone, checking to see if I somehow missed his call. There's nothing. "I don't know what's keeping him. He hasn't called." I put my phone back in my pocket. "Do you mind if I wait here for him to get home? I brought him dinner."

Caleb's all laidback and relaxed, probably still feeling the effects of the higher elevation. "You don't need my permission."

"Yeah, no. Of course not." I twist my fingers, hating the silence. "Sorry. If I'd known you were here, I would've brought you dinner too."

"You don't have to apologize."

"I can get you some more water, or there's even some mint hot chocolate in the cupboard. It's the only flavor of cocoa I drink."

"Are you always this nervous?" His brows drop in an amused way. Justin doesn't have an expression like that. I kinda wish he did.

"I'm not nervous." I tuck my hair behind my ear. "You're just lethargic, so you *think* I'm nervous. I'm just bubbly." I push a wide grin on my face. "I'm a really happy person by nature."

"Good to know."

Why is that good to know?

He lies there, staring at me, and yeah, I'm nervous.

"Are you feeling better?" Let's keep this conversation moving.

"Not really."

"You obviously changed elevation too much too fast. Where did you come from?"

"Thailand. Just landed this morning."

"Wow, yeah. That's a big difference. I think Telluride is almost 9,000 feet."

"I rode the ski lift higher up the mountain a few hours ago. That's when I really started to feel sick."

"That was dumb."

The corner of his mouth lifts. "Probably."

"For a minute, I thought I would have to take you to the ER."

"Nah, I'm tough."

Yes, you are. If muscles are any indicator.

His hand goes to his head, rubbing the side. "So, Summer, where are you from?"

"We don't have to talk. You can just rest."

"We should probably talk. Usually, I get to know women *before* I kiss them."

"I thought you said you didn't remember the kiss."

"I don't." His smile is playful, leaving me unsure if I can believe him. "So, where are you from?"

I decide to answer because it's not helpful to keep talking about the kiss. "From here...Telluride. What about you?" I'm acting normal. This is a normal conversation. "Where are you from?"

His grin is instant. "Phoenix."

"Right. You're Justin's brother." I drag out my laugh. "You'd obviously be from the same place as him."

"Unless we were the kind of twins that were separated at birth, and this is the first time we've met each other."

My lips lift. "But you're not."

"Nope."

I stare at him for a beat longer, waiting for him to say something else, but he doesn't. So I drop my eyes back to my hands.

"Justin said you do stuff with property management."

Knowing Justin has mentioned me to Caleb makes me sit a

little taller. "Yeah, my company is the largest in the area. We manage eighty percent of the properties around here."

"Impressive."

"It's not *my* company. I don't know why I said it like that. I'm just a regular employee. Well, not *regular* regular. I manage a hundred and twenty-five properties on my own."

Why do I sound like I'm reading off my resume?

Caleb's smile pulls wider. "Still impressive."

"Pfft." My lips vibrate. "You're the impressive one. You do, like, flips and stuff."

"Flips and stuff?" Caleb laughs while simultaneously narrowing his eyes. "Is that how Justin describes it?"

"Oh, I don't know." I tuck my hair behind my ears, wondering when I became so bad at small talk.

"I like your earrings."

"They're icicles." My hand jerks to my earlobe, feeling the jagged metal. "I like wearing Christmas earrings."

"Very cute."

"Thanks." He looks exactly like Justin but also different enough that he has become his own person to me.

"You're assessing me."

"I'm noting how you and Justin are different so we don't have another mistaken-identity moment."

"And how are we different?" He drops his arm into his lap. I guess his headache is easing.

"Just your mannerisms." There's no way I'm listing all the other things, like the muscles and the eyes, the stubble that is so long it might as well be a beard, and last but not least, the dreamy hair.

"For the record, I liked our mistaken-identity moment."

"So you do remember it?"

"Not really."

"Then why do you keep bringing it up?"

"I'm not."

I roll my eyes. "Well, I don't think Justin would like it very much."

"What wouldn't I like?"

I have whiplash from how fast my head spins to the front door. "Justin!" I jump out of my chair, run to him, and throw myself into his chest, hugging him close. "I'm so glad you're safe."

Loose arms wrap around my back, offering a half-hearted squeeze before he pulls away. "What wouldn't I like?"

"Uh..." My eyes pivot to Caleb, then back to Justin. I'm sweating and panicking. How do I confess? I've never been in this position before. I just have to explain the circumstances, tell the setup, then I can let him down gently with the details of the kiss. "Funny story. So I—"

"Your girlfriend kissed me," Caleb interjects with a winning smirk, and I suddenly have the urge to take my *very cute* icicle earrings and stab him with them.

six

CALEB

"YOU TWO KISSED?" Justin looks between Summer and me with raised brows.

"No!" She shakes her head, glaring at me, but I'm not scared. Summer is one of those bubbly people who could never be scary, even if she tried.

"She thought I was you and greeted me in a *very* nice way." I rest my head back on the pillow, not missing her knife-sharp stare directed at me.

"You said you didn't remember it."

"I don't, really."

Of course I remember it.

I mean, I wasn't all there when it happened. I didn't think she was real, just some hallucinated fantasy that came as a result of the altitude sickness. If I had known she was real *and* Justin's girlfriend, I would've never let it happen. But it did happen. And I most definitely remember the details.

I'm not into analyzing the way my brother's girlfriend kisses, but *dang!* that girl can kiss.

Justin turns to her. "You couldn't tell us apart?"

"All the lights were off, and your—*his*—back was to me," she stammers. "How was I supposed to know it wasn't you?"

"Maybe because he's totally jacked. His arms are, like, twice my size."

"I didn't notice his arms." Something about how Summer's eyes drop to the floor and how her head shakes makes me not believe her, but I smother my smile.

"Plus, his hair is longer than mine."

"Not that much longer," she defends. "But, like I said, it was dark. It wasn't that big of a deal. I just hugged him from behind and maybe kissed his neck a few times, then kissed *him*."

"What kind of kiss?"

"Um..."

"You're a lucky man," I throw out.

Her red lips purse as she shoots me another annoyed look.

"So like a *kiss* kiss," Justin clarifies.

"It felt like"—she teeters her head back and forth—"ten seconds."

Justin's eyes grow bigger. "So you kissed my brother for ten seconds, thinking it was me?"

"Why is this all about me? Why aren't you asking him why he didn't push me away or stop me?"

"I was hallucinating from the altitude. I really don't remember the details. But Summer seems to."

She glares at me again, and I shouldn't like messing with her this much, but I do.

"Are you okay?" Justin asks me. "Summer said you had acute mountain sickness pretty bad."

"It was so bad I kissed your girlfriend and didn't even know it."

Justin barrels over in laughter.

Summer's brows cinch. "You're laughing?"

Based on her expression, I think she was hoping for something along the lines of jealousy.

"Yeah, I would've loved seeing your reaction when you found out," he says between laughs.

"She fell in the dishwasher."

"So did you."

"No, I tripped over the dishwasher. I was really dizzy. The whole room was spinning."

Summer looks at Justin. "This isn't funny."

He straightens, calming his laughs. "It's a little funny."

"No, it's not. I *kissed* your brother. And he was so sick he almost died."

"You kissed him because you thought he was me, and he thought you were a hallucination. It's definitely funny." He walks to the table, opens one of the Styrofoam boxes, and nods in appreciation at the burrito. "My favorite."

"I also got you a Dr. Pepper because I figured you'd be up late working." Summer joins him by the food, nudging his drink forward.

"Don't worry about Caleb." He sits down in front of the food. "It used to happen all the time. We're identical. Nobody could tell us apart."

Her brows lift in skepticism. "You used to kiss each other's girlfriends?"

"I don't think we ever did that." His gaze drifts to me. "But we did swap places. I remember the last time. You wouldn't have passed Mrs. Jenkins's class or graduated if I hadn't taken that test for you."

"Chemistry, right?" I think back to a little over ten years ago.

"Wait." Summer takes a seat next to Justin. "You took a chemistry test for him?"

"It was really for our mom," I say. "She would've been devastated if I didn't graduate high school."

"And no one knew?"

"I'm sure Mrs. Jenkins knew when she saw Caleb's test score." Justin smiles at me, and in a small way, it feels like old times, like adulthood hasn't completely destroyed our relationship. He pokes his burrito with a fork. "This looks delicious. Thanks for picking it up, Sum Sum. I'm starving."

Sum Sum?

That's the worst nickname I've ever heard.

I give it two more months—the relationship, not the nickname.

"Why were you so late coming home?"

He does a dramatic eye roll. "Work is a long story, but once I did leave the office, I ended up getting in a car accident on the way home."

"What happened?" Summer's hand goes to his arm in concern. "Did someone hit you?"

"It was my fault. I was looking at my phone and didn't see the car in front of me stop. Luckily, we were going slow, so nobody got hurt."

"Why were you looking at your phone?"

"I was reading an email about our projected sales on Black Friday. It's going to be huge." Justin glances at me with a proud smile. I do my best to match his excitement because I'm trying to be a better brother, even though nothing about *projected sales* gets me excited, especially when I have a splitting headache.

"You've worked so hard, and it's going to be amazing." My eyes follow Summer's hand as she rubs it over his shoulder in an affectionate way. "I'm so proud of you."

The two of them continue the sales conversation while I cast my eyes over her and her sweet expression as she hangs on every last word Justin says. She's all wrong for him with her short blonde hair, bright-colored clothes, red lipstick, and that huge smile that fills up her entire face. She's the epitome of sunshine, and Justin is... What is Justin?

He's like a cirrus cloud, transparent, delicate, and detached.

Love the guy, but relationships aren't his strong point.

A woman who wears that shade of lipstick and greets her man the way she greeted me needs something more exciting than a cirrus-cloud man. She needs a storm cloud to keep her on her toes and match her energy. I'm not sure at what point in my life I became a meteorologist and started using cloud metaphors, but here we are.

"I told my family you had to work, but they were still bugged."

The tone of their conversation turns serious, sparking my interest.

"You guys were picking out a Christmas tree, yet you're acting like I missed the birth of my first-born child."

Summer stabs at her burrito, decimating the tortilla with each strike. "I'm just so tired of defending you to my family."

Apparently, there's trouble in paradise.

This personal topic is above my pay grade, so I turn my head away and close my eyes, as if that's enough to give them privacy. I would get up and leave, but that seems dramatic, and walking is still kind of hard.

"Then don't defend me."

"I want to defend you so my family doesn't hate you."

"Let them hate me."

When I gave their relationship two more months, I was being generous.

"They won't hate you if they get to know you. That's why I want you to come so bad."

"I get that, but you know my schedule the next few weeks."

"I know you're busy, but I thought you could take one night off to spend time with me and my family."

"What do you call Thanksgiving Day? I'm spending time with you and your family then."

"I call it a national holiday."

"Yeah, so I'm coming. I'll schmooze your family, eat the turkey, then get back to work."

Brutal, Justin. Just brutal.

"So it's turkey, mashed potatoes, then me. Glad to know how you prioritize things in your life."

I crack a smile, liking Summer's clipped reply.

"You're being ridiculous."

"And you're being selfish."

"I'm being selfish? You want me to put my entire business on hold, potentially lose thousands of buyers, so I can go to your family's Turkey Stuff?" I can picture the exact look on Justin's face right now, the I'm-right-so-why-can't-you-be-more-mature-about-this expression I've seen many times during our own family arguments. "There are more important things than stuffing a turkey."

I'm not sure what Justin is referring to, but it sounds mildly entertaining.

"I know that, but I'm asking you to show up for me one time since your business took over your life." Her words don't come out as a yell or even an angered demand. Her tone is more sad than anything, each word laced with deep longing that makes me feel bad for her.

"One time. That's all you want?"

"Yes, I just want my family to see how great you are and to finally get off my back about our relationship and whether or not you really care about me. To them, if you really cared, you'd come to the Turkey Stuff."

"I think I have a solution to our problem." Justin's chair scrapes across the wood floor like he stood up. "Caleb?"

Crap.

My eyes open just in time to see Justin sit down on the couch next to mine.

"I need you to impersonate me and go with Summer to her family party Wednesday night."

I rub my palm across the base of my neck. "I'm not sure that's a good—"

"That's your solution?" Summer is instantly beside him.

"Yeah, it's perfect." Justin shrugs. "Caleb doesn't care."

"Actually—" I try again, but my words are cut off by Justin.

"You need your family to see you with your boyfriend, and I need to work." His hand swings to me. "Enter my identical twin."

"About that," I start, but my words are suppressed again—this time by Summer.

"You're completely missing the point."

"I thought the point was to get your parents off your back about me being a bad boyfriend."

"No, it's more than that."

"Not really. Caleb's a warm body that you can take with you to your family party, and he looks exactly like me, and he has no plans. Problem solved."

"I want more than a *warm body*."

"Are you sure? Because it seems like you just don't want to go alone. That's kind of been the theme of our entire relationship. You can't even go to the bathroom alone."

"I go to the bathroom alone all the time. That would be weird if somebody went with me."

"You know what I mean."

"I want to go with *you* to my family party, *not* your brother."

Fair. Totally fair.

"Caleb has nothing going on. He doesn't care."

"Well, actually I—" I don't need to finish my thought because Summer does it for me.

"Oh, so I see how it is." She crosses one leg over her knee. "I'm just an item on your to-do list. It doesn't matter who's taking care of my needs as long as it doesn't interfere with your work schedule. I kiss your brother"—she throws her hand in the air—"no big deal! Just as long as you don't have to do it yourself."

Oh, boy. Things just got real.

"Is that what you're really mad about? That I wasn't jealous that you accidentally kissed my brother?" Justin's palms raise. "I'm sorry. I'm just not one of those guys who's insecure in my relationships."

"I just want you to care."

"I do care. I gave you a solution with my brother, but you won't even consider it, so I don't think you're really into solving anything."

"I'm into talking it through until we can come up with a compromise we both feel good about."

"And by 'compromise,' you mean talk about it until I give in, and you get what you want."

This is getting really awkward.

I should leave.

But I don't.

I sit and listen to the whole thing.

Twenty-two minutes later, the front door shuts.

"Sorry about that," Justin says as he takes a seat on the couch next to me.

"Don't worry about it. I love domestic disputes."

"So does Summer," Justin mutters under his breath.

I grab the remote on the coffee table, pretending like everything is fine. The arguing didn't bother me. I'm the type of guy who likes to have a knock-down-drag-out fight one minute and then get over it the next. But Justin is not that way. He hates facing conflict straight on and would rather pretend like it doesn't exist. Summer is good for him in that regard because she wasn't backing down.

The Monday Night Football theme plays as I get comfortable. A few minutes go by before I decide to continue the conversation. "So what are you going to do about her family turkey thing?" I'm still not entirely sure what this big event is she wants him to attend. Something about stuffing and turkeys. It's all very confusing.

"You could've helped me out with the twin-swap thing."

"Right, like I'm going to pose for you at her family party."

"It wouldn't be the first time we swapped for a girl."

"Trading places in high school is a lot different than swapping as adults."

"But Summer would be in on it."

"Summer doesn't want to be *in* on it. She probably feels super awkward because of the kiss."

"What? Now you guys aren't going to get along because of one stupid kiss?"

"I don't even remember the kiss." What he doesn't know doesn't hurt him. "I'm sure it's more awkward for Summer."

"I have to work Wednesday night, so I guess her family can just hate me even more."

"You know the relationship isn't going to last, right?"

He laughs, but it comes across as more frustrated than humorous. "Why? Because I won't go to one party, or because her family hates me?"

"Because you don't love her."

It's plain to see. I knew they weren't a good match within the first minute of seeing them together.

"We're not to that point yet. We've only been dating nine months."

"Nine months is plenty of time to get to that point."

He's been dating Summer for nine months but doesn't consider it serious—that's so like Justin. He can't commit to something unless he's overanalyzed it to death, including love. This relationship has probably been in the grave for the last four months, but neither one of them wants to admit it.

"Summer and I move slow, and you saw us at our worst tonight."

"So this was just an off night, and you do love her?"

"Are you part of the 'Define the Relationship' team? What's with the interrogation?"

"Asking if you love your girlfriend shouldn't feel like an interrogation."

"I told you, we're not that serious."

"Are you sure she feels the same way? Because she seemed pretty serious about you."

He rolls his eyes like he's been cornered and is finally ready to start telling the truth. "Summer might be more serious about the relationship than I am. I'm just so busy that it's hard to keep up with her. I mean, she said *I love you* after only five months."

"Did you say it back?"

His shrug is his answer.

"If you're not feeling it, why not just end things with her? Make your life a little easier."

"Because maybe I don't want to end things with her. I just haven't had the time to really think through how I feel about her, and until I do, it's easier to just keep things going between us."

"So you're buying time with her until you decide whether or not you love her?"

"I guess so." He shrugs again. "Besides, she loves this time of year. She's kind of clingy and hates to be alone. So even if I did decide I wasn't feeling it, breaking her heart right before the holidays would just be cruel."

No, cruel is leading her on. She's in love with him and doesn't even realize he doesn't feel the same way.

"I know it sounds bad, like I'm leading her on."

It's like he read my thoughts.

"It doesn't sound great."

"I *might* be in love with her. There's a lot about Summer that works with me. She's driven in her career, fine to work long hours beside me, she makes killer coffee, and she's had a lot of great ideas on the All-Weather Blanket."

That sounds like a list of compliments you'd give your employee, not your girlfriend.

He continues, "Like I said, my mind is just elsewhere right now, so it's hard to know how I feel."

My nod serves as my response.

"What did you think about her?"

Besides thinking she's an excellent kisser?

If I set the accidental kiss aside, as any good brother would, she's cute in a fun-loving kind of way—the type of woman you could tackle to the ground and she'd laugh about it. But at the same time, I could totally see her rocking a sexy dress and high heels. But that's just first impressions. We barely talked. My assessment could be all wrong.

"She seems sweet."

"She is. Not to mention thoughtful and kind. She reminds me of Mom, you know? That's why I'm just letting things between us play out for a little while."

If Summer is even half the woman Patsy Davidson is, then Justin should stop being an idiot and go buy an engagement ring right now.

"This whole fight will blow over. She just needs a night to sleep on it." He runs his fingers through his hair. "Honestly, I think she was just ticked that I didn't go ballistic over your kiss. That's what she was really mad about. Normally, she's cool about the work stuff and the sacrifices I have to make to grow my business."

"The blankets?"

"Yeah, the blankets." His words are clipped. "They're doing really well, by the way. Thanks for asking."

"I know they're doing well. Mom's been telling me all about how sales skyrocketed after your *Shark Tank* episode aired, and you said the sales projection for Black Friday is huge. I think it's awesome."

"It is awesome." The tenseness in Justin's shoulders relaxes when he sees I'm not going to tease him about his business. I probably would've when we were teenagers, but I've matured a lot over the years, and I respect him for working hard and building a company. If you're passionate about something, you should go after it. That's how I've always lived my life. Besides, who am I to dis on how someone chooses to make money? My own path hasn't been traditional.

"So now that you know about my problems with Summer, it's only fair I know why you're here."

"I just needed a break from filming and from always being on the go. What better time to take a break than the holidays? Spend time with family." I don't need to go into the whole part about me feeling like something is missing in my life—a grounding influence that is distinctly absent. When you've jumped off one tall bridge, it starts to feel like you've jumped off them all.

But even that isn't the real reason I came home.

My best friend, Lars, died two months ago, and although I knew it was coming—his leukemia had gotten worse over the last year—I wasn't prepared for how much losing him would make me miss every other relationship I'd lost in my life. I can't get Lars back, but maybe I can get my family back, and that's what my time in Telluride is all about.

Justin slaps his thighs before coming to a stand. "I'm sure Mom will be thrilled about your homecoming."

There's an edge to his words, the one that was there when we were kids, the childhood jealousy that I'm the presumed favorite son.

Kiss his girlfriend, no big deal.

But if our mom so much as smiles at me, he'll be wracked with jealousy.

That's where the real rivalry is at.

"I'll go visit Mom and Dad tomorrow." I keep my eyes on him. "But I'm not just here to see them. I want to hang out with you as well. Reconnect a little."

"Great, another person demanding I spend time with them," he jokes.

"Nah, I'm not here to stress you out. I'm chill to just hang out like this."

"I'd like that." His face lifts, and I know he means it. Twins have a bond that's meant to keep them close.

He turns and walks around the edge of the couch. "Well, tonight, I need to work, so we'll have to hang out another time."

"I'm not even a hundred percent yet, so no worries." I lift the remote, turning the volume to something so low you'd have to be sitting six inches away from the TV to be able to hear it. But I don't mind. It's the least I can do, considering Justin is letting me crash at his place for the next month.

We'll call it my first step toward reconnecting.

seven

SUMMER

SHE NEEDS a head count for food.

That's the excuse my mom went with.

As if one person is really going to sway the numbers that much.

I glance down at my phone and my mom's text, rereading it.

Mom: Hi, Summer. We're going to eat take-and-bake pizzas and salad tonight before we stuff the turkey. I need to get a head count for who's coming so I know how many pizzas to buy. Should I mark you down for one?

She thinks her text is an encrypted, multi-layered code that would take the entire FBI to figure out its meaning. But she's wrong. I got the message loud and clear. And because I'm not feeling any holiday spirit, I'm not giving her what she wants. I'm not letting her be right about Justin.

Summer: No, mark me down for two.

Mom: Oh, is Vivian coming with you tonight?

This woman and her manipulative mothering are unbeatable. Don't get me wrong. I love her to death. She's the sweetest lady around.

Actually, though, bringing my best friend, Vivian, isn't that bad of an idea. At least I wouldn't have to be solo at the party, and maybe if I brought someone outside our family, the conversation about Justin not attending wouldn't be too bad. I push my chair back, rolling far enough so I can see past my desk to Vivian's.

She chews on the end of a pen as she looks down at a piece of paper, giving me a perfect view of her Shirley Temple brown curls.

"Viv, what are you doing tonight? Want to come with me to my family's annual Turkey Stuff?"

She flips her head up, leaning back into her chair. "Is that the thing where your dad holds the Thanksgiving turkey by the wings and chases you around the kitchen?"

My brows drop. Out of our fifteen-year friendship, that's the takeaway Vivian got from my family's odd tradition.

"Uh, yeah." I can't seem to relax my furrow. "Kind of."

"Hmm." She nods twice, like she's thinking back to our teenage years when she stopped by my house on Thanksgiving Eve and witnessed the event firsthand. "Sounds fun, but I can't make it. I'm leaving work early so Sam and I can drive to Denver to spend Thanksgiving with my family."

My brows drop even lower. "Sam is spending Thanksgiving with your family?"

Her smile stretches wide. "Yeah, didn't I tell you?"

"But you've only been dating one month."

"I know." She shrugs happily. "It's kind of fast to meet the parents, but Sam said he didn't want to spend one second apart from me this weekend. So we're headed to Denver together."

Not one second apart, huh?

"That's great." I forcibly raise my brows into something over-joyed with excitement. "I'm really happy for you." If being happy for your friend includes feelings of hurt and jealousy.

No, I really am happy for Vivian. She wants and deserves the fairytale ending as much as I do. I just can't get over how fast, easy, and uncomplicated her relationship with Sam has been from the very beginning. I wouldn't even know what to do with a relationship like that. Everything is an uphill battle with Justin, and right now, we're at a steep incline.

"I'm happy too." Vivian sighs. "It's pathetic, but I'm totally over the moon for Sam. It's like we're seventeen, experiencing some crazy kind of love that no one understands. But you get it." She looks at me expectantly while I blink back at her. "You know, with Justin."

"Oh! With Justin." My voice and my nod are a bit too enthusiastic. "Right. I thought you meant that I get your and Sam's relationship. But no, I have my own crazy kind of love with Justin, so I understand what you're going through." I scratch my ear. "We're crazy in love. Like *crazy* crazy."

"Wait." Vivian sits up. "Why isn't Justin going to your family turkey thing with you?"

My shoulders drop. "He's working."

"Noooo!" Vivian slides out of her chair and runs to me, leaning in for a hug. "I'm sorry, Summer." She straightens, using the corner of my desk as her chair. "I know how hard things have been with his schedule."

My gaze turns misty. "I'm just so tired of going solo and then having to defend his intentions to my family." I press the heels of my palms into my eyes, staving off the tears. "It's stupid. I'm whining about the dumbest thing. I mean, there are people with real problems."

"It's not stupid." Vivian pulls my arms down so she can look me in the eyes. Her frown is the perfect amount of genuine best-friend sympathy. "It's hard. You love him, and you want your family to love him. There's nothing wrong with that."

"Why is it so hard for me when everything between you and Sam is easy? If it's meant to be, it should be easy, right?"

"Not necessarily."

"I think I'm just forcing it too much because I want to get married so bad." I flop over, resting my head on my desk. "Maybe my family is right. Maybe Justin doesn't really love me."

"Hey!" Vivian takes me by the shoulders, forcing me to sit up. "Justin is great. Remember when he brought you roses at work?" That was seven months ago, but still sweet. "And that night you locked your keys in your car at Walmart on your way to Denver, and he drove two hours round trip just to bring you your spare?" Again, that was more at the beginning of our relationship but still an amazing gesture. "He's a good guy. I know it's hard right now, but you're doing the right thing by supporting him in his business. Relationships aren't always about fun. Sometimes you have to work and put real-life stuff over the romance. And when you do that, your foundation will be so much stronger than everyone else's."

I look up with hope in my eyes. "You think?"

"I know." She squeezes my shoulder. "So just ignore your family. Stay focused on what you have with Justin."

"I'll try. I'm just so scared that if it doesn't work out with him, I'll be alone the rest of my life."

"You're not going to be alone." She rolls her eyes as if she's sick of hearing that same sentiment from me.

I don't want to be the annoying friend, so I change the subject. "I met his twin brother."

"Oh, how did that go?"

"We kissed."

Vivian practically falls off the desk in shock. "You kissed?"

"It was an accident. It was dark, and I thought I was surprising Justin in his kitchen with a kiss, but it was really his twin brother."

"Do they look that much alike?"

"Yeah, they're identical." I don't mention the ways Caleb has been blessed with a little extra oomph.

"Was it so awkward when you realized it wasn't Justin?"

"I fell in the dishwasher because I was so shocked."

Her hand goes to her heart. "I would've died of embarrassment."

"It's definitely not how I pictured meeting his brother for the first time."

Vivian grimaces. "Was Justin mad?"

"He thought it was funny."

"Well, that's good."

Is it?

I was annoyed at first. Me kissing another man, especially his brother, should have driven him into a fit of jealousy. But I guess I should look at it like Vivian and be happy that we all can move on from the disaster. No hard feelings.

"Yeah, it's no big deal." I cover up my annoyance with a smile.

"If they're that identical, it's too bad you can't use the twin to help with your family while Justin works."

Before I can tell Vivian that Justin suggested that very thing, her phone rings. "Back to work!" she calls as she runs to her desk. She slides into her chair as she answers, "Mountain Management. This is Vivian."

It's weird that Vivian mentioned the same twin exchange that Justin did. Where is everybody getting this idea? Was *The Parent Trap* on TV this weekend?

Another text comes in from my mom, and I pick up my phone.

Mom: So, I'll plan on you and Vivian tonight.

Janet Stanworth is relentless.

Summer: No, it will be me and Justin.

Even as I push send, I know my lie is a bad idea, especially after I just promised Vivian that I would ignore my family and focus on what I have with Justin. But it's like I can't stop trying to make him look good in front of my mom. And half of me is still holding out hope that Justin will come.

Mom: Great. I can't wait to see him.

It's almost like she knows I'm lying. That's why I open the text thread between me and Justin. Since our fight Monday night, he's texted a bunch of times, telling me he's sorry and that if I can just be patient with him, everything will work out. And he's right. It will all work out. But that doesn't stop me from sending him one last passive-aggressive text. I must've learned this tactic from my mom.

Summer: Hey! Just thinking about you. I'm getting ready to leave the office and am so excited I don't have to see this place for a few days. If you need a break from work tonight or if you're hungry, stop by my parents' house. We'll have pizza and salad. You don't have to stay long. Just come say hi. *kiss emoji*

I push send, hoping the flirty emoji keeps Justin from feeling irritated with me.

Justin: I had pizza for lunch. But thanks, though. I'll see you tomorrow. *kiss emoji*

His flirty emoji doesn't stop me from feeling irritated.

CALEB

I DIG another scoop of Rocky Road ice cream out of the carton and drop it into my bowl. Yesterday's grocery shopping was the best thing I've done with my time since I arrived at Justin's house. Besides Cinnamon Toast Crunch, the cupboards were bare of edible food. There were healthy options, but 'tis the season to be merry, and junk food makes me merry. Plus, I finally have my appetite back from the altitude sickness.

"I need to get the oil changed in my Bronco," I say to Justin as I put the container back in the freezer. The car has been sitting untouched at my parents' house for the last year. It might even need more than an oil change, but we'll start with that. "Do you have someone in town you like?"

"Uh..." Justin sounds distracted, and it's not until I walk out of the kitchen with my bowl of ice cream that he actually finishes his thought. "Lane's dad owns a shop. That's where I take my car." He says the whole sentence while squinting at his computer screen.

"Okay." My spoon brushes against my lips as the chocolate ice cream melts onto my tongue. "Who the heck is Lane? Should I know him?" I don't know why I would. My parents moved here three years ago, and I've only visited four times. I don't know anyone.

Justin nods toward his phone beside him on the table. "His contact is in my phone under *Lane's dad*."

Dropping into the seat next to him, I pick up the phone, adjusting it in one hand while still holding the bowl of ice cream in the other. I stare at the screen, seeing if the facial recognition will work on me. It does. My identical face unlocks the device perfectly.

"Lane's dad," I say to myself as I set the bowl down and swipe through his phone. I'm midway through the J's on his contact list when a text from Summer pops up. Actually, it's a picture, a selfie of her and an uncooked turkey still in its packaging, but the picture on the pop-up is too small to really see what's happening, so I click on the text. Her wide smile and red lipstick fill the screen. I stare for a second, noticing how her hair is flipped way past her part—I'm sidetracked, wondering how it got there and liking the wildness of it. My eyes drift to her pilgrim earrings, and my lips lift a little. She's gone away from Christmas, paying homage to Thanksgiving. Now I'm wondering how many pairs of Thanksgiving earrings she owns and what day she'll go back to wearing Christmas-themed ones.

I exit out of the picture but not their text thread. It's not snooping when your brother hands you his phone. I read over the last few texts.

Summer: Hey! Just thinking about you. I'm getting ready to leave the office and am so excited I don't have to see this place for a few days. If you need a break from work tonight or if you're hungry, stop by my parents' house. We'll have pizza and salad. You don't have to stay long. Just come say hi. *kiss emoji*

Justin: I had pizza for lunch. But thanks, though. I'll see you tomorrow. *kiss emoji*

"Dude, you're such a jerk." I backhand smack Justin's shoulder with the flick of my fingers.

He leans away from my slap. "What?"

"I had pizza for lunch?" My head shakes as I stare back at him, disgusted.

"What?"

I hold the open text thread in front of his eyes. "Summer clearly still wants you to come."

"You're reading my texts?"

"Not on purpose. She sent a picture." I shake the phone. "Throw the poor girl a bone."

"I'm working." He swipes the device away from his face. "Besides, I already made things right with her. She's fine."

"She's not fine. She's trying to get you to come without *telling* you to come." My eyes drop to the picture. "I feel bad for her."

Summer seems like a nice enough girl. She deserves more than Justin's indifference while he decides whether or not he wants her.

"You know, you could solve this if you wanted. You could go to the party for me."

"Not this again."

"I don't know what the big deal is. You used to love swapping. You thought it was funny."

"It's been a decade since we've done anything like that."

"That's not true. What about last year when your passport expired, and you couldn't get one in time for your international flight?" I roll my eyes but don't say anything because I know he's nailed me on this one. "You made me drive to Aurora, pose as you, say I had urgent travel—"

"Filming in Austria was urgent. We had a small window of time I could climb that particular mountain."

He gives me a sharp look before continuing. "Then overnight it to you in Wyoming."

"Montana," I correct.

"Whatever. The point is, I missed work, dropped everything, lied on an official US document—I could go to jail, by the way—

all for you, and you can't go to one stupid holiday party for me? I thought you wanted to work on our relationship."

"No, I said I wanted to hang out, reconnect. Posing as you doesn't fall under those categories."

"Oh, come on. Just do this one thing for me. It's not like you have anything else going on tonight. Plus, it will appease Summer's family and make them not hate me as much when I show up for Thanksgiving dinner tomorrow night."

"They're still going to hate you," I tease with a smile.

"But *less*."

"You're forgetting one major detail: Summer doesn't want to do this."

"Summer doesn't know what she doesn't know. She *thinks* she doesn't want to do this, but after she sees how well it works, she'll thank us for getting her family off her back."

"I don't know." I shake my head. "I still don't think it's a good idea."

"Why?

"Posing as you for her family feels like leading the poor girl on even more."

"I'm not leading her on. I'm still deciding. But if her family hates me, then she'll break up with me before I do decide. What if she's the love of my life, and this one little holiday party ruins everything? Do you really want to have that on your shoulders?"

My eyes pin him. "You can't manipulate me."

"Fine. Then just do this for me because I'm begging you to."

"I don't know. It's weird."

"What's weird?"

"The whole thing. Pretending like I'm in love with your girl-friend. It was one thing to do it with a date when we were teenagers, but a long-term girlfriend? It's too much."

"How?"

"Am I supposed to touch her? Don't you think we already crossed too many lines already?"

"Trust me, Summer will touch you whether you're

pretending to be me or not. She's just an affectionate, touchy person all around. Just follow her lead."

"I did that the other night, and we ended up making out."

Justin throws a pencil at me, the tip hitting my chest.

"Ow! That could've taken off my nipple." I rub the spot in question.

"Then put a shirt on for once." Justin tries to act mad, but the smile he's holding back tells me we're fine. "Listen, you don't have to touch her or pretend like you're in love with her. Just show up. Get to know the family. That's all I need. Then I can come tomorrow and do all the physical affection boyfriend stuff."

"Just show up?"

"Just show up." He nods. "I mean, you owe me that much for the passport, for staying here for free"—he glances around the condo—"for making everything messy."

My eyes follow his. There's a drip of chocolate ice cream melting on his kitchen table. My shoes and coat are thrown haphazardly in front of the door. The blanket I used while watching TV last night is crumpled on the floor beside the couch. There are soda cans and a bowl of yesterday's popcorn on the coffee table. And that's just what we can see. I know what the guest bathroom looks like. And I'm keenly aware of the pile of dishes in the sink. I'm sure my messes are a lot for my clean-freak brother.

I shift my gaze to him. "So you're implying that me posing for you tonight is like my payment for all the other things."

"Yes."

"And then we'll be even?"

"Then we'll be even." Justin shrugs. "Plus, it will mean a lot to me. You'd really be helping me out. I don't want to lose Summer, but I also can't risk neglecting my business."

His eyes are sincere, and in that moment, all I want is to be the kind of brother that Justin can rely on.

"Fine." I slap the table as I stand. "I'll go. But I'm only doing it one time. Just because I'm taking a break from work and don't have anything going on doesn't mean I'm available to stand in for you whenever you want."

"Yeah, just this one time."

"When does the party start?"

"6:30." Justin taps on his home screen, and we both glance down at the clock. It's 6:27 right now. "You better hurry. If you're really late, it will make me look bad." There's amusement in his expression, but I'm still annoyed.

"You make yourself look bad." I throw an irritated look at him as I walk toward my bedroom. "Follow me." I signal. "Tell me everything I need to know about her family."

"I don't know much." Justin's voice is behind me as I dig through the clean clothes in my bag. I haven't really unpacked yet, so wrinkles cover every shirt I hold up.

"Why don't you wear something of mine? You're impersonating me, after all."

I glance over my shoulder at his button-up shirt and iron-pressed slacks before turning back to my own clothes. "No, thanks."

"Anyway, I've only met her parents twice."

This piece of information causes me to pause and glance at him again with raised brows. "Twice in nine months?"

"Yeah, I've been busy."

"No wonder they hate you."

"Can we just stay focused here? Her parents' names are Marty and Janet. And then she has four sisters I've never met. Anna, Erin, Hailey, and Juliet, and she's the youngest."

Four protective older sisters. Yikes.

"I'm never going to remember all of their names, and my willingness to do this just went down a notch or two."

"I don't know what you're so worried about. We both know moms, sisters, and families all love you. It's me that they don't like. After twenty minutes, you'll have them eating out of the palm of your hand."

"That's probably true." I smell a gray long-sleeve shirt. It's a little musty from days in my bag, but nothing a little cologne can't solve. I throw it over my head and pull it down. "I'm going to the bathroom." I point my finger at Justin as I pass. "You text Summer and tell her I'm coming."

"Yeah, good idea." He reaches for his phone in his back pocket.

I don't really want to do this, and I know Summer isn't going to like it. So it's best if she knows beforehand what Justin has planned.

I don't want any surprises.

Surprises make things awkward.

SUMMER

SO HERE'S THE DEAL… It's best to be honest and forthright upfront. I live my life by that motto. I really do. I planned to tell my parents as soon as I got to their house that Justin wasn't coming, but when I walked through the door —*alone*—my mother immediately snipped, "I knew he wouldn't come," and something inside me cared more about not looking pathetic than being honest. So I lied.

"He's coming." I smile sweetly at her. "He's just coming straight from work, so we decided to have him meet me here."

"See, Janet"—my dad nods at my mom—"if Summer says Justin is going to be here, then he will. There's nothing to worry about." His smile lands on me, and I feel awful, as if I just told a six-year-old in the prime of his Christmas-magic life that there's no way a reindeer could fly, let alone have a red nose that glowed.

But I smile back at my dad because I'm in too deep now and because I have a plan.

I'll pretend to take a phone call in ten minutes and act like Justin got in a car accident, and that's why he's not here or coming at all. It's lying but on a very low-grade level. He *did* get in a car accident two nights ago that detained him. I'm just fudging the dates a little bit.

I change the subject away from Justin, pointing at the uncooked turkey in the roaster pan in the middle of the kitchen island. It still has the netting and packaging on it, but I pretend to know its poultry value. "That looks like a good one."

My dad beams. "Only the best for Thanksgiving."

I lean my head down by the turkey, holding my phone out in front of me. I flip my hair, smile big at the camera, and take a selfie with me and the turkey. I send it to Justin, not saying anything with the picture because what would I say? He's already made it clear and given me all the reasons why he can't come. So I let the picture speak for itself and set my phone down.

"What can I help with?" I pull out a stool.

"You can mix the Caesar salad." My mom pushes a bowl, a spoon, and a prepackaged salad bag in front of me.

I tear the bag open, dumping the lettuce into the bowl. "Where is everybody?"

"Carma's right there."

I whip around, noticing for the first time my great aunt, sitting at the kitchen table playing solitaire.

"Dang, two of diamonds," she mutters, flipping three cards over. "Where are you hiding?"

"Erin's family is out back, playing in the snow." I spin back around just as my mom gestures to the kitchen window. "Hailey and Juliet both texted and said they're going to be a few minutes late. And I haven't heard from Anna yet."

I glance at the oven clock, wondering when I should break the news that Justin got in a fender bender. It's 6:25 p.m., and anything past 6:45 is going to make him seem really late and just give my mom more cause to hate him. So we'll break the news at 6:42 p.m. The front door opens and slams shut, and immediately, the house is filled with excitement.

My nephews, Jack and Peter, run into the kitchen, each wearing one of those turkey feather paper hats that you make at school. "Grandma!" They run into my mom's legs, wrapping their arms around her thighs.

She pats their backs. "Are those turkeys or my grandbabies?"

"I'm a turkey!" Peter releases his grip first and bounces around the kitchen like a pinball, and it doesn't take long for Jack to join him.

"Sorry we're late." Anna plops an armful of two liters on the counter. "Lucy's diaper leaked right as we were leaving. We had to take her out of the car seat and change her outfit." Anna lowers her voice. "I think Jeff was in a hurry and put the diaper on wrong, and that's why it leaked."

"I heard that." Jeff comes around the corner, holding ten-month-old Lucy.

Anna flashes him a coy smile. "Heard what?"

"Well, the diaper doesn't matter. Because the kids' pizza just finished cooking. Boys, are you ready to eat?" My mom opens the oven, pulls out a half pepperoni and half cheese pizza, and slides it onto a hot pad.

Jack and Peter scoot onto stools, banging their fists on the table, chanting, "*Pizza! Pizza!*" but nobody seems to notice or care.

"I like your hats," I say to my nephews. "How come you didn't bring me one?"

Peter scrunches his nose. "Your head is too big."

"You're a girl. Girls don't get a turkey hat." Jack leans over his younger brother so he can see me when he talks.

"That's unfair." My brows drop.

"Girls get pilgrim hats," Jack explains.

"I don't need a pilgrim hat." I brush my hair aside. "I already have pilgrim earrings."

"Jeff," my mom calls over the noise, "will you open the back door and tell Erin the food is ready?"

"Yep." He shuffles to the other side of the kitchen where the door is.

Anna reaches across me, placing two plates of pizza in front of Jack and Peter. "Where's Justin?"

"He's coming from work. He'll be here any minute." The

front door opens again. "Maybe that's him," I say, knowing full well it is definitely *not* Justin, but I have to sell this lie if I want the car-accident excuse to actually work.

"We're here!" Juliet calls from the entryway.

"I guess it's not Justin." Anna's blue eyes skid to me. "Besides, he wouldn't feel comfortable just walking in the house, would he?"

"No." My shoulders drop a little. "He wouldn't."

"Sorry I'm late." Juliet gives my dad a side hug as she enters the kitchen.

"You're right on time."

I do a clock check, and my stomach pulls into a knot—6:32 p.m. Ten more minutes until the fake fender-bender call, and those ten minutes will go fast.

Pandemonium takes over the room as Erin's family comes in from outside. Cora and Berkley whine because they're cold. Juliet's six-month-old cries as she takes her out of her car seat and sits her in one of my mom's two highchairs. Jeff puts Lucy in the other highchair, and while all of that is going on, Hailey and her husband, Brian, and their twin seven-year-old boys show up, making the kitchen feel more crowded than a Pillsbury dough can.

Everything is loud and chaotic with my family, and I love it.

Like, *love* it.

I love how there are seven different conversations happening at once, how everyone talks over each other, how babies cry in the background, and how my nephews spill their drinks. How nobody can get around the kitchen island without their body parts skimming someone else's like you're trying to get out of your row at a movie theater. How the countertop is full of food, and the sink is topped with dishes. How my Aunt Carma swears over her card game and my mom warns her to behave in front of the kids. And I love that we all think it's normal. It's just how my family is.

My dad nudges Rick aside so he can open the oven and take

out another pizza. "When Summer gets married and starts having kids, we're going to have to knock out a wall and make this kitchen bigger, or else we all won't fit."

My dad's a sweetheart and has absolutely no idea that his well-meaning comment cuts me to the core. Marriage and kids are at the top of my to-do list—the *tip-top*. In seventh grade, in the college and career class, I wrote down that I wanted to be a wife and mom when I grew up. My teacher made me change it and choose an actual career path. As a side note, I did not choose an overworked property manager. I think I chose a school teacher because that would still be a good option for a mom because you have summers off.

The point is, I haven't crossed off the *start my own family* goal at the top of my to-do list. And it's fine. I'm young. There's still plenty of time to make all that happen. I know all of that. I repeat it to myself whenever I feel bummed about my current life situation, or feel jealous of my sisters, or when I'm frustrated about how slow things are moving between me and Justin. So I smile back at my dad and repeat it one more time. *I'm young. There's still plenty of time to make all that happen.*

"Speaking of Summer getting married"—Hailey looks around—"is Justin here?"

"He's on his way," my mother answers, but not in an informative kind of way. No, her tone is all skepticism and mistrust—and for good reason.

I glance behind her at the oven clock. 6:41 p.m. Close enough.

"Actually, this is him calling." I quickly hold my phone up to my ear so that nobody can see the screen and call my bluff on my fake phone call. "Hey, babe!" My words are loud and cheery as I exit the room. Even though I'm technically out of earshot of the kitchen, I keep the charade going as I pace the living room. "Are you serious? Oh my gosh! Are you okay?" I have the shock, the panic, and the worry down to a T as I pause and wait like I'm listening to Justin talk. "No, don't worry about it. There's nothing you can do." From the corner of my eye, I see my mom leaning against the wall between the kitchen and the living room. There's a disapproving, pinched expression hovering over her brows as her suspicions about Justin's attendance come to fruition. Now, my only goal is to soften her harsh judgment. "No, I'm just glad you're okay. That's the most important thing right now. I mean, you could've been killed if you weren't watching." I play the *killed* card to gain more sympathy. "Or seriously injured. It's amazing you're walking away without a scratch." I nod a few times, then end strong. "No, I know how much you wanted to come. You'll get to stuff the turkey next year." I pause, then push my lips into a frown. "Aww, don't have FOMO. We'll take lots of pictures. Okay. Sounds good. Bye."

I pretend like I'm ending the call before I flip around to my mother's crossed arms and pursed lips. I'm getting my story out there before she has the chance to speak.

"Justin was in a car accident! Can you believe it?" Like, seriously, does she believe it? I don't even give her a chance to answer before I add more details. "He's okay, thankfully. But pretty shaken up."

Her brows raise in her same cynical way. "So he's not coming?"

"He can't. He has to wait for the police to arrive and figure out whether or not his car is driveable or if he needs to call a tow truck. He's so bummed to miss."

My mom studies me for a second, and I worry she's going to call me out by dramatically shouting, "LIAR!" But instead, she nods and says, "That's too bad, Summer. I know how much you want him here."

There's a softness in her eyes that kills me. I *do* want him here, and any animosity or snippiness from her about Justin is because she cares, because she knows more than anyone how much I want this to work out.

She wipes her hands on her apron and heads back into the

kitchen, with me trudging after her. All eyes are on us when we enter.

"Justin's not coming?" I hate that that's Juliet's first assumption after the call.

"He got in a car accident."

Erin's eyes go wide with concern. "Is he okay?"

"Yeah, a woman clipped his back bumper, causing him to hit the car in front of him." That part is true, which is important for the pictures I'm about to show them, but this next part is a full-blown lie to strengthen my case. "When she hit him, he hit the car in front of him, spun through oncoming traffic, and ended up on the other side of the road, facing the opposite direction. He's lucky to be alive." Their faces and expressions show adequate concern and belief, so I keep going. "But from the sounds of things, he's fine, and there's minimal damage to his car."

"A Christmas miracle," my mom says with a smile so fake she's practically a flocked Christmas tree.

"Yes." I meet her gaze. "It would appear so."

"No, it's a *Thanksgiving* miracle," Miles, one of the twins, says.

"A *turkey* miracle!" Max shouts louder than his brother.

"That's right." My dad reaches across the pizza trays and ruffles both of their hair.

"Oh look, he sent me a picture." I flip to the photo from Monday night's accident I already had dialed up and show my family. It's a shot of Justin's car where his bumper was dented in from hitting the other car's fender.

Jeff points at my phone. "If he got hit first in the back, how come there's no dent there?" He's not asking to prove me wrong. He's just always thinking critically. It's annoying—especially right now.

"It was just a bump."

Jeff frowns. "A bump was enough to cause him to hit another car and spin across all the lanes of traffic?"

75

"Ice!" I interject. When in doubt, choose slick roads. "His tires spun out on ice." I don't even know if that's possible.

"Let me see." Erin's husband, Tommy, leans over my shoulder to take a look. That's when Brian and Rick join too. Now, all my brothers-in-law are discussing the trajectory and plausibility of my story. I want to take the picture away and hold it close to my chest so no one can look at it anymore, but that might give away my lie, so I stand there, letting them dissect it.

The doorbell rings. "I'll get it!" Finally, a way to get me and this picture out of here.

"What kind of salesman would knock on the door on a holiday?" my mom scoffs.

Anna laughs. "I don't think the Stanworth family Turkey Stuff is recognized as a national holiday."

"Not yet, at least," my dad chimes in.

"Maybe it's Bob Irvine," Carma says, keeping her eyes on her cards.

I back away from the men even as Rick gets the last word in.

"No, if the car hit him first, wouldn't the inertia take him in the other direction?"

Inertia? Are you freaking kidding me, Rick? All I wanted was a good excuse for my boyfriend. I've never been so happy to exit a room in my life.

I swing the door open, shocked by more than the blast of frigid air that hits my face.

Caleb stands on my front steps, the porch light illuminating him like a personal halo. His gray long-sleeve shirt fits snuggly over his chest and arms, making me wonder if there's a size at the store where he shops called let's-make-women-notice-how-in-shape-we-are (it's working, by the way). One curl from his wavy brown hair drops over his forehead, hanging above his dark brows and light-blue eyes. He smiles and shrugs, and that's when I panic.

"What are you doing here?"

His smile wavers. "Didn't Justin text you?"

"About what?"

"The swap."

I blink back at him, confused. Caleb takes a step forward like he's about to tell me a secret he doesn't want anyone else to hear. I'm momentarily distracted by his manly aroma that smells like Justin's body wash but with Caleb's own personal twist on it. Luckily, I have enough sense to stop myself from closing my eyes and savoring the smell.

"You know, the swap." His voice is low. "I'm impersonating Justin to make your family happy."

"I said I didn't want to do that."

"Well, Justin thinks you do."

"I don't."

"Are you sure?"

"Yes, I'm sure."

"Who's there?" My mom is right behind me, causing my heart to bang with sheer terror.

I do the only thing I can think of. I slam the front door in Caleb's face, then spin around to my mother, blocking the door from her reach.

"Salesman! Just like you said." My arm wraps around her shoulder, trying to ease her back into the kitchen. But Janet Stanworth can't be *eased*.

"Summer!" she scolds, wiggling out of my arm. And before I can stop her, she yanks the door open.

Caleb stands there in that awkward state of *Should I go or should I stay?*

"Justin? How did you get here?" Her shock is warranted. He's basically back from the dead—or at least back from his car accident that happened five minutes ago.

"Uh..." He looks at me, eyes asking what he should do.

Is he Justin?

Or is he Caleb?

Oh, for the love! We're in too deep now. I guess he's Justin. At least I won't be alone the entire night.

I take a step forward in damage-control mode. "She means,

how did you get here so fast after the car accident? You just called five minutes ago and said you weren't going to make it." There's a secret message in my stare that I hope Caleb understands, a fill-in-the-blanks-as-best-as-you-can type code. But we've only spent ten minutes together with him being conscious, and I was groping his chest and mauling his lips for part of that time, so I wouldn't say I know him well enough to know if he can read my mind.

"Yes, the car accident." He points at me, not missing a beat. "My brother came and switched cars with me so I could hurry and come here." Caleb's light eyes turn to me. "I just knew how much this night meant to Summer, and I couldn't leave her hanging."

Now it's his turn to have a hidden message—the reason he's standing on my parents' front porch, pretending to be my boyfriend.

"Well, that was so nice of your brother to do that."

"We trade things all the time. Cars, girlfriends, you name it. Nothing's off limits between us."

I turn my head to Caleb with a warning glare tailor-made just for him.

My mom completely misses what he said, inviting him in with a smile, and it's not even her fake, skeptic smile. She's genuinely happy Justin is here. It's amazing how far showing up one time goes with this woman. I've seen the flipside and what *not* showing up does to her, so this is a nice change for once. "Come in where it's warm."

Caleb eyes me as he passes, and there's another whiff of his lethal smell that confuses my senses. I need to shove a balsam-and-cedar Yankee Candle up my nose to keep the delicious smell at bay.

My mom grabs his arm and drags him toward the kitchen. "You guys will never believe who's here!" she calls before she's even entered the room.

I pick up my steps so I can be in on the big reveal too.

"It's Justin." My mom presents Caleb for my family like she's Vanna White.

"Surprise!" he holds out jazz hands, shaking them in the air, and I'm more surprised by that gesture than anything else tonight. Justin would never wiggle his fingers in excitement, and now I'm questioning how much this little ruse will really work.

"What about the car accident?" Rick asks, and I know if I don't stop him, he's going to come with a follow-up question about trajectory and inertia.

I step forward. "His brother went to the accident and switched him cars so he could come here. Let me introduce you to my family," I quickly say so Rick doesn't have a chance to linger on the car accident. "This is my sister Erin from Denver and her husband, Tommy, and her girls, Cora and Berkley."

Erin pushes her way to the front, extending her hand out. "You are way cuter in real life than in the pictures Summer has shown me."

"Is that so?" Caleb's amused smile flashes to me as he shakes her hand. His smug expression proves he doesn't need any praise added to his already self-inflated ego.

I ignore him, continuing with the introductions. "And that's Anna, Jeff, and their three kids, Jack, Peter, and Lucy."

"How's it going?" Jeff waves from across the room.

"And then we have Hailey and Brian." I point to her twin boys. "And Miles and Max."

Caleb's smile widens. "You're twins?"

"Yep!" Max nods.

"I have a twin brother."

My mom frowns at me. "Summer, you never told us that Justin has a twin brother."

"I didn't?" I peek at Caleb, a little embarrassed that I've never mentioned his existence to my family. "Yeah, Justin has a twin brother named Caleb."

His smile widens. "But Caleb is way better looking, more athletic, and definitely more charming than I am."

Like I said, super-inflated ego.

I give him a warning stare that does nothing to extinguish his amusement. So instead, I turn to my family. "Yeah, but Caleb is more full of himself than Justin is."

I don't miss his amused smile.

"I'm more athletic!" Miles chirps.

"Nuh-uh!"

"Yes-huh!"

"I don't know," Caleb breaks in, "you both look pretty tough and athletic to me."

"Okay." Miles shrugs, taking a bite of his pizza as if he's completely satisfied by them being equals.

"And this"—I gesture to Juliet's family—"is Rick, Juliet, and Bailey."

Juliet smiles as she leans forward to shake his hand. "We've talked on the phone before."

Caleb looks at me.

"You called Juliet to get some ideas of what to get me for Valentine's Day, remember?" I feel like a lawyer leading the witness.

"Yes." Caleb nods dramatically. "That's right."

"And you've already met my parents, Marty and Janet." I say their names in case Justin didn't debrief him beforehand.

"Yes, it's great to see you guys again. Thank you for letting me come tonight."

"And last but not least is Aunt Carma." Everyone swings their eyes to her at the kitchen table. She glances up at Caleb, eyes him with appreciation, says, "I didn't know we were getting dessert with dinner," then goes back to her card game.

I have a feeling Caleb is the *dessert.*

"Are you hungry?" my dad asks, handing him a paper plate with a cartoon turkey on it.

"Starving." Caleb smiles as he steps toward the buffet of food laid out across the counter. "Do we eat before we..." His words trail off, and he laughs. "I actually have no clue what we're doing here tonight—something about a turkey and *stuff*."

"We're stuffing the Thanksgiving turkey." My dad points behind him to the roaster pan and the waiting poultry. "It's a family tradition."

Caleb laughs. "What are we stuffing it with?"

My mom places two slices of pizza on his plate. "Stuffing."

"The kind you eat?" He kicks out a barstool and sits like he owns the place. "Like Stove Top?"

"Well, yes, but we make homemade stuffing and cook it inside the turkey," I explain.

"Do people do this?" He looks around the room. "Like, is this normal? The stuffing goes *inside* the turkey?"

Jeff laughs. "If you're asking if people make a party out of shoving food inside a dead turkey full of salmonella, the answer is no. It's just this family."

From the sink, my dad breaks into the same song he always sings whenever somebody mentions salmonella poisoning. "Salmonella! Dolcinia!"

Caleb jumps, obviously unprepared for someone to belt out opera, and I'm suddenly embarrassed by my family. I mean, I love them. But having a stranger with no skin in the game be thrown in the middle of all the chaos makes me hyper-aware of just how odd we are.

I lean in, feeling the need to explain my dad's sudden opera outburst. "He's singing a song from *Man of La Mancha*. It's a Broadway musical or something. I don't really know."

Brian walks past, tipping his cup to Caleb. "As you can see, nothing about the Stanworth family and the holidays are normal."

I'm sure he's rethinking this swap and planning his exit as soon as he can.

"We're weird." My cheeks flame even brighter as I grimace back at him. "Sorry you have to witness this."

"It's fine." He laughs, but not in a mocking way. It's more of an amused way.

"Justin! Justin, listen!" My mom taps his forearm, trying to get his attention. "You don't have to stuff the turkey. You can just watch."

"Are you kidding me? Stuffing a turkey has just become a bucket-list item." Caleb's smile is so big and animated that I can't help smiling too. "How did this tradition even start?"

My mom rests her elbows on the kitchen island as if they're instant best friends. I can't even wrap my head around how fast she went from hating him to loving him, but I'm happy to see her trying for me. "When we moved to Telluride, twenty-seven years ago, we were missing our families back east and had all of these little girls who wanted to help in the kitchen, so we decided to have them help with the Thanksgiving prep. They loved it so much that we just kept doing it every single year."

"That's awesome," Caleb says between bites of pizza.

Anna stands next to my mom. "So, Justin, tell us about the All-Weather Blanket that's been keeping you so busy."

"Um..."

Oh, no. He's going to crack under pressure and ruin this whole operation.

"Well, I took something basic that has been around forever, like a blanket, and improved upon it. Did you know blankets are the number one comfort item in the world?"

"I thought food was," Tommy says.

"Yes, food and blankets." He nods, glancing at me. My brows raise, but I don't help him dig himself out.

"Security blankets have been around for years," he continues when he sees I'm no help. "They've been comforting people in sad times, so we just wanted to capitalize on that."

"So you're trying to comfort people in all kinds of weather?" Bless Anna's heart for trying to make sense of his nonsense.

"Uh...yeah. People need security blankets for comfort in the rain and snow just as much as they need it in their bedroom or the hospital."

Erin looks confused. "I thought the blankets were just supposed to keep people warm and dry in all kinds of wet weather."

"That too." Caleb scratches his ear. Maybe it's time to bail him out.

"I'm the financial backer of the whole thing!" Carma grunts from the table.

Caleb's eyes shift to me for confirmation. I give a slight shake of my head, clueing him in on my aunt's delusion.

"That's right, Carma!" He smiles at her. "Although, I thought you were a silent investor."

"Pfft!" She blows a raspberry with her lips, and a drop of spit flings out. "I'm not the silent type."

"Anyway"—I turn back to my family—"that's enough of that."

"Yeah, nobody wants to hear about my boring blankets. Why don't you guys tell me something embarrassing about Summer." He turns to me with a mischievous smile. "Like, has she ever mistakenly kissed someone she wasn't supposed to?"

My jaw hardens. I am not amused. I repeat: *not* amused.

"I hope not!" Hailey laughs. "That would be really embarrassing."

He looks directly at Hailey. "Wouldn't it, though?"

Somebody thinks he's a funny man.

I kick his shin under the bar as I say, "Trust me, I don't get embarrassed."

"You don't get embarrassed?" His brows rise in surprise as he studies me.

"No, not really."

"Oh, come on. I'm sure one of these sisters of yours has something good on you."

"I know one!" Juliet bounces excitedly. "When Summer was in high school, they were reading the book *The Outsiders* in class, and when it was her turn to read out loud, she got to a word and pronounced it so-no-fay-gun and then asked the teacher what that meant. The most beautiful boy in school laughed from the back and said, 'You mean *son of a gun?*' She had to leave the class because she was so embarrassed."

"In my defense, the phrase was smooshed together into one big word like the character in the book had said it fast, so it was an easy mistake."

"I can top sonofagun," Caleb says.

I lift my chin to him. "I doubt it."

"Oh, I can." His blue eyes peek down at me in a playful way. "Senior year. English class. The word was manslaughter, and I said man's laughter. *Man's laughter.*" This makes my entire family cackle while I try to bite back my smile. "I just couldn't understand why the character in the book was getting fifteen to twenty for laughing." That's when I crack and laugh too. Caleb's face is dead serious, which makes everything even funnier.

"Justin won." Juliet points to him. "His story is better than sonofagun."

I can't help but glance around the room and notice how everyone is laughing and hanging on his every word.

And just like that, Caleb took Justin from public enemy number one to the most popular kid in school.

CALEB

THE STANWORTH FAMILY is loud but in a fun, buzzed-with-energy kind of way that's more contagious than off-putting.

"Justin, would you like a tour of the house while they get the turkey ready?" Summer's eyes tell me this private meeting away from listening ears is non-negotiable.

I hop to my feet. "Yep, I'd love a tour."

"We'll be back in a minute." She reaches for my hand and then stops abruptly.

"What's wrong?" Juliet looks at Summer.

"Uh...I was just trying to remember if I had washed my hands before I give Justin a tour."

"Oh, come on." Anna smirks. "We all know your 'tour' of the house is just a way for you two to go make out."

Summer's face pales. "We're *not* making out. We would never. Why would we?"

"Yeah, right," Hailey scoffs from the other end of the kitchen. "You don't have to pretend for us. Mom and Dad don't care."

"I don't care if you wash your hands before you make out. Just wash your hands before you stuff the turkey," her dad says as he dries a pizza pan.

Summer looks like a deer in headlights—eyes wide and frozen. She was fine for the last thirty minutes while I chatted with her family, but the mention of kissing me again has immobilized her.

I grab her hand, winking at her sisters. "We're not ruling anything out just yet." I tug her forward, calling over my shoulder, "And don't worry, Marty. We'll wash our hands before we stuff anything."

Once we're in the hallway, she pulls her hand back. "What was that?"

"That was me saving your butt from blowing everything."

She immediately folds her arms as if she doesn't trust me not to randomly hold her hand again. "When it comes to touching, just follow my lead."

"That's what Justin said to do."

"You and Justin talked about this?"

"Yeah, if I'm pretending to be your boyfriend, I wanted to know what level of touching I was signing up for." I smirk. "I want to be prepared in case you start kissing my back and neck again."

Her arms fold. "You seem to remember a lot more about the other night than you're letting on." There's a directness to her glare that's fun to draw out from her.

"Not really. Just a fleeting moment. A flash of a memory here and there."

"Tag! You're it!" Miles runs past us, followed by Jack.

"Maybe we should"—she points to an open room—"go somewhere we can talk privately."

I gesture for her to lead the way and follow behind. My eyes drop down her body, quickly glancing over her tan wide-leg pants and then back up to the white sweater with flowy see-through long sleeves. I'm not checking Summer out. I'm just getting to know her.

She spins around abruptly, and my eyes jerk away from her body faster than a shopaholic blows through her Christmas budget. I focus on the crown molding on the ceiling. Very nice stuff.

"So, Caleb..." She pulls back her shoulders like she means to intimidate me. "Can you explain why you showed up on my doorstep tonight?"

"Isn't it obvious why I'm here?"

"Not really. I don't remember agreeing to you standing in for Justin."

"You didn't, but Justin thought it was a good idea, so here I am. In fairness, he was supposed to text you and tell you I was coming so it wouldn't be a surprise. I don't know why he didn't."

"He probably knew I'd say no."

"I can leave if you want." I take a step like I'm on my way out the door.

"No." She grabs my arm, keeping me here. "You can't leave in the middle. That will look bad. Besides, I think my family likes you."

"I like them."

Her lips crease into a small smile, and she drops my arm. "You don't have to say that. I know we're a lot."

"What's wrong with a lot?"

"Nothing, I guess." Her fingers comb through her hair, and my eyes fixate on the bright-red polish that shines over each nail. I'm transfixed as she tousles the roots, flipping half her hair over to the other side. That's how she creates that wave thing from the picture earlier.

"Why did you agree to come for Justin anyway?"

"Uh..." I shift my eyes back to her face. "I owed him for a passport thing last year, and I'm staying at his house for free for the next month, so I figured I could help him out." Plus, I'm extending an olive branch, a goodwill gesture that will hopefully bring us closer together this holiday season, but Summer doesn't get to be privy to that information.

"Oh." She nods a few times while she thinks of the next thing she's going to say. "I feel like we're on *Who's Line is it Anyway?* Do you remember that TV show? We have to improv and think on our feet. It's kind of a rush. I seriously think I missed my calling in life. Who knew all these years I was a pro at acting? I should've been in drama class and plays. It's a missed opportunity."

"You think you're a pro? I just spouted off blanket facts like I own the place."

"Your blanket ramblings were a definite low point in the conversation."

"What? How can you say that? I thought I really nailed it."

"No." She shakes her head. "They won't be hiring you for *Who's Line is it Anyway?* any time soon."

Summer's family members aren't the only crazy ones. She's got some crazy in her too.

Her brows pinch together. "What?"

I shrug, not sure what she means.

She points to my mouth. "Why are you smiling at me like that?"

I didn't even know I was smiling.

"I'm not smiling." Somehow, my smile grows even bigger.

She covers her mouth with her hand. "I have something in my teeth, don't I?"

"No." I laugh. "You look great." She looks a little more than great, but she's not my girlfriend, so I'm stopping the compliment right there. "Besides, if you had something in your teeth, do you really think I would have a whole conversation with you and not say something about it?"

"I would."

"No, you wouldn't. You'd tell me."

"Never." She shakes her head. "I'd look you right in the face for two hours without saying something. Then I'd make you go home and discover the green leaf in between your front teeth hours later and wonder how long it had been there."

"That's just cruel."

"What can I say?" She stretches one arm across her chest, then swings her limbs, repeating the stretch on the other side. "I'm a cruel person." She twists her neck from side to side, then rolls it around in a complete circle. "So there are a few things about tonight you need to know. My dad is going to put the gizzard in his mouth and pose for a picture."

"Like the turkey's gizzard?" I tilt my head, watching her stretch on the other side.

"Yes, and then we'll hold all the grandbabies in the air with the turkey and take a picture."

"That sounds cute."

"It is cute." She pulls her arm behind her head, holding it at her elbow. "And then my dad will spank the turkey a few times— the grandkids love it."

"Spank the turkey?" My smile turns naughty. "That sounds kinky."

"Justin wouldn't say *kinky*."

"Well, I'm not Justin." I watch as she drops her arm and repeats the same thing on the other side. "Are you stretching?" I try to tone down my amusement, but I'm not sure it worked.

"Obviously." She jumps up and down, wiggling and loosening her body. "I have to be limber for the turkey stuff and for the fake-boyfriend performance of a lifetime."

"I see." I watch as Summer bends at the waist and touches her toes.

She twists her head and looks up at me from her bent-over position. "Right now, you're wondering why your brother keeps dating me, huh?"

At least she's aware of her crazy flag flying in the wind.

"No, actually, I'm wondering why you haven't done the most important stretch of all." I drop into a lunge with hands on my hips. I might have a crazy flag I fly sometimes too.

She walks around me, assessing. "Impressive, but that's not the most important stretch." She grabs her ankle and bends her knee, stretching her quad.

"What about high knees?" I start running in place, making sure my knees go way up past my hips.

"You guys are weird."

We both turn our heads to Anna. I don't know how long she's been leaning against the doorframe, but the judgment in her eyes says it's been a while. "We're ready to stuff the turkey." She pushes off the doorjamb and walks away, yelling into the kitchen, "They weren't making out—unless stretching is some kind of kinky foreplay thing they do."

We bust into laughter.

I point to where her sister stood moments ago. "Anna says *kinky*."

"That's probably why she likes you more than Justin."

In the back of my mind, I try and picture Justin fake-stretching with Summer. Or laughing this easily with her.

But I can't.

No matter how hard I try, I can't seem to fit Justin into anything about tonight.

SUMMER

I hand Max some canned milk. "Pour this over all the breadcrumbs."

"What about me?" Miles whines.

"You're in charge of the pepper."

"That's a big job." Caleb nudges Miles's shoulder.

"What's your job, Justin?" Peter asks.

"My job is whatever Summer says."

"You're the mixer man. Get in there and scrunch all the ingredients together," I boss Caleb.

"With my bare hands?"

"Yes, I believe you already stretched for this moment."

"Indeed I did." Caleb rolls up his sleeves and then slowly sinks his fingers into the stuffing. He looks over at my nephews, making silly faces, as if touching the stuffing grosses him out. The boys giggle and laugh as he plays it up.

Juliet is beside me, whispering in my ear, "He's cute."

I incline my head, keeping my eyes on Caleb. "You think?"

"Oh, yeah. He's adorable with kids. Did you see him holding Bailey and cooing at her? I've never seen her smile that big."

"He definitely has a way with people." But that's where my assessment stops. He's not Justin, so it wouldn't be fair to comment on whether or not he's cute.

"Whoa, Miles. You're really going to town with the pepper. Marty, don't you think that's enough pepper?" Caleb asks my dad, who's overseeing the entire project.

"You can never have too much pepper."

"Really?" Caleb watches as Miles shakes the dispenser even harder. Pepper dust flies everywhere, and like a domino effect, each kid surrounding Caleb starts sneezing directly into the stuffing.

"Mmmm." Caleb shoots me a wide-eyed glance. "That's going to be delicious."

"Don't worry." My dad is completely unfazed. "It will all cook out in the oven."

Caleb grimaces at me like he's unsure how factually true that is.

"Aww, you guys are cute together." Juliet bumps her hip into mine. "I can see why you've been defending him all these months. Justin's a keeper. You were right. We just needed the chance to get to know him better."

"Yeah, that's what I've been saying." I force a smile, but deep down, I wonder if she'd feel the same way about the real Justin.

"Okay." My dad grabs the pepper shaker from Miles. "It's time to put the stuffing inside the turkey. Everyone take a big handful and just shove it in." He twists the poultry, holding open the spot where the bird's neck once was. It's kind of gross to think about, so you just don't think about it.

Caleb takes the first handful and shoves it inside. He jerks his arm, acting like it's stuck. "Oh, no! I can't get it out!" He turns to the boys. "Help me!"

My nephews giggle as they pull on his arm, but it won't budge.

"Summer, we need your help," Jack calls me over. "We can't get Justin's arm out of the turkey."

"I wouldn't trust a man who sticks his arm up a turkey." Aunt Carma gives me a look like I should be scared. "That's why I never dated a gynecologist."

Caleb spits out a laugh just as my mom rushes to my aunt's side. "Carma, I think it's time for you to go to bed."

"Summer?" Jack says again. "We need your help."

"We're going to cook him in the oven if we can't get him out," Peter exclaims. "You need to come."

"Alright." I push my sleeves back as I walk over to the other side of the island. "Okay, make some room." I grab Caleb by the shoulders. It seemed innocent enough at first, but as my fingers close around the broad beasts, my stomach sparks with itty-bitty butterflies. That's when I decide touching him this way is more intimate than I originally thought. I pull harder than necessary—considering he's not really *stuck*—but I need my hands off his shoulders as soon as possible. We both fly back, sending a few pieces of wet stuffing flinging through the air. One lands on my shirt while another lands on my cheek above my lips.

Caleb straightens, laughing at me. "There's something on your face." His goopy, stuffing-drenched index finger swipes across my cheek, and my entire body floods with heat. Theoretically, nothing about this situation should cause that reaction. I can't explain it, but it's as real to me as Christmas and Santa Claus.

I wipe my cheek where the feel of his touch still lingers. "I got it."

His blue eyes search mine. What the heck are they looking for? I don't know, but I'm afraid of what they'll find if they keep searching, so I glance down. "I'm going to go wash my shirt."

I look back before exiting the kitchen. My dad is in Caleb's ear, explaining how they're going to cook the turkey tomorrow.

It's everything I wanted.

It's just with the wrong brother.

eleven

CALEB

SUMMER FOLLOWS my car to Justin's house after the turkey party is over. We walk the length of his driveway together, and it's the most awkward doorstep scene I've ever been a part of.

"Thanks for coming tonight." She takes the first step.

"It was fun." I step on the second stair.

"My family really loved you." She's on the third step.

"I liked them." We're both on the landing, standing in front of the door.

"Now you know what a Turkey Stuff is." She tucks her short hair behind her ear.

"Yep. I crossed off a bucket-list item I didn't even know I had." I shoot my hands into my pockets.

"I think they'll go easier on Justin tomorrow, so that's good." She fidgets with the button on her coat.

"That's the point." I nod three times in a row.

We stare at each other, smiles fading into more awkwardness as we both run out of things to say.

The front door swings open, and Justin stares at us with furrowed brows. "What are you guys doing?"

My shoulders lift. I have no answer.

"Hey!" Summer leaps into his arms, and he hugs her back this

95

time—we're talking full arms wrapped around her body in a bear hug.

I hang my head, walking past them inside the house. I kick my shoes off in just enough time to glance up and see Summer greet him with a kiss on the lips.

"Somebody's in a good mood." He smiles as he pulls back. "Things must've gone well."

"My family loved you!" she says, taking off her coat.

Technically, they loved *me*, but that wasn't the point of the evening, so I don't bother correcting her.

Justin throws his hands out like he's the man of the hour. "I knew my plan would work."

It's annoying that he's taking all the credit for Summer's happy mood.

"And guess what else?" He slings his arm around her shoulder, leading her to the couch.

"What?"

"I'm done with my work for tonight, so we can relax and watch a movie together."

"Really?" Summer beams up at him.

"Yep."

I'm annoyed again, but not for me. I'm annoyed on behalf of Summer.

If Justin has time to hang out, why didn't he go to the party himself and then come home and work? Oh, yeah, because she's not a priority in his life.

They sit down on the couch, cuddling into each other.

"Did you get the turkey all stuffed?"

"Yeah, do you want to see pictures?"

I flick my eyes to them while I scoop myself a bowl of ice cream.

Summer points to the picture on her phone. "That's Erin and Tommy and their girls, Cora and Berkley. My nieces weren't interested in the turkey, just my nephews."

I didn't get to hang out with Cora and Berkley that much

tonight. They were in the living room, playing dolls. I'll have to get to know them better next time.

Wait. I'm an idiot. There won't be a next time.

"Uh-hmm." Justin doesn't even look at the pictures on her phone. Instead, he nuzzles into her side, kissing her neck and ear.

"Hey, you need to know all of this for tomorrow." She laughs as she nudges him.

He pulls back, winning her over with his smile. What can I say? He's got a great smile. It looks like mine.

"I'm listening," Justin murmurs before diving back in to kiss her cheek and neck. For someone who's unsure how he feels about her, he's pretty sure he likes touching her.

I put the carton of ice cream back in the freezer and grab my bowl and spoon, walking past them on the couch. "I'm going to call it a night."

They stop their couple cuteness and glance up at me.

"Thanks for going with Sum Sum," Justin says.

My eyes dart to hers, hoping to find a shared hatred for the awful nickname Justin has given her, but her expression is unreadable, or maybe I just don't know her well enough to read it.

"Yeah, no problem." I walk down the hall, calling over my shoulder, "Be sure to try the stuffing tomorrow. You're going to love it."

I smile to myself as I remember how many kids sneezed in that thing.

twelve

SUMMER

"SO MILES and Max are the twins, and Hailey and Brian are their parents," I say as we walk up the front steps of my parents' house.

Justin squeezes my hand. "Summer, you've been drilling me about your family for the last half hour. Don't you think that's a little excessive?"

"You're right. Sorry. I just don't want you to forget anybody's name."

"It's fine if I do."

My lips stick out in a frown. "Not really. In their minds, you were with them last night, laughing and having a good time. There's no reason why you'd forget their names the next day."

He pushes the strap of his leather computer satchel farther up on his shoulder. I'm already low-key stressed about what my mom's going to think when he shows up ready to work on Thanksgiving.

"Don't worry. I won't use anyone's name unless I'm positive I have it memorized."

We stop at the front door. "And all my nephews love you. Well, they love Caleb. So you'll have to—"

"Relax." He caresses my cheek. "I've got this."

"Okay, you're right. They're going to love you as much as I do." I suck in a deep breath and push open the door.

I'm more nervous for Justin to meet my family than I was for Fake Justin, but it will be fine. We got all the awkwardness out of the way last night. Today is about enjoying the holiday with good ol' fashioned family time.

"We're here!" I call.

"In the kitchen!" my dad says over the banging pans.

The house smells perfect, like all the best food and holiday smells combined to make my happiest dreams come true. If I could bottle up this smell and save it all year long to pull out whenever I'm sad, I'd do it.

I grab Justin's hand and lead him back to where my parents are. It's nice to be able to touch without feeling bad about it. I'm a really affectionate person. The hugging, holding, and touching are important to me, but last night, I had to think twice every single time I touched Caleb. It's not like I *want* to touch my boyfriend's twin brother. So I'm glad today there aren't any constraints.

"Hey!" I say as we round the corner. "How's dinner prep?"

My dad is in front of a messy counter, peeling a stack of potatoes. "We are T minus two hours until the big meal, and things are going great."

"Justin, are you excited to try your homemade stuffing?" My mom smiles at him.

"Yes, Mrs. Stanworth. I can't wait."

Her brows drop, and she laughs. "Mrs. Stanworth? So formal for Thanksgiving."

He glances at me, and I shake my head, whispering, "Just Marty and Janet."

My dad eyes the leather bag at Justin's side. "Why don't you guys set your stuff down, and you can help peel potatoes? I have ten more pounds to go."

"Actually, I need to get some work done before dinner. Is there a quiet place I can go to work?"

My mom's eyes bounce from me to my dad. "A quiet place?"

I know what she's thinking. She's thinking, *why on earth is this guy working on the second-greatest holiday of the year?* And she's also thinking, *in about thirty minutes, when all eight grandchildren are here, there won't be a single quiet place in this entire house.*

"Sure." I pull on Justin's arm. "Let me get you set up in my old bedroom upstairs."

My mom shakes her head. "Cora and Berkley are in your old bedroom, and Erin wanted to put the girls down for a quick nap before dinner. And the other room has Erin and Tommy's things in it."

"He can't have my room," Aunt Carma says behind us. She's sitting at the kitchen table again, but this time, she's knitting. "I don't want him snooping around my stuff."

Justin's brows dive into a deep V as he watches my aunt. It's as if he has no clue who she is, even though I know I've told him a million times that my Aunt Carma moved in with my parents three months ago.

He finally drags his eyes away from her. "What about the basement?"

My dad's lips twist downward. "I don't think it'll be very quiet down there. That's where all the kids go to play." He looks at my mom. "I guess he could use our bedroom."

"Eh." My mom's not even trying to hide the annoyance in her eyes. She has a weird love affair with her bedding. For as long as I can remember, her king comforter and decorative pillows have been off-limits, and letting my boyfriend, who she barely likes, lounge on her bed while he works on Thanksgiving is not going to fly.

"No, that's okay." I shake my head. "We'll find somewhere else."

My mom shrugs. "Well, that only leaves the laundry room downstairs, and there's nowhere to sit in there."

Justin smiles at my parents. "Don't worry about me. I can work anywhere." He points behind him to the front room. "I'll just set myself up out in the living room, and then it will be like I'm still here and in on the conversation." He shifts his smile to me, and I do my best to match his enthusiasm.

"Great. I'll just make sure you have all that you need." I walk out of the kitchen, but not before I catch my mom's eye roll to my dad, and I know all the progress from yesterday has suddenly been erased.

CALEB

"Mama, dear, can you please pass the mashed potatoes?"

Instead of just passing me the bowl, she jumps out of her seat and carries it to me, spooning a pile of the creamy food onto my plate.

"You don't have to do it for me." I laugh.

"Dadgummit, Patsy. What's next? Are you going to hand-feed the boy?" My dad's words come off as harsh, but really, he's just a big teddy bear.

"I know." My mom shakes her head, a sheepish grin smeared across her face. She sets the bowl down and returns to her chair. "I'm just so happy Caleb's home for Thanksgiving. I could cry." I smile back at her, noticing the fresh prick of tears she blinks away.

I feel bad that I haven't come around more. I've been really selfish with my time. I know that now.

She's skinnier than the last time I saw her. She's always been a slender woman, but the older she gets, the more her thin frame carries a fragileness that scares me. There's also a shakiness in her movements that wasn't there before. Or maybe it was there, but I was too busy thinking about my next big trick that I missed it. But with everything that happened with Lars, now I'm constantly looking for the warning signs of death, as if I can somehow stop it from taking another person that I love away from me.

My mom dabs at her eyes with her linen napkin. "I just wish that Justin and Summer could be here too. Then we'd be together as a family for the first time in four years."

"I wonder how Thanksgiving is going over at Summer's house," my dad says.

I hate to admit it, but I've wondered the same thing. Did the stuffing have too much pepper, even though Marty said you can never have too much? Did Jack, Peter, Miles, and Max fight over the wishbone? Did Juliet's pumpkin pie that she slaved over all day yesterday turn out? For people I just met, I'm way too invested in the Stanworth family Thanksgiving dinner.

"There's no way their turkey is as moist as mine." My dad sits a little taller, as if a moist turkey is the peak of his existence.

"Don, stop saying the word *moist*." My mom scrunches her nose. "I don't like it."

"What don't you like about it?"

"I don't know. It's like nails scratching over a chalkboard. It just gives me a funny feeling."

"Moist gives you a funny feeling?"

"Yes." She half-heartedly covers her ears.

"How does moist give you a funny feeling?"

"I don't know, Don. It just does."

I bite back my smile, happily listening to my parents go back and forth in quite possibly the dumbest argument of all mankind.

But I love it.

I've missed it.

I know it isn't much, but it's the grounding feeling I've been chasing this last year. The life roots that actually matter. I couldn't explain the emptiness inside me until two months ago when I sat in the middle of Lars's funeral and heard his family talk about the kind of man he was.

Sure, there were talks about the tricks he pulled, the mountains he'd climbed, the bridges he'd jumped off, but that was all secondary to the real person he was. It wasn't the daredevil stunts that defined his life. It was how he treated the ones he loved.

I knew if I died right then, the entirety of my life would be defined by the cool things I'd done and not the relationships I'd fostered, and that's not what I want. So I came home, and now I'm eating Thanksgiving dinner, discussing the cringe factor of the word moist.

"Well, I hope Justin is having a lovely meal with Summer's family." My mom looks at me as she scrapes a small portion of sweet potatoes onto her fork. "Caleb, have you met Summer yet?"

"We've had a few chances to get to know each other."

"And what do you think? Do you think she's the one?"

I push a few kernels of corn around my plate. "What do I think?"

Well, for starters, I think she's all wrong for Justin. There's a quirkiness about her that will eventually annoy him. She's way too needy—not in a whiney way, but in a constantly craving attention sort of way. She thrives on loving and being loved in return, and Justin is never going to fulfill that need in her life. He's always going to be working toward the next big goal. But I can't say that to my mom, not when she's pinned her hopes and dreams of becoming a grandmother on Justin and Summer getting married. So I lie.

"It looks promising." Then I shove an entire spoonful of potatoes and gravy into my mouth before I have to say anything else about Justin and Summer.

SUMMER

"Geez, what's with Dr. Jekyll and Mr. Hyde in there?" Anna asks as she carries a stack of dirty dishes into the kitchen.

"What do you mean?" I move the roaster pan so she has somewhere to set them all.

"I mean, Justin just asked my boys not to jump on his back because he's working when, last night, he was the one initiating the wrestling."

Hailey whips around from her spot by the refrigerator. "Okay, thank you! I was waiting for someone to say something. It's like he is a completely different person. Aunt Carma told him she had some ideas for 'their' blankets, and he got all defensive, like he had no clue what she was talking about."

My grip tightens on the dish I'm drying. I hoped my family wouldn't notice his change from last night. But going from the life of the party to the workaholic in the corner is a pretty big difference.

The thing is, Justin can be the life of the party like Caleb. Okay, not *exactly* like Caleb, but he's still a really fun guy. Work is just bogging him down right now.

"Um...I don't think he feels well," I say. "He was up all night working, prepping for Black Friday, and I know he has a migraine, so he's just a little off tonight." I embellish the details, hoping it's enough to convince them. "Not to mention stressed about the sale tomorrow."

Anna nods. "I guess that makes sense."

I'm glad when the conversation moves on to something else, but I notice how my mom doesn't join in on any of the new topics.

"How come you're so quiet?" I finally ask.

"Am I?"

"Yeah."

She scrubs the side of a pot where food is stuck to the glass. "I'm just worried about you."

I should be happy that her mother's intuition is so on point.

Maybe I would be if I were a child about to run in the road before checking both ways, but I'm a grown woman who can fend for herself.

"You don't need to be worried about me. I'm fine." My defenses close over my chest like one of those heavy-duty Carhartt work coats.

"Are you sure?" She eyes me. "Because something seems off between you and Justin."

"Nothing's off." I say the words in my cheery tone even though I feel the friction in my heart.

"You've always been so happy and bubbly—the summer sunshine that brightens every room—but the last few months, something has changed. You've lost the light in your eyes."

Her words hurt, cutting deep into my soul more than anything else ever has. She's not trying to hurt me or be rude. Everything she's saying comes from a place of love. I know that. It just hurts because there's truth behind it, a truth I don't even want to admit to myself.

I'm not happy.

My gaze drops, and I focus on the next plate that needs drying.

"I think that's why I've been so hard on you about Justin. I blame him for the dimness, but then he showed up last night, and I saw the old you return, and I thought that maybe these last few months I'd been too harsh." She pauses her scrubbing and looks at me. My eyes slowly drift to her. "But I see the sadness again today, and I don't know what to do about it. I want my happy, cheerful baby girl back."

What do you say to your mom after something like that?

Tears start to well behind my eyes, and I glance away before she has a chance to see them.

"I don't know what you're talking about," I say. "I've never been happier."

"Okay." She goes back to scrubbing. "If you don't want to

face the red flags in your relationship, then I'll keep my mouth shut."

Justin working one holiday does not mean our relationship has red flags. Things were so much easier and enjoyable last night when I didn't have my mom scrutinizing every little thing about us.

"Hey." Justin pops his head in the kitchen. "Should we go? I could really use some time at home to get some work done before the Black Friday sale hits at midnight."

"You guys can't go. We're going to play games," Hailey says from across the kitchen.

If I want my family—and my mom—to approach my relationship with Justin differently, then I need to pave the way. Lead by example. I can't keep getting butt-hurt every time he doesn't meet my family's expectations, because like my mom said, she's noticing the sadness. So I smile, knowing everyone is watching my response. "Why don't you go home and work? You have such a big day tomorrow that you need to prepare for. I'll stay and play games, and Juliet and Rick can drive me home."

"Are you sure?" There's complete shock on Justin's face that I gave in so easily. Heck, I'm shocked. "I hate to leave you on Thanksgiving."

I force my smile even wider. "I know, but it's better this way."

"Okay, then." He leans in, kissing me on the cheek, then whispers in my ear, "Thanks for understanding." That's me, the most understanding girlfriend of the year. Hooray! He waves at my mom. "Janet, thanks for dinner. It was delicious."

My mom gives a polite nod, but I know inside she's biting her tongue, holding back all the things she wants to say to Justin. And after he leaves, she'll unleash all those grievances on me. The *I told you so's* of *I told you so's*.

thirteen

CALEB

A CAR DOOR SLAMS OUTSIDE, and a few seconds later, a heavy knock bangs out in the family room. I glance at the clock. It's eleven twenty-two at night. The only person who would be coming over to Justin's condo this late is Summer.

My bedroom door is cracked open enough that I can hear them greet each other, but I turn the TV in my room down (I just installed it tonight so I don't have to keep watching television in silence while Justin works at the kitchen table) so I can listen to the rest of their conversation.

"I thought the whole drive over about what you said earlier this week." Summer's voice is animated, and she's a little out of breath from either talking too fast or climbing the four short steps up to his front door.

"What did I say?"

"That I just needed a warm body to take with me to my family parties so my family would get off my back about us."

"Okay."

"But it's not just about having someone there. It wasn't enough that you came to Thanksgiving dinner tonight. My mom was still bugged. She just won't let it go. I need more than a warm body. I need somebody who's going to interact."

"Summer, if this is about today, you know I had to work, and I thought you were cool—"

"Justin, I'm not mad at you."

"You're not?"

"No. In fact, I think you're right about how we can solve our problems."

I lean forward, becoming more and more interested in this conversation.

"I just need Caleb to come with me and pose as you. It solves everything."

My mouth drops open.

"That's what I was saying." Justin isn't even trying to hide how thrilled he is about this.

"I mean, it was so great Wednesday night. I wasn't alone. My family was satisfied. I didn't have to defend you or explain why I'm still with you when you never come around. Everyone was happy. And then afterward, I got to come here and spend time with you, and we didn't have to fight. It was just like old times. Easy."

"I know. I felt the same way."

"But when you left early tonight, all of my family's old opinions about you resurfaced. And my mom thinks I've lost the light in my eyes. It's exhausting, you know?"

"Yeah, I'm sick of it too."

Justin completely breezes past her mom's concerns. It's baffling.

"So I think we should do it. I think we should just have Caleb be your holiday stand-in. It will solve all our problems these next few weeks when you have to work while my family has so many demands. And then after the holidays, when things calm down, you can come as yourself."

I think Summer's being a little too optimistic about how seamlessly this will work out for her.

"Alright." Justin laughs. "Let's do it."

"Do you think Caleb will?"

Finally, someone who's asking the right questions.

"I don't know. He told me the other night that he would only do it that one time."

"Well, is he home? Should we ask him?"

"He's home, but the sale goes live in thirty-five minutes. It's crunch time for me."

"Yeah, sorry. This is bad timing."

"He's back in his room. You can go ask him if you want."

She'll never come back here alone.

"Okay, I'll just check. It doesn't hurt to ask, right?"

I did not see that coming.

I go into scramble mode—turning the TV up to hide my eavesdropping, pushing dirty dishes under the bed, throwing a pile of clothes across the room to the corner, and combing my fingers through my hair. I lie back just as a soft knock taps on my door.

"Come in." Now I'm the one breathing heavily.

Summer pushes the door open. Her eyes travel to my bare chest, then to the ceiling. "Sorry. I didn't know you weren't dressed."

I glance down at my sweats. "I'm dressed."

"Do you not like wearing shirts?"

"You knock on *my* door at eleven-thirty at night and then judge me for what I'm wearing to bed?"

"You're right. You can wear whatever you want in your room." She nervously runs her finger along the dresser, grabbing my car keys and swinging them around her finger. "Or *don't* wear what you want. Either way." Her hand closes over the key fob, and instantly, the car alarm blares outside. Blinking lights flash through the window as she fidgets with the remote, trying to find the button that stops the sirens. She's all craze and panic until the alarm stops, and she gently places the keys back on the dresser. "That was unexpected."

"Summer, do you want something from me?"

I know exactly what she wants, but I'm not letting her off the hook that easily.

"Uh, yes." She places her hand on her hip, decides she doesn't like that pose, and switches to swinging her arms at her sides like holding still isn't an option. "Justin and I were wondering if you'd be willing to, um..."—she clasps her hands together, looking up at the ceiling again—"you know, um..."

"Spit it out."

Her blue eyes flash to me. "I am!"

"No, you're not. You're tiptoeing around whatever it is that you want."

"Fine." She runs her fingers through her hair, flipping it over to the side in her signature way. "I need you to stand in for Justin for the rest of the season."

Even though I knew that was coming, I pretend to be surprised.

"Like stand in for Justin at work?" Playing dumb adds to my amusement.

"No!" she groans. "What do you know about running a business?"

"A lot, actually."

"No, I need you to stand in for Justin as my boyfriend, like you did last night." She bites her bottom lip, waiting for my reply.

"Why?"

"Well, you know, Justin is so busy, and my family is obsessed with whether or not he's going to show up. My mom is worse than a junior high attendance secretary. It's bizarre. So I just thought it would be easier to have you come for him and take some of the pressure off."

"Easier for who?"

Her weight shifts. "Me and Justin."

"And what do I get out of this?"

"Rent?" She gives me a half-smile like she's testing her answer.

"Rent?"

"You said yourself that you owed Justin for staying here for the next month. This is how you can repay him."

"I think I'd rather just pay him money."

"Do you have money?" Her brows raise in such an innocent way that I'm not even bugged at how rude her comment sounds.

"I'm sure I can figure it out."

"Then what do you want? How can I sweeten the deal so you'll agree to do it?"

"You can't sweeten the deal. There's nothing that I want."

"Oh, come on. Everyone wants something."

"Not me."

I mean, I want to have a better relationship with Justin, but fake-dating his girlfriend isn't going to give me that.

"Well, then, do it for the rent," she offers.

"So let me get this straight. You want to use me as your fake boyfriend to make your life easier in exchange for staying at my twin brother's house during the holidays?"

"Okay, look." She sighs. "I know it's not a good deal for you, and I know it means spending a lot of time with my crazy family and me, and then there's the lying..."

"Yes, there's a lot of lying that goes into it."

"Just don't think about the lying. It's not meant to be mean-spirited or hurt anyone. Think of it as a way to help your brother out. It would really mean a lot to Justin if you did this."

"If it means so much to Justin, why isn't he the one asking me to do it?"

"Fine. It means a lot to both of us."

I shake my head, prepping to tell her no.

"Please!" she quickly adds, sensing my answer isn't going her way.

"Sorry, I can't do it. Things like this are fine every once in a while, but over the course of a month, it's just not a good idea."

Her entire countenance drops as she leans against the dresser. "You're probably right. It's not a good idea. I'm just so desperate for my family to like Justin that I'm not thinking straight."

"They'll like him—*eventually*—when he shows up." Or he won't show up, and you two will go your separate ways.

"I hope so." She straightens, inching toward the door. "Well, sorry to bug you." She grabs the handle and pulls the door shut as she exits.

I don't move at first. I just stare absently at the shut door. Saying yes to their charade would've been easy. It's not like I have anything going on. A holiday party here and there would've been fine, but I just couldn't bring myself to do it.

fourteen

CALEB

OUT OF ALL THE places my parents could've picked to move to, Telluride was a pretty awesome choice. The mixture of terrain, scenery, and ski culture is right up my alley. I spent the day skiing, hitting the slopes with all the other non-shoppers. It was the perfect way to clear my head, get my heart pumping, and burn off some of my mom's apple pie from last night's dinner.

When I got home, Justin had set up some sort of office at his house. The family room and dining room were overtaken by computer screens and All-Weather Blanket employees. I'm not sure why they decided to work from home instead of at their actual office. Maybe it made them feel better about working so hard on Black Friday. Either way, I wasn't about to stay at his condo, where the business testosterone was at an all-time high.

After a hot shower, I drive into downtown Telluride, where Christmas lights decorate Main Street, and holiday wreaths hang on doors. Finding a parking spot is hard. It's like the entire community is here for an event—I don't even know what one. I guess I'll be surprised by whatever small-town experience this city throws at me tonight.

I stop at an outdoor vendor, waiting in line for hot chocolate because what's the Christmas season without a warm drink in your hand? Live holiday music plays a little farther down the street, and kids run up and down the sidewalks, weaving in and out of shoppers holding bags of sale items in each hand. I look around, taking it all in. The holiday ambiance is exactly what I didn't know I needed. I thought I was coming to Telluride to build on family relationships, but as I look at all the families huddled together, I realize family relationships are deeply rooted in the small things like this. In tradition.

"Justin?" I feel a tap on my shoulder and turn to face Summer's brother-in-law, Brian. "Dude, I've been calling your name for, like, twenty seconds."

"Oh, sorry. I didn't hear you."

And my name's not Justin, so that probably didn't help either.

I stare blankly at Brian, trying to decide what to do. The real Justin is back at his condo, working. I was just there ten minutes ago, and judging by the stack of orders piled in front of him, there's no way he's planning on taking a break and meeting up with Summer and her family tonight. So it's probably safe and harmless to let Brian believe I'm Justin.

"You getting some cocoa for Summer?" Brian cups his hands near his mouth, breathing hot air onto his fingers.

"Summer's here?" I spin, keeping my head on a swivel.

"That's funny." Brian taps my chest, laughing away my question. "The light parade is about to start. I don't want to wait in line and miss the twins' reactions. Will you grab a cocoa for Hailey too?" Before I can protest, he's shoving dollar bills into my hand. "We're set up in front of the bookstore. Come find us when you have the goods."

"Wait."

Brian takes a few steps backward. "And you better hurry. Like I said, the parade is about to start."

I grind my teeth together, looking down at the wad of cash in my hand. The way I see it, I have three options. I can steal Brian's money and go home, avoiding the entire Stanworth family. I can buy hot cocoa, deliver it to them, and explain that I'm *not*

Summer's boyfriend. Or I can buy hot cocoa, deliver it to them, and pretend to be Justin like everyone wants.

I've never seen a light parade before and don't even know what it is. It would be a shame to miss it. I'll always wonder about it. Plus, going back to Justin's condo with all the people there seems lame.

"Next in line." The girl at the hot chocolate stand smiles back at me. "What can I get you?"

My eyes dart down to where the bookstore is.

What could it hurt? It's just one night.

"Sir? What can get you?"

"Uh." I glance back at her. "I guess I'll take two hot cocoas."

SUMMER

He's going to try and make it—that's my answer every time someone in my family asks about Justin.

"He's going to try and make it." If you add a confident smile, it cuts down on the follow-up questions by 40%. Actually, I just made up that statistic to sound cool. A confident smile does nothing to help, especially with my mom.

"Hey, I just bumped into your boyfriend," Brian says as he walks past me to his camp chair at the end of our row.

My head kicks back. "My boyfriend?"

He points behind me down the street. "Yeah, he's in line getting hot chocolate." He kisses Hailey on the cheek. "Don't worry. I told him to get one for you."

"Wait. You're talking about Justin, right?" I can't get past my confusion.

"Of course I'm talking about Justin."

"Why are you acting so shocked? You said he was going to try

117

and make it," Juliet says while bouncing Bailey in her arms. If I didn't know better, I would think she was holding a pile of blankets, not a baby.

"I know." I lean back in my chair, trying to look down the sidewalk for more information. That's when I see Caleb walking toward us, holding two Styrofoam cups. A gray beanie is pulled over his head with the perfect amount of hair wisping out the front and back. He looks like a model straight out of a holiday magazine. All he's missing is the dog and the log of wood on his shoulder.

The pieces click together. Justin must've forced him to come even after he said he didn't want to do the swap. I feel stupid. Caleb is literally being held against his will all because I'm sick of dealing with my family on this one topic.

I hop up, jogging to greet him.

"Did Justin make you come again?"

"What? No." He shakes his head, glancing over my shoulder to where my family sits. "I didn't even know you guys were here. I just randomly ran into Brian."

"Why wouldn't we be here? It's the holiday light parade. Bob Irvine decorated the fire truck that Santa is standing on, and Donna O'Day is singing "All I Want for Christmas is You" on one of the floats."

"I don't know who those people are or what a light parade is."

"It's where...forget about it." I shake my head, reaching for the cocoas. "You don't have to stay."

"Really?" He moves the cups out of my reach. "Are you going to tell your family that I popped by in between work just to bring you some hot chocolate, and then I'm leaving again? That's stupid. Of course I have to stay. Now, if you'll excuse me, I have a delivery to make."

I spin and watch as he walks toward Brian and Hailey with their drink. The rest of my family greets him with smiles while the kids run up and hug his legs. My eyes drift to my mom. She's already watching me. I lift my chin and smile in an I-told-you-so kind of way, grateful that her prediction of Justin not coming was proved wrong.

Caleb picks up each of my nephews and swings them around. Then he walks over to where Cora and Berkley sit, kneels in front of them, and has a twenty-second conversation with the girls.

He looks around as he stands. "Where's Carma?"

"She stayed home," my dad answers. "It's too cold for her."

Caleb lifts his hands to the side. "I can't believe she's going to miss Donna O'Day singing a Mariah Carey classic."

"That's what I said." My mom wraps a blanket around herself before sitting down.

"What about Bob Irvine's lights?"

"On the fire truck." Caleb points at my dad. "I hear it's going to be epic this year."

His eyes dart to me, and he winks like he just nailed his big improv moment. I roll my eyes, not giving him any credit for his performance. But inside, I'm smiling.

Police sirens in the distance cause all the little kids to scream with anticipation.

"Summer, you coming?" Caleb grins, giving me the feeling that he's actually excited to be here. "The parade is starting."

"Yes, I'm coming." I walk to his side, watching as a few police motorcycles fly past, clearing the street.

Caleb whistles with enthusiasm.

I eye him. "You act like you've never seen a parade before?"

"I've never seen a *Christmas* parade."

"It's pretty much the same as a regular parade, just everyone strings Christmas lights on their floats and plays Christmas music as they pass. That's why they do it when it's dark." He nods. "Oh, and at the end, Santa Claus rides on top of the fire truck. He's the finale."

"That sounds awesome." His smile grows. "I bet the kids love it."

"Yeah, they do." I stare into his blue eyes, feeling something I can't place. Mostly gratitude—I think—that I don't have to be alone.

"Hey, down in front," Jeff calls behind us. "Nobody can see over you two."

"Oh, sorry." I move to my seat, then realize there's only one chair. Justin was never coming, so why would I bring an extra chair for him?

Caleb sees what I see. "Don't worry about it. You take the chair, and I'll stand back behind everyone."

"No, this is your first time seeing the parade. I want you to have a good view."

"Hello?" Anna snaps at us. "Why don't you two just share the chair so we all can see? Summer can sit in your lap."

Our eyes lock for a second. Caleb is not moving an inch until I do.

"Yeah, sure," I say.

He leans down, placing his drink in the cupholder, and then takes a seat. I couldn't be more awkward as I try to find the least-intimate way to sit in his lap with minimal touching. I slowly sink lower, placing my butt on the edge of his kneecap. Nothing about this position is comfortable. His kneecap rolls in between my cheeks as I situate myself, and suddenly this feels more like a proctologist appointment than a holiday parade.

"You can't sit like that. Your butt is too boney."

"My butt? What about your boney kneecap?"

"Kneecaps are supposed to be boney." His hands grab my waist, pulling me back to his chest so I'm fully sitting in his lap with his arms loosely at my sides. "There. Are you comfortable?"

Am I comfortable? That is the question.

The easy answer is yes, I'm physically comfortable.

That also happens to be the complicated answer. *Why do I feel so comfortable in Caleb's lap?*

It's fine. Sitting on someone's lap is a totally acceptable thing to do at Christmastime. I mean, millions of kids sit on Santa's lap, and nobody seems to care, so I shouldn't make a big deal out of this.

I shift my gaze to the lighted float in front of us while discreetly pushing his hand away from my hip so it's resting more on the arm of the chair than against my body. "That's better."

He snickers, but I ignore it.

We sit in silence for a second, watching the passersby, until he shifts his position, causing my blanket to crunch under his touch.

"What the heck is this? Do you have a tarp wrapped around you?"

I give him a pointed side-eye, lowering my voice. "It's the All-Weather Blanket."

"Oh, nice! I've never seen one up close," he whispers between us. "It's like a tarp muumuu. Perfect for all kinds of weather."

"That's kind of the point." I bite back my smile. "It's a really great product—very warm."

"It better be a great product since it's Justin's first love."

My eyes fall to my lap.

"Sorry." Caleb leans down, trying to catch my gaze. "I didn't mean it like that."

I lift my head, feigning indifference. "It's fine. I know what you meant." I hold his stare for one more second, just to prove how *fine* I am, before glancing back to the high school marching band performing "Little Drummer Boy" as they walk by.

"Do you come to this parade every year?"

"Yeah, ever since I was a little girl."

"We didn't have anything like this in Phoenix." His words are innocent, but the warmth of his breath tickles my ear, sending goosebumps down my neck to my spine, involuntarily making me shiver.

"Are you cold?" His voice has that manly protective layer behind it that most girls love. That *I* love...in situations where the man saying it is not my boyfriend's twin brother.

"No, I'm fine." It was just your freaking warm breath on my ear.

"I would wrap you up in my arms, but—"

"No." I whip my head to him, using my palm as a stop sign. "We're good."

His lips turn upward like he finds my interruption amusing. "But *instead*"—he reaches for the cocoa in the cupholder—"I'll offer you some hot chocolate to keep you warm."

"Oh." I glance down at the cup. "Thanks, but I only like—"

"Mint-flavored?" He pushes it toward me. "I know."

He *knows*? How does he know? I can barely remember telling him that. And I can barely remember someone doing something thoughtful for me. I'm usually the one giving thoughtful gifts.

"Thanks." I take the cup from his hand, feeling the warmth of his fingers during the transfer.

"I'm curious," he says, watching me lift the cocoa to my mouth.

"About what?" I turn back to the parade because that's what we're here to see and because all this close-proximity eye contact with Caleb isn't necessary.

"You want me to pretend to be Justin, but you brushed my hand away when you thought I was touching you too much. How did you think the whole physical relationship was going to work?"

I nervously glance at Juliet sitting next to us, but she's leaning close to Rick as they try to get Bailey to look at the parade. "I hadn't gotten that far." I lift my chin, zeroing back in on the floats. "But it doesn't matter because you didn't agree to do it."

"Yet, I'm here tonight."

"That's not my fault."

"I know. It's fine. I'm actually enjoying myself."

I peek back at him. "Good."

It is good, right? If Caleb is enjoying himself, maybe he'll be more willing to stand in for Justin if I *really* need him to—if it's, like, Christmas Day or something. On second thought, Justin better not be working on Christmas Day—that's a worldwide non-negotiable holiday.

A few floats down, the famous Mariah Carey song plays, and my mom jumps to her feet.

"It's Donna!" She points down the street.

"How do we know Donna?" Caleb whispers in my ear, causing chills to crawl over me again.

"She's my mom's best friend. They work at the high school together. They are both the secretaries."

"Gotcha."

My entire family stands, clapping along as Donna's float pulls in front of us. The car slows to a snail pace, letting Donna have her moment in front of friends. She sings the entire bridge of the song and then finishes with the last chorus.

Caleb claps as she hits her last note, then looks back at my mom. "What a cover!"

"Isn't she good?" My mom cheers with him.

He whistles as the music ends, then to my surprise, he starts chanting, "Donna! Donna! Donna!"

In a matter of seconds, the entire crowd around us joins in on Caleb's chant. Donna kisses her fingers and throws them at Caleb before her float moves on. The chant fades, but that doesn't mean Caleb has. He high-fives my brother-in-law and then turns around, high-fiving my parents.

Then he sits down.

He waves his fingers, signaling for me to *come here,* and I'm not even going to comment on how sexy his bossiness is combined with his glimmering eyes.

I sink down to my seat in his lap, staring at him the entire time.

"What?" His eyes bounce from me to the parade.

"You high-fived my mom."

"So?"

"Who are you?"

"I'm just a Donna O'Day groupie. Has she recorded anything? Can I find her on Spotify?"

My lips drift into a smile. "No. She's a high school secretary from Telluride."

"Too bad. I'm a fan of Double D."

"Double D?"

"Yeah, Donna O'Day."

"Technically, wouldn't that be DO?"

"I guess so." He shrugs. "But I like Double D better."

I laugh, turning my gaze back to the parade. Everything about Caleb and this night is unexpected.

"Hey!" The woman on the float in front of us points at me, shouting over the noise, "Did you grow up here?"

My brows lower in confusion. I don't recognize her or know why she's talking to me. "Yeah, did you?" If I had an angel sitting on my shoulder, maybe she could've stopped me from sounding so rude and indifferent with my reply, but when I answered, I didn't have that luxury, so my words came out clipped with arrogance.

"I wasn't talking to you." She repositions her finger so she's pointing at Caleb. "I was talking to him."

My entire family breaks into laughter over what a presumptuous idiot I am, but the woman in her ski-bunny snow outfit—that somehow still manages to be sexy—keeps the conversation going as she moves farther down the street.

"You're the YouTuber, right? Caleb Davidson." She even cups her hand around her mouth so that her shouts can reach us as she floats away. "I love you! Call me!"

Caleb laughs, dropping his head with a modest charm that's annoyingly cute.

"Oh my gosh, Summer." Erin leans across her girls to make fun of me. "You were so put out and cocky with your answer, and she wasn't even talking to you."

"I was not put out or cocky," I defend. "I just didn't recognize her."

Jeff laughs behind us. "Yeah, because she wasn't talking to you. She was flirting with your boyfriend."

"Not even her boyfriend." Juliet looks back at Jeff and Anna. "She was flirting with her boyfriend's twin." I stiffen, worried that somehow Juliet figured out that Caleb isn't the real Justin, but she looks directly at him and asks, "Is your twin brother a YouTuber?"

"Yeah, he does daredevil stunts and tricks in different places around the world."

"He must be pretty famous if a woman can recognize him while standing on a float in the middle of a parade," my dad says.

Caleb shrugs with more of that modest charm I'm trying not to notice.

"How many followers does he have?" Tommy asks.

"Um..." His blue eyes flash to me. "I don't really know. A few."

"What's his account? I'll look it up." Tommy has his phone out, ready to investigate.

"His channel is down!" I blurt. "So you can't look it up."

I don't know what Caleb's account looks like, but I can't risk someone from my family finding it and noticing that Caleb looks a lot like the version of Justin they know. I mean, yes, they're identical, so they're going to be similar, but we don't need anyone drawing any comparisons between the two of them, because the more time I spend with Caleb, the more I see exactly how different they are from each other.

Tommy frowns. His fingers hover above his phone like he might try to Google him anyway just to fact-check me, so I use the art of distraction to put out this fire. "Look!" I point down the street. "Santa's coming!"

The kids bounce and squeal with delight while all the parents get their phones ready to record. Crisis averted.

I glance over my shoulder to Caleb, just checking in to see where he's at with the events of the last two minutes. But he's already watching me, and the swaggering sparkle in his eyes starts a new crisis, but this time in my heart.

CALEB

"WE'RE NEVER GETTING out of this traffic." I look back and forth at the gridlock of headlights stopped along Main Street.

"That's why my family parks just outside of town." Summer shrugs, but you can barely see the action under the massive All-Weather Blanket parka draped over her.

"Yeah, well, you guys know the secrets of Telluride better than us outsiders." I open the back door of my Bronco and put her camp chair inside, slamming it shut again. "What do you say we walk around town and look at the lights while we wait for traffic to clear out?"

I'm not sure she'll say yes. I think the only reason Summer agreed to ride home with me instead of Juliet was because it would look bad in front of her family if she didn't.

"Yeah, okay." Her face brightens. "I love the downtown area at Christmastime."

I gesture to the sidewalk, and we fall into an easy stroll as we walk together.

"So there's one thing we need to clarify," she says.

"What's that?" I wrack my brain, trying to remember if I said or did something I wasn't supposed to.

But Summer turns to me with a playful smile spread across her lips. "You get shoutouts from women in parades?"

I laugh. "Yes, apparently so."

"I wish I had known that before I made a complete fool of myself in front of my entire family and every other person in earshot."

"I thought it was cute." Not *cute*. It was cute, but she's my brother's girlfriend, so probably not how I should describe the moment.

"Did you know that woman?"

"Nope. Never seen her before in my life."

"Then how did she recognize you?"

I smile, eyeing her. "You've never seen my YouTube channel before, have you?"

"No." A guilty laugh puffs out, dotting the air with her warm breath. "I'm sorry. I haven't."

"That's fine."

Am I a little disappointed that Summer hasn't looked me up? Nevermind. I'm not answering that.

"Are you, like, a 'big' deal in the daredevil world?" Her use of finger quotes is mildly offensive.

"A *big* deal?" I smile while simultaneously shaking my head in disbelief. I've never had to prove my coolness factor to a woman before. They just kind of already know.

"Yeah, like, do you have...what did Tommy call it?" She zones out, thinking for a second.

"Followers?" I offer.

"Yes, followers. Do you have followers?" Her voice lowers like she's afraid to ask in case I don't. "You know, besides your mom and the woman on the float."

I flip around, walking backward while I laugh at the irony of the conversation.

"It's okay if nobody follows you. I think it's great that you still do what you love."

"Tell you what." I lean into her with a smug expression, my

face inches from hers. She stops walking, gazing at me with those expressive blue eyes. "How about you look me up sometime and then let me know what you think?"

She swallows. "Look you up?"

"That's right." There's an edge of cockiness to my voice, and I don't even care.

"Okay." She steps around me, distancing herself as she continues our walk. "Maybe I will."

I turn on my heels and catch up to her. "I do think it's kind of interesting, though. You expect Justin to know every little thing about your family, your brothers-in-law, and your eight nieces and nephews, but you don't know anything about his *one* identical twin brother."

Her brows draw together as she shrugs. "Well, I'm super close with my family."

"And Justin and I aren't close?"

She turns her eyes to me. "Are you?"

"Not right now." I drop my head, embarrassed about how bad that looks to someone like Summer, who lives for every second with her family. "But that's one of the reasons I came home. I thought we should spend some time together, work on our relationship."

"Well, you'll have to get in line." A bitter laugh tumbles over her lips. "Looks like we're all vying for Justin's time and attention."

"He's been really busy the last few weeks, hasn't he?"

"Ha! Try the last few *months*." She puts on a fake smile and I wonder if it's the same thing Summer's mom sees when she watches her talk about Justin. "But it's just temporary, so it'll be fine, and once he starts coming around more, my family will forget all the times he's left me high and dry, and I won't have to be alone at family parties anymore."

"Do they really give you that hard of a time when he doesn't show up?"

"They just aren't convinced he cares about me. To them, if he really loved me, he'd show up to the things that are important to me, even if he's busy. But Justin hates it when I say that. He's sick of my family being so heavily involved in our relationship. I don't blame him, but..." Her words trail off, and I get the sense she's holding something back.

"But what?" There's a sadness behind Summer's normally cheery disposition that makes me feel for her.

"I just thought things would be easy when I found the right person. We'd immediately bond with each other's families, and everything would click. But that's not how things are going. I don't know." She lifts her shoulders. "Maybe Justin isn't the right one, and I should just break up with him like everyone says."

I'm glad she's at least aware that she and Justin have problems. It makes him leading her on not as bad. I can't personally see their relationship working out, but I'm not about to be the person who encourages her to break up with my brother, even if he isn't sure how he feels about her.

"Justin's a good guy." When in doubt, take the high road.

"I know, but I barely see him on weekdays, and when I do see him, it's because I popped by his house or contacted him. I'm just not a priority in his life. So, although he's a good guy, maybe he's not a good guy for me."

This is turning south quickly—like if I don't turn the tide, Summer will leave this conversation and immediately go break up with Justin. And then when he asks, 'Where did this come from?' she'll say, 'Your brother,' and then he'll hate me, and we'll never have a chance at having a close relationship.

It's suddenly a pivotal moment in Justin's and my relationship, and before I think through what I'm agreeing to, I say, "Let me help with your family. I can stand in for Justin and take some of the pressure off."

Summer looks at me with an adorable furrow on her brow. "I thought you didn't want to."

I thought I didn't want to either, but here I am, trying to keep their relationship afloat.

"It's not a big deal for me to hang out and pretend to be Justin. I'm happy to do it if it will help you guys make it through the holidays." Because after the holidays, maybe Justin will wake up and realize that Summer and her family are great.

"Really?" Her lips teeter between a half-smile and disbelief.

"Yep. Count me in." We're probably only talking about one or two more family activities until Justin can come himself.

"But why change your mind all of a sudden?"

"Justin is a great guy, and it would be a shame for you to miss out on something with him just because he's busy right now." I'm taking one for the team. Helping Justin. Being a better brother. I've been him the last decade—so focused on my career that I didn't take the time to foster the relationships that matter most to me. By standing in for him, maybe I can stop Justin from making the biggest mistake of his life.

Summer's half-smile grows into something electric and cute. I keep using that word to describe her, and I don't know why—it just fits. She's the epitome of cute.

"Thank you!" She bounces toward me, flinging her arms around my neck. "I'm just so grateful you're going to help me out."

I stumble backward, surprised by her spontaneous hug. That same smell of hers floats around me, triggering the memory of holding her in my arms in Justin's kitchen a few days ago. But now that I know her a little better, holding her feels different. It's more meaningful than the kiss we shared, although the kiss was pretty epic too.

She tilts our bodies back and forth like a teapot being poured before she releases me and spins around.

I smile as I watch her carefree side take form. I've only seen it once before, when we were stretching at her parents' house before the turkey stuff, but I like it.

I like seeing Summer happy.

That's probably an underlying reason why I said yes to this

whole twin-brother swap, but I'm not admitting that, even to myself.

sixteen

CALEB

TALK ABOUT A WEIRD ROLE REVERSAL.

I'm dressed in jeans and a flannel button-up while Justin sits across from me in sweats. He's moved his workstation away from the kitchen table to the couch. His laptop rests in his lap with a stack of papers piled next to him.

I should be in sweats, settling in for some college football games, but instead, I'm waiting for Summer to get here so we can go to her parents' house for turkey flautas. But I'm not even upset about it. I'm kind of looking forward to hanging out with the Stanworth family.

"Are you sure you're okay with this?" I've asked Justin this question a billion times since last night when I agreed to be his holiday stand-in.

"Dude, I already told you. I'm more than okay with it. You're saving me by going to Summer's family party. Like, honestly, I can't thank you enough." His smile reaches his eyes. "And when work calms down, we should go snowboarding or something. Make a day of it. Hang out like we used to."

"That would be awesome." It's the entire reason I'm here.

"You'll have to go easy on me, though, or else I won't be able to keep up with you."

"Nah, you've got skills."

"Not like you."

There's a knock at the door. It's Summer, but I don't move to get up. It's not my house, and she's not my girlfriend to greet.

"Can you grab that?" Justin's eyes drop to his computer.

"Sure." I stand, walking to the door. I open just as she lifts her hand to knock again.

"Oh." Her eyes widen, and I wonder if her surprise is from the door opening when she was about to knock or from the fact that I answered instead of Justin.

She's in bright-red pants with a hot-pink sweater under her black coat. The bright colors suit her, matching her bold lipstick and wavy short hair. It all just works for me, which is probably a really bad thing.

"Come in." I hold the door open for her. "Unless you want to leave right now."

"No." She points inside. "I'll say hi to Justin before we go."

"Yeah, of course."

She walks past, and it's like her intoxicating smell is working overtime tonight, teasing me with its goodness. And the worst part is, I don't even know what the scent is. Like if I could say, '*That's coconut. I love coconut. That's why I like how Summer smells,*' then it would have nothing to do with her, and I'd feel better about myself.

"Hey, Sum Sum." Justin waves from the couch without even turning his neck to see her.

"Hi!" She walks over to him, leaning down to kiss his cheek.

Is he going to say what I can't—that she looks amazing? That her bold choice of colors is cute and flirty? That her bright red lipstick makes her blue eyes pop? That she smells incredible? I wait for it, but Justin lets me down by not saying anything.

Summer takes a seat on the other end of the couch. "How are the Black Friday sales coming?"

"So good. Way better than we even anticipated."

"That's because people love your blankets." She brushes her

hand over the back of his neck, combing her red fingernails through his hair.

I linger by the kitchen, acting like I have something else to do while I wait. It's weird if I just sit and watch them interact. Maybe I should pull out my phone. Yeah, that's a good idea. I reach into my back pocket for the device, opening my email app. The lack of activity in my inbox has me peeking at them once again.

"We're going to be crazy busy the next few weeks getting these orders out before Christmas."

Her lips lift as if she's happy, but everything else about her expression dims. "I bet."

"That's why Caleb is here." He turns over his shoulder to me, adding a smile. "To keep you from feeling neglected."

I lift my lips in fake happiness, like Summer did two seconds earlier.

Keep her from feeling neglected?

That sounds like it entails much more than just attending a family party.

"Well, babe"—Justin leans into her—"I'll see you when you get home, and maybe we can watch a movie or something."

"I'd love that."

I tuck my phone back in my pocket, glancing up to see the end of their kiss.

Summer pulls apart, shooting her embarrassed eyes to me. "Sorry." She brushes her fingers over her lips, and I'm secretly hoping she doesn't do anything to ruin her bright-red lipstick that I've grown to love.

"You don't have to be sorry for Caleb. He knows how we feel about each other. Why else would he agree to this?"

Why else? That is the question.

"Yeah, I'm just here to help." Because no other reason is morally acceptable.

Summer hugs Justin before she stands and meets me by the door. I hold it open for her to pass.

"Should we take my car?" she asks.

135

"I don't mind driving."

"You two kids have fun," Justin calls as I close the door behind us.

We walk to the Bronco, where I open the passenger door for her.

"Oh, thank you." She's so surprised by the action that I wonder if Justin doesn't typically hold her door open for her. I'm starting to feel like he's the world's most inattentive boyfriend, and I want to smack him upside the head for it.

"It's freezing!" she says when I get in my side of the car.

I crank up the heater. "Where's your All-Weather Blanket when you really need it?"

"It didn't go with my outfit, so I left it at home."

"I like the pink and red. You look very *fun*." That's an appropriate way to finish that sentence. It's not at all how I want to finish it, but it's appropriate.

"Thanks."

"So, tell me about tonight's tradition."

"Well"—she twists in her seat so she's facing me—"we take the leftover turkey from Thanksgiving and make flautas with them. It's a turkey-stuffed corn tortilla that we deep fry. You know, like a taquito."

"I've had flautas before."

"Really?"

"Yeah, do you think the Stanworth family has cornered the market on Mexican food?"

"No, I just...well..."—she fidgets with her sleeve—"when I told Justin, he acted like he'd never heard of them before, so I just assumed everyone in your family is the same."

"I lived in Mexico for two months a couple of years ago."

"You lived in Mexico?"

"Yeah." I shrug.

"Why?"

"We were filming a few stunts there, so we stayed in an Airbnb right in Mexico City."

"Who's *we*?"

"My partners and film crew."

Her head kicks back. "You have partners and a crew?"

"I'm guessing you didn't look up my YouTube channel last night."

"Oh." She tucks her hair behind her ear, showing off Santa-hat earrings. "I completely forgot. I can look it up right now." She grabs her purse like she means to dig her phone out.

"It's not a big deal." I reach my hand out, placing it on top of her wrist. "You don't have to look it up right now."

"Are you sure?"

"Yeah, I'm sure." My fingers still have her wrist. I should pull back, but I don't. I'm making sure she's not going to take her phone out. Besides, it's a wrist—the least-intimate body part next to maybe the ankle.

"I promise I'll look it up tonight."

"Don't worry. I'm just teasing you." I finally pull back. It was time. "So you asked who I travel with. My partner and I usually get to a location first. His name was Lars."

She leans forward as if she's not sure she heard me right. "Was?"

"Yeah." I shrug indifferently, but my fingers tighten over the steering wheel, keeping my emotions steady. "He passed away two months ago."

"From one of your tricks?" Her concern is so high I can't help but smile amidst my pain.

"He had leukemia."

"Oh." Sadness weighs her shoulders down.

"Lars wasn't only my business partner. He was my best friend. It's been really tough." I barely get the words out before emotion swallows them up. I glance away, clearing my throat.

"I'm really sorry, Caleb. I'm sure it's been tough." Now it's Summer's turn to reach out. She rubs my forearm in a comforting way, and I'm surprised how much one little touch makes me feel better.

"Thanks." I clear my throat again, forcing my emotions back.

She squeezes my arm, offering a closed-lip smile before she tucks her hand into her lap.

"Losing Lars has kind of made me reevaluate my life."

"That's why you came to Telluride and why you want to work on your relationship with Justin?"

"Yeah. I haven't told him that, but losing someone you love changes you. Makes you prioritize family and friends."

"I love that." Her expression falls. "Not the part about your best friend passing away, but what it's inspiring you to do."

I smile. "I know."

She sits back in her seat, looking out the front window of the car. "I'm not very good at it, but I try to live my life that way. Put relationships first."

"What are you talking about? You're the best person at it. I've never known anyone who cares about the relationships in their life as much as you do."

"You think?" Her giant smile shows how much my words mean to her.

"Yes, you're all in. All the time." It's something that I really like about Summer.

She thinks over my words. I steal a glance in between watching the road and can't help but love the small smile on her lips as she looks out the window.

"So now that Lars is gone"—she turns to me, and I quickly flip my eyes back to the road—"are you done with your YouTube channel?"

"No, I'm just taking a much-needed break. My heart isn't in it anymore. Maybe in a few months I'll feel differently."

"I wish I could take a break from work."

"You don't like your job?"

"I hate it." She sighs. "My boss keeps giving me more properties to run without a pay raise. I'm just overworked and tired of the whole thing, you know?"

"So why don't you quit?"

"It's not that easy."

"Why not? If you hate your job and it's making you miserable, why don't you quit?"

"Because I need money, and the job options in Telluride are slim to none." She taps her fingers on the armrest of the door, glancing out the window. "I don't know. I just keep hoping that someday I'll get married and become a mom and that I won't have to work anymore."

I haven't met many women who talk about motherhood and marriage like Summer. Most women I date don't act like having a family is the dream. To them, it's a death sentence. And to each his own, but Summer is different in that way. I can see why Justin said she reminds him of our mom. Patsy Davidson's dream life was being a mom too.

When I don't immediately respond, Summer turns her head to me. "That sounds stupid, doesn't it? Like something someone would say in the 1950s."

"It's not stupid if that's what you want."

"That's what I want." She stares at me in her genuine way that somehow encapsulates vulnerability, honesty, and sweetness all in one glance. If I'm not careful, Summer's gaze is something I could easily get lost in, losing hours of my day. So I force my eyes back to the road because her parents' house is up ahead, and somebody has to slow the car and park it. Since I'm driving, I guess that's my job.

"Are you sure you're ready for this again?"

I shift into park. "Your parents want to feed me a delicious meal. It's not that big of an imposition."

"They'll want to play games too."

"I like games."

"I should probably warn you..." She leans in, a touch of flirtiness in her eyes. "I'm really competitive."

I lean in too, meeting her halfway between our two seats. "So am I."

Her lips tug into a small smile. "We'll see."

"I guess so." I like the buzz of playful tension pulling between us.

"Alright, *Justin*. Let's do this." With that, she opens the car door and hops out, leaving me with the disappointing realization that I'm only here to pretend to like Summer.

Actually liking her is out of the question.

seventeen

SUMMER

"JANET, DINNER WAS AMAZING." Caleb turns behind him to my mom as my parents follow us to the door.

She taps him on the forearm. "I'm so glad you liked the *flaw*tas."

Caleb's eyes hold a glint as they swing to me. How my mom pronounces flautas has been one of his favorite things all night. She just can't quite capture the Spanish pronunciation.

"And Marty"—he points to my dad—"I want a rematch of Rook. I know I can beat you."

My dad straightens with pride. "Nobody can beat me. It's all about knowing how to play your trump cards."

"Well, then I'll have to settle for beating Summer." He shoots me a cocky smile that should be outlawed for how dangerous it is.

"I just had an off night. I'll destroy you next time we play." I feel my mom's eagle eye on me. She's constantly watching us, assessing every single interaction and touch.

Caleb waves to my parents as he opens the front door. "Thanks again."

"We'll see you next week?" my mom asks, gathering more information to hold over my head. "At the Noel Night in town?"

His eyes dart to me. "Summer hasn't given me the full holiday schedule yet, but that sounds fun. Let's plan on it."

The way my mom smiles back at Caleb breaks my heart. She's cautiously opening up to a lie, and it's all my fault. But this situation is just temporary, a means to an end. She can feel that way about Justin too.

"Okay, well. We'll see you then." I loop my hand through Caleb's arm, letting him escort me down the walk. I glance behind my shoulder, seeing one of my mother's brown eyes as the door shuts. Her hawk-eye treatment is getting creepy.

"Is everything okay?" Caleb asks at my side.

"Uh, yeah." I flip my focus forward and gasp at the exhaust billowing out the back of his car. "Did we leave your car on this whole time?"

"No, I came out here a few minutes ago and turned it on so it would be warm for you." He opens my door, waiting beside it for me to get in.

Caleb's sweet and simple gestures keep piling up.

"You did that for me?"

"Not really. I did it for myself. I hate to be cold." The teasing in his eyes says differently.

I drop into my seat and watch as he walks around to his side of the car.

"We did it," he says as he backs out of my parents' driveway. "Another successful holiday party without anyone knowing I'm not actually your boyfriend."

"Thanks for coming. I know it's a lot. I owe you big time. Whatever you want."

"Whatever I want?" Caleb eyes me with a smirk that's so irresistibly charming I wish I could take back my words like a shopping spree at Target when you don't have any money. Why is his smile so gosh darn attractive?

"Okay, not *whatever* you want."

"That's not what you said. You said, 'Whatever I want.'" His smile tilts, and his eyes dart to me. Even in the darkness, I can see the gleam behind his stare. "I'll have to think long and hard. Make it something really good."

I playfully narrow my gaze. He matches my stare as best he can while driving. Our smiles hold as we study each other.

"I'm low-key scared to find out what you want as payback." My phone buzzes in my purse, and I dig through, trying to find it. The light from the home screen brightens with the beginnings of a text.

"It's from Justin." I go quiet as I read the whole message.

Justin: I think I'm getting a cold or the flu. Can you stop at the store on your way home and get me some NyQuil and decongestant with an antihistamine?

"Oh, no."

Caleb looks over at me. "What is it?"

"Justin doesn't feel well. He wants us to stop at the store and get some medicine."

"Medi-sinny?"

My mouth falls open. "See? You do remember everything from that night."

"Not true." He shakes his head, returning his gaze back to the road. "I have a vague memory of saying that one word wrong. Everything else is foggy."

He might be teasing me right now, but I'm not in a power position to question it.

It's not like I want Caleb to remember, with perfect recollection, the kiss we shared. It's better if he doesn't remember it. But up until the moment I realized he wasn't Justin, it was probably the best kiss of my life—like, drive-me-insane-with-desire, destroy-every-other-kiss-after-it kind of connection. So it's annoying that he acts like he doesn't remember any of it. Not to mention offensive. I'm offended the best kiss of my life doesn't live rent-free in his mind. Because it has put down a deposit, moved in furniture, and repainted the walls in my head.

"So, go to the store?" His question pulls me back to the moment.

"Yeah, if you don't mind."

Caleb makes a quick lane change and pulls into the parking lot of Clark's Market.

"I can just run in really quick if you want to stay in the car."

"Like I'm really going to make you go in alone." He opens his car door and climbs out before I can even protest.

I scramble after him, catching up as he passes my side of the car. Normally, I would hold his hand or cuddle in close to stay warm, but nothing about our relationship is normal. So I keep my hands to myself.

"So what are we buying?" he asks as we enter the store.

I point to the pharmacy side. "NyQuil and decongestant with an antihistamine."

"There goes your night."

"What do you mean?"

"Sounds like Justin is trying to knock himself out with drugs. So much for watching a movie together."

"Yeah, I forgot about that." I trail my fingers along the shelf full of cold and sinus medications. "We'll have to do it another time."

"Or I could watch a movie with you."

His offer sends a thrill—that definitely shouldn't be there—swirling through my stomach. "Yeah, sure. That would be fun."

He turns his head to the pharmacy counter. "Hey, look at that."

"It's a cash register." I look at him like he's crazy. "Are you suggesting we rob the place?"

"No." He walks over to the microphone sitting on the counter and wiggles it. "I dare you to talk into it."

"Is this how you want to be repaid for standing in for Justin with my family?"

"No." The corner of his mouth curls upward. "This isn't my thing. This is just a dare."

"A dare?"

"That's right."

I look over my shoulder for a sixteen-year-old employee who might catch me, but the aisles are clear.

"Unless you're too scared to talk into it."

"I'm not scared. I told you I don't get embarrassed."

"Prove it." Behind his expression is the perfect amount of challenge and flirtatiousness.

I grab the microphone, leaning down to speak into it, changing the tone of my voice to sound more official. "Attention, customers. Would Caleb Davidson come to the pharmacy?" He lifts his brows at me in response. "I repeat: Caleb Davidson to the pharmacy. Your Viagra is ready."

The look on his face kills me.

He tears the microphone from my hand so fast I can barely stand from how hard I'm laughing. His lips go to the tip. "That was *vitamins* for Caleb Davidson, not Viagra. Vitamins, folks. But Summer Stanworth, your hemorrhoid cream is ready."

Now, it's my turn to reach for the speaker. Caleb lifts his arm, holding the speaker up so it's out of my grasp. I still go after it, and he spins his body with me following. He twists more, and our bodies get tangled up in the microphone cord as we fight to control it.

"Fine! You win." I take a step back but can't go anywhere. The cord is wrapped around my waist several times, holding me close to Caleb. I peer up at him—not the best idea if you're trying not to make things feel intimate. Eye contact intensifies everything.

His lips pull into a smirk as his ocean eyes stare down at me. "We're stuck."

"It looks like it." My heartbeats go from regular to erratic, but I don't pull away. I just keep staring into his beautiful eyes like it's my job to be this close to him.

Why are neither of us moving to get *un*stuck?

"Excuse me!" We turn our attention to a slender guy with a

Jim, Store Manager tag pinned on his vest. "That microphone isn't a toy. It's for Clark employees only."

"Sorry." An involuntary laugh spits out, and I scramble to get undone from the cord binding me to Caleb's chest, something I should've done five seconds ago.

"Yeah, sorry." There's humor in Caleb's voice as he unwinds. "We were just—"

"I know what you were doing." The manager's glare intensifies. "I'm going to have to ask you to leave the store. Immediately."

I step over the last little bit of the cord, freeing myself. "Can we at least pay for our stuff first?"

"No, you need to leave now."

"But what about our Nyquil?"

Jim the Manager reaches into our shopping cart, taking away the medicine. "You've lost your privilege to buy it."

Caleb loses it. Laughter spills out of him in loud bursts, infuriating Jim even more.

And that's how we end up being escorted out of Clark's grocery store by the night security guard.

eighteen

CALEB

JUSTIN SITS up from his spot on the couch the second we come through the door. His tired eyes go to Summer. "Do you have the NyQuil?"

"Uh..." She pulls on the lapels of her coat. "About that." Her gaze shoots to me, and there's so much humor in her stare I can't help but smile. "We got kicked out of the store."

"What?" His expression distorts to something confused and pinched.

"Yeah, Summer got us in trouble, and the manager made us leave without buying anything."

"What?" Her jaw drops at the same time her expressive blue eyes drill me. "It was all your fault."

"My fault? You're the one who grabbed the microphone and started talking into it."

"Because you dared me."

I take my coat off, hanging it up. "I didn't dare you to say Viagra."

"And I didn't dare you to say hemorrhoid cream."

"So you didn't get me any medicine?" Justin interrupts.

"No," we say in unison.

He murmurs and grunts as he stands. "I can't believe you guys. How am I supposed to sleep with a stuffy nose?"

Summer walks to him. "I'm sorry. I can go back out."

"Forget about it." He waves her away. "I'm going to bed. We'll talk tomorrow."

We watch in silence as he stomps down the hall to his room. Summer sighs, her posture deflating.

"Don't worry about him," I say, heading to the kitchen. "It's just a man cold. He'll live."

"You think?" She meets me by the kitchen, resting her elbows on the bar.

"Yes, I get them all the time." I open the freezer, popping my head around the door. "Do you want some ice cream? We have mint."

Her expression grows from concerned to happy. "I would love some."

"Two mint chocolate chips coming right up." I grab bowls and begin scooping the treat into them while Summer walks to her purse and pulls out a piece of paper.

"It's good we have a chance to talk because we need to go over the upcoming schedule." She sits at the bar, flattening her paper on the counter.

"What's that?" I place the bowls in front of us.

"I made you a calendar of all the planned holiday events you need to attend."

I glance at the paper as I sit down. It's a Christmas calendar, something you can make on your computer. She even added clipart in the squares to match each event. I smile at how adorable it is. The sweetness and innocence of it perfectly matching Summer.

"Why are you smiling?"

I eye her. "Did you make this yourself?"

She gives me a pointed look. "No, I had a Christmas elf make it."

"That would explain the little graphics."

She punches me in the shoulder. "I like the graphics."

I grab the side of my arm where the sting of her punch is barely detectable. "I do too." I point at the paper. "There's a tree for the Noel Night tree lighting and a cookie with Christmas Cookie Decorating. It's cute."

"It is cute."

"That's what I said."

She rolls her lips together, giving me a skeptical expression, as if she doesn't believe a grown man like myself can think a Christmas calendar with holiday clipart is cute. But when Summer makes it, it is cute.

She points at the paper. "Well, looking ahead to next week..."

Instead of following her finger, I take a second to breathe in her smell, wishing for the life of me I knew what it was. My eyes cast over her blonde hair and the perfect waviness that complements her short haircut.

"Next Wednesday is Noel Night." She glances up at me excitedly, and I quickly flip my gaze to her eyes, hoping she didn't notice I was staring at her hair. "Have you ever been to Noel Night?"

I shake my head. "Nope."

"You're going to love it. Everyone in town gathers for the lighting of the ski tree."

"Please tell me Bob Irvine is going to be there. I'd like to officially meet the man, the myth, and the legend."

Her eyes glow. "I can't believe you just threw out Bob's name."

"Your family talks about him so much. I need to meet this guy."

"We do talk about him." She smiles with that same gleam in her stare. "And he will be there. He's in charge of lighting the bonfire."

I would expect nothing less from Bob.

"After the tree lighting, we'll ride the gondola to Mountain Village for ice skating."

"Bob Irvine, a ski tree, and ice skating? It sounds awesome. But it's been fifteen years since I went ice skating. I think it was a cruise ship when I was thirteen years old."

Her eyes study me and my smile. "Thank you."

I'm surprised by her sudden seriousness. "For what?"

"For being excited about all these traditions that I love. It's so much more enjoyable when I don't have to defend each activity. Or feel stupid for loving them."

"You're welcome." I keep her stare a few seconds longer, liking how alive everything inside my body feels. I drop my eyes to my bowl of ice cream. I wish I didn't have to. I wish I could gaze into her animated eyes as long as I wanted.

"Then next Thursday night, we're getting together with my best friend Vivian and her boyfriend to decorate Christmas cookies to take to the nursing home. On Saturday, we visit Irvine Ranch, where we'll see Santa and go on the sleigh ride." She glances up at me with a guilty expression. "Wednesday, Thursday, *and* Saturday. That's three activities next week. I hope it's okay."

I cast my eyes over her pretty face and how she bites her bottom lip when she's nervous. "It's not a problem."

Our stares stay on each other a little longer this time before she glances down at her spoonful of ice cream. It's like the more time we spend with each other, the longer we allow our gazes to hold.

"I don't need to go through each activity with you. All the information is on the calendar. You can figure it out."

"I'm sure I can."

"And the best part is, if you stick to my schedule, you'll have the perfect Christmas season."

"The perfect Christmas season? That's a pretty bold statement."

"Not a bold statement. It's truth." Her shrug comes with a side order of cockiness that I absolutely adore. "This is a tried-and-true Christmas agenda. Stick with me, Davidson, and you'll be so jolly this Christmas they'll be begging you to be Santa Claus."

I scrunch my nose, shaking my head at her. "Who's *they?*"

"I have no clue." She lifts her shoulders, dropping a spoonful of mint chocolate chip into her mouth. "But they will." She taps her calendar a few times with the tip of her spoon. "'Cause this is a recipe for success."

"I like your confidence." *More than I probably should.* "But, you know, I had a different plan for the season. Maybe we should do both plans simultaneously and see whose activities are better."

"You had a plan?" she says over another spoonful of ice cream. "I don't believe it."

"Why not?"

"Because men don't plan."

I reach for my phone and open my notes. I angle the screen so she can read the list of activities I had brainstormed for my stay in Telluride.

"Ice climbing, snowshoeing, fat biking, backcountry skiing." Her gaze darts to me. "These aren't holiday activities. They're recreational suggestions."

"Same as yours." I gesture to the calendar.

"Not the same."

"We're doing these." I lift the phone in front of her face.

"You can do them." She pushes my arm away. "You have my blessing. On your off days from me, go and recreate."

"No, we're doing them *together.*"

She eyes me like I'm crazy. "I'm not doing all of that."

"Have you ever done any of it before?"

"I know how to ski, but I haven't done any of the other stuff."

I click my tongue. "I'm disappointed in you, Summer. I thought you liked adventure. I took you for the kind of girl who's up for anything."

"I am."

"Then what's the problem?"

Deep down, we both know what the problem is.

"I just don't think any of the stuff on your list sounds very Christmasy. So I don't want to do it."

"Too bad. You said I could have whatever I want as payment for being your fake boyfriend, and this is what I want."

"You want me to ice climb and backcountry ski...with you?"

"That's right." I twist my barstool so I'm facing her. My knees brush along the side of her leg, but I pretend not to notice. "And then we'll see who came up with the better holiday plan. Me or you."

She glances down the hall. "What about Justin?"

"He can come too." We both know he won't. "If you want me to do all of your activities, then you have to be willing to do all of mine. It's only fair."

"Okay, fine. But"—she holds her finger in front of me—"I'll only do them if they don't interfere with what I already have planned."

"Great." I lean over the calendar, rubbing my palms back and forth. "Looks like you have nothing planned for tomorrow. So let's knock off ice climbing."

"Tomorrow? We're going to your parents' house for a make-up Thanksgiving dinner since we missed the one on Thursday."

"That's in the evening. I'm talking about tomorrow afternoon. We'll ice climb and then go straight to dinner at my parents' house on the way back through."

"Don't you have to make a reservation first?"

"Don't worry about the details. I'll handle everything."

"Alright." Her eyes drift to Justin's bedroom door. "I guess that would be okay."

It's totally okay.

First thing in the morning, I'll even invite Justin to come along too.

nineteen

SUMMER

"WHEN YOU SAID you'd handle everything, I didn't think you meant you'd be our ice-climbing guide." I look down, watching as Caleb tightens a harness around my body.

His fingers currently are, and have been for the last minute, brushing against my waist and thighs—*innocently*, of course. I glance across the snow to another woman getting innocently manhandled by her guide as he straps her into a harness. If a stranger can do that to her, surely my boyfriend's brother can do it to me.

He peeks up at me with blue eyes and a smile. "Why wouldn't I be our guide? I do this all the time."

Oh, he does this all the time. Naturally.

At least I look cute in my new all-white snow clothes. Not that I'm trying to look cute for Caleb. Actually, I got the snow pants and jacket as a Christmas present from my parents last year. The functionality of the snow clothes is low. They are more about being fashionable than warm, but at the time, I just wanted to look good while outdoors. I remember being excited about wearing them in front of a date during an outdoor activity like this one. At the time, I thought I might wear them in front of Gil, but our short-lived holiday romance fizzled out soon after. So I shoved them in the back of my closet, thinking about next Christmas: *Next Christmas, maybe I'll have a serious boyfriend and can wear my new snow clothes during the holidays...with him.* I do have a serious boyfriend. I'm just not ever with him.

Take today, for example. Justin said he was sick and didn't want to go out into the cold. It's a perfectly acceptable excuse for not coming ice climbing with us, and yet, it feels like an *excuse.*

"All set on the harness." Caleb straightens. "Why don't you sit on that rock, and I'll strap your crampons on?"

"My what?" I lean forward to hear better.

"Your *crampons.*" He holds up some shoe things. "They're clawed foot pieces that strap to your boots so you can get leverage on the ice."

"That's a horrible name. Somebody didn't think through that name enough when they decided to use it." I sit on the rock, looking at Caleb expectantly.

His smile turns impish. "I need your leg."

I half-heartedly lift it, causing him to reach down and grab my ankle. I don't know if it's his hand on my leg or his blue, blue eyes glimmering back at me, but the whole two seconds send an electric charge to my heart.

He props my foot against his chest, fastening the crampons to my shoe while I glance around the park.

"I can't believe this whole place is man-made by sprinklers dripping over the rocks."

"And I can't believe you've never been to the Ouray Ice Park."

"I know what it is, and I know about the ice-climbing festival they have every year, but for some reason, when you're a local, you're the last person to try out the fun things you live around."

"It doesn't have to be that way. Maybe you just need someone to explore your surroundings with." He drops my foot, tapping my knee, signaling he's ready for my other foot.

"That's the tricky part." I give him the next leg. "Up until now, I haven't really had anyone."

"What about before Justin?"

"Have you seen the size of Telluride? There's not a huge pool of men to choose from. Mostly, I've just had casual relationships with out-of-towners who come to work for the winter."

His eyes dart to mine. "Out-of-towners like me?"

Definitely not like you.

I brush away the stirring in my chest with an easy-breezy smile. "Yep, out-of-towners who are only temporary."

"Yeah, that's exactly like me. Temporary." He finishes with my boot, dropping it to the ground. A flash of hurt skims through his eyes before he turns around to the gear bag. "And last but not least, protective headgear." He faces me again, holding a helmet, and all traces of whatever I thought I saw before are gone.

I pull off my beanie and stand. Caleb takes a step forward, fitting the helmet over my hair. My stare stays on him as he fastens the loop under my chin. He shaved yesterday, not all the way smooth, just a trim, so his facial hair becomes stubble once again. I can't picture what he'd look like with smooth, clean-cut skin. Actually, I can...because of Justin.

His fingers skim against my skin below my chin, sending a shot of warmth funneling through my body like hot cocoa rolling down my throat.

"All done." But he doesn't step back. Instead, his hand moves from the helmet strap to my ear, lightly taking the tip of my earlobe between his fingers and rubbing them over the metal. "I like today's earrings," he says without looking at me, and it's a good thing because I think my expression is a cross between shock and delight. Dropping his hand, Caleb returns to the bag, leaving me melting behind.

My fingers go to the exact spot he just touched as if I can somehow stop the sensation. "They're the Grinch," I say under my breath.

Is it safe to climb an ice waterfall when your body temperature is this high? I would say no—fire and ice are not good combinations. Safety hazard.

The next time Caleb turns around, he's holding a rope. "I'm

going to climb up first and set the ropes. Then I'll come down, and we'll go up together."

"You're going up twice." I glance at the seventy-foot frozen wall.

"Somebody has to set the ropes—unless you want to."

"Nope, I'm good. I'll just watch from the ground."

And that's exactly what I do. I *watch.*

Caleb effortlessly climbs over frozen ice, whipping ropes and carabiners around like he owns the place. His athleticism is impressive. I admire and respect what he does.

Do I find him incredibly attractive right now?

No.

Absolutely not.

I'm sticking with admiration and respect—feelings you can have for any human being, whether he's your boyfriend's twin or your boss.

A few minutes later, Caleb's feet hit the ground.

"Very impressive." I clap. "You looked like the abominable snowman up there, scaling ice walls like a pro."

His chest lifts up and down from exertion, but he still manages to throw me a smirk. "You're comparing me to a Tibetan yeti known for being large, hairy, and apelike?"

"No!" I laugh.

He twists his body, looking at the ice. "Because I thought I looked dead sexy climbing that wall, but I guess not."

"You did." I startle, catching myself. "I mean, I admire how you can climb the ice so fast. I respect your *skills.*" Nothing more. "That's why I said you were the abominable snowman, because you looked like you were in your element. Like you belonged on an ice wall." And because nothing about a yeti is sexy, it's a very safe comparison. Ice climbing with your boyfriend's good-looking twin brother is all about staying safe.

"It's your turn. Let's get you up there." Caleb hands me two curved ice pick things. "When you use the ice tools, think of flicking the wrist rather than swinging your whole arm." He demonstrates the motion with his own hand. "And keep your legs wide for a greater base of support. You're almost making a triangle —your legs wider than your upper body." I try to mimic his position and get a nod of approval from him like he's satisfied with my effort. "I'm going up first. I'll be a few feet above you, but don't worry, your rope is attached to me, and I'll be belaying you the entire time in case you slip."

"So I won't fall to my untimely death?" I tilt my head, lifting one shoulder.

"You're too important to me to let that happen." He clicks a carabiner onto my harness and starts his ascent, leaving me wondering what the heck he meant by that.

I'm too important to him *because* I'm his brother's girlfriend. That's what he meant. Phew, I'm glad I sorted that out.

"You coming?" Caleb flashes a charming smile over his shoulder. He's already ten feet up. How did he get that high so fast?

"Yep, yep. Right behind you." I flick my tool into the ice sheet and kick my crampon-ed foot until I have enough leverage to pull myself up.

And we're off!

"There you go!" Caleb says above me. "You're a natural."

I just focus on the moves, flicking and kicking as I go.

"I feel like I have the upper-body strength of a jellyfish," I say as I pull myself to the next level.

"If you get tired, that's what the belay is for."

"It's un-*belayable!*"

"Oh, you're even making jokes. Next, you'll be singing 'Ice Ice Baby.'"

I flick the tool into another frozen piece and lift myself higher. "It's looping through my head as we speak."

"How did I know?"

I glance at Caleb above me as he hoists himself to another level. I take a second to study him as he climbs, the smoothness of his movements, the ease of his strength.

He looks good—pure athleticism and confidence.

"You're checking me out, aren't you?"

My head drops. "What? No! I'm climbing. You can't get"—I look down, checking my progress—"twenty feet off the ground without focusing on climbing."

He drops his eyes to me with a cocky smile. "It's my butt, isn't it? I know how good it looks in a harness."

I laugh as my mouth falls open. "No comment." Great answer. Very Switzerland-esque.

"Don't worry, I won't tell anyone."

I roll my eyes, focusing on each flick and kick as if my life depends on it. I'm halfway to the top when part of the ice protrudes, making it difficult to climb upward.

"You can go to the left if you want to take a little easier route," Caleb calls to me.

Easy sounds good right about now, so I shift to the left, kicking my foot into the ice, but it doesn't catch. Instead, both feet slide out from under me. My hands tighten around the tools like I can muscle a save with my jellyfish upper body, but the weight is too much. My heart panics as I slide downward. I'm quickly yanked to a stop by Caleb and his belay rope.

"Oh my gosh!" My eyes shoot to him. "You saved me!"

His smile is calm and relaxed. "I'll always be here to catch you."

There's a place in the back of my heart, a hidden cavern where I hide my deepest, darkest secrets. Right now, that cavern wishes Caleb was talking about more than ice climbing.

CALEB

"WHAT'S the next step for a pro ice climber like myself?" Summer looks over at me from the passenger seat of my Bronco with an expression that's so serious it can only be sarcastic. "I mean, do I guide tours, climb without ropes, enter contests?"

I try to match her same playful seriousness. "All of the above."

There's a cocky-cute undertone to her shrug. "I'm probably going to need gold-encrusted crampons."

I smile, amused by everything this woman does and says. "Probably so."

She shifts her eyes to her window, tapping her fingers and shimmying her shoulders to the beat of "Last Christmas" playing on the radio. "You know, my dad loves this song. One winter, when I was in middle school, I worked for him at his office after school to earn money for Christmas. Whenever this song came on, he'd turn the radio up in his office so loud that the entire workplace could hear it. He never said anything or even came out. But when the song was over, he would turn the radio down again and go back to work as if nothing had happened."

I watch Summer tell her story, her eyes casting to the scenery out the window, a slight smile crossing her lips. She looks like a giant marshmallow in her white, puffy snow coat that makes her bright-red lipstick stand out. Who wears lipstick to go ice climbing anyway?

Summer does, and it totally fits.

"I thought your dad was a general contractor. What was he doing in an office instead of at a job site?"

"He's more *general* than *contractor,* even though he'll never admit it."

"After talking to him, I got the impression he was the Tarzan of contractors, swinging from one scaffolding to the next."

"No," I spit out with a laugh. "I don't think the man's ever been on a piece of scaffolding in his life." Her brows lower. "When did you have this conversation with him?"

"I think it was the night of the Turkey Stuff when you were in the bathroom. He told me about all the house remodels he does in Telluride and how when he tears off sheetrock, the walls are crookeder than a dog's hind leg."

"Yeah, he loves that saying." She glances at me as I make a right turn off the highway. "Where are we going? I thought we were going to your parents' house for dinner with Justin."

"We are. We're just taking a little detour first."

She reads the road sign in front of us. "Ouray Hot Springs?"

"Yeah, have you ever been?"

"Once, when I was little, we stayed at the hotel and did the hot springs, but that was years ago."

"I thought we could go try them out."

"I'm in snow clothes."

"They have swimsuits we can buy in the shops. Besides, if we go straight to my parents' house, we'll get there early before Justin and be waiting around. We might as well kill some time before dinner."

She glances at the clock on the dash, obviously doing the math on the dinner start time. "I have wanted to go back as an adult."

"Today's the perfect day."

Her eyes dart to me. "Maybe I should call Justin first to make sure he isn't getting to your parents' house early."

"Yeah, you can give him a call."

She holds her phone up to her ear, biting her lip while waiting for him to pick up. After a second, she clicks off the call. "He didn't answer."

"So, should we check out the hot springs?"

"I guess that would be alright."

I pull the car into a hotel parking lot.

"I thought we had to be a guest at the hotel to use the hot springs here."

"Being a hotel guest is encouraged." A mischievous smile covers my mouth before I jump out of the car.

"So we're sneaking in?" She stands and slams her car door behind her.

"Can you handle that?"

"Pfft. Of course, I can handle that."

"Just act like you belong."

She heads for the front of the hotel. "That's what I was going to say to you."

We walk through the lobby doors, and the receptionist smiles at us from her spot at the front counter. I return the smile, leading the way into the hotel gift shop.

"What if we can't find a swimsuit to buy?" Summer casually walks around the shelves of over-the-counter medicine and magnets.

"Then we'll have to go naked."

Her head jerks up with a freaked-out expression that ruins my joke.

I start laughing. "I'm kidding. If they don't have suits, we'll have to come back another time." My eyes catch some in the corner. "But I think we're in luck."

We walk to the back of the small shop, flipping through the hangers.

"Oh, no!" Summer groans.

"What?"

"They're ugly." She holds up a white bikini with deer heads on each triangle and on the bottoms. Her lips quiver as she watches my expression go from confusion to comical until we both crack with laughter. "I think it's a play on having a nice 'rack,'" she says through her giggles. She flips the tag around, reading the description out loud. "The classic three-point top that better reflects the advantages of the body. Sexy-hot, cheeky design"—her blue eyes look up at me with a playful glow before she continues reading—"that will give you a new look and make you stand out in the crowd."

"Or stand out in a herd."

Summer snorts, drawing out my own laugh. There's something so satisfying about making her laugh.

"I will *not* be standing out in a herd today."

"You have to wear it. It's amazing."

"No, it's hideous."

"Look, there's a matching men's elk swimsuit for me. I'll wear one too." I hold it up to my waist, showing off the antler pattern strategically placed in the middle of the crotch.

"That's gross. I refuse to be these people."

I grab the hanger from her before she can put the bikini back. "You're wearing it. What size are you?" My eyes drift up and down her body as if they've magically become a tape measure, but when they land on Summer's face, all signs of laughter have faded into a playful, pointed stare.

"Um, do you mind?"

"I wasn't checking you out. You look like a marshmallow in your snow clothes." I start walking backward toward the cash register. "If I were going to sneak a peek, I wouldn't waste it on when you're wearing your snow clothes. I'd make sure to steal a glance when you're wearing *this*." I hold up the bikini.

Summer's cheeks turn pink, and it isn't from the cold outside.

But I said *if*.

If I were going to check her out.

I never said I would.

And I never said I wouldn't.

I LEAVE MY PHONE, WALLET, AND KEYS UNDER THE floormat in my Bronco and run back inside the hotel lobby to change out of my snow clothes into my swimsuit. Summer's already in the women's bathroom, changing, but I still make it out first, walking toward the floor-to-ceiling windows while I wait.

Large snowflakes slowly drift from the sky. It's not the kind of snowfall that will collect on everything. Mostly, it makes the day magical and, dare I say, *romantic*.

"I can't believe I'm wearing this."

I flip around, expecting to see the deer bikini, but instead, Summer stands in her white coat zipped up over her chest with her bare legs hanging out from under the hem. She still has on her black snow boots and beanie. The rest of her clothes are rolled up and bundled in her arms.

It's like winter-sexy-cute. I didn't even know that was a thing, but it just became one of my favorite looks.

I'm flustered by her exposed legs barely being covered by her coat, but I avert my eyes as any good brother would do. "It's a memory."

She lifts her brows in a teasing way. "Wearing a rack over my rack is a memory?"

"When in Telluride." My smile hitches at the side. "Besides, I have a rack over my crotch."

She lifts her chin, glancing away. "I'll take your word for it."

"Come on." I laugh. "Let's sneak into one of the hot springs." I lead the way outside, feeling the freezing air against my legs.

"There's a fence around the hot springs, and we don't have a hotel key card to unlock the gate."

"Maybe someone can let us in with their card." I glance over the property. There are a few people in the springs on the other side, but the tub up ahead is vacant. Having a hot spring all to ourselves sounds much better than crowding in on the others, so I lead the way to the empty spring. "We'll have to climb the fence."

"If we do that, won't everyone know we're trespassing?"

I throw her a smile over my shoulder. "Are you scared of getting in trouble?"

"Did it look like I was scared last night when I used the pharmacy speakerphone?" She marches ahead of me with indignation in each step, like she's proving a point. She drops her pile of clothes on a lounge chair and removes her coat, keeping her boots on to trudge through the snow to the fence.

And suddenly, visiting the hot springs was the worst idea I've ever had—or the best, if you forget about the fact that she's my brother's girlfriend. Because my brother's girlfriend looks pretty phenomenal in that ridiculous swimsuit.

I know because I looked.

And then I looked away.

I mean, there's still a level of *looking* that has to happen to see what the heck she's doing, but the studying and the admiring of her curves has stopped. Scout's honor, and I'm not even a scout.

Summer attempts to climb the fence—*attempt* being the best description of what's happening. I remove my coat and meet her by the fence, assisting where possible. But there's really no way to assist her besides pressing my hands on her butt and pushing upward. As tempting as that sounds, I decide to forgo the butt-grabbing.

"Here, let me go first."

She steps back, giving me room. I grab the top of the fence and pull my body up, hoisting myself over until I hit the ground on the other side.

She tilts her head at me. "Show off."

"Me? Showing off to impress you? I would never."

I totally would, and right now, I'm hoping it worked.

She grabs the fence like I did and climbs until her body reaches the top. I raise my arms, placing my hands on her body, helping her get down over the other side.

It's a tough job, but somebody has to do it.

My fingers glide across her hip to her back, holding her body to me as I carefully lower her to the ground. It's a slow and sexy— I mean, painful. It's a slow and *painful* process with lots of drawn-out eye contact and skin-to-skin contact as her feet steady herself.

"Thanks." Her blue-eyed gaze stares at me, and I feel every heated moment of the exchange as a molten feeling spreads through my body.

"You're welcome." We're still chest to chest with arms tangled around each other, bodies smashed together, faces inches apart, and lips...let's not forget about the lips. They're inches apart too. But actually, I try to forget about Summer's lips and that kiss of ours every dang day.

"It's freezing," she finally says.

"Yeah, it is." I take a step back, removing my body and arms from her.

We kick off our boots, leaving them by the hot spring, and slowly sink into the steaming water, making sure we're sitting a respectable distance apart.

If Summer were my girlfriend, I'd pull her to me and enjoy the privacy of a vacant hot spring. Instead, I rest my head back and close my eyes. "Your swimsuit is very ugly, by the way."

"So is yours." I hear the humor in her voice. "Hmmm." She sighs. "This is nice. Especially after ice climbing. I know my arms are going to be so sore tomorrow."

"Oh, really? Because thirty minutes ago, you said you were a pro ice climber." I crack one eye open, smirking, but hers are closed. With her head back like that, I make a mental note not to look at her bare shoulders or follow a snowflake as it melts against the delicate skin between her neck and collarbone. I'm all about mental toughness.

"Pro ice climbers can still get sore," she defends.

I close my eyes again because it's easier than looking at Summer and then feeling guilty that I looked at Summer.

I'm not an idiot. I knew what I was getting myself into when I suggested the hot springs, but I didn't think it would be this hard. But it's just a stupid attraction. It's not like I'm going to act on any of it.

We sit silently for a few minutes with our eyes closed, soaking in the heat. The gate opens and closes, causing me to sit up. A man in a security outfit with a long black coat stands above us.

"Excuse me?" His disapproving expression can't be good. Summer opens her eyes, straightening beside me. "You both need to exit the property before I call the police for trespassing."

"Oh, we're not trespassing," Summer quickly says, but the security guard's glare cuts through her confidence, and she crumbles under pressure. "Okay, we are. We're trespassing. I'm so sorry."

He points behind him. "Leave. Now."

"Sure." I stand, glancing around for towels. "Is there a towel we can use to dry off?"

"No," he grunts. "Towels are for hotel guests only."

"Yeah, but it's freezing outside." I puff out a humorless laugh. "Can't you just let us dry off?"

"Nope. You should've thought about that before you trespassed."

"It's okay, Caleb." Summer stands and climbs out, grabbing her snow boots. "We'll just use our coats."

I follow after her, putting on my boots. The guard holds the gate open for us, making sure we actually leave the premises.

"Where are our clothes?" Summer gasps.

I peek around her, looking at the exact lounge chair where we left the pile outside the fence, but it's empty.

"Did somebody take our clothes?" I ask the security guard.

"I have no clue." He slams the gate, gesturing to the sidewalk that leads to the parking lot. "I need you both to leave."

"But somebody stole our clothes." Summer is shaking from the cold with both arms wrapped around her wet body. I can see her gigantic goosebumps from two feet away.

"That sounds like karma to me."

"But—"

I wrap my arm around her shoulder, escorting her forward. "Let's get you to the car before you freeze to death."

She spits out a laugh that's full of disbelief. "But what about our clothes?"

"I don't know. I think the security guard is trying to teach us a lesson."

"Can he do that?" She cranes her neck, trying to see over my arm to where he still stands behind us by the hot spring.

"Well, we did break the law by trespassing."

A fist goes into my side, and I hunch over in stunned pain. "Caleb Davidson, this is the second place in a matter of twenty-four hours you've gotten me kicked out of."

"Ouch." I rub the area where she hit with my free hand. "Don't blame me. You've gotten yourself kicked out of these places."

"Well, you're a bad influence on me."

We get to my car, and I swing the passenger door open for her. I flash her a charming smile. "And you're a bad influence on me."

twenty-one

SUMMER

WE TALKED about stopping and getting clothes before we showed up for dinner, but since the Davidson's live in the middle of nowhere between Ouray and Telluride there wasn't really a place to stop and shop. Plus, the whole '*No shoes. No shirt. No service,*' thing presented a problem. We have shoes, but definitely lacking in the shirt department. That's why we pull up to the Davidson's house in our swimsuits.

"I'd let you wear my pants, but I don't have any." Caleb's smile is chock-full of humor.

I do my best to maintain a serious glare. "This isn't funny."

"It's kind of funny."

"No, it's not. My brand-new snow clothes got stolen along with my underwear and bra. We got kicked out of a hotel by a security guard. I'm wearing a *cheeky* deer bikini. I'm wet and freezing, and I'm supposed to go inside your parents' house and have dinner with your family with no clothes on. What about this is funny?"

His lips twitch, and I know he's going to lose it. He covers his mouth with the palm of his hand, trying to hold in his laughter.

"It's not funny!" My irritated facade falters, and I show a smile that I desperately try to hide from him. "It's not!"

But it's no use. We both give in and spend the next minute laughing at how ridiculous the day has turned out.

Caleb reaches for the handle. "Let's make a run for the front door before we turn into an icicle."

"On the count of three?" I hold my handle too.

"One, two, three!" We count in unison and then climb out of the car in a rush.

Caleb waits for me to catch up to him. His hand extends, and I'm so cold I don't even think twice about grabbing it and running to the house with my hand in his. We're still laughing when we reach the front door—the alternative is freezing to death.

He twists the knob, and we barrel inside but stop the moment we see his mom, dad, and Justin looking at us with blank expressions.

"Summer?" Justin's expression is not amused.

"Caleb?" Patsy frowns at her son.

"What are you guys doing?" I follow Justin's gaze as he assesses our deer bathing suits and then stops on our hands... currently still joined together.

I yank my fingers out of Caleb's grasp. "Our clothes got stolen at the hot springs, and they kicked us out."

"Without giving us towels," Caleb adds, and I'm relieved to have someone help explain.

"So we had no clothes and had to come here for dinner like this."

"We thought about stopping and buying clothes." Caleb looks at me. "But there wasn't a lot of open stores to choose from, especially on a Sunday evening."

There's a distinct V between Justin's brows as he listens to us rattle off excuses. "What are you wearing?"

I nervously cover my body with my arms. "It was the only swimsuit they had at the gift shop."

"I thought you were going ice climbing." The accusatory look on Justin's face hasn't softened once since we arrived.

"We did." Caleb shrugs. "But we were so close to the Ouray hot springs, and Summer hadn't been there for twenty years, so we made a quick detour."

"Oh, honey!" Patsy jumps up from her spot on the couch. "You must be freezing." She grabs my hand, pulling me toward the bedrooms. "Let's get you some clothes."

"What the heck, Caleb?" Justin says as we exit the room. "You show up here with my girlfriend with no clothes on?"

"Relax. We're in swimsuits," Caleb snaps back. "We told you what happened."

"You can wear something of mine." Patsy smiles as she walks, but there's an anxiousness in her eyes.

"Thanks." I follow her down the hall, straining to hear the conversation in the family room.

"It just doesn't look good," Justin says.

"Is that what you're mad about? How it looks?"

"I'm not mad. It's just classic Caleb. You never think before you do something, and now you've dragged Summer into it."

"Don't mind them," Patsy tells me over her shoulder.

"I think Summer can decide for herself what she wants to be dragged into," Caleb defends.

"Hey, hey," Don says. "Let it go. Your mother worked hard on dinner and wants a nice evening."

"We're not fighting," Justin says.

"Good. Keep it that way."

"I think I have an old sweat outfit you can wear. It's light pink. Don and I were pigs for Halloween a few years ago."

"Patsy?" I touch her arm, pausing her steps. "I'm really sorry if I've caused any problems today."

She places her hand on top of mine. "Oh, stop. These boys have been fighting over toys ever since they were babies. Whatever Caleb had, Justin wanted. Whatever Justin had, Caleb wanted. Not that you're a toy. I'm just saying that's how it goes with them. I'm used to it. Don't think another thing about it." Her hand squeezes mine. "Now, let's get you warm."

"Okay." I smile, but as hard as I try not to think about it, Patsy's words dance through my head.

These boys have been fighting over toys ever since they were babies. Whatever Caleb had, Justin wanted. Whatever Justin had, Caleb wanted.

Everything about that feels unsettling.

"DO YOU HAVE ENOUGH INVENTORY OF BLANKETS TO fill all of those Black Friday purchases?" Don asks as we sit around the dining table.

We finished eating a half hour ago, but everyone stayed put, talking.

"We were anticipating a big holiday season, so we have more than enough," Justin answers.

"That must keep you really busy." Concern brushes across Patsy's brows. "Are you making enough time for Summer?"

Justin rubs my shoulder. "Summer's been so understanding about my work schedule. Especially during the holidays."

"And Summer, how's your work going with all the properties you're managing?" Patsy asks.

There's a distinct difference between Justin's family and my family. When you talk at Justin's house, all eyes are on you. It's silent as everyone listens to you speak. At my house, you have to fight to get your words heard. Everyone talks over everyone. So when the Davidson family turns their attention to me, it feels like a lot. Or maybe it's a lot because I feel the weight of Caleb's stare from across the table.

"Work is busy, but it's going good."

"You're being modest, babe." Justin rubs my back. "Summer manages more properties than anyone else there. She's killing it. I wouldn't be surprised if, in a few years, she's running the entire office as the manager."

I smile at Justin, leaning into his touch.

"Do you even want to run the office?" Caleb asks.

"Of course she does," Justin answers for me. "Summer loves her job."

I glance at Caleb. His brows lift as if he's daring me to speak up and tell Justin how I really feel about my job. But I look away instead.

"And let's not forget about everything Caleb has accomplished with his YouTube channel." Patsy beams at him before turning to me. "Have you seen Caleb's videos?"

"Uh..." I hesitate because this is the third time I've had to admit that I haven't looked him up. "Not yet, but I've seen him ice climb in real life, and that was pretty impressive."

"Is it really that impressive to climb ice?" Justin scoffs. "Don't the guys holding the ropes on the ground do most of the work?"

"They are unbelayable," Caleb mutters, drawing out my smile.

"Climbing is only part of what Caleb does," Patsy says. "He does the most incredible tricks. I can't even watch them because they're so dangerous. Who would've thought all that jumping and flipping off my furniture as a child would help make Caleb famous?"

"So you are famous?" I smile at him. "The girl at the light parade wasn't a one-time fluke?"

Patsy's brows drop. "I thought you said you didn't go to the light parade because you had to work?"

"I didn't go." Justin shakes his head. "Caleb and Summer went."

Patsy glances at her husband, and I know what she's thinking. She's trying to figure out why Justin's girlfriend is hanging out with Caleb so much. She doesn't understand the complexity of my family dynamics and Justin.

"Caleb and I bumped into each other at the parade," I explain. "I was with my family, and we invited him to sit with us."

173

"Yeah, but that's not the whole story." Justin looks at me. "Tell them about our holiday arrangement."

No, thanks, Justin. I'd rather not.

"What holiday arrangement?" Don asks.

"Caleb has agreed to impersonate me in front of Summer's family so they don't get irritated with how much I'm working the next few weeks." He makes my family sound overbearing and difficult.

"Well..." Patsy glances at her husband, then at Caleb.

"Don't look at me." He lifts his hands in the air. "It was Justin's idea."

Don frowns. "It was your idea?"

"Great plan, right?" Justin puffs his chest out like he's proud of the arrangement he's made. "It worked when we were younger. Why not now?"

"I never liked it when you were younger, but I guess if you're all okay with it." The smile that Patsy is faking isn't fooling anyone.

"It's only a few family parties." I lean forward, hoping to explain. "Justin's been working so hard. I don't want to be a burden on him or his schedule. So we figured this would be a good compromise so my family wouldn't feel slighted. My mom has the tendency to keep score on stuff like this."

"And so that Summer wouldn't have to spend the holiday season alone." Caleb's blue eyes drill me, and although his statement is innocent and true, it feels loaded with all sorts of meaning, like the moment he told me on the ice that he would always be there to catch me.

I feel my cheeks flame under his stare. What is it about that statement and that look that warrants blushing? I don't know, but I drop my eyes, hoping to stop the spread.

"It seems a bit complicated," Don says. "Are you sure you all know what you're doing?"

"Don't worry, Dad," Justin reassures. "There's nothing complicated about this."

It feels a little complicated when I have one Davidson twin sitting next to me with his arm around me, and the other sitting across from me with a heated stare that could puddle me if I held his gaze for too long.

Patsy jumps to her feet. "Maybe we should start clearing the table. It's getting dark, and I don't want you guys driving back to Telluride too late."

On her lead, everyone stands and begins gathering dishes, taking them into the kitchen. I drop off my first round to the sink and return for more. As I pass through the dining room walkway, I almost run into Caleb.

"Sorry." I glance up, expecting to see the usual whoopsy face that two people give each other when they almost crash, but Caleb's smile holds more than that.

He bends down, putting his lips near the side of my face. "I can't believe you haven't looked me up yet. This feels personal now."

I eye him. How can a man wearing his dad's flannel pajamas look so good? "I'm starting to think you're obsessed with your online profile."

"Aren't you just the least bit curious?" His mouth teeters into a crooked smile.

I am.

After today, I really am.

"Nah." I shake my head.

"And why didn't you tell Justin that you hate your job and hope you're not working there in a few years?"

"It's hard to say."

Excelling at my job is one of the things Justin loves about me. I'm not about to tell him I hate it and wish I could quit.

"It didn't seem hard to say when you told me."

"That's because you're you."

"I'm taking that as a compliment." There's that same heated stare like Caleb's pupils have been switched out for flames. Every second I stare into his eyes, my heart gets softer and softer. Mushier and mushier.

"Oh." Patsy comes behind us, trying to get through.

I do this whole jump-scare thing, moving as far away from Caleb as possible.

"Traffic jam," I say, trying to act like the conversation between me and Caleb is just normal traffic-pattern problems, but I don't think Patsy Davidson is buying it.

CALEB

"Thanks for dinner." Summer hugs my mom in the entryway.

"It was no problem at all. Just glad to see you guys." My mom pulls back with a sincere smile that reaches every corner of her eyes.

"I'll wash your sweat outfit and bring it back next time we come over."

"Oh, I don't care about that."

"Alright, let's go." Justin tugs on Summer's arm, pulling her to the door. "I want to do a little work tonight now that I'm feeling a little better."

Summer's eyes find me. I'm leaning against the back of the couch with my arms and legs crossed. I've been waiting—*hoping*—for her to look my way. "Thanks for teaching me how to ice climb."

"Yeah, no problem. You're a pro." She smiles like she understands my reference. "And sorry for getting your clothes stolen. My bet's on the security guard."

She laughs. "Yeah, me too."

"Summer?" Justin says impatiently.

"Yeah, I'm ready." She gives one last wave, and they walk out the door.

It's weird. I came with Summer, and now I'm the one leaving alone. Watching her walk out the door with Justin sucks more than it should.

My mom whips around with an accusatory finger pointed at me. "Caleb John Davidson!"

"What?" My brows drop as I look back and forth between my parents. "What did I do?"

She walks toward me, and I feel like I'm twelve years old again, when she found out I jumped off the roof into a pile of mattresses. Her finger hits my chest with more force than a tiny sixty-year-old woman should have. "What's going on between you and Summer?"

"Nothing." I shrug.

"First, you show up to the house naked in the dead of winter."

I roll my eyes. "We were not naked. We had a four-point rack."

My mom ignores my joke, still hitting me with her finger. "And then you spend the rest of the night flirting with Summer right in front of your brother."

"Whoa." I straighten. "I was not flirting with Summer."

"You were looking at her." She turns to my dad. "Don, was he looking at her?"

"You were looking."

"Looking at someone is way different than flirting with them."

"No, you were looking at her with bedroom eyes. That's how you were flirting."

"I was not." I throw my arms up, knowing this is one battle with my mom that I'm not going to win. "She was sitting across from me at the table. Where else was I supposed to look?"

"And I don't like you impersonating Justin."

"It was his idea. Not mine."

"Well, you didn't have to go along with it."

"They needed my help. What was I supposed to do?"

"It's just asking for trouble." My dad shakes his head. "Summer is his girlfriend, not yours."

"I know that. You don't have to worry." I push off the back of the couch and start walking toward the kitchen.

My mom follows behind. "When you show up at our house naked after spending the day together, I'm going to worry."

"I was teaching her how to ice climb. She'd never been before." I face my mother, placing both my hands on her tiny shoulders. "I promise. Summer and I are just friends. And she could really use a friend right now with how much Justin is working."

I feel her shoulders lower, releasing some of her pent-up tension. "Alright, but promise me you won't cross any lines or even get close to the lines. That's when bad things happen."

"I promise."

But even as I say the words, I know in my heart that's one promise that's going to be hard to keep.

twenty-two

SUMMER

THAT NIGHT, after Justin dropped me off, I went down the Caleb Davidson rabbit hole. I'm so far down it I wouldn't be surprised if I ran into Bugs Bunny down here.

There are hours of videos of him doing death-defying tricks. BASE jumping, sky diving, rock climbing, hang gliding, zip lining, bungee jumping. You name it. If it's dangerous, Caleb has probably done it and done it in style or shirtless or in a way that's incredibly appealing.

His last video was posted three weeks ago. He swung from the rafters of a bridge in Thailand, threw five flips and five twists—a quint-quint (his words, not mine)—before a parachute opened up, dropping him into the water below. Speedboats holding his crew immediately zoomed in, making sure he was okay. Other crew members filmed the stunt from different angles—on top of the bridge, from the ground, from the river. It was an elaborate affair.

Before that, he BASE jumped off the side of a cliff, using a trampoline to get extra air. It would've been too easy to just jump. His body flipped and twisted as he fell, looking like some kind of Olympic diver.

He's incredible.

And a pretty big deal if you consider sixty-two million YouTube subscribers a pretty big deal.

How did I not know this?

Justin always acted like his twin brother was a joke, like he was barely getting by with his reckless *hobby*. But this is way more than a hobby. This is a multimillion-dollar business. Caleb has merch, diehard fans, and loyal followers who want to know everything about his life. He's created a brand centered around him.

I click through video after video, watching as he preps his tricks, analyzes the risks, tests the safety of his equipment, and—my favorite part—smiles at the cameras. So much of his carefree personality comes through in each video. I can see why people adore him. He's charismatic, exciting, surprising, and charming. No wonder he wanted me to look him up. He wanted me to see him in his element. Ever since he arrived in Telluride, I've been comparing him to Justin. But on his channel, he's himself—larger than life.

My eyes glance at the clock on my nightstand. It's almost midnight. I've been at this Google search for a while. But even though it's late, I open my phone to Caleb's name, happy that we decided to exchange numbers last night after my family party.

Summer: 62 million followers.

I hold my phone in my hand, hoping it's not too late for him to respond. My lips spread into a smile the moment his text comes through.

Caleb: They're called subscribers.

Summer: Same thing.

Caleb: Not really.

Summer: I'm embarrassed that I called myself a pro at ice climbing today when the real pro was my guide. From the looks of things, you didn't even need to use ropes to climb that waterfall.

Caleb: Sounds like somebody finally watched my YouTube channel.

Summer: I glanced through it.

Caleb: And?

And everything I thought I knew about Caleb has been flipped upside down. He's not reckless and immature. He's daring and *wildly* attractive.

Summer: And I'm impressed.

Caleb: Good.

I can picture his smile right now—smug and full of charming swagger.

Caleb: What do we have planned for tomorrow?

Summer: Nothing. Some of us have to go back to work. We don't have 62 million followers, which makes it possible for us to take a break during the holidays.

Caleb: Subscribers.

Summer: Same thing.

Caleb: Not really.

I bite the side of my cheek, but the action does nothing to suppress my smile.

Summer: The next activity on the calendar is Wednesday. Noel Night with my family for the tree lighting and ice skating. Come prepared to be my fake boyfriend.

Caleb: Looking forward to it.

What's he looking forward to? The entire night as a whole, or being my fake boyfriend? I'm dying to know, but at the same time, I'm happy for my ignorance.

Summer: And Thursday is Christmas cookie decorating with my friend, Vivian.

Caleb: Keep Friday afternoon and night clear for back-country skiing.

Summer: Backcountry skiing? What about avalanches and other dangerous winter stuff?

Caleb: Don't worry about the details. I'll handle everything.

That's the exact same thing he said to me about ice climbing. After seeing everything Caleb is capable of, I wouldn't be surprised if he knows how to stop an avalanche while it's tumbling down a mountain.

Summer: Okay, you're on for Friday.

Caleb: And I'll be sure to invite Justin too.

My shoulders sink with guilt. I hadn't thought about Justin one time during this entire text conversation.

What does that say about me?

I don't know, and I don't want to analyze the answer to find out.

twenty-three

SUMMER

"SO WHAT ABOUT YOU?" Vivian asks after she tells me about Thanksgiving with Sam and her family. "How was your weekend?"

"Good." My mouth widens into a smile as I tap my fingers over my desk.

Vivian squeals. "I recognize that look. Things must've gone well between Justin and your family."

The giddy smile from two seconds ago falls into a frown. "Not really."

Vivian's brows push downward. "Then why were you smiling?"

My fingers brush over my mouth. "Oh, I wasn't smiling like how you think. I just had a really fun weekend with my family and"—I infuse as much casualness into my voice as possible for this next part—"with Justin's brother."

"Wait." Vivian sits up taller. "The twin? The one you kissed?"

"Yeah, we went ice climbing yesterday." I scoot my chair under my desk and begin organizing everything. I pick up a stack of papers and straighten them. I sharpen a few pencils.

"You mean, you *and Justin* went ice climbing with the twin you kissed?"

I give her a sharp look. "Stop bringing up the kiss."

"Did you kiss him or not?"

"I kissed him."

"Then I feel like it has to be brought up." She waves her hand, signaling to continue the story where we left off. "So you and Justin went ice climbing with the twin?"

"No." I dust off my computer keyboard. "It was just me and Caleb."

Vivian shoots forward, grabbing me by the shoulders, forcibly shaking me. "Why are you holding out? Tell me what's going on."

"Okay, okay." I remove her hands from my body to stop the shaking. "Wednesday night at my family Turkey stuff, Caleb just showed up unannounced instead of Justin."

"Why?"

"Because Justin told him to come in his place to impersonate him like you suggested like week."

"Wow! So what did you do?"

"My mom was so happy that Justin was there, at least a guy she thought was Justin, and I was happy that I didn't have to defend him for not coming, so I just...you know." I shrug. "I let everyone think that Caleb was Justin."

Vivian gasps, closing her hand over her mouth. We stare at each other for a whole two seconds before she lowers her fingers enough to speak. "Did your family know it wasn't the real Justin?"

"No." I shake my head. "They loved him. It was a great night. My mom was finally off my back about our relationship, and I could just enjoy the tradition like old times."

"Did you guys kiss again?"

All my reactions happen at once. My brows bunch, I frown, and my head kicks back. "No! Why would we kiss? I'm with Justin."

"Because he's pretending to *be* Justin."

"No, we barely touched. It was all very brother-of-my-boyfriend kosher."

"So what happened next?"

"Well, Justin came the next day to Thanksgiving."

"The real Justin?"

"Yes, and he was distracted the whole time with work because of the Black Friday stuff, which made my mom mad again, and I don't know... I hated feeling like we were back to square one despite all the progress we'd made from Caleb showing up the night before. After how hard Thanksgiving was, Justin and I talked, and we decided to officially ask Caleb to be his holiday stand-in. So on Friday and Saturday, Caleb came with me to my family parties."

"And nobody knew?"

"Nobody knew."

"And Justin is okay with it?"

"Yeah, it was pretty much his idea."

"And the brother doesn't care that you and your family take up all of his free time?"

"No, he's been really cool about it." I don't know why.

Why does Caleb not care? I'll have to dive deep into analyzing that at some point. Or maybe I don't. Maybe Caleb's motivations don't matter.

"You're living your own personal version of the movie *The Parent Trap*."

"I know. Young Lindsey Lohan would be so proud."

"You're not going to fall in love with the brother over Justin, are you?"

"No!" I'm overcompensating my answer with loudness. "It's not like that. Caleb and I are just friends. I'm one hundred percent committed to making things work with Justin. I wouldn't be doing this whole charade if I didn't have all my eggs in the Justin Davidson basket."

"Okay." Vivian studies me as she nods. "How did you end up ice climbing alone with Caleb?"

"Oh, that was what Caleb wanted in exchange for going to all of my family parties."

Her brows lift. "To ice climb?"

"Not that exactly. He wants me to do some of the holiday things on his list with him. So this weekend, we're going backcountry skiing."

She shifts her position on my desk, switching what leg crosses over the other. "So in exchange for spending time with you, Caleb wants to spend even more time with you?"

"That's correct."

"That has disaster written all over it."

"It does not. He's not from here and doesn't have any friends. Justin and I are all he has. And if Justin isn't busy, he'll come backcountry skiing with us too."

"I see." Vivian's brown eyes stare into my soul, scrutinizing me. "And did you have fun ice climbing yesterday?"

I smile, thinking about all the times we laughed and joked. "Yeah, I had a lot of fun."

"See?" She points at me.

"What?"

"There's that same smile again. I haven't seen you smile like that in months." She isn't pointing at me. More like my mouth. "That smile is trouble."

I hit her hand away. "I'm not smiling the way you think I'm smiling. I'm smiling because a few funny things happened. Like we got kicked out of a hotel, and our clothes got stolen."

"I thought you were ice climbing."

"We were. It's a long story." I shake my head, moving on. "The point is, I can still have fun with Caleb and be in love with Justin. In fact, it's better for our relationship. Take yesterday, for example. Justin worked all day while I had fun with Caleb, and neither of us felt annoyed with the other person. And then that night, we spent some time together. It was the perfect situation."

"As long as you don't spend so much time with his brother that you end up falling in love with him."

"Pfft!" I laugh. "You don't have to worry. That's not even a possibility."

"Okay." Vivian slides off my desk like she's ready to work. "I just hope you know what you're doing."

I smile with all the confidence of a woman in control of her life. "Yep. Everything is under control."

twenty-four

I DOUBLE-CHECK Google Maps one last time, making sure I'm at the right apartment complex to pick up Summer for Noel Night. Picking her up at her house makes this feel more like a date than a brotherly service project, but Justin is still at his office working, so it seemed pointless for Summer to meet at his condo. And driving separately to meet up with her family didn't exactly sell our story that we're a couple, so that's how I end up knocking on her apartment door.

"Hey!" Summer swings the door open, greeting me with one of her dazzling smiles.

If hearts could sigh, mine would be sighing hard right now. It's so good to see her. She's been in my dreams every single night, but the real version of Summer Stanworth is better than anything my mind can conjure up.

"Hi."

Her eyes drop to the present tucked under my arm. "What's that?"

"It's a gift." I hesitate, suddenly feeling a little stupid about what I've done. "For you."

Her brows lift in excitement, easing the nerves from one second ago. "You brought me a gift?"

I push the package forward. "Yeah, it's just a little something."

"I love gifts!"

Somehow, I could've guessed that.

She carries the package to her kitchen counter, leaving me to follow her inside, shutting the door behind us. I take a quick glance around the apartment. Actually, an apartment isn't what I would call this place. It's a shrine to Christmas. A perfectly decorated, no-inch-spared, Christmas wonderland.

From where I stand by the door, I see four Christmas trees, each decked out in ornaments—a large one in the family room, a smaller one on the kitchen counter, one in the corner by her kitchen table, and one down at the end of her hallway. Strung Christmas lights dangle from one side of the family room to the other, creating a colorful canopy of holiday glow. Different replicas of Santa Claus seem to be her favorite decoration. Glass statues, stuffed dolls, and pictures of the jolly old man are everywhere. Real garland is spread across every shelf and above every cupboard, making the entire place smell like a Christmas tree farm.

"Wow, you've gone all out on the decorating."

"Uh..."—she scratches her head, glancing around—"just ignore that about me."

"I love it. It's festive."

"Or tacky, but let's go with festive."

Summer tears into the present like a five-year-old who just got the okay from his parents to open his first gift on Christmas morning. She opens the box, looking inside, and her smile grows to its full width. What I thought was dazzling before has just been topped. Her blue eyes swing to me with excitement.

"New snow clothes?"

"Well, I felt bad that I got your others stolen."

She pulls the coat out first. "These are way nicer than the ones that got stolen. I think my mom bought those off Amazon." She eyes me. "This is name brand. It probably cost you a fortune."

"No, it wasn't too bad." She lowers her chin, giving me a playful, pointed stare. "Okay, fine. It cost me a fortune." But she's worth it. "In my defense, all the activities I'm asking you to do are outside, and I didn't want you to be cold like you were ice climbing."

"How did you know I was cold?"

"The shivering and dancing around to keep yourself warm was the first giveaway. "My seriousness shifts into something a little more flirty. "I mean, if you were my girlfriend, I'd keep you warm myself."

I'm glad when her eyes fill with a little flirtiness. "But you can't do that."

"No, so I figured you better have warm snow clothes."

"Very true." She throws me a smile as she tries on the coat. "I like the color."

"Yeah, I thought you'd look good in the mint. I tried to get white again, but they didn't have it."

"I love mint-green."

I know. Unfortunately for me, my mind keeps a running list of all the things Summer likes and dislikes. She's an addiction I can't shake.

She leans over the box, pulling out the snow bibs and holding them up to her body. Her head pops up with another one of those smiles that are brighter than the strands of Christmas lights hanging in her family room. "Thank you!"

"That's it?"

"Were you hoping for more than a thank you?"

"No." I laugh. "I thought you would fight me on it and not accept the present."

"I love giving thoughtful gifts and watching people use the things I bought for them. I don't want to be a hypocrite by not accepting your thoughtful gift. So thank you. I love it."

"You're welcome." Everything inside lightens with a new kind of satisfaction I haven't felt before, and now I'm generating a list of ideas of what I can get Summer for Christmas just to feel this same feeling again.

At Christmas, Telluride looks like it came straight out of a holiday card painting, especially with the fresh dust of snow from yesterday's storm. Summer and I walk toward Elk's Park, where the traditional lighting of the ski tree takes place. A huge fire glows up ahead as Summer and I make our way through the crowd.

"My parents have a spot saved for us up front by the tree, so we have a good view of the lighting."

"How early do your parents have to get here to save spots for you guys?"

"I don't know. Like two hours ahead."

"That's commitment to the tradition."

"Oh, us Stanworths are one hundred percent committed to Christmas."

"Yes, I gathered that from your apartment."

"Be nice!" Summer pushes her shoulder into mine, knocking me off balance as I walk.

"How did your Christmas obsession start?"

"It's Christmas enthusiasm, not an obsession."

"Oh, I see." I smile at her rationalization. "So, how did your enthusiasm for Christmas start?"

"Well, it's my birthday, December 24th, so I've always loved this time of year."

"Wait. It's your birthday on Christmas Eve?"

Summer's smile is adorable as she shrugs. "Yeah."

Noted. A Christmas birthday fits her perfectly.

"Since it's my birthday month, celebrating the season feels like I'm celebrating me all month long." Her mouth twists into a grimace. "And not just me. Also, the birth of our Lord and King."

"How kind of you to share the holiday with Him."

"I know Christmas isn't really about me and *my* birthday, but I still love it."

"You would be the type of person who loves their birthday so much they celebrate for an entire month."

"There's nothing wrong with being excited I was born."

"I completely agree."

"Wait." She looks at me with skepticism behind her stare. "You completely agree?"

"Yeah, I love birthdays."

"Hmm." Her focus turns forward again.

"Does that surprise you?"

"A little." Her shoulders lift. "Justin would hardly let me celebrate his birthday, so I just assumed you'd be the same way."

"There's a lot about me and Justin that is different."

"Yeah, I've noticed." She peeks at me but doesn't elaborate.

Now, I'm dying to know what differences she's noticed and how she feels about those differences, but I don't ask because knowing all of that doesn't help anything. Her liking Justin more than me sucks. But if she likes my differences better, I can't go behind my brother's back and pursue her. So basically this is a no-win situation.

"I see your family up ahead." I nod toward the seventeen-foot tree made out of old skis.

Summer grabs my hand without hesitation and all I can think about is how great it would be if she were really mine, if I weren't pretending to be Justin right now. But really, I'm not pretending. I'm completely myself around her and her family. The only thing that's fake is my name. And I guess my job. And my backstory. Okay, there are a few things that are fake. But the feelings and relationships I'm building are genuine.

"Hey!" Her sisters cheer when we walk up.

"You made it just in time," her dad says, waving us over. "Bob Irvine is about to light the bonfire."

I give Summer a side smile. "I can't believe I'm going to see the real Bob Irvine in action."

"You should feel blessed." And although I know she's only teasing, blessed to be here is exactly how I feel.

Janet walks toward us, leaning in for a hug from Summer. As she pulls back, her eyes drop to our linked hands. Summer wasn't lying when she said her mom watched our every move. Because of that—and that reason only—I tug Summer so she stands in front of me, unlocking our fingers. I wrap my arms around her shoulders, hugging her from behind. She lifts her hands, placing them on my arms, and rests her head back on my chest. I let my cheek fall against her head. The smell of her shampoo drifts up to me and strands of her hair tickle my chin and lips as I hold her. It's perfect.

There are justifiable reasons for this position.

It helps show Summer's mom that Justin cares for her daughter.

It's cold outside and cuddling close together is a proven method to stay warm.

It keeps Summer in my eyesight so we don't get split apart (this one's a stretch. I know).

But there's one *major* reason why this position is a bad idea.

I like holding Summer in my arms.

And that's when I know I'm in trouble. Like I'm-falling-for-my-brother's-girlfriend-and-I-don't-even-care kind of trouble. Families break apart over this kind of stuff all the time. It's a dangerous, dangerous road. And even though I feel myself being sucked in by Summer's charms, I don't turn off the vacuum. I don't distance myself from her force. Instead, I keep coming back for more.

twenty-five
SUMMER

THE GONDOLA between downtown Telluride and Mountain Village fits eight to ten people comfortably. After the ski tree lighting, my family crams into one gondola to head up the mountain to the ice-skating rink. Our gondola has twenty people in it. Yes, half of them are my nieces and nephews with little bodies, but that doesn't make things less crowded. So, when it was time for me to take a seat, nothing was left except a spot on Caleb's lap. This is the second time I've had to sit on his lap in less than a week. I feel like I'm in a never-ending game of musical chairs, and I keep losing. Or winning depending on if you ask my head or my heart.

When I sit on Caleb this time, I forgo the awkwardness and scoot into his lap so we're both comfortable. I'm also forced to wrap my arm around his shoulder. *Forced?* It's not like there's a gun to my head, but placing my arm around him was a space-saving move that had to be done.

The lights from the houses below and how the moon glows over the majestic San Juan mountains make everything extra.

Extra magical.

Extra fun.

Extra *romantic*.

But it's fine because we're not alone. We're with my family, singing Christmas carols. So, nothing about how Caleb's thumb rests against my thigh, how his warm breath hits my neck, the up close and personal view of his jaw, or the sensational smell of his cologne is romantic or thrilling.

It's just a normal family outing with regular heartbeats. Yep, my heart *always* beats this fast and heavy.

Miles gets a little too animated with his singing, bouncing up and down in his seat. He bumps into Caleb, pushing his fingers into the tips of mine. And since I removed my gloves for the gondola ride—*like an idiot*—that skin-to-skin contact destroys me. It's not like Caleb and I haven't held hands before, because we have. But things are different tonight and the light brush of his hand against mine feels like I'm holding my fingers inside an electrical socket. How long do I have to keep my hand here until I can pull away without my mom being suspicious? Because we all know she purposely sat next to us to keep tabs on our relationship.

When a boisterous version of "Jingle Bells" starts, I inconspicuously pull my hand back, shoving it in my coat pocket as if my fingers need more warmth, which is hilarious since Caleb's touch creates my own personal bonfire. I could ditch every layer I'm wearing and still be overheated.

It's not *Caleb*. It's just this time of year and the glowing lights and the fact that I've felt so lonely lately with Justin's work schedule. That's what it is. That's what it *has* to be.

"We're almost to the top," my dad says from his spot next to my mom. But she's so eager to look out the window at the station that she twists her body, bumping into my arm that's draped across Caleb. My fingers brush against the side of his neck, and it's like a jolt goes through his body. A massive shiver shakes us both, and he lifts his shoulder to his neck, where my fingers skimmed.

"Sorry," he says in response to his earthquake of a shiver.

I can't help but smile. "Are you ticklish?"

"Something like that." His blue eyes meet mine. His stare is full of so much passion, I'd be a fool to think that shiver had anything to do with him being ticklish. We're sitting close. We're like eyeball to eyeball, which should be awkward, but instead, the stare-down is charged with chemistry and heat and everything it's not supposed to be charged with. Attraction fizzles through my chest.

Thankfully, everything pops when the gondola doors open.

Caleb looks like a giant panda on the ice— clumsy, always falling, ending his fall with a roll. I literally have to cross my legs, one over the other, so I don't pee my pants from how hard I've been laughing.

He gets to his knees, using the wall for support to climb to a stand. "I'm embarrassed at how bad I am at this."

"Don't worry." I smile, slowly skating a circle in place. "This is a judge-free zone."

"But you're totally judging me, right?"

"Absolutely." I smirk. "I thought a guy as athletic as you would be able to stay on his feet."

He holds onto the wall, walking on his blades instead of skating. "We haven't talked about what you really think of my job."

"Is this the part of the night where you're hoping I'll shower you with compliments?"

"A shower?" His lips stretch into a grin. "Do you have that many compliments to give?" Even though he's holding onto the wall for dear life, Caleb is strutting toward me like a man who knows how charming he can be.

"If I do have compliments for you, I'm keeping them to myself. Your ego doesn't need any more stroking."

"My ego?" His brows raise. "I'm holding onto a wall so I don't face plant. I have zero game right now."

"Do you want some help?" I slowly glide toward him, the tips of my skates hitting into his, putting our faces mere inches apart.

"I thought you'd never ask." There's a rough quality to his words that sends my stomach swooping.

His gaze stays on me as he lets go of the wall and places his hands on my hips. He's wearing gloves and I'm wearing a coat, so it makes absolutely no sense why I feel Caleb's touch so severely, but I do. His fingers press against my waist in a way that drives my senses crazy. The man has more game than he even realizes. I rest my hands on top of his, holding them against my body. A few of my fingers hook over his, and I slowly skate backwards, pulling him along.

"Look who's the show-off now." Caleb's blue eyes squint into a playful glare that's more flirtatious than it should be.

"Aunt Summer," my nephew Max says as he skates by, holding Brian's hand. "I'm beating you!"

I'm grateful for the interruption. We all could use a grounding reminder of what we're doing here.

Caleb's here in place of Justin.

The touching and flirting are *for* Justin's sake so he can win over my family.

Got to keep some perspective here.

"Way to go, buddy." I smile at Max as he passes then I shift my eyes to Caleb's skates. It's a safer place to stare than directly at his blue eyes or handsome face.

"You're getting better. You have *some* coordination."

"I think I look better climbing ice than skating on it."

No, I can confirm he looks pretty good doing both.

Don't think about it.

"How did you get into all your outdoor sports?" Casual small talk is the key to keeping things casual.

"I don't know." He shrugs with a boyish smile that my heart begs me to commit to memory. "I've always loved the rush that comes from doing something challenging and dangerous, something not everyone can do."

"Would you say you're an adrenaline junkie?"

"I used to be."

"And you're not anymore?"

"I used to live for the excitement of an intense moment, the feeling that my own strength and skill saved me from danger during high-risk activities. The more tricks I nailed, the more I wanted to do something bigger and get a bigger rush. I was addicted to the high and the endorphins that came with it. I thought if I stopped planning and throwing new tricks, I wouldn't be happy. I didn't think I'd ever be able to find something else that would fill my life with as much thrill, uncertainty, and excitement."

"Did you find something?"

Caleb stares back at me. It's more than the usual conversation eye contact. It's different and loaded with feeling. "I think I have."

I swallow, sensing the weight of his words—they're heavy.

Thanks for nothing, small talk.

I lose focus, and the back of my skate catches the ice. Down I go, falling backward, dragging Caleb with me. My butt lands first, breaking my fall, but that doesn't stop my head from smacking the ice too. Caleb lands on top of me, watching the whole thing play out.

"Summer!" One hand goes behind my head while he shakes his glove off his other hand. "Are you okay?" The now glove-free fingers caress my cheek.

"Ow!" I groan, shifting my eyes to his. "I think my head cracked the ice."

"You might have a concussion." His concerned gaze flits around my face as his hand continues to brush my hair back, sweeping over my cheek with a tenderness so sweet I could dip a piece of fruit in it like fondue.

"I'm okay. My butt took the brunt of the fall."

"Are you sure?"

I nod, liking this worried side of him. I have to stop my mind from brainstorming other ways I can get hurt so that he can take care of me.

"I'm glad you're okay." He smirks.

"Me too," I whisper.

"Summer, there's something I need to tell you."

"Do I have blood spilling out from the back of my head?"

"No." A soft laugh puffs over his lips as he trails his fingers up and down my cheek again, but this time, the action is slower, more intense. "I'm actually an excellent ice skater. I just pretended like I wasn't so I could touch you."

My lips grow into a small smile. "The oldest trick in the book. I should've known."

"It's not like me to waste on opportunity."

Charming. Caleb's smile and his gaze are charming the heck out of me.

Attraction warms inside my chest. It starts a low-lying simmer, but quickly gains intensity, and suddenly, the moment shifts. The weight of his body on me feels like a blessing instead of a burden. His touch turns from tender to sensual. His gaze from concerned to passionate. As if I'd trained my heart to do it, my beats speed up, building the moment into something bigger, something I want more of.

The second my eyes drop to his lips, Caleb's off me, awkwardly climbing to a stand.

He lit a match inside my body and then immediately blew it out before the fire could spread. My chest drops, and I exhale a tension-filled breath.

I'm blaming the head injury for my two-second lapse in judgment.

The night's over.

It has to be.

Time to go home to Justin.

twenty-six
CALEB

"YOU JUST MADE short ribs on a random Thursday night?" Summer sits at the bar in Justin's kitchen. She's dressed in a Christmas green jumper with Frosty the Snowman earrings. Her hand rests under her chin as she watches me pull the pan out of Justin's oven.

After last night's almost kiss—no, let me rephrase—it wasn't an almost kiss. It was an almost thought. I almost *thought* about kissing Summer. That's way different than an almost kiss. It's more innocent because I didn't think about it. I shut the whole thing down like a mental ninja before my mind even went there. But after all of that, I'm glad that tonight's activity is cookie decorating with Summer's friend. Vivian can act as a chaperone and I can hold a cookie instead of Summer. Great plan.

"I didn't make short ribs. I made *dinner*. It shouldn't matter what night of the week it is." I lift up the tinfoil, checking the tenderness of the meat. Perfection. "Do you want some before we go?"

"If you have enough, I'd love a taste."

"Coming right up." I cut off two slabs of the ribs, putting them on plates with a side of string beans.

"Do you like to cook?" she asks as I set her plate down in front of her.

"Yeah, I like cooking, and it's a good thing, or else I'd just eat cold cereal and ice cream every day."

"I don't think I've ever seen Justin cook anything." She holds the rib on each end of the bone and takes a bite. Her eyes drift to me as she chews. I don't even bother looking away or hiding my smile. "What?" she finally asks.

"I like how you went all in on the ribs with your hands. Most women would've used a knife and fork."

"I'm barbaric like that." She smiles over another bite. "This is really good, by the way."

"Let me see if you're just being nice." I tear into the rib, the meat falling off the bone easily. "Mmm." I nod as I look at her. "It is good." We spend a few seconds taking more bites before I ask, "So, tell me about your friend that we're decorating cookies with tonight."

Summer straightens as she wipes her mouth with a napkin. Surprisingly, her red lipstick stays put. How that's happening is the world's best-kept secret, but I'm grateful for it. "Her name is Vivian, and we've been friends since kindergarten. Best friends, actually. We do everything together. We both even work at the property management firm."

"Best friends are important. I'll try to channel my inner Justin."

"Actually"—her gaze drops, and I sense some embarrassment —"she knows about our little arrangement, so you can just be yourself tonight."

"She knows?"

"Yeah, I tell her everything, so..."

"And you still want me to come?"

Summer's eyes pop wide, confirming the embarrassment I thought I saw earlier. "Oh, I guess you don't have to come. You're just the stand-in for Justin, so if Viv already knows, then there's no reason for you to be there."

"I think I have to come. I mean, if we're really going to see whose Christmas agenda is better, I need to experience everything you have planned."

Her expression lifts. "Yeah, that's true. I totally forgot about that part of the deal."

"Plus, you already came to pick me up. I wouldn't want your drive over here to be a waste."

"Gas is so expensive these days." She nods. "And you're feeding me dinner, so I owe you some Christmas cookies for dessert."

"You do owe me that." We smile at each other, eyes hinting that we both know our excuses to hang out are flimsy at best.

Summer is the first to look away. Her eyes drop to her plate, and she picks up the next rib, taking a big bite. Barbecue sauce paints the side of her cheek, but she doesn't notice.

"You have some sauce—"

"Oh." She wipes at the wrong side of her face.

"It's..." I point to the other side, and she wipes again, somehow still missing it. "Here." I raise my hand, slowly brushing the thick sauce off her cheek with my thumb. Her blue eyes watch me, and her breath hitches as my skin connects with hers. It's silly that I used my finger instead of a napkin, but it's also the best decision I've made in my entire life. Because touching Summer gives me all the butterflies that accompany falling in love. "I think I got it." I reluctantly pull my hand away, but the sensation in my chest stays. It's like the rush of freefalling through the air, spiraling and turning as I go. Up until this point in my life, no other feeling has ever matched that. But with Summer, there's a tangible rush that I could easily get addicted to. Let's be honest. I'm already addicted.

"Thanks." She peeks at me, and I wonder if she feels it too. Hoping that she does would mean that I'm the worst brother in the entire world. But I'm starting to think Justin could never care for her the way I could.

The front door opens, and as if on cue, Justin waltzes into the kitchen, and everything I thought I was feeling moments ago crumbles into guilt—like, make-you-feel-like-you-suck-at-being-a-brother guilt.

"Hey, I'm glad I caught you guys." He throws his computer bag down on the counter.

"Oh, yeah?" The smile Summer wears seems strained.

Justin comes to her side, picking up the last rib on her plate. "I've been texting you both. Don't you ever check your phones?"

"Mine is on silent in my purse." She watches him take a bite of her food. "You're home earlier than usual. Are you going to finish up work here?"

"No, my head will explode if I look at another spreadsheet. So I thought I'd go with you tonight."

My heart plummets as if somebody put Santa's bag full of presents in the center of it.

"With me?" She glances at me, then back at Justin.

"Yeah, aren't you going to Vivian's or something?"

"Yes." She smiles, and I still feel like there's something tense about it. "That was the plan."

"Well, I'm here and not working, so let's go."

"Uh..." Summer's eyes flick between the two of us.

Justin's lips push downward. "I thought you'd be more excited. This is what you wanted, right?"

"Yes, of course." She flips her smile into something full of animation. "I'm just surprised. That's all."

Justin turns to me, patting me on the back. "Looks like you're off duty tonight. You can go do something you actually want to do."

I lift my eyes and nod.

The problem is, hanging out with Summer is what I actually want to do. I was looking forward to meeting Vivian, decorating cookies, and I'm not even going to say what else I was looking forward to because it doesn't matter now.

"Caleb, you can still come if you want to," Summer offers—a pity invite that makes everything worse.

"Why would he come?" Justin's hand goes to Summer's back, rubbing her neck and shoulders.

Watching him touch her is a gut punch that sends shock waves to my heart, making the whole thing ache—a miserable ache that's only going to get worse when they walk out the door together. Because I'm not going with them. I refuse to be the third wheel, watching all night with a front-row seat as Justin touches her.

"I'm good." I stand from my stool and start gathering our plates. "I've wanted to go night skiing ever since I got here. Conditions are perfect for that."

"I'm good." I stand from my stool and start gathering our plates. "I've wanted to go night skiing ever since I got here. Conditions are perfect for that."

"Are you sure?" Summer asks as she puts her coat on.

"Yeah, you guys go have fun."

She glances at me with an apology, as if she remembers ten minutes ago when I was making up any excuse under the sun to be with her.

I'm such a freaking idiot.

The massive sting in my heart is added proof of my idiocy.

"Alright, we'll see you later." Justin smirks at me as he holds the door for Summer. "Don't wait up."

I've never wanted to punch my brother in the face as much as I do right now and he hasn't even done anything wrong.

SUMMER

"Did I surprise you by coming tonight?" Justin squeezes my hand in the car. I study our interlocked fingers, noting the differences between his hand and Caleb's. Justin's skin is smooth, almost baby-like, while Caleb's palm is calloused from...I actually don't know what the callouses are from. Maybe from climbing or—

"Sum Sum?"

"Sorry." I turn my gaze to Justin, remembering his question in the first place. "Yes, I was very surprised. Don't you have work to do?"

"There's always work, but I'm sick of it, and I thought my baby could use a little time with me instead of my clone."

I give a forced laugh because Caleb is nothing like Justin's clone.

I hated leaving him alone at the condo. He seemed so excited about coming. That's dumb. He probably wasn't excited, just being polite. We're decorating Christmas cookies, not sitting front row at a Trans-Siberian Orchestra Christmas concert.

But I'm going to forget about Caleb.

Justin is finally taking a night off work, and we're going to enjoy it.

"I wish you could've taken work off last night when we went to Noel Night with my family. You would've loved it." I twist in my seat as my excitement takes over. "Bob Irvine spilled some gasoline on the snow right before he lit the bonfire, and then—"

Justin's phone rings, interrupting my story. He glances at the dash. "Sorry, babe. I have to take this. Hello?"

The conversation is on speaker throughout the car. It's Jordan from work. She's over marketing and is all excited about how she landed another spot on QVC next week for the All-Weather Blanket if Justin wants to take it.

"Jordan, you are amazing. I owe you big time!"

"No problem, boss. I'll work on ad text tonight and have it ready for you tomorrow."

"That sounds great. We'll see you then." He clicks off the call and turns to me with a never-ending smile. "Can you believe that? Another shot at QVC. I just hope I have enough inventory for all the orders we'll get."

"Yeah, that's awesome. I'm really happy for you."

He shakes his head as he grips the steering wheel. "I just can't believe how this company is taking off."

"It's no surprise. You've put in a lot of hard work."

"And hard work pays off." He keeps his focus forward, not saying anything else.

"So anyway." I decide to jump back into my story about last night because I wasn't able to finish it when Jordan called. "Bob Irvine spilled gasoline on the snow, and somehow one of the sparks from the bonfire landed where the gas was, and the whole thing lit up, but the fire immediately melted down to the grass, and then..." I pause, glancing at Justin. Nothing about him seems like he's paying attention to me. "And then my Aunt Carma dipped Bob down and planted a huge kiss on his lips. Miles and Max bumped into the ski tree and knocked the whole thing over. Donna O'Day signed a record deal with Justin Bieber's agent. And Caleb and I got married and rode off into the sunset."

Justin finally looks at me. "That sounds great, babe."

"Yeah, it does." I flip my body in the other direction, facing my car window. It takes twenty seconds for Justin to even notice.

He rubs my thigh. "Hey, what's wrong?"

"You're here. But I still feel like you're a million worlds away."

"Sorry, it's just this new QVC thing has my mind reeling, but I'm here." He squeezes my leg. "I promise I'm here."

"Okay." I let my frustrations go because we get so little time with each other. I don't want to spend it fighting. "Tomorrow afternoon, Caleb wanted to take us backcountry skiing. Since you need a break anyway, it will be the perfect time to check out a little early on a Friday and get outside."

"With this upcoming QVC—"

"I know, you're busy again."

"Plus, you know I hate the cold."

"Telluride is a tough place to live if you don't like cold weather."

"I know. I'm missing my Arizona winters. I hope I can move back there sooner rather than later."

My lips press downward. "You're not planning on staying in Telluride?"

"I hope not. My goal has always been to build my company up big enough that I can move it somewhere warmer or sell it."

"But warmer weather would be a terrible place to sell blankets."

Justin laughs. "I'm not selling them there. I'm just talking about factory headquarters."

"But what about your parents? They live here." *And what about me?*

"Relax." Justin smiles. "I'm not talking about moving anytime soon. Just someday."

"Someday?"

"That's right."

Justin's someday is giving me a lot of anxiety. I've pinned my hopes and dreams on marrying a man that doesn't want to stay in Telluride by my family. The realization feels devastating.

We ease into silence the rest of the way to Vivian's apartment, and I think about Caleb even though I said I wouldn't.

What would we be talking about if he were here?

Would I feel happier?

Because, right not, I don't feel happy at all.

CALEB

FOUR HOURS LATER, I COME HOME TO A DARK CONDO. Summer's car is gone, and Justin's bedroom door is closed like he's already gone to bed for the night. I didn't intend to stay at Mountain Village, skiing, this late. I just wanted to stay late enough so I wouldn't have to see Summer and Justin cuddle on the couch, kiss goodbye for the night, or interact at all. Because seeing is believing, and when I see Summer and Justin together, I believe that she's really his girlfriend. When we're alone, it's easy to forget that fact.

I toss my keys on my dresser and plug in my cell phone on the nightstand—it ran out of battery a couple of hours ago. After I change my clothes and get ready for bed, I sit down on the edge of my mattress to glance at my phone.

Twelve missed text messages.

All from Summer.

I open up the app and start reading the first.

Summer: You should've come. We have plenty of dough here if you still want to stop by.

Summer: My mom requested a cookie for Donna O'Day. I think you're going to like this one.

A picture of a tree-shaped cookie with green frosting and the letters DD written in white frosting show up next. I smile as I glance over the picture.

Summer: I also did my best deer rack for this cookie, but I don't think it turned out very well.

There's a picture of a circle cookie with antlers made out of white frosting. I never would've guessed a deer rack. It looks more like a spider web, but I smile because I can picture Summer leaning over the cookie, trying to make something for me.

Summer: I'm super proud of these ones.

Two bell cookies are in the next picture. One says *man's*

laughter, and the other says *sonofagun*. I smile again—or maybe I never stopped smiling.

> **Summer:** I was going to bring you home some cookies if we had extra, but I lost track of time with this last batch.

There's a picture of a pan of brownish-black cookies left unfrosted.

> **Summer:** So I guess you're not home. Actually, this is a cell phone. You could be home or anywhere and still see these messages.

> **Summer:** You're probably snowboarding or skiing. I don't really know which one you like to do best.

And the last message was left eighteen minutes ago.

> **Summer:** We missed you tonight. I'll see you tomorrow for backcountry skiing.

I read through all the messages and study the pictures again before tucking my phone away.

My eyes stare into the darkness of my room as I lie back on my pillow. Summer texted me when she was with Justin.

Me.

twenty-seven

CALEB

I CARVE my skis into the snow, sliding to a stop. Summer is right behind. She stabs her poles into the snow before pushing her goggles up. Huge flakes fall around us, landing on her pretty face and immediately melting into drops of water on her skin.

"Oh, my gosh!" Her chest heaves up and down from exertion. "I think I'm too out of shape for this."

"You're doing great. I'm actually really impressed with your skill level."

"Well, you don't grow up in Telluride without knowing a thing or two about how to ski."

"It shows." My smile tilts into a tease. "I'm happy I didn't have to tether you to me and drag you down the mountain."

"It could still happen. Don't rule it out just yet." She looks at the darkening sky. "Are we going to get caught in a storm?"

"Nah." I hand her the bottle of water, and she unscrews the cap, taking a long drink. I glance up, looking at the ominous clouds in the distance. Yes, we're totally going to get caught in a huge storm, but I don't want to worry Summer because I have a plan. "It's a shame Justin couldn't come," I say, changing the subject.

She swallows one last gulp. "Did you know he doesn't like the cold?"

"Yeah, I think I knew something about that." I take a swig of the water and then put it in my backpack. We grab our poles and start an easy glide side by side.

"Justin says he wants to move back to Arizona someday."

"Not surprising, I guess."

"It was surprising to me."

"Because you...want...to...marry...him?" I can barely get the words out. I hate everything about how they sound as they come off my lips.

"I mean, I..." She shrugs instead of finishing her answer.

"It's alright, you don't have to tell me." I'm not sure I even want to know.

"There's nothing to tell. We've never talked about marriage— or I should say, Justin has never talked about it."

"But you have?"

"Just in general terms. We've been dating for nine months. I always thought after that much time it would be easy to know if things were right."

"And is it easy?"

"Sure. We've been through the most difficult times in a relationship. Him starting a new business and having to work all the time." She pauses, letting her breath catch up to her increasing heart rate. "If we can make it through this, I'm positive we can make it through anything." She sounds like she's convincing herself more than she's convincing me. "Our relationship is reliable. Sturdy. I mean, take his work schedule, for example." She hesitates again, catching her breath. "We never get any time together, but when we do, things are great. Like really, really great."

From what I've seen, nothing is *great* about their relationship. They don't communicate well. Summer's needs are barely being met. Justin's unsure and leading her on. I just don't get it. I don't get why Summer keeps fighting so hard to stay together. But I nod a few times out of politeness.

"Why aren't you saying anything?" she finally asks in response to my silence.

"If things are so great between you and Justin when you're together, then why were you texting me last night when you should've been decorating cookies with him?"

She digs her poles into the snow, lurching her body forward. "I was decorating cookies with him."

"And texting me."

"I was trying to be nice. I felt bad that you didn't get to come decorate." She sucks in a deep breath. "Plus, you need to know what decorating cookies is like to see how great my Christmas activities are. That's why I was texting. I needed to send you pictures."

"Okay."

"Okay?"

It seems like the lamest excuse ever, but okay. Pointing out that I think she's bored with Justin seems like a jerky thing to do. Calling her out on her bull crap won't help anybody. I want Summer to come to those conclusions herself, not be coerced into them by a guy who shouldn't have an agenda. But the way she smiles at me and how she gazes in my eyes makes me want to have an agenda.

"What?" She turns to me. Her nose and cheeks are pink from the cold, and her beanie is tilted to the side under her goggles just adding to how cute she looks.

"Nothing. I was just thinking how difficult it would be for you to move away from your family to Arizona if you did marry Justin."

Her skis slice through the powder. "Yeah, that was my first thought when he told me he didn't want to live in Telluride forever."

"But you know, Erin moved to Denver with Tommy," I offer,

trying to give her some hope even though hope is the last thing I want her to have.

"I know. I guess that's just what you have to do in life even though you hate it." She flips her head to me. "What about you? Do you have a home?"

I laugh because her questions are so innocent. "Yes, I have a home."

"And where would that be?"

"It's in Arizona."

"The Davidson brothers just can't seem to get enough of that place."

"Well, our parents moved out here for a slower pace of life, but Phoenix will always be home to me and Justin."

"I see." The disappointment on her face is endearing and gives me encouragement I shouldn't have.

"I say that, but really I haven't been home to Arizona for a while."

"So it just sits vacant?"

"No, I rent it out as an Airbnb."

"Oh." Her brows drop at the exact same time her lips purse into a frown.

"What?" I try to steal a glance at her while gliding my skis forward. "You don't like that?"

"Home and family are so important to me. I can't imagine having a home and never living in it. Like all your Christmas decorations would just be a waste."

I smile at her. "I don't have any Christmas decorations."

"That's what I'm talking about. I think it's sad that you don't have any Christmas decorations."

"Is it really my lack of Christmas decorations that makes you sad, or just my lifestyle in general?"

"I don't know. I guess your lifestyle in general. I just can't imagine not having a home and a family and everything that comes with it. So much so that I'm stressed that if I marry Justin, I'll have to move away someday."

"I think home can be anywhere you make it as long as you're with the people you care about."

"I guess."

"Did I ever tell you the real reason why I came to Telluride?"

"Because of Lars. You wanted to build better relationships with your family."

"That's definitely part of it. Lately, something's been missing in my life. No matter how many bridges I jumped off, I couldn't shake the feeling that I wanted more, that I *needed* more. Losing Lars showed me how important having a family is. Yeah, I have an empty house in Phoenix, but I don't always want an empty house. I want to fill it with a future that gives me more excitement than free-falling through the air."

"And what's in that future?"

"A family of my own. I'm ready for that in my life."

"Caleb, if that's what you want, then I have no doubt you'll make it happen. You're the kind of guy that puts your mind to something and lets nothing stand in your way until you accomplish it."

"I think achieving this goal will be a little harder than other things I've done in my life." Especially since the more time I spend with Summer, the more I think about what it would be like to build a life with her—the one woman I can't have.

"Eh, you're cute enough." She smiles. "I'm sure some woman somewhere out there will take pity on you."

Her statement makes me grin. "You think I'm cute?"

"Uh..." She smiles, looking down. "I said you're cute enough. I didn't say that I find you cute."

"It's the same thing."

"No, it's not." Her teasing smile could break me. "I'm not even attracted to you. I'm attracted to Justin."

This statement makes me smile even bigger. "You know we're identical, right?"

"Your chromosomes are identical. But everything else looks completely different."

"So you're not attracted to me?"

"Nope."

Summer is so full of crap. I can hardly stand it. The attraction I've been feeling is not one sided. She's fighting it, but it's definitely there.

"I guess that's a good thing," I say. "Or all this time we're spending together would be considered dangerous."

"Exactly." She looks straight ahead, avoiding my gaze. "This plan works because we're just pals."

Pals.

Nothing has ever felt so depressing in my life. I don't want to be Summer's pal. I want to be a heck of a lot more than that.

"In fact, *pal*, I'll race you to the bottom of the hill." Summer tips her skis over the edge before taking off. I give her a few seconds lead, knowing I can easily overtake her. But I love that she's trying.

SUMMER

I CAN BARELY SEE CALEB EIGHT FEET AHEAD OF ME. THE storm has picked up to a blizzard, shooting snowflake daggers at the side of my face. I zipped my coat up over my chin, and with my goggles, there's only a half inch of space the sideways snow can access, but it's enough to freeze my skin

"The storm came in faster than I was anticipating," Caleb yells over the wheezing wind when I get to the bottom of the hill.

"I can see that." I dip my chin further into my coat. "Are we close to our car?" Despite having lived at the foot of the San Juan mountains my entire life, I don't actually have a clue where we're at.

"Not super close."

I glance up at the darkening sky. The storm doesn't seem to be lightening, and we only have about thirty minutes until all light from the sun vanishes completely. "Can we make it to our car before the sun sets?"

He looks up and then looks both ways. "I don't really think so."

My brows raise, lifting my goggles with them. "So we're going to die out here? Great!" I throw my arms up. "I didn't even get to plan a wedding or get married. I'll just die as a lonely, single woman. Think about how depressing my 'survived by' list will be in my obituary. It will just be *survived by her family* with no husband or kids."

"We're not going to die out here," Caleb says. "And last I checked, you're not single." There's a hint of bitterness in his voice, but it's hard to see through the snow if his expression matches what I thought I heard.

"I'm not like you. I can't live off the elements and survive with a small fire. My body will be completely frozen in forty-five minutes. I'll probably skip the whole frostbite stage and go straight into an ice block." An animal howls in the distance, and everything about me goes still. "What was that?" My eyes move around, but my head doesn't move. "Was it a wolf? Maybe a bear. I'm not even going to have time to freeze to death because an animal will eat me." I glance at Caleb, and this time, I can see his giant smile despite the pounding snow.

"Summer, you're not going to freeze to death or get eaten by an animal. Look." He points behind me. "There's a hut right over there."

I squint through the snow, making out a small structure. "A hut?"

"Yes, haven't you heard of the San Juan hut system? You can backcountry ski to each of them or go from hut to hut."

I've heard of them before but never seen them. You need a reservation, but who cares? Surely, they won't let us freeze to death for the sake of no reservation.

"We're saved." My chest exhales with relief. "We're so lucky we just happened upon one by accident."

"It wasn't an accident." Caleb's smile turns guilty. "We just skied part of the Sneffels Range, and that's the North Pole Hut... that I have a reservation for."

All I heard was North Pole Hut. Excitement fills my face. "The North Pole! I love that they named it something Christmasy."

Caleb's lips turn downward, as if that wasn't the reaction he expected. I go back through his words, picking up on the one detail I should've focused on in the first place.

"Wait. You have a reservation for the North Pole Hut? Like you were planning on us getting snowed in and sleeping there alone *together*?"

"No!" His hands immediately fly up in innocence. "Not alone. The hut sleeps eight people. I just reserved three spots on the off chance we didn't make it down the mountain before the storm hit. It was a backup plan."

"But now it's *the* plan?"

"You said yourself you don't want to die out here. And we won't be alone. I'm sure whoever else reserved the other five spots will be here soon. We just got here first."

"The whole thing seems sketchy, but it's better than dying." I use my poles to push my skis forward until I have enough momentum to ski over to the hut.

"How is it sketchy?" Caleb asks, coming in hot behind me.

"You planned to have a sleepover on the mountain the entire time, and you didn't even tell me."

"No, I said it was a backup plan. Just in case."

He gets to the padlock on the door and removes his glove, punching in the code.

I glance up at the hut. It's small. A twelve-by-twelve cabin with a metal roof and a few windows that are covered by snow drift. The San Juan Mountain Range rises and falls all around us, with snow-covered pine trees towering over our heads. It's majestic, even in a blizzard. Quiet and peaceful. And if I let my mind run wild, I would call it romantic. But I'm not letting my mind run wild. I'm not going to think about all the ways being snowed in a mountain hut with a manly man like Caleb Davidson is romantic. I'm not going to think about the cozy fire or the dim lighting. I'm not even going there. Because five other strangers will be with us in this hut. It's a backcountry skiing adventure, not a page out of a romance novel.

twenty-eight

CALEB

I THROW another log on the fire, sparking it to life. "Is that better?"

I glance over my shoulder at Summer holding both her hands in front of the flames, gathering as much warmth as she can. Her beanie and coat are off, leaving just a white long-sleeve thermal shirt under her mint snow bibs. She ran her fingers through her hair a bunch of times, trying to fluff it up after wearing a hat all day. But then, finally, she gave up and tossed all her hair to one side, creating that perfect little wave that matches her fun-loving personality.

"Yeah, the fire's great. I won't freeze to death after all."

"I brought us some food." I set my backpack on the table between us and dig through it.

"I don't know, Davidson. The more you say, the more this doesn't sound like a backup plan. You came a little too prepared."

I love how Summer calls me *Davidson* sometimes. Is that something reserved just for me or a habit from her relationship with the other Davidson brother? I'm telling myself it's just a *me* thing.

"Every smart adventurer never leaves home without the

proper gear, including food, for the journey. So, yes, I am prepared, but not in the way you think."

"Sure." She smirks at me, and I smirk right back.

"If you're going to give me attitude, I don't have to share my sustenance with you."

"Fine. I'll behave." She peeks over the edge of my bag. "What did you bring?"

I pull out a small box of Cinnamon Life cereal.

Summer's gaze flicks to me. The reflection of the fire makes her already animated eyes dance.

"Did you really bring cold cereal up the mountains?"

"I did." I pull out a metal canteen full of milk. "It's the only way to go."

"Most people pack baked beans or protein, but not you. You bring empty carbs."

"I mean, it is called *Life*. I don't think anything can be more sustaining than that." I pour her a bowl and top it off with milk. "For the lady."

"Thank you."

I do the same thing for myself and sit across from Summer. "How is it?" I ask over a mouthful of squares.

"Surprisingly good."

"What's better, this or my ribs?"

"This." There's a smile behind her eyes that tells me she's lying. "I'm a big cold cereal fan."

"So am I."

We stare at each other for a few bites before her eyes bounce around the hut. There's the fireplace we're sitting in front of, a small sink, a propane stove, a wood stove, and then padded bunk beds.

"I can't believe this place," she says. "It's like an Airbnb in the mountains."

"It's pretty cool, huh?"

"It's amazing. Something I'd never be able to experience on

my own." She turns her gaze to me, taking another bite of her cereal. "Have you stayed in one before?"

"No, this is the first time. It was on my Telluride Christmas season wish list."

Her mouth grows into a smile. "Well, then, I'm glad we made it come true."

"Me too."

There's a lot of smiling and staring happening between us, and when you add in the low firelight, it's just a lot for a man who's not supposed to be feeling what I'm feeling for my brother's girlfriend.

I jump to my feet. "I almost forgot. I brought you some mint hot cocoa."

"You packed that in for me?"

"Yeah, of course. You can't be in a mountain hut without hot chocolate, and since you prefer the mint flavor, I had to make sure I had it."

"That's so thoughtful." She reaches across the table and puts her hand on my forearm. "Thank you."

My entire body warms from her simple touch. "You're worth the extra thought."

The sincerity behind her eyes falters, and she pulls away. "Where do you think the other skiers are?" She eyes me. "There are other skiers, right?"

"Yes, I took the last three spots in the hut. Everything else was already reserved." I place a pot of water on the stove and light it.

"It's completely dark outside. Do you think they're dead? Should we go search for them?"

"I'm sure they're fine. They probably have headlamps and are still making their way here."

"Headlamps. Yeah, I guess that's true."

"Or they've decided not to stay the night."

"So we'll be here alone?"

"We've been here alone the last hour, and it's been just fine."

"Right." She nods, flipping her hair again so it's still to the side.

"Can I ask you something?" I stir the hot chocolate over the stove, glancing at her behind me. "When you thought you were going to die, you said that you didn't get to plan a wedding or get married. You said you'd die a lonely, single woman."

"Is there a question in there?" She smiles out of the side of her mouth, and suddenly, all I can think about is how amazing it would be to kiss that crooked smile, to reopen the feelings we started the night we met—feelings I find myself thinking about when I have nothing else to think about.

"Um..." I glance down at the pot, doing whatever I can to keep my thoughts where they should be. "My question is, why do you fear being alone so much?"

"Oh." Her eyes drop. "It's stupid."

"Try me."

"It's really stupid, but I'll tell you." She peers at me through the dim hut. "Once, when I was thirteen, I went to a popular kid's party with my friend Jody. The party was way out of our league, and we had no business being there, but we took a chance at going because we had each other. Within minutes of arriving, Jody found a cute boy and ditched me—like left the party. I had no one to talk to." She shrugs as if the action will help her not seem too vulnerable. "I know it's just a silly junior high party, but I felt so alone and uncomfortable—more than I ever had in my entire life."

"Why didn't you call someone to pick you up?"

"I tried, but no one in my family was home. I locked myself in a bathroom until the party was over."

I walk over to the table, sitting Summer's mint hot cocoa in front of her. "Were you crying or just sitting in there?"

She rolls her eyes. "I was weeping like a baby."

"No shame in that."

"Well, I ended up staying in the bathroom for three hours until I was the last one there, and the kid who threw the party had to drag one of his parents out of bed to drive me home. I was humiliated and traumatized, and I vowed I would never fly solo again. So I don't. I always make sure I have a plus-one, especially if it's a non-family event." She twists her lips into a grimace. "And lately, even if it is a family event. I just hate being the only one not married. I'm like the seventh wheel, and I'm sick of it."

I nod, casting my eyes over her. Me spending the holidays with her isn't only about her family not liking Justin. It's about Summer not feeling alone or like she's the odd man out. If I could, I'd make sure she was never alone again.

"It's stupid. I know." She blows on her cocoa before taking a sip.

"It's not stupid if it left that big of an impression on you. I get the sentiment. I've been living my life with Lars for the last decade, depending on him for all my social interaction, and then he died, and instead of staying out there and sticking it out by myself, I came running home. I think it's okay to admit you don't want to be alone."

"I'm glad to hear I'm not the only one who doesn't want to fly solo." She presses her lips into a closed-lip smile before taking another sip. "Mmm. This is the best mint hot cocoa I've ever had."

"It's probably the mountains and the hut making it taste so good."

"And the company."

I stare back at her, feeling the excitement inside my chest flare to life. "You're not too bad yourself."

Summer blushes under my compliment, and I wish I could reach out and run my fingers through her hair just so I can watch each piece flipped over fall back to its place.

There's an unspoken rule when it comes to brothers—it's even more of a rule when it comes to *twin* brothers. You can't fall for your brother's girlfriend. And yet here we are. I've never envied Justin as much as I do right now. And I've never wanted what he has until I met Summer.

And now she's all I want.

The crackling fire, the smokey wood, and the dancing flames against the cabin walls add to my need to touch her, feel her skin against mine, and ease the tension building in my chest.

I would give anything to kiss her again. To know, this time, she was kissing me because it's me and not some version of Justin she wished for. I want it so bad I'm willing to go against all my principles. I inch toward her. Summer holds still like she's just as interested in my next move as I am. Her eyes watch me, and maybe it's the dancing flames reflecting, but I swear I see a flicker of desire pass through her gaze. My body floods with a million responses. But there's only one response that I need to pay attention to:

The thought in my mind that Summer is not mine, and I can't do that to Justin.

No matter the fact that he doesn't really love her.

No matter how much I care for her.

No matter that I think she might care for me too.

I have to stop.

I take my inching forward and apply it to a stand, raking my fingers through my hair. I've never been more frustrated in my entire life—mentally, physically, emotionally. I'm a wreck. And the worst part is, there's nothing I can do about it. There's no way to ease the longing.

She's not mine.

I pace the tiny hut. "I don't think the other skiers are coming."

Summer stares at me, and I don't even try to hide my frustration. "Maybe we should go to bed."

"Yeah, we probably should."

Because if I go to sleep, maybe the suffocating ache and the never-ending temptation will finally stop.

SUMMER

I'VE NEVER BEEN IN THIS POSITION WHERE DOING THE right thing feels wrong.

One time, when I was six years old, I thought about stealing candy from one of those buckets at the candy store. I really wanted that watermelon hard candy, so choosing the right in that situation felt wrong.

But tonight is different. Choosing Caleb feels wrong, and yet I'm tiptoeing to his bunk and climbing under his covers, scooting next to his body. He stirs, and even through the darkness, I know his eyes are on me.

He doesn't hesitate.

His body turns into mine, and his hand runs through my hair, dragging my mouth to his.

There's a small satisfaction in knowing he wants this as much as I do.

His kiss is like all my favorite Christmases combined into one. He tastes like peppermint candy, and the ridges of his arm muscles feel like an icicle, minus the cold part.

The kiss moves and shifts, taking me back to Justin's kitchen and the way Caleb held me there with strong hands pressed against my back, keeping my body close to his.

Now I'm a falling snowflake, fluttering through the sky, dancing and drifting through the air with every passing second of this kiss until the snowflake lands on our lips and the heat between us turns into flames.

Flames? Really?

Like our mouths are on fire?

That's weird.

But I like it.

I like it a lot.

This kiss is so hot our mouths are on fire.

Everything deepens, and I'm feeling more and more passion.

"Summer?"

We don't break apart.

"Summer? How could you do this to me?"

Justin's tortured face is all I see.

"How could you?"

His chest opens, and his heart splits down the middle, but instead of blood, eggnog pours out of his open wound.

Eggnog tears stream down his face as he repeats again, "How could you?"

I jolt upright, banging my head on the bunk bed above me. "Ow!" I immediately grab my forehead, checking for blood—not eggnog, *thankfully.*

Caleb is instantly by my side, sitting on the edge of the bed. "Summer, are you okay?"

"Uh, yeah." I scoot back from him, a good idea given the circumstances that woke me. "I just had a bad dream."

A very bad dream that was actually a great dream, but terrible because it was so great.

"Do you want to talk about it?"

"No!" I hold my hands up, stopping the conversation from going any further.

"You were mumbling a lot. Are you sure you don't want to talk about it?"

"I was mumbling? What was I mumbling? Like, could you make anything out of what I was saying?"

Please let it all be unintelligible.

"I couldn't understand anything. But I didn't think it was a bad dream. I actually thought you were happy...you know, enjoying yourself."

Oh, I enjoyed myself, that's for sure.

"No, it was a nightmare," I say. "Not a happy dream."

The backs of Caleb's fingers caress my cheek. It's the backs of his fingers with knuckles and all that jazz, something a school nurse would do to see if I have a fever, but because of the schmexy dream, his backs-of-the-fingers touch feels *real* nice.

"Your face is ice cold."

That's his assessment? Really? Because I'm feeling all sorts of hot.

Caleb stands, looking at the dying fire. "We're out of wood. Let me go outside and see if I can find some more."

"No!" I reach my hand out, grabbing his arm. And again, it's just a freaking arm, but touching it fills me up with butterflies. "You can't go outside in the storm for more firewood. That's ridiculous. I'll just wear my coat to bed and bundle up."

"I don't want you to be cold."

"It's fine." Even as I say the words, my teeth chatter.

"That's it. I'm going out."

"No! I forbid it!"

Everything is dark, but not too dark that I can't make out the shape of Caleb's amused smile. "You forbid it?"

"Yes, I forbid you from going outside in a blizzard and catching a cold and dying and leaving me here all alone to fend for myself."

"Well, I can't let you be cold. I mean, we could..." His words drift away as his eyes bounce from his bunk to my bunk.

"We could what?"

He scratches the back of his neck. "I was just thinking that we could bring up our body temperature by, you know, sharing a bed."

"Like, you sleep in here with me?" I point down at my bunk.

"In a totally platonic way. You know, just keep each other warm."

"That is survival 101. And we are snowed in."

"Why do you keep saying it like that? *Snowed in?*"

"Something I saw on Hallmark." I wave it away. "So you and me in one bed *together* when there are seven other beds?"

231

He counts all the bunks. "Yes, there are seven other empty beds."

"But we're cold," I say.

"And there's no more firewood, so we're going to get colder."

"Unless we join forces and share a bed."

"That's right."

I reach for my coat slung over the back of the chair in front of me. "And I could put my coat on so it wouldn't even feel like we're touching."

"Yeah, we don't even have to touch. Just radiate heat."

"And then you wouldn't have to go outside in the middle of the night in a blizzard to find firewood," I say as I push my arms through my coat.

I don't know why, but at this late hour, everything about this plan sounds completely logical and necessary.

"And maybe if I'm close by," Caleb offers, "you won't have any more bad dreams."

"Let's not talk about the dreams." I shake my head.

"So, should I climb in your bunk with you? For the sake of heat?"

"Yes, for the sake of heat."

I scoot over, pressing my back against the log wall. Caleb climbs under the covers. The bunk is only a twin, so even though we're not trying to touch, we're right next to each other. Two heads, one pillow, thighs brushing against each other. Feet fighting for space at the bottom of the mattress. But it's fine. I'm in snow clothes. They're basically like a winter chastity belt. I can't feel anything in these things.

Except for maybe my pounding heart.

In the dim light of the embers, we stare at each other. And maybe eye contact is all it takes to feel Caleb's presence.

"Are you comfortable?" I ask, like some sort of bed host.

"Yeah, are you?"

"I'm fine." As fine as a girl can be who's sharing a bed with a man who's not her boyfriend—that sounded bad. Let me rephrase: as fine as a girl can be who's sharing a bed for heat's sake. We've got subzero temperatures out here.

"Are you warm?" he asks.

"Getting there. What about you?"

Caleb nods. "Getting there."

"So I guess we go to sleep?"

"I guess so."

Caleb smiles. "Sweet dreams, Summer."

But what he doesn't know is that I already had a sweet dream, and it was centered around him.

CALEB

SUNLIGHT WAKES ME.

I lift my eyelids, still feeling a sleep haze, but everything awakens when I feel Summer curled up next to me. Curled up is the best way to describe her position. I'm on my back with my arm wrapped around her shoulder and body. Summer is on her side, curled like a ball into me. But the best part is her head on my chest.

I can't see her face. She's tucked under the blankets up to the crown of her head, probably to keep her nose and cheeks warm. But I can smell her hair and feel her body next to mine. I would've thought that holding her in my arms would ease the longing and the ache I feel for her but I can already tell it's only going to make things worse. I've had a small taste of what it's like to hold her, to wake up with her in my arms, and it's not even a fraction of enough. I already crave more.

But like any good brother and good guy would do, I slide my arm out from under her and slowly inch my body away. I don't want Summer to wake up embarrassed about cuddling into me or feel guilty about how we chose to keep warm last night. She doesn't need that added stress in her life.

I stand and put my boots on. After that, I boil some water over the propane stove so Summer can wake up to a hot cup of mint cocoa. We'll have a quick breakfast. Then we'll ski out of here to make it back in time for the festivities with her family later today.

Before I wake her with a steaming cup of hot chocolate in my hand, my eyes sweep over her one last time, remembering how she felt in my arms. I smile, grateful for the memory—just like the kiss I'm not supposed to remember either.

twenty-nine
SUMMER

CALEB and I are going on hour twenty of hanging out. A person can do a lot of things in twenty hours. You can ski up and down a mountain, stay in a hut, and cuddle with your boyfriend's twin brother—just to name a few. Technically, I don't know for certain that Caleb and I cuddled. When I woke up, he was already awake, but there was this feeling inside my chest, this peacefulness that last night was the least lonely I've felt in my entire life, and something tells me it's because Caleb slept beside me.

Then something tells me I should feel guilty for feeling so content.

But then again, maybe there's nothing to feel guilty about.

I should just ask him.

I tap my fingers on the side of his Bronco as we make our way to Irvine Ranch to meet up with my family. "So what happened last night?"

Caleb eyes me. "What do you mean?"

"Or this morning. What happened between us?" I scratch the side of my ear. "You know, when you woke up?"

He smirks, and it's one of those smirks that tells me he knows more than I do, and I hate that. "Does it really matter what happened between us?"

"Well, yes. I need to know if I did something that I need to tell Justin about. Like if I cuddled with you."

"Were you trying to stay warm?"

"Yes."

"Then I think whatever happened was innocent enough. Especially since you said yesterday that you aren't attracted to me."

"Right. I'm not." I never thought I would talk to a man about whether or not I'm attracted to him, but here we are again, having this same conversation, which is unfortunate since I'm lying.

"So, then, we're good." He shrugs. "You don't need to worry."

"Great." I smile in a way that can only be construed as over-done. "I'm glad we cleared that up. I won't mention it to Justin. It was just two outdoor adventurers trying to stay warm."

"Now we're outdoor adventurers? I thought we were *pals*."

"Both." I lift my chin, glancing out my side of the car. "We can be both."

Just as long as that's all we are. Maybe it was the mint hot chocolate or the freezing temperature last night, but the lines between what Caleb and I are, and can be, blurred for a little bit. But we're back on track. Caleb is here on behalf of Justin.

"You're going to love our Irvine Ranch Christmas experience today." I change the subject—part of getting us back on track. "The whole town comes to sit on Santa's lap and enjoy sleigh rides. It's really magical. My family goes every year because Bob Irvine is—"

"Your dad's best friend." Caleb smiles at me. "I know. It's one of the Stanworth family's claims to fame."

"Not the only one," I mutter under my breath.

Caleb pulls the car into the marked parking lot covered in snow. I glance at the clock. We're a little early. The whole event doesn't start for twenty minutes, but I see my family up ahead by the picnic tables.

I flip the passenger sun visor down and look in the tiny

mirror. "Ugh! I look like I just slept in a hut and skied down the mountain. Oh, wait. I did do that." I wipe the mascara stains away from the bottoms of my eyes.

"I think you look beautiful."

I slowly turn my head. Caleb's staring at me, radiating genuineness from his eyes, reminding me of the only other time he told me I was beautiful. It was right after we met, when he had altitude sickness. At the time, I dismissed his comment and chalked it up to him being so out of it that he was talking nonsense. But with the way he's staring at me across the car, I believe he meant it then as much as he means it now.

"Thank you." My words come out as a whisper as I drop my eyes.

"Should we go say hi to your family?"

"Yes." I clear my throat, opening my door. I meet Caleb around the back of his car, and he grabs my hand. I look down at our joint fingers. Holding his hand feels exciting and right and wrong all at the same time.

"You okay?"

I whip my head up, meeting his gaze. "Yeah, I'm fine." I take a step forward, dragging him with me.

"There's Summer and Justin." My mom turns to us. "You guys aren't going to believe what happened. Christmas is ruined."

"Janet," my dad huffs, "Christmas is not ruined."

"What's going on?" I glance around.

"Santa and Mrs. Claus aren't here yet," Jeff says, nodding toward his kids, playing right behind him. "Their sleigh got stuck in the snow, if you can believe that."

"Oh, no." I frown. "What about all the kids coming to sit on Santa's lap today?"

"Bob's looking for someone to fill in until the real Santa can get here," my dad explains.

"I'll do it." Caleb shrugs, lifting my hand up with his shoulders.

"You'll do it?" Anna looks at him like she's shocked.

237

"Yeah, Summer and I can be Mr. and Mrs. Claus until the big guy gets here."

"I don't look like Mrs. Claus."

"Oh, come on." He nudges his shoulder into me. "It'll be fun."

My mom walks up to Caleb, placing her hands on his shoulder. "You've saved Christmas."

I roll my eyes. Caleb has Janet Stanworth eating out of the palm of his hand.

"I THINK YOU NEED A BIGGER BELLY." I STUFF ANOTHER pillow under Caleb's red Santa jacket and then poke it, testing the squishyness factor.

He pokes my pillow-stuffed chest in response.

My jaw drops, and I twist my body away from him. "You can't poke Mrs. Claus in the boob."

"Why not? You poked me in the stomach."

"I poked a pillow."

"So did I."

I tilt my head, giving him a pointed stare. "Are you sure?"

His eyes dart to my chest and the hot dog-shaped pillow I stuffed in that area to fill out the red velvet dress. "Yes, I'm sure. Unless you've somehow turned into Dolly Parton in the last ten minutes."

I walk over to the mirror, taking my first look at myself since I put the white wig and costume on.

Caleb is right behind me. "You look more like Mrs. Doubtfire than Mrs. Claus."

I hunch over with laughter because his assessment is so true.

"Ho, ho, ho!" he says in his deepest voice, but every time he tries to move his mouth, his fake white beard falls off. "Merry Christmas!"

"Stop!" I say through my giggles. "I'm going to pee my pants from laughing so hard."

He sticks his beard on, pushing it down with added effort. "That has to be good enough." He smiles at me through the mirror, holding his arm out for me to loop mine through. "You ready, Mrs. Claus?"

I suck in a deep breath to try and control my unsolicited laughter. "I guess."

We march out of the ranch to the line of waiting children. My mom bounces up and down while simultaneously clapping. I can't even look at Juliet, Hailey, or Anna for fear that I will die laughing again.

Caleb and I sit in the huge velvety chairs, and one by one, kids come up to talk to us.

"Hey, little man!" Caleb says in his best Santa voice. "What do you want for Christmas?" He listens patiently as the little boy rattles off seven different PlayStation games. Even under that ridiculous fake beard, he still looks handsome—even more so when you add in how sweet he's being with the children. He was even nice to the one little girl who screamed in his face and then whacked him across the cheek.

The next little boy sits on his thigh and immediately starts crying. "Ho, ho, ho! Don't cry!"

But the little boy can't be consoled, and his mom sweeps in and whisks him away, apologizing for how sad he is.

"Summer?" Caleb whispers. "Summer?" he whispers a little louder.

"What?" I smile at the family that's next in line.

"I think that kid peed on me."

My eyes shoot to his leg and the round, wet spot on his thigh where the little boy had just been sitting.

That's when I lose it for good.

I can't help it.

And you know what else I can't help? Just really, really liking Caleb Davidson.

It's a problem.

thirty

CALEB

"HOW MANY TIMES do I have to wash my pants to get urine out of them?" I ask as I climb out of my Bronco in front of Justin's condo.

Summer giggles so hard she snorts. "I can't believe you got peed on."

"I bet Bob Irvine has never been peed on before."

Summer shakes her head with more light laughter as she takes the front steps two at a time. "I bet Bob Irvine has never dressed up as Santa Claus."

"Hey, we should watch *Christmas Vacation* tonight. Keep the laughs going."

"I'd love to. We could pop some popcorn and light a fire." I twist the door handle and push open the door.

"Do you think you have stuff to make s'mores?"

We both step inside and immediately pause.

The lights are off, and candles are lit everywhere. There are some along the fireplace mantel, on the hearth, and in the middle of the kitchen table. Fancy china that Justin probably bought today is laid out for two. Soft music plays in the background, and there's a pathway of rose petals on the floor, leading to the table.

Justin stands next to it all with arms spread wide. "Surprise!" His eyes go straight to Summer, and so do mine.

Her smile falters. "What's all of this?"

"This is an apology and a thank you."

He walks to her, wrapping his arms around her waist, and brings her body into his for a kiss. I have to look away. Two seconds ago, Summer felt like she was mine. We planned on watching a movie and making s'mores in the fireplace, and now she's kissing my brother.

It's the worst.

She pulls back. "An apology and a thank you?" I don't miss the way her eyes bounce to me. I search her gaze, selfishly hoping to find something that lets me know she hates this as much as I do. But her eyes dart back to Justin before I see what I want.

"Yes. An apology for me being so busy that I've neglected you and a thank you for you being so great to support me even when my schedule has been crazy."

He hugs her again, and her eyes meet mine. I wish I knew what was happening inside her head or why her gaze drifts to mine when she should be totally focused on Justin. He's giving her all the attention she's wanted. She should be the happiest woman around. But instead, she's looking at me with an expression I can't read.

"You didn't have to do all this."

"I know. I just wanted to." He walks over to the table and pulls out her chair for her. "I just want us to have a romantic night together."

"Uh…" I take my coat off and hang it on the hook by the door. "I'm going to go shower."

"Caleb, you don't have to leave," she says as I head to my room. "You can eat dinner with us."

I spin around, slowly walking backward. "You guys deserve a night together alone. I'll give you some privacy."

Justin smiles. "Caleb, you'll be happy to know that, after this week, we won't be needing your services anymore."

My services?

Nothing has ever sounded so cheap and tawdry before.

"We need to get all blanket orders out by the fifteenth so they make it in time for Christmas. So, depending on what Summer has this week, it will be your last time filling in for me."

"Oh." I can't even muster a fake smile or a fake *'Great!'* to go along with my *'Oh.'*

"I bet you'll be glad."

I nod as my eyes pull to Summer. She's looking down at the ground, and I'm hoping she's feeling as depressed about this opening in Justin's schedule as I am.

But why would she? I'm not the man she wants.

"And"—Justin points to me—"I have a thank-you dinner planned for you as well."

I lift my brows like I'm super interested. I have to, or else I'm afraid he'll figure out that I'm disappointed not to have a justified reason to hang out with Summer anymore. "Oh, yeah?"

"Yeah, Monday night is my company party up at the Mountain Lodge. It's one hundred dollars a plate, and I want you to come and have a steak on me for taking such good care of my girl." He slings his arm around Summer's shoulder, tugging her in close to his side.

His girl.

I'm such an idiot.

Summer is *his* girl.

"Yeah, no problem. A steak sounds great." I force a wide smile. If I can't have the girl, I might as well have a filet mignon on my brother's dime.

"Summer, of course, will be my date. But"—he wags his brows up and down—"I've already secured someone for you."

"A date?" Summer whips her head up to him.

Justin looks at her. "Jordan from my office. She's already agreed."

Summer frowns. "Caleb doesn't need you to set him up with somebody. He's only here in Telluride for a few weeks."

243

"All the more reason to go out with some hottie."

Her eyes swing to me. "You don't have to go with her."

"Why not?" Justin says. "She's perfect for Caleb. Dark-brown hair, tall, thin, and she loves the outdoors and traveling on her own. You'll love her. She's very independent."

Jordan literally sounds like the opposite of Summer.

Her eyes never leave mine. "Is she even Caleb's type?"

Does Summer know that *she's* my type? This bubbly woman with a playful smile and a kind heart who happens to be obsessed with Christmas and her family is my type down to her very festive earrings.

Justin shrugs. "I think Jordan is perfect for Caleb."

My eyes watch Summer, how her jaw hardens with what looks like jealousy, and I decide right then and there that maybe Summer should have a taste of her own medicine. Feel what I'm feeling.

"You know what?" I look at Justin. "I'd love to go with Jordan."

"You would?" Summer's jaw drops.

I shoot her a pointed stare. "Yes, I would."

"Alright!" Justin smiles wide.

"Set it up." I keep walking backward. "It's a date!"

Before I round the corner to my room, I catch Summer's pursed lips and frustrated glare.

MY PHONE BUZZES ON THE NIGHTSTAND NEXT TO MY bed, waking me. I glance at the clock. It's a little past midnight. I must've fallen asleep watching *Saturday Night Live*. I pick up my phone. The text is from Summer.

Summer: I never got the chance to thank you for this

weekend—backcountry skiing and for today at the ranch. I'm really glad I didn't have to go alone.

I tap my fingers on the side of my mattress, trying to decide what I should say. I know what I want to say, but *should say* is what I have to go by.

Caleb: Sure, no problem. That's what I'm here for.
Caleb: Are you still with Justin?

Is she texting me while cuddling with him?

Summer: No, I just got home. I was tired.

Relief coats every corner of my heart.

Caleb: I'll be at Justin's company party on Monday night. You can just tell me then if you need me this week.

Summer: Do you still have the calendar I made you?

Caleb: I think it's around here somewhere.

I turn my head to the side. Summer's Christmas calendar is on the dresser next to my bed. Is it weird if I admit that I've been looking at it every night before falling asleep?

Summer: I was going to say you could just check the calendar for the activities this week, but since you lost it...

My shoulders drop. I feel like the biggest jerk. I would never *lose* Summer's calendar. Heck, I'm surprised I don't have the thing framed. But she's not mine, and at some point, I have to face that.

Summer: There are only two things this week. Dinner with my family for my dad's birthday, and the Telluride Mistletoe-Down Hoedown and Dance.

I pick up the calendar, confirming what she said. There's a Christmas cake graphic by her dad's birthday and a cowboy elf by the Mistletoe-down Hoedown.

Summer: And do you have any activities for me this week that I need to plan on from your holiday activity list?

Caleb: No. I think I'm good.

I hit my head on the headboard behind me, hating how cold I sound.

Summer: Okay, then. I guess I'll see you Monday night at Justin's work party.

Caleb: Sounds good. See you then.

I bang my head three more times against the headboard before setting my phone down.

thirty-one

SUMMER

IN THE NINE months that I've been dating Justin, I've never once been jealous or felt threatened by Jordan Neeley until tonight.

Her gold-sequined mini dress with a low cut and puffy sleeves is gorgeous. It screams holiday party and shows off her long, tan legs perfectly. Why are her legs so tan anyway? It's the middle of winter, for crying out loud.

She brushes her long, dark hair back from her shoulder as she continues her life story. "Then, after college, I moved to Switzerland for a year—"

"By yourself?" Caleb asks.

"Yes, I just wanted to be alone. Fly solo. Really get to know me and my inner voice."

Pfft! My inner voice.

That's code for: I don't have any friends or family.

"What did you do in Switzerland?" Justin asks.

"I spent the year exploring, hiking, and climbing the Swiss Alps."

I do my best to hide my eye roll as I shake some salt onto my baked potato.

"I've been to Switzerland several times," Caleb says. "What was your favorite part?"

I must shake my salt for too long because Caleb grabs my hand. He doesn't even look at me. His fingers pry the salt out of my grasp, while his other hand pushes the pepper into that same palm. He nods once, like he's really fascinated by Jordan's answer, and when she turns to look at Justin, he leans in and whispers in my ear, "You can never have too much pepper."

That's what my dad says. He remembered.

I peek over at him. Don't even get me started on how devastatingly handsome Caleb looks in black pants, a white button-up shirt, and a black tie. He went from Mr. Mountain Man to a lady-killer in the blink of an eye. Even his wavy, brown hair seems more tame tonight.

But it's not even how good he looks dressed up that's killing me. It's him. It's his smile and the easy way he converses with people, setting everyone around him at ease. That's always been what I admired about Caleb, but watching him put Jordan at ease has me feeling frenzied with jealousy.

"All that travel is right up Caleb's alley," Justin says. Since when did he become such a little matchmaker?

Jordan twists her body to face Caleb. "Yeah, I looked you up on YouTube before our date."

Is this really a date? I mean, we're at an office party. Just because it's only the four of us at the table and it's at a fancy mountain lodge doesn't mean this is a double date. We're just here to celebrate All-Weather Blankets and the company's success this year. It's not a *date* date.

"Oh, yeah?" Caleb gives her one of his charming smiles—one I'd hoped was only reserved for me. "It takes some women over a week to be curious enough to look me up, but you did it without even knowing me."

This time, I don't try to hide my eye roll.

"Well"—Jordan's perfect blush appears right on cue—"ever since Justin told me what you do for a living, I've been more than a little curious about it. I've always hoped we'd have a chance to meet."

"And now we have."

"And now we have," she repeats but a little slower.

Wow, I could really learn a thing or two from Jordan and that sultry smile.

Justin gives me a discreet elbow nudge under the table and a smile that shows just how proud he is of himself for setting them up. It's on par with Janet Stanworth's *I-told-you-so* looks.

"These rolls are delicious!" I randomly say, smiling around the table as I pick up my roll from off my plate. "So soft."

"You haven't posted a video in a while, though," Jordan says, ignoring my bread compliments. "What made you decide to take a break?"

"You know what would be really great on these rolls?" I say, trying to gain as much attention as I can. When Caleb looks at me, I smile innocently. "Butter. Butter would be so delicious."

He reaches for the butter tray, then grabs my roll, buttering it up for me all while answering Jordan. "It's the holidays. I just thought a break would be nice." When he finishes, he hands it over, never looking at me once.

I suppress my smile by taking a big bite.

Caleb buttered my roll. He didn't butter Jordan's. There's something really cute about that.

It makes me happy that he didn't tell Jordan that something was missing in his life. That his best friend, Lars, died and that he wanted to honor him by having more meaningful relationships. Jordan thinks she knows Caleb, but she doesn't know him like I do.

"Taking a break is always a good choice." Jordan smiles. "I love this time of year."

"You know who else loves this time of year?" Justin's hand goes to my shoulder. "Summer."

Unfortunately for me, I just stuffed my mouth with the last half of my roll. I try to chew it down, but there's so much freaking soft dough that it's going to take a second. I answer anyway.

"Yesh." I chew some more. "I...loooveah... Chrishmash...time."

Jordan gives a polite nod despite probably being disgusted by my mouthful of yeast. "I noticed your poinsettia earrings," she offers. "Very fun."

I don't want to be fun.

I want to be sexy like Jordan. Instead, I'm the fun and cute girl with poinsettia earrings and red lipstick that matches my red swing dress. I totally should've gone for the backless red dress from the Shein online store, but it seemed like too much trouble to buy one of those sticker bras for the backless dress. Plus, if someone complimented me and asked where I got it from, I wouldn't know what to say because I don't know how to pronounce that cheap online store. Is it *sheen* or *she-in*? Who really knows? All of that steered me away from the sexy backless dress and into the swing dress Shirley Temple would wear.

And now I'm regretting it.

Jordan is still looking right at me. "Justin told me about your little holiday swap."

My eyes drift to him. "You told her?"

"I didn't know it was a secret. Besides, Jordan asked how you were handling my demanding work schedule. I told her you were being incredibly cool about it." Justin squeezes my shoulder, bringing me in to kiss my cheek. He leaves his nose right next to my ear, and with Caleb sitting on the other side of me, it feels awkward, or wrong, or just...*something*.

"Don't worry. I won't tell anyone." Jordan smiles at me. "I'm just so fascinated by it all." Her eyes bounce back and forth between me and Caleb. "How do feelings not get complicated when you guys spend so much time with each other, pretending to be boyfriend and girlfriend?"

"Summer is Justin's girlfriend," Caleb immediately says. "I've known from the beginning that all she wanted was for

Justin to spend time with her. I've only ever been standing in for him."

I turn my eyes to Caleb, noticing the stiffness in his jaw and the tenseness in his shoulders.

"Told you it was the perfect situation," Justin says, drawing me close again. "Isn't Sum Sum so chill?" His physical affection and doting are all I've wanted for the last four months, and now that I have it, I don't know what to do with it.

Jordan glances down at her watch. "We better go set up the company slide show so it's ready after dancing."

"You're right." Justin scoots his chair back and stands. "Will you two be okay here alone for a second?"

"I'll take care of Summer as if she were my own girlfriend," Caleb says with a dryness that's a little alarming.

"When I get back, you owe me a dance." Jordan trickles her fingers up his arm and across his back as she walks away.

"Wow." My mouth drops open. "She is forward."

Caleb shrugs. "I don't know what you're referring to. All she said is that I owe her a dance."

"Yeah, she said it as she fondled you. I mean, you guys just barely met."

"You're joking, right?" Caleb gives me an incredulous smile. "Within one second of meeting me, you were fondling me more than she was."

"Oh, please." I look away. "I thought you were Justin."

He twists in his seat, facing me. "You know there are holes in your story."

"How so?" I eye him.

"For starters, I'm bigger than Justin. Do you really expect me to believe that you didn't notice the height or the bulk difference?"

"It was dark, and I don't pay attention to that kind of stuff."

"What about my hair?"

"What about it?"

"It's longer than his."

"Didn't notice." I lift my chin.

"And at that time, I pretty much had a short beard or long stubble—however you want to say it."

"I hadn't seen Justin in a couple of days. I thought maybe he was growing it out."

Caleb leans closer, his warm whispers dusting over my neck and ear. "What about how I tasted or smelled or held or kissed you?"

Holy, Hannah! His closeness lights my skin on fire.

My head slowly turns to his, our noses less than an inch apart. I can see the flicks of dark blue in his eyes and the coarse stubble that covers his chin. There are a few specks of light freckles that dot the bridge of his nose and cheeks. I've never noticed them before. Probably because I've never allowed myself to really look at him this close up.

His gaze dances over my face. "Surely, you felt a difference in all of that."

"You sure are spouting off a lot of details for someone who doesn't remember anything about that night or that kiss."

Caleb's smirk turns as naughty as all the kids on Santa's list. "I remember every. Single. Second." Somehow, he inches closer, making me hold more still than I ever have in my entire life for fear that if I move even a bit, I'll scare him away. My heart pounds and thrashes inside my chest as his gaze skewers me. "I remember what it was like to hold you in my arms. I remember how your body melted into mine. How you took control but then resigned to my touch. I remember how you smelled, and the taste of your lips." Chills drop over my body like a blanket as each of his soft words puff across my skin. "I'll remember that kiss for the rest of my life. It's the kiss that screwed me up for every other kiss after it."

My breath goes ragged as I stare back at him. His words grip my chest, squeezing my heart with thrilling tension. The tip of my tongue sweeps over my lips at the same time my eyes drop to his mouth. All this talk of kissing, has my mind thinking about kissing Caleb Davidson again.

"Got the PowerPoint all working," Jordan says as she walks up to Caleb's side.

We jerk away, but it looks too suspicious, so I go into damage-control mode, opening my mouth into a wide smile in front of Caleb. "Are you sure I don't have anything in my teeth?"

His brows hover above his eyes.

I lean in closer to him, glancing over at Jordan to make sure she's looking. "Are you sure they're clear? Look again."

Caleb gives a half-hearted eye roll and leans into me like before, but this time, instead of saying the sexiest things I've heard in my entire life. He looks at my teeth.

"They're fine," he mutters. "But if the tables were turned, you wouldn't tell me if I had something in my teeth."

"No, I would not." I lean back to my spot, feeling satisfied that I smoothed over that whole we-got-a-little-too-close moment.

"Are you ready to dance?" Jordan asks.

"Absolutely." He smiles up at her. How? How can he melt me into a puddle and then smile at Jordan Neeley like she's the only woman in the room?

I don't know, but I hate him for it.

And I hate him for how confused I feel right now.

thirty-two

CALEB

"I REALLY THINK this is the last time Caleb will have to go in my place," Justin says, placing a rushed kiss on Summer's cheek. "I have to finish the books from the QVC orders we got earlier this week, and then I'll be a free man." He spins in his chair at the kitchen table, facing me. "You don't mind, right, Caleb?"

I'm sitting on the couch, putting on my freshly purchased cowboy boots that I bought today just for this occasion. "Nope."

Summer glares at me from the kitchen table. It's one of her harmless glares that's more of a pout than hurtful. "Are you sure you don't already have plans to go to the dance with Jordan? You two seemed pretty cozy the other night at the Mountain Lodge before leaving together."

Is it wrong to take pleasure in Summer's jealousy?

"Yeah, Jordan was pretty tight-lipped at work yesterday about what happened *after* you two left the party together." Justin tips his smile. "Did you guys kiss?"

I look at Summer with a gloating smile. "I'm not the type to kiss and tell."

"You kissed her." Justin points at me. "You *so* kissed her."

Summer lifts her chin, trying to act like she doesn't care, but jealousy hangs off each of her movements. "That's what I was saying. Maybe Caleb already has plans to go to the dance with Jordan."

I stand, straightening my legs in my new tight Wranglers and fixing my giant Telluride belt buckle just right. "Don't worry, Summer. I'm all yours tonight."

Her jaw hardens, and she looks away.

"Perfect." Justin claps. "I promise this will be the last time."

"But Justin, this is the Mistletoe-Down."

"I know." He places his hand on the top of her head, running his fingers through her hair until there's no more, and he's left resting his hand on her shoulder. "We'll go to the Mistletoe-Down together next year."

Wow. A few weeks ago, he wasn't sure about Summer, and now he's promising things for next year. Why the sudden shift?

"It's not just that." She bites her lip, all while blatantly avoiding my stare. "There's mistletoe everywhere at the dance."

"A good decorating choice since it's called *Mistletoe-Down*."

She huffs in her spot, getting annoyed. "You don't get it. There's mistletoe *everywhere*." Her eyes peek at me, then glance away. "What if...you know..." her voice lowers. "What if Caleb and I get stuck under one?"

"Then you kiss." Justin says it so matter-of-factly that I have to believe he's either the most distracted, oblivious man not to see what's really going on here, or he doesn't *really* love Summer. I'm hoping it's the latter.

"You want us to kiss?" She gives him a pointed stare.

"I don't *want* you to kiss, but if you find yourself accidentally under some mistletoe and people are watching, then you have to kiss. We don't want people wondering about our swap."

Summer leans forward, ready with a rebuttal. "But—"

"It's not like you two haven't kissed before." Justin laughs, looking between us. His gaze lands on me and stays. "It will be like kissing your sister."

"I doubt that," I say under my breath.

"Try not to throw up." He laughs again, but when he sees

neither Summer nor I laughing, his tune changes, and he gives me a look. "I'm not saying you should search out a mistletoe. This is only if the situation can't be avoided."

"Understood," I say.

If the situation *can't* be avoided.

"And if it can't be avoided, just keep it chaste. A little peck."

"Sure." I walk to where Summer sits at the table and hold my hand out. "You ready?"

Her eyes bounce from Justin to me, and when our stares connect, I don't even hide my appraising of her.

I thought Summer couldn't top the red dress from the other night—she was killing me in that thing—but tonight, she looks incredible in a green velvet button-up with two pockets over her chest. All the buttons are white pearls, making the top seem fancy for Christmas. I can imagine her finding this in a store and being so excited to wear it to the Christmas hoedown. But the best part of her outfit is the denim mini skirt, gold snowflake belt buckle, and red cowboy boots. She looks like she walked straight out of a cowboy's winter wonderland.

Out of *my* winter wonderland.

I pull her to a stand, and we stare at each other for a second, her hand still in mine.

Man, if given the chance, I'd never let her go.

"Don't stay out too late," Justin says behind us as we walk hand in hand to the door. There's a level of stress in his voice that I haven't heard before when it comes to me hanging out with Summer. I don't blame him. If I were Justin, I wouldn't trust her with me tonight either.

I'm not even sure I trust myself.

"Text me!" he says.

Then I leave with his girlfriend.

257

"So, do you think Jordan will be here tonight?" Summer asks as we enter the old cultural hall where the hoedown takes place. I'm glad she's talking. She spent the entire car ride here, staring out the window, away from me.

"I have no clue if Jordan's coming to this thing or not."

She goes up on her tippy toes and cranes her neck like she's looking over the crowd for her. "If she's here, I don't mind letting you two dance."

"You don't mind?"

"Yeah, why not?" She tries smiling, but there's fake written all over it. "You two seemed really enamored with each other."

"Enamored?"

"Yes, smitten. Fond of."

"I know what it means."

"Great." She looks at me with that same fake smile. "So you two should try and dance together tonight."

"And how will you explain to your family that your boyfriend is dancing with another woman?"

Her face gets flustered.

"That's what I thought."

"But if we see her, you can still talk to her."

This is getting ridiculous.

I lean in, crowding Summer with my closeness. "Do you *want* me to be with Jordan?"

Summer holds still, her eyes flitting across my face. "No."

"Good. Because Jordan's not who I want."

Her chest rises with an unsteady breath. I grab her hand and weave her through the crowd, glancing up at the ceiling. That's a heck of a lot of mistletoe. The entire decoration committee just became my best friends. They weren't joking around when they named this dance the Mistletoe-Down. There's mistletoe every five feet, under every archway, every doorway, at the center of every table (although, I don't think it counts if you're not standing under it). Avoiding getting caught under mistletoe tonight will be harder than avoiding snowflakes in a snowstorm, but I'm not complaining. I welcome the challenge.

There are two seats saved for us at the table where Summer's family sits.

"Don't you two look cute," Juliet says as we walk up. "I need to get Rick a pair of pants like that."

"These old things?" I twist, lunging one leg forward, maximizing the tightness around my butt.

"That's what I call eye candy," Aunt Carma says with absolutely no emotion.

"You like that, Carma?" I spin so she has a better angle of my butt.

"I may be old, but I can spot a firm butt from a mile away."

"Carma!" Janet chastises. "That's not appropriate for a Christmas event."

"Since when are *firm butts* not appropriate at a Christmas event?" Marty asks his wife.

She laughs, pushing his shoulder.

"Do we need to ask Justin and his *firm butt* to leave?" Jeff jokes.

"I bet Summer's not bothered." Rick laughs. "You know she likes Justin in his Wranglers."

"I haven't even noticed." She turns her head in the other direction, avoiding my butt.

I straighten, placing my lips next to her ear. "I don't believe that at all." She pulls her shoulders back, fidgeting like my closeness affects her more than she's letting on. "I've noticed how good you look." I inch my foot forward so I'm even closer and take a chance by lightly placing my hand on the small of her back. "Tonight and the other night at the party."

Her head flips as if I've said something that has piqued her interest. Her blue eyes peer up at me, and there's so much tension bubbling between us we're like a wine bottle ready to pop and spill over. "Jordan was dressed like a golden goddess. I guarantee you didn't even notice me."

I lean in more, lowering my voice to just whispers that graze her ear. "Red dress that perfectly matched your red lipstick." I lightly brush my finger over her lips, feeling her shiver below my touch. "Fitted on top, then it fanned out like one of those dresses from the 1950s. But the best part was when you were dancing, because your dress twirled upward, and I saw a little more of your legs," I tease.

Summer playfully elbows me in the side, causing me to step back. She gives me the first natural smile of the night and lowers her voice so only I can hear. "Justin would never say that."

"I'm not Justin right now."

SUMMER

CALEB STANDS IN THE MIDDLE OF THE DANCE FLOOR with a crowd around him. "When I say *Merry*, you say *Christmas!* Merry!" He points to everyone else.

"Christmas!" the crowd yells in unison.

"Merry!" He does it again.

"Christmas!"

"Merry!"

"Christmas!"

Then Caleb starts jumping up and down, and the whole crowd, including me, joins in on the merry mosh pit until a Christmas version of "Cotton Eye Joe" starts playing.

Caleb hunches over, stomping one foot and clapping his hands. Everyone follows his lead, stomping their feet. The wood floor below us moves and vibrates, sending dust flying in the air.

He looks at me, charming me with a smile that threatens to win my heart completely. He's just so much fun to be around. He's happy, the life of the party, the one that brings the energy and makes everyone else have a good time too. But Caleb's more than a good time. He's sweet, and thoughtful, and remembers small details. And at this moment, in the middle of the Mistle-toe-Down, I'm wondering why I'm with Justin and not with him.

All the reasons we started this swap have vanished. I'm happy, my mom's happy, my family isn't questioning my life choices anymore. I haven't even thought about my family problems for over a week. Caleb solved everything—not because he was pretending to be Justin, but because he's *him*.

"Conga line!" he shouts, grabbing my hands and putting them on his waist to follow him around the dance floor. In a second, the rest of the crowd joins in and marches behind us until the song ends.

I clap, and he whistles, and we both smile at each other through our heavy breaths.

"That was fun." The fact that I know he really means it sends my heart soaring with happiness I didn't even know was possible.

"Let's go grab a drink," I say, and Caleb doesn't hesitate to take my hand and lead me off the dance floor before "Boot Scootin' Boogie" takes over.

"Here you go." He takes two water bottles from the ice bath on the table and hands me one.

I practically drink the entire thing in one big gulp but stop when I hear my name.

"Summer?" I turn around, and Vivian tackles me into a hug. "I thought I saw you out there tearin' up the dance floor."

"Oh, it's not me." I pause, wondering if I should say Caleb's name or pretend like he's Justin. Vivian is the one person who knows about the swap, but for fun, I want to see if she'll figure it out. "Justin's the one who's the big-time dancer."

Vivian side-eyes him. "Hey, Justin."

"Hey!" He shakes her hand, not having a clue who she is. "It's good to see you."

"Same." Her smile curls upward as she studies him. Then she

leans in, whispering in my ear so Caleb can't hear. "I thought you said they were identical?"

"They are," I whisper back.

"Not *that* identical. This version is all sorts of cute." She winks at me as she pulls back.

The song ends, and everyone claps.

"Next up, we're going to slow things down with a Christmas classic sung by Donna O'Day." The DJ sweeps his hand to the side, ushering in Donna.

"Double D! Double D!" Caleb starts to chant, and it takes off like wildfire.

Vivian laughs, giving me another goofy grin.

"Oh, my!" Donna says as she takes the stage and the microphone. "That's a nickname I haven't heard before." She points right at Caleb. "We can thank Justin Davidson for that."

His smile drops as the chant dissipates, and for the first time, I feel really bad about forcing Caleb to pretend to be someone else, because he's the type of guy who deserves to stand out as himself.

Just as I'm about to introduce him as himself to Vivian, she pushes us out on the dance floor. "If they're going to play a slow one, you two better get back out there."

CALEB

DONNA O'DAY HOLDS THE MICROPHONE UP TO HER LIPS and sings the first lines of "Blue Christmas." It's the first slow song they've played all night. I've put in a solid hour and a half on this dance floor. I've earned the right to slow dance with Summer.

I reach my hand out to her. "May I?"

She doesn't answer. Just slips her fingers in mine. I spin her under my arm, then pull her body close so we're chest to chest.

Her delicious scent washes over me, and I can't stand not knowing what it is that makes her smell so good.

"I have to know," I say. "What is that smell?"

"Oh, no!" Her eyes go wide, and she dips her nose down, smelling her armpit. "Do I have BO?"

"No." I laugh. "You smell amazing. You always smell amazing."

She straightens. "Oh."

"But it's killing me because I can't figure out what scent you use."

"It's probably my bubble gum shampoo."

I smile, breathing her in again. "You would smell like bubblegum."

Her grin stretches even wider. "I would, wouldn't I?"

We dance in silence for a moment, swaying back and forth. I've never paid much attention—okay, maybe in junior high—to how much of a full-body contact sport dancing is. My arm is wrapped around Summer's back, with my fingers curling into her waist. My other arm is holding her hand. Our bodies are pressed together, and her free hand rests around my neck, her fingers grazing the skin just above my shirt collar. I pull her even closer so our hips touch and the side of our cheeks brush against each other. I want to close my eyes, but I can't be one of those guys who closes their eyes while they dance—although everyone here thinks I'm Justin, so maybe it would be okay.

I settle on keeping my eyes open but paying attention to how she feels in my arms and the sensational feeling that holding her has spurred inside me. Every time Summer is in my arms, it feels like I'm never supposed to let her go, and yet, after tonight, I have to let her go.

"So I guess this is one of our last activities before Justin's going to be back," I say into her ear.

"Yeah, that's what he said." We slowly move together to the melody of the music. "You're probably so happy to be done with me."

I lean back enough to see her blue eyes. "Nothing could be further from the truth." She doesn't look away like I think she will. Instead, she holds my gaze. "And you? I bet you'll be happy to be done with me."

"Nothing could be further from the truth."

We both smile, knowing that's the most either one of us can say out of respect for Justin.

Summer leans back in, placing her head on my chest and I'm a goner, completely lost over this woman. I can't concentrate on anything but her. And the sad part is, she doesn't even know how crazy for her I am.

What if I threw my hat in the ring? What if I told Justin that he better bring his A-game because I'm bringing mine? Would we shake hands and say, 'May the best man win,' or would he never speak to me again? I came to Telluride to build a stronger relationship with him, and now I'm willing to toss it aside for a woman—but not any woman. It's Summer, the brightest light I've ever seen. The one woman who took my dark life and turned it into sunshine.

"Hey, look, you guys." Hailey points above us. "You're under the mistletoe."

We both look up. There's a large mistletoe centered directly above us.

"You have to kiss." Hailey smiles as she and Brian dance beside us.

Summer shakes her head. "Um, I'm not into PDA."

Hailey gives her a pointed stare. "You're hilarious. I've never met anyone who's more into PDA than you."

Summer's eyes drift back to me.

"Dude, take your chance." Brian elbows me. "You can't pass up mistletoe."

Take my chance.

Throw my hat into the ring.

I glance at Summer. I'm not going to do anything she doesn't want to do.

"Mistle-toe!" Janet sings the word as she and Marty dance by.

Summer looks around, noting how everyone in her family is watching us.

I smile, trying to ease whatever she's feeling inside and repeat Justin's words back to her. "Only if the situation can't be avoided. It's not like we haven't done it before."

She lifts her chin up to me, her eyes saying she's on board.

It's like the moment I step out on a bridge, my toes curling over the edge. I look down, and I second-guess everything. Did we calculate the free-fall correctly? Is the chute going to open at the right time? Are we sure the wind won't pick up at any second? Do I remember how many flips and twists I'm going to throw? In those last seconds, before I bend my knees and jump, it seems like the craziest idea I've ever had, and yet I know it will give me the best rush of my entire life. I'm out of control but so in control there's no doubt in my mind that I'll jump.

And jump I do.

I drop my mouth to hers, feeling the instant adrenaline jolt my entire body.

Her family cheers around us like our kissing has made all their dreams come true.

Little do they know, it's made all *my* dreams come true.

Just when I'm about to end the kiss and pull away, Summer keeps me there.

We were walking at the edge of the waves before, tiptoeing over jagged rocks, being careful not to fall, and then suddenly, we dove headfirst into the giant curl of water. I don't know how it happened, but I'm happy to be submerged.

My hands drift along her cheeks until my fingers dig into the back of her hair, tipping her head up to me, holding her lips to mine. She reacts by moving her hands to my lower back, clinging to my stupid cowboy shirt like she needs it for support or she might fall over.

The passion intensifies and so does every feeling I've been suppressing every time I've held back my affection because she wasn't mine to adore. Right now, she feels like she's mine, and I completely adore her.

Our lips graze and brush, bodies push and pull, and heartbeats pound and stall as the excitement builds between us. It's like each second the kiss goes on, our knowledge of each other multiplies until I feel like I know what she needs better than any other man out there.

It's as good as the first kiss in the kitchen but better because we're both fully aware. We have all the information, and we're choosing this moment *together.*

There's a whistle and a catcall from someone in Summer's family.

And that's enough to break the spell.

She pulls apart abruptly, eyes glazed over with tears.

"I can't," she whispers.

The song ends, and she walks away.

I want to chase after her, but I know she needs a second to wrap her head around what we just did.

Jeff slaps me on the back, leading Anna off the dance floor. "You really went for it with that kiss, didn't you?"

I lift my brows, offering a fake chuckle. "Yeah, I guess I did."

And I don't even regret it.

thirty-three

SUMMER

HEADLIGHTS SHINE through Caleb's Bronco windows as we wait for our turn to pull out of the parking lot.

We haven't spoken since the mistletoe kiss, which was easy to do since it happened fifteen minutes ago, at the end of the dance.

I glance out the window, the awkward silence so thick I can practically taste it.

"Are we going to talk about this?" Caleb finally asks. Apparently, the silence is choking him too.

"I'm a cheater!" I burst, throwing my hands up in the air.

"You are not a cheater." He rolls his eyes.

"Really"—I flip my head to him—"because I just kissed a man that isn't my boyfriend."

"It was an accident."

"It was not an accident. We both knew what we were doing."

"No, finding ourselves under the mistletoe was an accident. I followed all of Justin's rules. I avoided it all night until I couldn't avoid it any longer."

"You didn't follow all of his rules. It should've been a peck, but my whole family was there, cheering us on, and I don't know what happened."

"I know what happened."

267

"You do?" I stare at him expectantly, waiting for him to enlighten me.

"Yeah, we're attracted to each other. We've been dying to kiss for almost three weeks now, so when given the opportunity to kiss, we kissed."

My brows drop. "You've been dying to kiss me for three weeks?"

Caleb smiles. "Every single day we've been together."

I want to smile.

NO! I can't smile. This is bad. So incredibly bad.

"No." I shake my head. "That's not what happened. We haven't *wanted* to kiss."

"It is what happened. You just don't want to admit it because you think it makes you sound even more like a cheater."

"That is not true!"

It's entirely true, but like he said, I don't want to admit it.

"Whatever happened tonight was just an unfortunate part of the swap."

"Nothing about that kiss felt unfortunate to me," he mutters under his breath.

"Can we just not talk about it anymore?" I reach for the radio, turning the dial to the first channel I can find. I sit back in my seat, letting the music fill the car.

Until I realize what song is playing.

"Jessie's Girl" by Rick Springfield, and it's at the chorus, which is the worst part because it's diving deep into the fact that he wishes he could be with the woman Jessie's with.

So freaking awkward.

Caleb abruptly leans forward and changes the station to something else. He has obviously had enough of that message.

Thank goodness!

But then I realize what the new song is: "Two Princes" by the Spin Doctors. It's also on the most damning part of the song where it talks about choosing between two different guys to marry.

It's the middle of December. Where are all the Christmas songs?

We both jump forward to change the song, our hands tangling together by the buttons.

"I got it," I snap.

Caleb pulls back, and I take my sweet time finding a song on the radio that has nothing to do with a love triangle.

CALEB

"HEY!" JUSTIN COMES OUT FROM THE KITCHEN WHEN we walk through the door.

"Hi," Summer and I mutter.

We avoid eye contact with him as we take off our coats and hang them up.

"How was the hoedown?"

Summer folds her arms, staying at her spot by the door. "Good."

"Good," I give the same answer.

"Okayyyy," he drags the word out as he watches us. "Are you sure?"

"Yeah." I offer a half-hearted smile as I walk to the couch. I turn around, leaning against the back of it, kicking my feet out.

Justin eyes Summer. "Did something happen with your family?"

"Nope."

"So nothing's wrong?" He walks to her, hooking his finger under her chin, forcing her to look up at him.

"Nope."

"You guys are acting weird."

I feel like Justin has me in one of those interrogation rooms with the lights shining in my face.

"Fine!" I straighten, throwing my arms out. "I kissed her, okay?"

Justin's accusatory glare pulls to me. "You kissed her?"

"It was under a mistletoe," Summer explains, but when and where it happened doesn't really matter at this point. What matters is how I felt when we kissed.

"Yes, I kissed her, and I liked it."

Summer's mouth drops in shock as she looks at me. I don't know what about my confession is such a big surprise. Could she not tell during the kiss that I was feeling it?

"You liked it?" Justin's voice raises.

"Yeah, I liked it a lot. I'm not going to lie to you about it."

He turns to her. "Did you like the kiss?"

She bites her lip, looking down. "I didn't hate it."

Her words draw the biggest smile from me that I think I've ever had.

The happy moment is short-lived.

"I'm going to kill you!" Justin flings his body at me, and we both fall back onto the sofa. Summer screams, making this brotherly squabble seem more intense than it really is.

"Whoa!" I try to fend him off. "Last time I kissed her, you laughed. This time, you went from zero to sixty with no gas."

"Last time you kissed her, you were hallucinating." He pushes away my attempts to push him away. "What's your excuse this time?"

"Mistletoe?"

"I can't believe you kissed my girlfriend."

"You told me to!"

"No, I told you to avoid it!"

"I can't do this." Across the room, Summer gathers her coat and purse. "I don't know what I was thinking."

Justin and I both sit up.

"Sum Sum, don't go!"

"Summer, wait!"

She ignores both of us and walks out, slamming the door behind her.

"Look what you did!" Justin drops his body on me again.

We wrestle for a minute on the couch, then roll off the side, knocking into the coffee table. Now we're on the ground, wedged in between the table and the couch, with no room to wrestle. He takes me in a headlock, and I let him feel like he's winning because, in this particular situation, I'm in the wrong.

"For the record, I did avoid the kiss," I grunt. "Until I couldn't."

"Until you didn't *want* to avoid it."

"That's not true." I grab his hands, unlocking them from around my neck, and push his body off me. The force slides the coffee table back—cheap Ikea furniture for the win—giving us more space to roll around and wrestle.

"I knew you had a crush on her." Justin makes a fist, and just when I think he's going to punch me in the face, he gives me a noogie, twisting his knuckles into my hair.

"Ow!" I swipe away his hand from my head and roll our bodies so now I'm on top. "If you knew I had a crush on her, then why did you let me keep taking her out."

"Because I didn't think Summer would ever go for you." He squirms, trying to get out from under me, but I hold him there.

"Why wouldn't she go for me?"

I sit on him, holding his arms down with my knees. Then, as if I've reverted back to my ten-year-old self, I start knocking on Justin's forehead. He twists and tries to move his head, but he can't escape the knocking.

"Say uncle!" I call, giving him the code word for how to make all the knocking stop.

"Uncle!" he yells, and I sit up, thinking the fight is over, but Justin knees me and flips me over, gaining the advantage. Now he's the one sitting on me. "You always do this."

"Do what?" I wiggle, trying to get out from under him.

"You always want what I have. Even when we were kids, you just can't stand it when I have something better than you."

"Don't be stupid." I push his face away, but he grabs my arm, pinning it under his knee.

"Take it back!" He moves his cheeks like he's gathering spit.

"Take what back?"

"Take back that you have a crush on Summer, or I'll spit on you." He leans over my face, slowly releasing a trail of saliva from his mouth. The liquid precariously hangs in the air above me.

"I'm not taking it back. There are no take backs." I turn my face away. "Don't you dare spit on me!"

Just as I say the words, a drop of Justin's saliva hits my cheekbone. There's a pause as if we're both waiting to see how the other will react. That's when burst into laughter until he rolls off my body, landing on his back on the floor next to me.

I wipe my cheek with my sleeve. "I cannot believe you just spit on me."

"And I can't believe you played knuckles on my forehead."

We laugh again, chests heaving up and down from our stupid wrestling match. After a minute, the laughter fades, and we're left with our thoughts as we stare at the ceiling.

"I'm sorry I kissed Summer and liked it. Just so you know, it was the mistletoe."

"Why do people feel like that tradition is ironclad? Like if you don't kiss, the whole world will explode?"

"I don't know." I shake my head, letting a few more seconds of silence pass. "But the truth is, I wanted to kiss her." I turn my head to him. "You're right. I do have a crush on Summer." It's more than a crush, but I figure we'll take baby steps before I reveal how much I really feel about her.

"Yeah, I know." Justin pushes out a heavy sigh. "I've seen the way you look at her."

If how I look at Summer portrays even half of what I feel, then I'm in trouble.

"So if you're still unsure about her, and you think your relationship is headed nowhere, I'd love to have a chance to date her for real."

Justin's brows drop. A touch of anger flashes in his eyes. "Dude!"

"What? You told me a few weeks ago that you were unsure."

"I was unsure then, but after how cool she's been about my work schedule and how supportive she's been of me and my business the last few weeks, I realized that's important to me in a partner. And honestly, seeing how you look at her has opened my eyes. You've helped me see how great she really is."

Glad I could be of service.

Justin leans up on one elbow. "I know I've been busy and took her for granted, but I plan on making it up to her because I want me and Summer to work out. I really do love her."

That statement knocks the wind right out of me.

"So even though you have a crush on her"—Justin looks me right in the eyes—"you have to stand down."

"Stand down?'

"Yeah, for me."

I guess the finders-keepers rule doesn't apply here, no matter how much I want it to.

I came to Telluride to strengthen my relationship with Justin, but I hate how it's all shaking down. At the end of the day, he's my brother—my *twin* brother—and he's asking me to walk away. I'm being forced to bow out of this race no matter how much I don't want to.

"Yeah, of course." I extend my arm out. "I can stand down."

"Thanks." He takes my hand, shaking it. "You're a good brother."

But is being a good brother enough if I don't have Summer?

thirty-four

SUMMER

I GLANCE through the peephole in the door of my apartment.

It's Justin—apparently, he and Caleb didn't kill each other. Things looked pretty dicey when I left them wrestling on the floor an hour ago.

I draw in a steadying breath, uneasy about how this is going to go down.

I'm a cheater.

I cheat.

I knew this about myself from my ninth-grade biology class when I had to look at Corey Gillis's answers to pass the final, but I didn't know it would bleed into my love life as an adult.

Justin knocks again. "Summer, I know you're in there. I saw your eye in the peephole."

That's embarrassing and enough to cause me to pull the door open.

Justin dives into my arms, hugging me to him. At first, I'm taken aback. I expected a *how-dare-you* speech or even a *this-isn't-working* intro, leading him into a breakup speech. But a hug? I never saw that coming. I wrap my arms around him, and he sighs

—*sighs*—as if he's never been more content in his entire life, which seems crazy because I've never been less content.

"Can you forgive me?" he finally says.

My brows hover somewhere between confusion, and did I hear him right?

"Forgive you?" I pull back so I can see his face. "I'm the one that needs forgiveness."

"No." Justin shakes his head, stepping around me so he's all the way inside my apartment. He faces me just as I close the door. "I forced you into this silly swap with Caleb. It's all my fault."

"It's not all your fault. I agreed to it and let things go too far. I never should've—"

"I don't even care," Justin stops me. "Whatever happened between you and Caleb doesn't matter to me. All I care about is whether or not I've completely lost you." He steps toward me, taking my hands. "Have I been so absent that I lost you?"

I blink back at him. What is even happening? Five minutes ago, I had written off my love life completely, and now, Justin is in my apartment, looking at me like he used to, like he really *wants* to look at me.

"Summer?" he prods.

"Sorry." I shake my head. "I'm just so confused. Did I ruin your and Caleb's relationship?"

"No. In fact, we're better than ever."

Better than ever?

"How is that possible?"

"Come sit down, and I'll explain everything." He tugs me over to the couch, pulling me to sit next to him. "I've been a distracted idiot who took you for granted. I know that now. But I don't want to be that guy anymore. I want us to go back to how things used to be before, when I wasn't so bogged down with work." He smiles perfectly, squeezing my hand. "I love you, Summer."

This isn't the first time Justin has said that to me, but it does feel like one of the more sincere times. And although the sincerity is there, I'm lacking something. Fireworks maybe? The jolt of excitement I should feel when the man I love tells me he loves me too.

"What about Caleb?" I ask.

Probably not the best response after all the sweet things Justin just said to me. But I can't help it. Caleb's face was the first thing that flashed through my mind when Justin said he loved me.

"Don't worry about Caleb. He already said he was standing down. From now on, it will just be you and me."

"Caleb said that? He said he was 'standing down'?"

I hoped he would do the opposite, tell Justin he has feelings for me and fight for a chance to stay in the game. Unless he doesn't have feelings for me. Unless this whole swap was a game, a way to stay entertained while in Telluride.

"Yeah, Caleb knows he overstepped his bounds."

Overstepped his bounds. Standing down.

I thought—*wondered*—for a second if Caleb was the better brother for me. But it doesn't matter if he's the better brother for me. He's standing down. He doesn't want me. I should be happy about that. Happy because Justin is the steady one—the brother you marry. I was getting confused, but Caleb's disinterest clears everything right up. And I hate how much it hurts.

"So can you forgive me if I promise to never let my work come between us again?"

I blink back at him, willing my head and my heart to forget about Caleb.

"What about my family? They mean the world to me."

"I know, and I promise to try harder to get to know them better."

"And all my family parties?"

"I'll be there. Just make me a copy of that calendar you gave Caleb, or I'll just go steal it off his nightstand since he won't be needing it anymore."

Caleb still has my calendar? He acted like he lost it. What am I saying? It doesn't matter. He's probably already thrown it in the garbage and moved on from spending time with me like he moves from one trick to the next. I have to focus on Justin.

"I don't want you just to be there at my family functions. I want you to interact."

"I will." He lies back, pulling my body with him so we're cuddling on the couch. "I promise I'll be more present when I'm around them. You don't have to worry, Summer. This whole experience woke me up. I'm ready to be the man you want."

The man I want.

Justin kisses my forehead, and I smile up at him, even though in the back of my mind I know Caleb's really the man I want.

Too bad he doesn't want me back.

thirty-five

CALEB

THE LAST THREE days have been all about high adventure in Telluride. The biggest risks I could take, the fastest speeds I could reach, the highest point I could climb, but none of those activities did anything for my heart. It didn't dull the pain, quiet the memories, or ease the ache. I'm just as miserable as I was three nights ago when Justin said he loves Summer.

He freaking *loves* her.

And lucky for me, he realized it right in time.

Worst case scenario.

It takes Justin walking out his front door for me to realize that I'm just sitting in my Bronco in front of his condo like some kind of depressed lunatic. When he notices me in the front seat of my car, his steps pause, and he half-heartedly lifts his hands as part of an unspoken question of *What are you doing?* I push out a heavy breath and turn the car off. I grab my bag and coat and climb out, meeting him in front of it.

"Where did you go today?" he asks.

"Fat biking in the snow."

"Cool. I've always wanted to try that, but I don't really like the cold."

"Yeah, I know." That dislike put me in a hut alone with Summer, waking up with her in my arms. I try to mute the thought. "Where are you off to?"

"Uh..." He looks around awkwardly as if he feels dumb telling me. I want to say, 'Dude, I already know where you're going. I have a calendar with all the events that I can't seem to crumple up and throw away.' His eyes land on me again. "Dinner. It's Summer's dad's birthday."

"Oh, right." I try to smile because even though I'm hurting, I don't want to make things worse for Justin. The last few nights, he and Summer have been hanging out at her place instead of the condo, probably because they feel weird around me.

I don't know how long it will take for the weirdness to pass.

Maybe it never will.

Or maybe after Christmas, I can go somewhere across the world, away from Summer Stanworth and all my tormenting thoughts of her.

"Tell Marty happy birthday." I lift my coat kind of like a wave and head toward the house.

"What are you doing tonight?" he calls after me.

I shake my head, not even bothering to turn around. "Same old."

Because now that I don't have Summer to hang out with, I don't have anyone.

SUMMER

"Happy birthday, dear Dad! Happy birthday to you!" We all clap as my dad blows out his candles.

"We should've gotten him trick candles," Justin says beside

me. I smile at him, grateful he's trying with my family. He even turned his phone off tonight so he wouldn't be distracted. But as much as he's here, he's not Caleb, and I worry my family will notice.

"We don't do trick candles anymore," my mom says. Her eyes flick to Justin, but not in the warm way they used to look at Caleb. That warmth has faded as the night has gone on.

"Why not?" he asks, putting his arm around my shoulder and squeezing me into his side.

My mom eyes the gesture before answering. "One year, the trick candles flicked back on and lit the pinata on fire."

Justin laughs. "How?"

"It was sitting on the counter next to the cake," Anna explains. "I think it was Erin's fourteenth birthday."

"From that moment on, we've never had trick candles or pinatas," Juliet adds.

"That's wild." Justin smiles at me, and I smile back again.

This is what I wanted, so why doesn't it feel like I thought it would?

"So, Jeff, how often do you have to travel for work?" Justin nods in thanks at my mom when she hands him a plate of birthday cake.

"We talked about this last week, remember? I'd just gotten back from Atlanta."

"Right." He shakes his head, eyeing me. "I forgot."

"Justin, what did you think about that Black diamond trail at the top of the mountain?" Brian asks.

"I wouldn't know. I don't really ski."

Brian's face crumples into confusion. "The other day, at the hoedown, you said you were going to hit it tomorrow."

Rick leans forward, suddenly interested in the conversation. "Wait. I thought you loved to ski."

"Not really. That's more my brother." I nudge him with my knee under the table. "But yes," he quickly adds, thanks to my nudge. "I was going skiing but had to work instead, so I don't know about the Black hill."

"Black *diamond*," Brian corrects.

"Right." He tries a smile before taking a bite of his cake.

This is a nightmare.

Nobody tells you how difficult it's going to be to acclimate someone back in after a swap. I mean, it's probably the number-one reason why people don't do swaps—that and the fact that it's lying and toying with people's real emotions—but still, someone should've warned me.

Juliet and Hailey eye me from across the table, and it's the kind of stare-down that gives me sweaty pits. It's like they know. Not *know* know, because a twin swap is so far-fetched they wouldn't even consider it, but they're definitely suspicious about something.

I could tell my family, fess up to all my wrongs. It wouldn't be so bad now that Justin is fully committed to me, but it's easier just to pretend like it never happened and move forward in life with the real Justin by my side.

Aunt Carma slowly walks behind us, holding onto the back of the chairs for support.

"Where are you going, Aunt Carma?" I ask over my shoulder.

"To the bathroom," she mutters. "If I can make it there."

"Justin will help you." I nod at him, and he immediately jumps to his feet.

"I'd love to help."

She pushes his hand away. "I want the other Justin. I like him better."

"Uh..."—my eyes lock with his before shifting back to my aunt—"there isn't another Justin. I only have one boyfriend."

"One boyfriend, two personalities," Rick coughs under his breath. He said it so low I'm not even sure I heard him right until Juliet elbows him in the side. That's when I know for sure.

"Fine," she grunts, holding onto Justin's forearm. "You can stay."

I watch them walk out of the party room toward the back of the restaurant, where the bathrooms are. My eyes study the back of Justin. Even the way he walks and carries himself is different than Caleb. And suddenly, I panic that my family might know more than they're leading on.

CALEB

"OH, THIS IS A BAD IDEA," I SAY TO NO ONE OTHER THAN myself, and then I open the door and step inside the restaurant where the Stanworth family is currently having Marty's birthday dinner.

I hear them in the party room. You could hear this family from two miles away. But the universe sends me a lucky draw when I catch a glimpse of Justin escorting Aunt Carma to the bathroom. I wait until they round the corner before rushing to where they're at. I'm careful to keep my back to the party room. I'm not here to ruin anything for Summer. Although, I would give anything to see her, see what kind of holiday earrings she has on tonight and what shade of red she has spread across her lips.

I pop my head around the corner, making sure the coast is clear. It's so clear that even Justin is not here. He either went in the ladies' restroom with Carma, or he's in the men's room. My guess is on the men's room.

I push the bathroom door open, keeping my head on a swivel. Justin stands at a urinal, taking care of business.

"Don't freak out," I say, standing next to him.

The second he sees me, he swears.

"I said don't freak out."

He zips up his pants. "Caleb, what are you doing here? Summer's family is going to see you."

"I'm here because Jordan has been trying to get ahold of you all night."

"I have my phone turned off." He immediately pulls it out of his pocket and turns it back on.

"Your website crashed, and they can't access the rest of the orders. And if they don't have the orders—"

"They can't ship them out tomorrow in time for Christmas." Twenty texts ding one after the other once his phone comes to life. "I have to take care of this." He sets his phone down on the sink and starts unbuttoning his shirt.

"What are you doing?"

"You need to go out there for me so I can do this."

"No way." I step backward, shaking my head. "You told Summer we weren't doing this anymore. If she sees me, she'll probably hit me."

"Summer is not going to hit you. Besides, I'll text her and explain everything."

"Right, like you did the night of the Turkey Stuff. Where was her warning text that night?"

He takes his shirt off and hands it to me. "Put this on."

"No." I fold my arms. "I'm not doing it."

"Don't do it for me. Do it for Summer."

That's a low level of manipulation, but it works.

"Fine." I pull my Henley over my head and grab his shirt from him just as he drops his pants.

"We have to hurry. I'm sure Aunt Carma is almost done and will be waiting."

"I can't believe I'm doing this," I mutter.

"It will be fine." He grabs his phone, typing out a text while I finish getting his clothes on. "There." He holds the screen in front of me. "See. I already warned her."

I turn and look in the mirror, assessing our differences. "You have a five o'clock shadow, and I have full-on stubble. They're going to think you're some kind of werewolf that goes into the bathroom at night and starts growing hair."

"It will be fine. Nobody's paying attention to me that much."

Really? Because when I'm with her family, they pay a lot of attention to me. Never mind. This isn't a competition, and if it were, I already lost.

"Just fix your actual hair."

I get my fingers wet and slick my hands through my hair, pushing my waves down so they're a little more straight like Justin's.

"What are you doing in there?" Carma knocks on the bathroom door. "Did you fall in?"

"Crap, you better go." Justin pushes me toward the door. "I'll text you if I can make it back. If not, you'll have to drive Summer home." Before I can say anything, he opens the bathroom door and pushes me out.

Aunt Carma smiles. "Oh, you're back."

"I am," I say as I offer her my arm.

She pats my hand before holding on to me so we can walk back. "I like you better than the serious one."

I smile, knowing somehow Carma is on to us. "What about Summer? Who do you think she likes better?"

"Definitely you."

"Really?" I smile big.

"But what do I know? I'm only a silent investor."

"I'm upgrading you to a fifty-fifty partner."

"Tell that to the stuffy one. He'll fight you on it."

"Don't worry about him. He owes me."

I escort Carma to her seat. Actually, I don't even know which one is her seat, so I let her lead the way. Summer stands at the end of the table with her back to me. Her and her sisters are looking at some of her dad's birthday presents.

I could continue with Justin's plan and pretend to be him, but I don't want to pretend anymore, especially when he promised her the swap was over, and now, on their first real night together with her family, he bails. Summer's going to be massively hurt and disappointed when she sees me, and I don't want to make things worse by being Good Time Charlie when she's hurting.

There's only one option. I have to end things now.

"Hey, guys," I say, getting everyone's attention. Summer turns around with her sisters and goes bug-eyed when she sees me—she clearly didn't get Justin's message yet. I send a subtle nod in her direction, letting her know that everything will be okay. "I just had a huge catastrophe at work. Our website crashed, and without it up and running, my staff can't access the orders to get them fulfilled and in the mail by tomorrow morning, so I'm going to have to bail on the party a little early." I look at Marty with a teasing smile. "I had scheduled an exotic dancer to come out of a giant cake, but I'll have to cancel it and save it for next year."

Her dad chuckles. "That would give me a heart attack."

"What's an exotic dancer?" Jack asks Anna.

"Whoops." I give Anna an apologetic smile as I back up. "That's my cue to leave. I teach the children new things, then go to work."

"Well played." Brian gives him an air pound.

"In all honesty"—I look right at Summer—"I am really sorry that I have to leave. It was my intention to stay the entire evening with you guys. If there wasn't a huge emergency at work, I wouldn't be leaving. I'm really sorry."

There.

I said what Justin should say if he were here.

And now I'll leave so Summer doesn't have to keep pretending.

I give her a slight smile as I make my exit.

"Wait," she says as she gathers her things and kisses her dad on his cheek. "I'll go with you."

Those simple words lift my entire world.

SUMMER

"You didn't need to leave the party," Caleb says as he pulls out of the restaurant parking lot.

I watch the lights of the town pass by through my window. "It's fine. The party was winding down anyway."

"Did you read Justin's text?"

"Yeah, when you were scraping the snow off the car." I sit back in my chair, annoyed that he once again chose work over me. Things were supposed to be different. He promised.

"I know what you're thinking."

"You don't." I shake my head because my head and my heart are so confused, I don't even know what I'm thinking.

"You're disappointed that Justin left. But it's my fault. He didn't even know about the work thing. I came over to the restaurant. I was the one who told him about the crisis. He never would've known about it if it wasn't for me."

I turn to look at him. "Then why did you do it?"

"I don't know. I wish that I hadn't. If I could go back, I would let him figure it out when the night was over."

"How did you find out?"

"Jordan told me."

"I get it." I turn my head to the window again. "You just wanted to help her."

"No." He taps his fingers on the steering wheel as if he's frustrated. "Me coming here had nothing to do with Justin or Jordan. I think, deep down, I hoped I'd get to see you."

I keep my eyes on the window, avoiding Caleb's probing stare. Because if I look at him, I'll end up asking why he didn't want me and that's the last thing I should be asking or wondering about. I'm with Justin. I did all of this so I could be with Justin. He's the end game.

"I know you're mad, but be mad at me. Don't be mad at Justin."

"I'm mad at the situation. You know, he didn't have to go through the trouble of changing clothes and having you come out. He could've just told me. Told my family." I finally look at him. "Like you did."

"I told your family because I don't want to pretend anymore."

I smile, but it's full of sadness. "I don't either."

thirty-six

CALEB

"HERE WE ARE." I pull into Summer's apartment complex.

"Thanks for the ride." She immediately grabs the door handle like she's going to jump ship while the car is still rolling to a stop.

I wish I could do something to help the situation. I hate seeing her like this.

"Hey, hey." I touch her arm, causing her eyes to dart to my hand. "I'll walk you to your door."

"That's okay. It's not necessary." She's climbing out of the Bronco while I put it in park and turn off the ignition.

I catch up to her just before she reaches the stairwell. "Why are you in such a hurry? Do you really want to get away from me that bad?"

"No, I'm just tired of all of this." She stops walking and faces me. Gentle snowflakes fall from the sky, looking more threatening when they drift into the light of the lamppost. "I just want it all to be easy."

"What?"

"Love and relationships."

"It's not supposed to be easy."

"It was easy for my sisters and for Vivian."

289

"You're on the outside looking in on their relationships. The grass is always greener on the other side."

"Well, I want green grass." She throws her arms out, dips her head back, and yells into the night sky and falling snow. "Why can't falling in love be easy?"

I look at her with the moonlight on her face, puffs of cold air drifting away from her mouth each time she breathes, and I can't help myself or stop myself.

"I love you." Her head pops up, and she looks at me. "I wasn't planning on telling you that—it just came out. But now that I've said it, I can't take it back. I love you so much it hurts."

Her brows fold together, and tears fill her eyes. "What are you—"

"I know it's not what you want to hear, but I just need you to know. At least once. You asked why falling in love can't be easy. Falling in love with you was the easiest thing I've ever done. So easy that I didn't even know it was happening at first, and then I did, but I didn't care because you're you, and you fit perfectly with me."

"No." She shakes her head as one tear falls down her cheek. "You can't say that. Justin is—"

"My brother. I know. Justin is my brother, and he's a great guy too, but that doesn't stop me from loving you."

Another tear falls. "What am I supposed to do with that? It's crazy." She puffs out a humorless laugh as a new tear drips down her face.

I step in front of her, holding her ice-cold hands. "It is crazy. But I'd rather our love story be crazy than easy."

"*Our* love story? Caleb, he's your twin brother."

"I know, and it sucks." My eyes go misty. "It sucks big time. Trust me, no one knows how much it sucks more than me. But I still want you, despite the messiness, despite the hurt feelings, because you're happy, caring, sweet, fun, silly, and you've made me fall in love with Christmas and your family right alongside falling in love with you."

"I can't." Two tears fall, and she swipes the remnants away. "I can't do that to him. Being with Justin was always the end plan. It's the entire reason we did the swap."

"Justin will be fine."

"How do you know?"

"Because he doesn't love you like I do. And he certainly doesn't make you happy."

"I'm happy."

"You're not. Not like you are when you're with me." I place my hands on her shoulders, dipping my head down to see into her eyes. "Summer, we could be wild and crazy and madly in love together. Just imagine it. Imagine how happy we'd be together."

She shakes her head, her voice shaky from emotion. "You only think you're in love with me because it's Christmas."

"Don't do that." I pull back.

"No, it's true. It's just the magic of the season that's making you feel this way."

"Don't say that." It's my turn to shake my head. "I don't want you to say that, because I know these feelings between us aren't because of Christmas magic. They're real. You've felt them too." I gently cup her cheeks. "I know you've felt it too. I've seen it in your eyes."

Her face is stone, except for the tears as she keeps up with her same reverie. "When the holidays are over, and you go back to your regular life, you're going to realize I'm right."

"I don't want to go back to my regular life. I want to spend my life with you."

"Caleb." Her lip quivers with emotion, and I know what she's about to say. "Caleb, I can't." She shrugs innocently, like the thousand other innocent things I've watched her do the last few weeks. "I can't do that to Justin. It's not possible."

I drop my hands. "You're taking the easy way out."

More tears spill down her cheeks. "It doesn't feel easy."

"You're making a mistake." I shake my head. "He doesn't love you like I do."

"Stop saying that." She closes her eyes, squeezing the moisture out. "You don't know that."

"I know he doesn't appreciate all the little things I love about you. How you toss your hair to one side without even knowing it. How you match different shades of red lipstick to whatever color you're wearing that day. How you think of others and react with genuineness every time." Her lips tremble as tears roll down her face one after the other, but I don't stop. I can't walk away until she understands how much I completely adore her. "Justin doesn't stay awake at night and wonder what kind of earrings you'll be wearing the next day. Or look at the cute calendar you made a hundred times a day just to make sure he doesn't miss one second of hanging out with you. Or wish that you'd make him a calendar full of cute little graphics for every single month of the year, just as proof that you're going to spend every day together. He doesn't love how you're up for anything, even if it means getting yourself kicked out of somewhere. He doesn't appreciate how happy you are or how your sunshine touches everyone around you. And I know he doesn't appreciate your love and devotion to your family like I do."

Summer still shakes her head like my words aren't enough, so I say more, hoping that something will make her see. "I get it. You've been together a long time. So it might feel easier to stay with him. But, Summer, I don't need nine months to get to know you. It only took me a few days to fall head over heels for you."

"But you don't even live here. You have an adventurous life all around the world. That's not me. That's not who I am."

"Do you think I care about any of that?" I grab her hands again. "You're what I've been missing. You're the relationship that I want to create and put first. I only want to be right where you are."

She looks down at our joined hands and then lifts her head, eyes brimming with fresh tears. "I'm sorry," she whispers.

One second, I was floating through the sky, feeling the rush of adrenaline. And then the next second, my parachute didn't open, and I hit the ground, my heart breaking into a million little pieces.

I let go of her fingers and take a step back, tears taking over my vision.

"Caleb, I'm so sorry," she whispers again.

"It's okay." I blink, sending moisture trickling down my face. I try smiling even though the action betrays the heartache crushing my chest. "I had to try, right?"

"I don't know—"

"You don't have to say anything." I wipe my cheeks, trying to regain a shred of manliness. We stare at each other, snowflakes falling around us, melting on tear-stained cheeks. This is the end of the road for me and Summer. I know I need to walk away. But how do you walk away from the woman you love?

You just do it.

Because you don't have any other choice.

I nod once—the only goodbye I can muster.

Then I turn and leave.

SUMMER

THE VERSION OF SUMMER THAT EATS AN ENTIRE PAN OF brownies has returned.

And I changed into sweats—a must for any woman who is sad and eating her feelings.

My apartment is dark, except for the low glow of Christmas lights strung around my tree and hanging across my ceiling. I have Kenny G's *Miracles* Christmas album softly playing in the background. It sets the mood—kind of. There's not a Christmas album out there that could entirely capture my sadness, confusion, hurt, aching, and pain.

Two hard knocks on my door cause me to jump.

My heart explodes with a nervous excitement I can't explain.

It's almost like I'm hoping it is Caleb and hoping that my answer will be different this time.

I fling open the door.

It's the other Davidson brother.

Justin stands before me in Caleb's clothes, and I don't know what happens, but I lose it. Tears pour out of me like it's Niagara Falls.

"I'm sorry, babe." He opens his arms, and I fall into his chest, sobbing against the smell of Caleb's shirt. I soak in the scent, wishing I was a sponge that could hold it forever.

Justin brushes his hand over my hair and gently helps me to the couch.

"Shh. It's all going to be okay." He drags me down so I'm leaning against him, cradled in his arms. I cry like that until I fall asleep, until I'm no longer able to feel the weight of sadness that saying goodbye to Caleb caused.

thirty-seven

SUMMER

I DIDN'T TELL Justin about Caleb's love confession the other night or tell him that was the real reason I sobbed for hours in his arms. Justin thought it was about him letting me down, and I didn't feel it necessary to drive a wedge between the relationship. So I let it go. I don't care.

That's been my motto this last week since my dad's birthday party.

I don't care, because caring about things I can't control got me into this mess where I feel confused and sick to my stomach all the time. So, I'm trying something new.

If Justin chooses work over me, I don't care.

If my family hates Justin, I don't care.

If I'm not happy all the time, I don't care.

If love isn't what I built up in my mind, I don't care.

If I chose the wrong brother, I don't care.

At least I won't have to be alone.

Besides, not caring has its benefits. There's less smiling and pleasing everyone. There's less disappointment because you're already planning on your expectations not being met.

Yes, this is the new *indifferent* Summer.

"Summer?" my mom says, and I snap my head up, remembering I'm on table-setting duty.

"Sorry." I glance at the plates in the china cupboard in my parents' dining room.

"Do we need Christmas plates for the little kids, or do you want them to eat on paper plates?" I start counting, making sure my mom has enough.

"Summer?" she says behind me.

I hold my finger up, still mid-count.

"Summer," she repeats my name but this time with a little more force behind it, causing me to turn over my shoulder and look at her. She's wearing a Christmas apron with a dish towel thrown over her shoulder. Her eyes look sad, full of worry.

"What's wrong?"

"That's what I wanted to ask you."

"Nothing's wrong. It's my birthday and Christmas Eve—the best day of the year—why would anything be wrong?"

"That's what I've been asking myself. This is usually your favorite day, so I can't figure out why you look so sad." She shifts her weight, placing her hand on her hip. "It's about Justin, isn't it?"

"No, I don't care about Justin." I wince, catching how bad that sounds. "I mean, everything's fine with Justin."

"He's going to propose to you tonight. Did you know that?"

"What?" I gasp, abandoning the Christmas plates and facing her.

"He came over last night and asked us for your hand in marriage."

I cover my mouth with my fingers, then drop them enough to speak. "What did you say?"

I half expect my mom to have turned him down.

"What did you want us to say?"

"Yes?"

"Why are you answering like you're asking me?"

"I'm not." I straighten, fixing my tone so my answer comes

out the way it's supposed to. "Of course I want you guys to give your permission. To say yes. You know how much I want to get married."

"That's what worries me. You are so eager to get to the next phase of life that you're willing to settle." She shakes her head, moving her finger back and forth. "Actually, I take that back. I'm not sure if you're settling or not. One minute, I think Justin's the perfect guy for you, and I tell myself to relax, and then the next minute, there are twenty thousand red flags, and it's all I can do to keep my mouth shut and not warn you."

"Not this again." I roll my eyes, dropping into the dining room chair. "Mom, Justin is a good guy."

She pulls out the chair next to mine and places it in front of me, sitting down. "I never said he wasn't a good guy. But you'd be dumb not to look at his flaws and at least think about whether or not you can handle his emotional roller coaster your entire life."

"What emotional roller coaster?"

"Summer, I know what's going on here."

"You do?" I'm half relieved the secret is out and half scared. She lifts her chin. "Justin is bipolar."

"Oh, no." I drop my head into my hands.

"Don't tell me you haven't noticed it too. One night, he's the life of the party, and then the next time we see him, he's serious and formal and doesn't remember anything from the last conversation. It's like he's a completely different person."

That's because he is a completely different person.

"It's bizarre. No wonder you're so sad all the time. It's difficult dealing with mentally imbalanced people."

"Mom"—I laugh, shaking my head—"Justin is..."

"I don't know why you're laughing. Mental illness isn't funny. It's real, and he needs help."

"I know that," I defend, not wanting to seem like I'm making light of the situation, but that isn't happening here. It's time to tell her the truth as soon as she lets me get a word in. "I can explain—"

"Summer, you don't have to shoulder this burden alone."

"Mom."

"No, let me say this." She holds her hand up. "Justin and his split personalities are a lot to take on. You don't have to agree to marry him tonight. You can, and you *should* take some time to think about if you can handle it. And in the meantime, I suggested to Justin that he get on some medication if he isn't already—you know, to control the swings in his personality."

"Oh, my gosh! You did not tell him that." I'm dying. In my efforts to make things easy, I've made them more difficult than climbing Mt. Everest.

"I did. I told him that I would give him my blessing if I saw more of the side of him that really cherished you. The guy that came to the Turkey Stuff, the light parade, family game night with *flaw*tas, Noel Night, or even the Mistletoe-Down. Those were the times I saw how good you two are together. I saw it in his eyes and in yours—you love each other. But every other time, you both had lost the light, the spark between you. So I told him he needed to look at his medication doses or see what he did those particular days to control his mood swings, and if we can get that side of him always, I'd be happy to welcome him into the family."

Everything she's mentioning are times when Caleb was with me. Not Justin. I don't even know what to make of that, and I can't think through it right now because if I don't stop my mom, she'll have Justin committed to a mental hospital before the end of this conversation.

"Mom!" I put my hands on her shoulders to get her attention.

"What?"

"Justin does not have bipolar disorder."

"Are you sure?"

"I'm sure."

"Then I don't know what to think!" She throws her arms up, moving my hands off her. "We've all been trying to figure this out. I mean, Juliet even suggested that maybe there are two of them—

you know because of the twin brother. But that's just crazy. Summer, the whole thing is crazy!"

I knew Juliet was sniffing this out.

My mom puts her hands on my knees again, looking me in the eye. "But if I knew that he was going to be the good Justin all the time, I wouldn't hesitate to give him our blessing. Because when he's good, he's really good for you. And when he's the other guy, you're not your best self. I want him to make you happy all of the time, not just some of the time. You're my baby girl."

I close my eyes, drawing in a steadying breath.

"There's something I need to tell you about the guy you're describing. The good version of Justin that you love."

"Okay."

"He's not bipolar. He's—"

"Hello?" The front door opens, and a lot of noise fills the house. "We're here!"

My mom gets a guilty expression. "It's Erin." She glances at the clock. "They just got here from Denver."

I love how she's explaining it to me as if I didn't know Erin and Tommy were driving in for Christmas Eve.

"It's okay," I say, pulling her to a stand. "I can explain things later."

"No, just quickly tell me."

"It's not something that I can just quickly say."

"Grandma?" Cora calls.

"Go." I smile, pushing her toward the living room.

"Okay, but we'll talk later. Don't marry him until we've talked."

I think she means *don't say yes to his proposal until we talk,* but I wave her away anyway.

I sit, letting our conversation sink in for a second.

Justin is going to propose.

My mom thinks he's bipolar.

And she wants me to be with the guy that's been hanging around all holiday season.

My *I don't care* motto isn't going to solve this problem.

CALEB

"HAVE YOU EVER TASTED BETTER EGGNOG THAN THIS?"
My dad lifts his glass to me.

I stare at him for a second. "Why are you always trying to compete for the best meal or drink?"

"Because I do have the best eggnog around."

I hold my cup up to him. "You're right. It is the best."

"I'm going to let the beef brisket cook a little longer." My mom breezes into the room and sits on the edge of the couch. She twists her fingers like she's anxious.

"Mom," I say with a smile, "you don't have to be nervous about the food. We'll eat whenever it's ready."

"I'm not nervous about the food."

"Then what is it? You've been high-strung ever since I got here."

She looks at my dad.

He kicks out his recliner, leaning back. "Just tell him. He's going to find out anyway."

I glance between them. "Tell me what?"

"Well, it's supposed to be a surprise. But..." She hesitates just enough that my anticipation is at an all-time high. "Justin stopped by this morning and picked up Grandma's ring. He's proposing to Summer tonight." She smiles at me, but the longer she stares at my expression, her smile drops. Something on my face gives it away. "Oh, no." Her shoulders fall. "You love Summer too."

"No." I shake my head, intending to lie, but then I decide that it's not worth lying to my parents. "Okay, fine." I sigh. "I love Summer too."

My mom nods in her wise way. "That's why."

"What?"

"That's why Justin wanted the ring all of a sudden. He's proposing to Summer so you can't have her. It's just like when you were kids. If you had something, he wanted it. If he had something, you wanted it."

"Mom, that's not what's happening here."

"Then tell me why Justin has spent the last nine months saying things weren't serious with her, and then the second you show interest, he's asking for her hand in marriage?"

"I hope you're wrong." I stand, swiping my hand through my hair. "For Summer's sake, I really hope you're wrong."

"Maybe I am wrong." My mom wrings her hands again. "I just thought it seemed really sudden."

I rub my hands over my face. I thought it seemed sudden too. Not the timeline. Just his jump in feelings.

"What are you going to do?" my dad asks.

"Nothing." I place my hands on my hips, looking out the window without really seeing anything. "Summer already made her choice."

"Justin said they might stop by later tonight, after he proposes."

My eyes dart to my mom. "I can't be here. Not right now."

"Where will you go?"

"I think I'll go up the mountain. Maybe ski a little."

"On Christmas Eve?" my mom gasps. "Caleb."

"Don't worry." I hug my mom close. "I'll be fine. I just need to get out of here for a little bit."

thirty-eight

SUMMER

"CORA'S GOING to be Mary, and Peter will be Joseph." My mom taps each one of them on their heads as she sets up our own family nativity play.

"Lucy can be baby Jesus!" Jack points to his little sister.

"Yes, and Berkley can be an angel."

"What about Aunt Carma?" Peter asks. "Who can she be?"

"She's the angry innkeeper who has no room," Jeff answers.

Aunt Carma sits in her recliner across the room with her eyes closed. "I heard that."

"She has no room but great hearing." Brian laughs.

I tip my lips upward, almost smiling.

"Hey." Justin leans in, whispering in my ear. "Is everything okay? You seem distracted."

"Everything's great." I smile at him like I'm perfectly calm, even though a tornado whirls around in my chest.

We made it through dinner without Justin proposing, and I'd be pretty surprised if he got down on one knee during the nativity story. So it must be after. After this, he's going to propose.

"Okay, birthday girl. I was just checking." His sweetness is killing me.

I can't breathe. It's like there's something wrong with my lungs, and my chest, and my freaking heart.

"You know"—I suddenly stand—"I think I'll go to the restroom before the play starts."

"Do you want me to come with you?" I know he's asking because he'd rather die than be left here all alone with my family.

"No, that's okay. I'll be right back."

I feel my mom's eyes on me as I exit the family room. I pass the bathroom and head straight to the stairs, taking them two at a time until I am upstairs in my old bedroom. I flip on the lights and pace the room. There are pictures of me and my sisters growing up and a few of me and Vivian. I stop and stare at one picture in particular. It's of Vivian and me on the last day of ninth grade. We were so young and naive about love back then. It was easy to be that way. We didn't know the mess life would throw at us like falling in love with twin brothers. I brush my hand over the photo, wishing I could go back to that time when love and happily ever afters were simple. Fifteen-year-old Summer stares back at me, jogging my memory, and I'm suddenly digging through my drawers, searching for my old journal and the list of qualities I wanted in a husband that I wrote out long ago, before I knew Justin and Caleb, before my heart and mind were confused —back when falling in love was simple.

I toss old clothes and knick-knacks aside, desperate to find the book, as if that one list holds the answers to all my problems. At the bottom, under everything else, I see a glimpse of the blue book with sheep jumping over the moon. I pull it out, flipping to the back, to the page that I started when I was fourteen, after my friend's mom told me and Vivian that if we wanted to find the man of our dreams, we needed to start making a list of what we were looking for. My desire to grow up and get married led me to go straight home and start thinking of things. Unlike Vivian, who wrote down every single positive trait out there, I only added qualities that were really important to me. And each year, as I got older, I would add a new item that I discovered meant a lot to me, either from watching my sisters date or from dating boys in high school.

It's been ten years since I've read the list.

I can't even remember what's on it, but the second I turn to it, I see written in big, bolded letters: *My Future Husband.* I smile as I trace the words and my cutesy teenage handwriting.

1. Handsome.
2. Makes me laugh.
3. Makes me want to be a better person.
4. Is happy and makes me happy.
5. The life of the party.
6. Adventurous.
7. Kind and thoughtful.
8. Loves my family and they love him.
9. Very, very rich.

I think item number nine was heavily driven by my teenage immaturity, but everything else holds true to what I really want. And by the time I get to the last item, a single tear trickles down my cheek.

10. Adores me and tells people he adores me.

Somewhere over the years, I lost sight of the things that really matter to me in a partner. My mom is right. I have been settling for the last few years, dating anyone that I could so that I didn't have to be alone. Then I found Justin, and I thought that he was everything I was looking for. I'd finally found my happily ever after. I wanted it so badly that I convinced myself our problems were temporary. I even convinced myself that I was happy. But I'm not happy—not with Justin anyway.

When I look at this list, I don't think of Justin.

I think of Caleb.

I mean, they're identical twins, so item number one is pretty well covered either way, but Caleb is the one who makes me laugh and challenges me to be better. His enthusiasm for life is contagious, and he's always the first one to turn any activity into a party. Sometimes, he's more adventurous than I can even keep up with, but I like that he pushes me to try new things. He's always thinking of me and remembers what I like or what I've said. My family likes him better than me, and I'm pretty sure Caleb is fond of them too.

But the most important one is that he adores me. I can see it in the way he smiles when I do something silly or immature and feel it in his sweet touches, but it's how he says it so boldly and out loud without shame that really lets me know how he feels.

I forgot that I wanted that in a man.

Or maybe I gave up thinking that actually existed.

But it does exist, and it's what I want.

Up until this moment, I haven't allowed myself to really think about what I really want. Because what I wanted seemed wrong. You can't fall for your boyfriend's twin brother. It's a cardinal sin —the number one rule when it comes to love and family relationships. Falling for your boyfriend's twin is crazy, but Caleb has convinced me I want crazy. I don't want a good enough relationship with Justin. I want wild and exciting. Because that's how love should be. And I've finally woken up and realized it.

thirty-nine

SUMMER

WHEN I WALK into the living room, all heads turn to me. I glance around, feeling a little offended that they're being so blatantly rude about how long my bathroom visit was—and it wasn't even a bathroom visit.

"What?" I say in defense.

That's when Justin's head pops up. I didn't see him at first. It's like he was leaning over to tie his shoe.

Oh, my gosh.

He's kneeling on one knee, not tying his shoe.

He's proposing right in the middle of the nativity play. Something about that feels really sacrilegious.

My heart pounds, each beat saying, *You love Caleb. You love Caleb.*

I reach my arms out in a panic. "I don't want you to propose!"

The lines on Justin's forehead crease. "Uh, I wasn't. I spilled my drink all over your mom's carpet and was trying to clean it up."

My eyes shoot around the room to my family. "Then why is everyone staring at me?"

"Because your boyfriend spilled cranberry juice all over mom's

307

carpet," Anna says, and I get it. The carpet is only four months old—the pride of my mother's heart. Second only to her bedspread and decorative pillows.

"I wouldn't marry this one either," Aunt Carma huffs from her recliner in the corner. "I'd hold out for the other one with the Wrangler butt."

"Wait." Justin straightens, coming to a stand. "Did you say you *don't* want me to propose?"

Oh.

I really jumped the gun on that one.

But at this point, I have to rip it off like a Band-Aid. Like one of the really adhesive kinds that will leave gray sticky residue on my skin if I don't just take care of it immediately.

So that's what this is. I'm taking care of everything in one sweep. I'm letting Justin down. I'm owning up to my deceit.

"I don't want you to propose because, over the last few weeks, I fell in love with your brother."

"I knew it!" Juliet squeals, punching Rick in the shoulder. "I told you that the twin is Justin."

"The twin is Justin?" My dad leans forward like he can't follow. "Then who's the twin?"

"You love Caleb?" Justin stares blankly back at me.

"Who's Caleb?" my mom interjects.

"The twin," Hailey says.

My dad shakes his head. "I thought the twin is Justin."

"Dad, shh!" Erin shushes him so she can hear me and Justin talk.

"I didn't mean to fall in love with him," I try to explain to Justin amid the noise, but how do you explain something like this? "It just happened. We spent so much time together, and you were always working."

"Oh, my gosh!" Erin sighs. "It's like *While You Were Sleeping*."

"Except this one is While You Were *Working*." Tommy laughs at his joke before he even gets it all out.

"So it's my fault you fell in love with my brother?" Justin's ability to tune out my family is pretty impressive.

"No, I'm not saying it's your fault. But you can't be surprised. You sent us off on date after date—with your blessing—while Caleb pretended to be my fake boyfriend. Love is blind, but not *that* blind."

"You have a fake boyfriend?"

"Dad!" Juliet exclaims. "Keep up. Summer pretended to date Justin's brother so that…" She pauses, turning to me. "I actually have no idea why you would do that."

"Because I was sick of defending Justin to all of you. Every time he didn't come to a family party, you were all so disappointed and told me over and over that he didn't really love me. And look"—I gesture to Justin—"he proposed. See? I told you he loved me."

"For the record, I did not propose. I was on one knee to clean up the fruit punch."

"Cranberry juice," Aunt Carma corrects as if Justin's beverage is of utmost importance right now.

"My mom said you were going to propose tonight."

Justin flips his head to her like he's disappointed she couldn't keep one little secret.

"I had to tell Summer." She stands by her gossip. "You were like two different people."

"He *was* two different people," Hailey adds.

My dad frowns. "Justin was two different people?"

All four of my sisters turn, chastising him in unison. "Dad, keep up!"

"Well, which one do I like?"

"You like the twin, Caleb," my mom says to him.

Justin throws his arms out. "Do you have to pick favorites right now? Because I can hear you."

"Can we go somewhere to talk privately?" I grab his arm, pulling him out of the line of fire from my family and into the kitchen. He keeps his head down, avoiding my gaze. "Justin, look at me." His blue eyes reluctantly drift to mine. "I really am so sorry."

"Was this your plan all along? Get me around your family just to humiliate me as payback for never getting to know them?"

"No." I reach for him to try and console him, but he pulls away. I don't blame him. I just blew up Christmas and our relationship and the Davidson family. It was quite a bomb that I dropped. "I shouldn't have said anything in front of everyone, but I saw you on one knee, and after what my mom said, I just thought you were asking me to marry you."

"I was going to wait until later when we were alone."

"Honestly, I'm surprised that you thought proposing was a good idea."

"I thought it was a good idea because I thought that's what you wanted." The bitterness in his words makes me feel terrible.

"It is what I wanted. One month ago, I would've given anything to have you ask me to marry you." I gaze at Justin, seeing traces of the man I fell in love with months ago. His drive, ambition, and need to succeed all attracted me to him—until those same qualities sucked the life out of our relationship. I can see that now.

"So if Caleb hadn't come along, everything would've been fine?"

"We had problems way before Caleb showed up. We both know an engagement between us would've been for the wrong reasons. For me: so that I wouldn't be alone anymore and could finally get married. And you: a proposal out of duty, something to appease me, a reward for putting up with your crazy work schedule. Eventually, our real wants and needs would've come through, and we would've ended things. I'm just glad we didn't waste even more time not saying how we really feel for the sake of being polite."

"Summer, I was ready to commit to you, and I was going to try and be around more."

"I know, but I don't want to ask you for more than you're

able to give right now, and you don't want to feel guilty all the time when you don't meet my high expectations. That's not how either of us wants to live our lives."

Justin doesn't immediately say anything. He just looks down, running his hand over the countertop. "Caleb loves you." He looks up. "Did you know that?"

I nod.

"So I guess it's my turn to stand down?"

"I don't want this to ruin your relationship with him."

He laughs, but no smile accompanies it. "Caleb is my twin brother. It would take more than a woman to break us apart. We're family."

"So you're not mad at him?"

"I didn't say that. I'm furious with him. I might even punch him the next time I see him. He deserves it. He stole my girlfriend right out from under me. I definitely will punch him next time I see him." The corner of his mouth lifts like he's teasing. "But he's a good guy, and I've seen the way he looks at you. He can give you more than I can right now."

It's like he's giving us his blessing without actually saying he's giving us his blessing.

I pull Justin into a hug. "I think you're going big places, and I can't wait to see all of your hard work pay off."

His arms wrap around me, and we hug in my parents' kitchen for a few minutes, letting this moment be the end of us—something that should've happened months ago.

But at least it's happening now. Before it's too late.

I COME INTO THE LIVING ROOM. MY FAMILY IS QUIETER than ever before as they watch me.

"Justin left. I snuck him out the garage so he didn't have to face all of you and the embarrassment."

"We know," my mom says. "We had Peter sneak a cell phone in while you were talking and leave it on the kitchen table. We heard your whole conversation through the speakerphone." She holds up another phone, showing me. "I think Justin took it pretty well."

"So do I," Juliet agrees. "All things considered."

My mouth falls open. "I can't believe you guys. That was a private conversation."

"Really?" Anna folds her arms. "You're going to judge us when you've been lying for weeks about who Justin—or should I say *Caleb*—really is."

"That's fair." I bite my lip. "Should we just call it even?"

"Summer, it's sad that you thought you had to go to such great lengths to make us like Justin."

"You guys are the most important people to me. I need you to love whomever I love."

My mom steps toward me, placing her hands on my shoulders. "Well, we love Caleb."

"I do too." I smile as tears gather in my eyes.

"Then let's go get him," she says.

"Right now?"

"Yes!" my family says together.

"What better time is there to go after the man you love than Christmas Eve?" Erin smiles. "Plus, I want to see it, so you need to do it while I'm in town."

"Call it a birthday present to yourself," Juliet encourages.

"I think he's at his parents' house. That's probably where Justin is headed. I can't show up there and confess my love to Caleb after I just broke Justin's heart. They're mom will kill me."

"Sure you can!" my dad says as he jumps to his feet. "And I'll drive you."

"I'm coming too!" Peter bounces up and down.

"We'll all go in the van." My dad gestures for everyone to come with him.

"We can't all fit in the van," I protest.

312

"It's a twelve-passenger van!"

"Yeah, and there's like twenty of us."

"Try me." He marches out the front door, and before I can stop them, my family is up and following after my dad.

And I guess I wouldn't have it any other way.

If I'm confessing my love, my family may as well be there to witness it. I owe them that much.

forty

SUMMER

"CALEB IS NOT AT HIS HOUSE!" I yell to my dad in the driver's seat. "His mom said he left four hours ago to go skiing by Mountain Village."

My dad immediately spins the steering wheel, turning the car in the opposite direction. We all go flying, trying to brace ourselves by holding onto the rows of seats.

"Marty!" my mom yells. "This isn't a car chase, and half of us don't have seatbelts on."

"I'm just trying to get Summer to Mountain Village before Caleb leaves."

"The traffic is going to be terrible," Jeff says. "Tonight is the Christmas Eve Torchlight Parade, where they ski down the mountain, lighting it with torches."

Brian seems more excited about that community event than he is about my love life. "I've always wanted to go to that."

"The mountain is going to be closed for skiing." I bend lower, trying to look out the window. "We're never going to find him."

"Try calling him again," my mom says from the front seat of the van.

I shake my head. "His phone is off."

"What did his mom say?" Rick asks from the back seat. "Was she mad that you turned her sons against each other?"

"I did not turn her sons against each other," I say over my shoulder. "Patsy was very sweet and understanding about it."

"You fell in love with your boyfriend's twin, and you're telling me that the mom was sweet and understanding about it?"

"Shut up, Rick!" I snap.

Peter pokes my arm. "Aunt Summer, we don't say shut up."

"I'm sorry, buddy." I ruffle his hair. "You're right."

"Mom, you need to wash Summer's mouth out with soap," Peter tells Anna.

"Soap? Really?" I look at my sister. "That's kind of a harsh punishment."

"Maybe we should wash Summer's mouth out with soap because she kissed her boyfriend's twin brother," Rick snickers from the back row again.

"Shut up, Rick!" Juliet barks at her husband.

"I'm going to park here." My dad quickly jerks the car to the right, illegally double-parking in front of a red zone.

My mom frowns. "Marty, you'll get a ticket."

"I'll expense it to the company," Aunt Carma says from the very back of the van where there's no seats. I almost forgot she came with us.

Everyone seems satisfied with that answer, even though Carma has no authority to expense a parking ticket, and they all shuffle out of the van like one of those clown cars.

"Get in line for a gondola." Tommy rushes ahead, fighting the crowd. "It looks like they just shut down the mountain for skiing so they can light the torches. If Caleb is here, we might be able to find him at the bottom of the hill."

We wait our turn, squeezing into one gondola again. It's standing room only.

I'm pressed against the window, looking down at the large crowd gathered for the Torchlight Parade. "This isn't going to work. We'll never find him with all of these people."

"Who are we looking for?" Jack asks. His little nose presses against the glass.

"Caleb." I shake my head, realizing there's no way my little nephew would know him by that name. "I mean Justin. You know, that guy you love playing with?"

"He's right there." Jack points out the window.

The gondola gets even more crowded as everyone pushes forward to see where Jack points. They all start talking at once.

"I don't see him."

"Where is he?"

"Jack, where are you pointing?"

His little finger hits the glass. "Right there. In that other gondola coming down the mountain."

My eyes follow Jack's finger, and in another gondola going down the mountain, across from ours, stands Caleb. Our eyes catch as we slide past each other. It takes him a second to notice me in the stuffed gondola, but when he does, his hands press against the glass. I smile, and he smiles, but we're moving away from each other faster than we can communicate, and as quickly as I see him, he disappears from my sight.

My heart sinks. I missed him.

"Well, that was anticlimactic," Aunt Carma huffs. She's the only one who's actually sitting in a seat comfortably. "I guess we should just go home."

"No!" Erin groans. "We are seeing this out before I have to go back to Denver tomorrow night."

My phone vibrates in my back pocket. I grab it, seeing Caleb's face on the screen.

"It's him!" I scream with excitement, and my sisters do the same. "Caleb?"

"Summer?"

"Caleb?" I can barely hear him with how loud my family is being. I try plugging my ear, but it doesn't help. "Caleb?"

"Summer? I'll come to you."

"You'll come to me?"

"Yes, get off at the next stop."

"Okay." I end the call and turn to my family. "He's coming to us."

There's a big cheer, and my mom starts chanting, "He's coming to us! He's coming to us!"

My sisters jump up and down and hug me, and it's like a party —a love confession birthday Christmas Eve party.

THIS HAS TO BE THE LONGEST EIGHT MINUTES OF MY life. We're huddled together at lift four, holding our breath every time a new gondola goes by.

"What if he doesn't come?" Rick asks. "What if he leaves you here on this mountain?"

"Rick, you're being awfully annoying tonight." My mother frowns.

"I agree." I glare at him.

"I see him!" Hailey yells, pointing at the next gondola and we instantly forget about Rick and his annoying comments.

Caleb stands by the door with a couple making out on the bench behind him. Talk about being the third wheel.

"Summer, are you nervous? Juliet shakes my shoulders. "What are you going to say?"

"I don't know." I haven't even had a chance to think about what I wanted to say. I was so focused on just finding Caleb that I didn't even gather my thoughts, and now it's too late. I'll have to wing it.

The doors of his gondola open, and he steps out, walking to me. I love the confident purpose in each of his strides as if he knows exactly what he wants. And what he wants is *me*.

"Don't make him go the whole distance. Go to him." My mom pushes me, and I stumble forward a bit but meet him in the middle.

"Are you engaged to Justin?"

"No, I—" I start to say, but Caleb scoops me in his arms, hugging me to him. I don't think we've ever hugged before—not for real, not without any rules or boundaries.

It's so freaking amazing.

His grip around me tightens, and in his arms, I feel more wanted than I ever have in my entire life.

My family cheers behind us, but all I focus on is Caleb's soft whispers in my ear. "I really hope that you came here for me and not the Torchlight Parade, or else I'll feel really dumb."

"I came here for you." I smile, pulling back so I can see his face. "Caleb, I—"

"Yes," he says.

"Yes, what?"

"Yes to whatever you're about to say."

My brows jump, and I can't hide my grin. "But you don't even know what it is."

"If you really came here for me, then nothing else matters. I'm yours. Whatever you want."

My smile stretches wide. "You're mine?"

"I always have been, from the moment you kissed me that night in the kitchen."

"And I'm done playing it safe." I pause because this moment feels big. "I love you, and I want us to be together. And I'm sorry—"

Caleb grabs my coat, jerking my body forward into a kiss. It's surprising and exhilarating all at the same time. The want behind his tug and the desire in how his mouth covers mine makes everything in my body dance with happiness. By the way my family screams and cheers behind us, you would think they were in the middle of a Taylor Swift concert. But I don't even care. I'm devoted to every second of Caleb's tender kiss.

The sweetness is genuine. The passion is electric. And the butterflies are strong.

This is how a kiss is supposed to feel.

For the longest time, I felt like my kisses were gestures Justin didn't need.

But Caleb makes it seem like I'm giving him life.

I forget about the things I should say or want to say and freely kiss him back. Fireworks go off above us—like real fireworks, not the kind in my body—and the crowd around us cheers. It must be the start of the Torchlight Parade, but I don't even care to stop kissing Caleb and look.

For all the times I fought my feelings, hid them away like they could be ignored and forgotten, I'm not doing it anymore. I press my body to his, feeling the warmth of his mouth as his lips brush over mine.

The crowd applauds even louder, and more fireworks go off. We both turn our faces toward the mountain, momentarily breaking apart. Skiers fly down the mountain, lighting each torch, one by one, until the entire zig-zag ski slope glows with firelight.

You couldn't plan a more romantic backdrop if you tried.

"It's beautiful," I whisper as Caleb holds me close.

"You're beautiful." He kisses my lips one more time, soft and sweet. "I haven't been able to tell you that nearly as much as I've wanted to."

I nudge his shoulder, gazing into his eyes. "I'm the one that should be telling you things, like how I shouldn't have turned you down last week. I was stupid and taking the easy way out, thinking somehow that I owed it to Justin to stay with him because that's what was fair. But I want you. I've wanted you since the night you stood in my parents' kitchen with your forearm up a turkey, making everyone laugh. And then again, when you started a chant for Donna O'Day during the Light Parade. And when you got me kicked out of the grocery store and a hot spring. The more time I spend with you, the more parts of you I find that I love. You're everything that I've wanted since I was a little girl. And I'm not saying all of this because I can't stand being alone or not having a significant other in my life. I'm saying it because I want to experience new things by your side. It isn't about not being alone. It's about being *with* you. Like you said, falling for you was easy, but admitting that I loved you was hard. I just didn't want to hurt Justin."

"But you told him?"

"I told him everything."

"And how did he take it?"

"You're right. He'll be okay."

"He might not like me for a while." He grimaces.

"Yeah, family dinners could be a little awkward at first, but we'll get over it."

"I can't believe you're here." He cups my cheeks with his frozen hands. "Happy birthday."

I smile, forcing his hands to move with my giant grin. "It is my birthday."

"I got you something." He drops his hands, reaching into his pocket.

"You got me something?"

"Of course."

"And you have it with you?"

"I know." He shakes his head. "It's weird that I've just been carrying it around with me on the off chance that I would see you. But I wasn't exaggerating when I said I'm yours. Even when I thought you didn't want me, I was still yours." He creates a fist with one hand, grabbing my palm with the other. "Now, this isn't much. I still thought you were Justin's girlfriend when I bought it, but I saw it and thought of you." He opens his fist, dropping two earrings into my hand. I bring them up to my face so I can study them.

"What is it?" my mom calls behind us. "What did he give you?"

I smile, darting my eyes to Caleb. "They're snow globe earrings."

"Because she loves Christmas earrings," my dad explains to anyone in the family who didn't already know that fun fact about me.

"I know it's stupid. But I saw them, and I thought of you, and I haven't seen you wear snow globes yet this season, but obviously, there were a lot of days that I didn't see you, so if you already have some like that, then—"

I stop his rant with a peck. "Thank you. I love them so much."

"What did she say?" Aunt Carma snips. "I can't hear."

"She said she loves the earrings," Juliet tells her.

Caleb eyes my family. "They know about the swap, right?"

"They know." I spin around, gesturing from him to my family. "Caleb, I'd like you to meet my family. Family, this is Caleb. The other Davidson twin."

He gives a little wave. "I'm sorry I lied to you guys."

"You can be forgiven if you wear those cowboy pants again," Aunt Carma says.

"Gladly." Caleb nods at her.

My mom steps forward, grabbing his arm. "You'll be forgiven if you take care of Summer and promise to always make her laugh and bring out her sunny side."

"That's my only goal."

"Then all's well that ends well."

More fireworks light up the sky, and someone in the crowd spontaneously starts singing "O Holy Night." I look around. It doesn't get much better than this.

Caleb must think the same thing, because he leans down for another kiss. We keep this one a little more chaste—you can't make out to "O Holy Night." It just doesn't feel right.

"We did it," I say, letting him wrap me in his arms. "Between the two of us we managed to have the perfect holiday season."

"I think we can do better than this."

I pull back, looking at him with wide eyes. "Better than falling in love at Christmastime?"

"I was miserable the majority of the month because I couldn't be with you. So yes, I think we have a lifetime to do way better than this."

I smile, hugging him to me. "Fine. I'll give you a lifetime of perfect Christmases."

"Hey, Summer," Caleb says, tapping my shoulder. "Isn't that the security guard from the hot springs?"

I glance to where Caleb is looking, and sure enough, it's the same guy. "Yes!"

"He's wearing my snow clothes, and isn't that woman beside him wearing your white snow outfit?"

"I knew he stole them! Should we go get them back?"

"Nah." Caleb slings his arm around my shoulder. "He needs them more than we do."

I glance up at Caleb, seeing the reflection of red fireworks sparkle in his perfect blue eyes. Snowcapped mountains tower over us with magical stars in the moonlit sky. This is everything that I love: family, my birthday, Christmas, and Caleb.

epilogue

CALEB

ONE WEEK LATER

"I CAN'T BELIEVE we're back at the scene of the crime." Summer leans against my chest, giving me the perfect opportunity to wrap my arms around her stomach and hold her close. Her bubble gum shampoo stands out from the smell of the fire burning in front of us. I bury my nose in her hair, breathing in that addictive scent.

She tilts her head, glancing over her shoulder at me. "I would hardly call this ski hut a crime scene."

"It's a place where an illegal offense was committed."

"And just what illegal offense are you talking about?" Her mouth lowers in a frown, and my eyes follow, momentarily distracted by her red, pouty lips.

"We slept together." My words come out so matter-of-factly like the answer is obvious. "When you had a boyfriend."

"Oh, my gosh!" Her elbow jabs me in the stomach before she turns her head to rest it against my chest again. "We did not *sleep* together. We laid beside each other to keep warm with lots of space between our bodies. There's a big difference."

325

"We may have started with space, but that's not how we ended. When I woke up, you were all over me."

Summer's head twists, and she looks at me with wide eyes. "No, I wasn't!"

"You were. I can't say I blame you for cuddling with me." I smirk. "I know how much you wanted me."

Another elbow jabs me before Summer snuggles into my arms. "Cuddling with you was an accident."

"I'm not sure it was an accident on my part." My fingers find hers, tangling our hands together. "And there's something else you should know."

"What?"

"It's a confession."

"Should I be scared?"

"There weren't any other skiers coming that night to the hut. I had every spot reserved."

This admission makes her sit up and twist around to face me. "You little liar!"

The smile on her mouth tells me she's not really upset with me.

"I wasn't trying to lie. I was easing your mind. You might not have stayed if you knew we were the only two staying in the hut together."

"You're right. I wouldn't have stayed." Her face turns solemn. "I have a confession to make as well."

"Should I be scared?"

"I had a schmexy dream about you that night. That's why I woke up."

My smile is instant. "You dreamed about me?"

Now, it's her smile that's instant. "About kissing you."

I don't think anything has ever made me happier.

She playfully punches my shoulder. "Oh, don't look so pleased."

I roll my lips together, trying to play things cool. But the thing is, I'm so in love with this woman I can't play things cool. I can't be smooth or suave or anything. Summer has completely screwed me up. My heart is helpless.

"So I was right." I smile bigger. "This hut is a crime scene. There were dreams and cuddling and—"

She holds her fingers over my lips, stopping me. "I maintain everything was innocently done. I had no intention of hurting Justin."

"I know. Neither of us did. I'm just joking. And I promise Justin will get over it."

"Are you sure? Because things have been so awkward this week."

"He just needs space. That's why we're at a ski hut on New Year's Eve and not at his condo, cuddling in front of the fire. And that's why I just bought a house in Telluride."

A smile falls over her lips. "You bought a house?"

"I did."

"What about your house in Arizona?"

"There's nothing in Phoenix that I want." I gather Summer into my arms, pulling her back into me. "If you're in Telluride then that's where I need to be."

"But what about your job?" She turns her head, trying to look up at me.

"There's plenty of dare devil things to do in Telluride. And, every once in awhile if you want to see the world, we can take a working vacation."

She snuggles in close. "I'd love to see the world with you."

"But tonight, it's just you and me in the middle of nowhere. That's how I want it." I dip my lips down to her ear. "And here, we need to sleep in the same bunk to stay warm."

"Or you could just chop more firewood."

"Why would I do that?" I brush her hair aside so I can kiss her neck.

"Okay, fine." She sighs as my lips graze her collarbone. "You can keep me warm tonight."

That's exactly what I plan to do.

"But first"—she turns her head so her lips hover next to mine —"we have to ring in the new year with a kiss."

Her lips brush against mine, and I don't hesitate to pull her close, taking full advantage of the moment.

SUMMER

Six Months Later
Interlaken, Switzerland

"I can't do it!" I yell to Caleb above the wind and noise. "Jumping out of an airplane is the craziest idea I've ever had."

"No problem." He smiles, and even through his goggles, I see how the action reaches the corners of his eyes. "We'll take these parachutes off, turn the plane around, and spend the rest of the day soaking in a hot tub, looking at the Alps from the ground. Not the air."

I bite my bottom lip as I glance out the open door of the plane. This is scenic beauty at its finest. Crystal blue lakes. Snowy precipes. Stunning glaciers. I'd never be able to experience any of this without Caleb. In the six months we've been together, he's shown me more of the world than I ever imagined seeing. I thought I was living life to the fullest, but he's taken me on a wild and crazy ride that's made me happier than I ever dreamed I could be.

My eyes shift to his.

"Summer, if you want to jump, I'll always be here to catch you."

It's the same thing he said on our first adventure ice climbing, and he's lived up to it every day since.

"Okay, I'll jump with you." I reach my hand out to him, and he immediately grabs it.

His smile grows. "On three?"

I nod. "On three."

"One, two, three!"

I jump, holding hands with Caleb the entire time.

CALEB

Christmas Eve
One Year Later

"DON AND PATSY, AS OUR GUESTS, YOU TWO SIT ON THE COUCH, facing where the kids will put on their nativity play." Janet Stanworth directs my mom and dad to their seats on the sofa.

"We don't need to be Front Row Joe." My dad says that, but he sits down in the front like he intends to stay.

"Look at all these cute costumes!" my mom gushes as she glances around at Summer's nieces and nephews.

Summer smiles at me from across the room as if watching my mom and dad join in on the Stanworth family Christmas makes her as happy as it does me.

Aunt Carma huffs from her recliner. "We didn't do a play last year because *the twin* spilled his punch."

"Aunt Carma, we didn't do the play last year because we went chasing after Caleb, remember?" Juliet smiles at her.

"Eh." She purses her lips, glancing away.

Marty stands in front of everyone, silencing them with his hands. "This year, before we start the play, I'd—"

A hard knock at the door stops him.

329

Jack waves his shepherd's staff in the air. "Bob Irvine!"

"It's not Bob Irvine." Marty walks to the door. "It's Justin and Jordan. They were just running late."

Marty swings the door open. "Justin! You guys made it."

"Hey!" Everyone cheers as they walk into the family room hand in hand.

Jordan gives a little wave. "Thanks for letting us crash your Christmas Eve party. I don't have any family in town and Justin wanted to spend the holidays with you guys."

"It's more than okay." Janet's smile is big and warm. "We've been through a lot with Justin. He's one of us now."

Justin laughs good-naturedly, swinging his arm around Jordan's waist. "Thanks, Janet." His eyes dart to me. "I'm happy to be here."

I smile back at him, grateful he's here too. It's been a rocky year. I'm pretty sure he hated me and Summer for the first few months after she left him for me. There were a lot of unanswered texts and calls, but now everything is back to normal. Actually, it's better than normal. Justin and I are closer than we've been in years and I have Jordan to thank for that.

"Where's Bob Irvine?" Aunt Carma snaps, craning her neck around the room.

"It wasn't Bob Irvine at the door." Juliet places her hand on Carma's leg. "It was Justin and his girlfriend Jordan."

"*The twin* has a girlfriend?" Aunt Carma scrunches her nose. "I don't like it."

Marty waves his hand in Carma's direction, dismissing her. "As I was saying before the knock on the door, this year, we have something special planned before we start the Christmas play." Summer's dad looks right at me. "Caleb, I'm turning things over to you."

Summer's brows drop in confusion. She watches in silence as I walk to her, grabbing her hand. I lead her to the front of the room.

"What are you doing?" Her confused smile makes me smile.

"It's a birthday surprise. I have to top the snow globe earrings from last year."

She touches the dangling jewelry hanging from her ear. "I don't think you can top these. I love them."

"Well, let me try." I drop to one knee, reaching under my pants to where the ring box is hidden in my sock.

The second she sees the velvety red box, she gasps along with all four of her sisters.

"Summer"—I open the box, showing a pear-cut diamond ring—"we've spent an entire year together—gone through every season and experienced living life to the fullest—and I can say with absolute certainty that you are the woman for me. I love you more today than I did one year ago when I saw you pass by me in the gondola. And I'm so happy that I was the wrong *right* brother because you are who I want." Her eyes glisten with tears as she laughs. I glance around, looking at each person in her family before meeting her gaze again. "And I know how much you love everyone in this room and how much they mean to you, so it's only fitting that I ask you to be my wife in front of them. So, Summer Stanworth, will you complete my heart by becoming my wife? Will you marry me?"

She leans down, kissing my lips quickly. "Yes!" She laughs through her tears. "Yes! I will marry you."

I slip the ring on her finger and come to a stand. She jumps in my arms, and I hug her close, lifting her feet in the air.

Everyone claps, and before I lower her to the ground, I kiss her the way I plan on kissing her for the rest of her life.

With absolute adoration.

THE END

also by kortney keisel

Famously In Love (Romantic Comedy)

Why Trey Let Me Get Away

How Jenna Became My Dilemma

The Sweet Rom "Com" Series

Commit

Compared

Complex

Complete

Christmas Books (Romantic Comedy)

Later On We'll Conspire

The Holiday Stand-In

The Desolation Series (Dystopian Royal Romance)

The Rejected King

The Promised Prince

The Stolen Princess

The Forgotten Queen

The Desolate World

acknowledgments

I'm a sucker for love triangles and forbidden love stories. They get me every single time. So, despite the fact that love triangles are known for being one of the most hated tropes, I set out to write the story I wanted to read. Plus, I really love the movie *While You Were Sleeping* and wanted to write something with that same vibe. That's how The Holiday Stand-In started. It's a project that was for me.

Along the way, I realized that I couldn't just write it for myself. I kept thinking about what readers would want or hate...I can't help it. So, while I can handle a lot in fictional stories, I tried to make my love triangle appeal to the masses. I'm not sure if I achieved that, but I worked really hard to walk the line of falling for an identical twin in a way that, hopefully, readers could still love and root for the characters.

I had a lot of help along the way. My sister Stacy is the best. When she's in my corner, I know my book will be better than what I can do alone. Thanks, Stacy, for spending your free time reading my book when you are so busy with your family. You are the world's best grandma, and somehow still find the time to be the best sister/book partner I could ever ask for.

A huge thank you to Madi. I can always count on you to give it to me straight. I rely on your honesty so much, and I know if something passes your approval, then I'm headed in the right direction.

Meredith, you are always so helpful with your ideas and

letting me know what you like or what you wish would happen. Thanks for reading.

Thank you, Chelsea, for your love and excitement over this book. That alone made it so much easier to push through and finish. Your messages made me feel like maybe the story didn't suck. Thank you! Thank you!

Thanks to Kurt, who read the book while on vacation when he could've napped or done pretty much anything else. You are my favorite person in the whole world. Thanks for being my biggest supporter.

Thank you to my readers. I am always floored by how much you love my books. The glowing reviews. The word of mouth. The shares on bookstagram and Facebook. The messages. The emails. It all means so much to me. I couldn't do any of this without you.

I also want to thank Melody Jeffries for this adorable cover and also my editor, Jenn, for getting this book back to me so quickly. I have so many talented women in my corner.

I always end my acknowledgments by thanking my Heavenly Father and Jesus Christ. I say it every single time, but I couldn't finish any book without Their help. I literally pray for words to come, and somehow, they always do.

about the author

Kortney loves all things romance. Her devotion to romance was first apparent at three years old when her family caught her kissing the walls (she attributes this embarrassing part of her life to her mother's affinity for watching soap operas like Days of Our Lives). Luckily, Kortney has outgrown that phase and now only kisses her husband. Most days, Kortney is your typical stay-at-home mom. She has five kids that keep her busy cleaning, carpooling, and cooking.

Writing books was never part of Kortney's plan. She graduated from the University of Utah with an English degree and spent a few years before motherhood teaching 7th and 8th graders how to write a book report, among other things. But after a reading slump, where no plots seemed to satisfy, Kortney pulled out her laptop and started writing the "perfect" love story...or at least she tried. Her debut novel, The Promised Prince, took four years to write, mostly because she never worked on it and didn't plan on doing anything with it.

Kortney loves warm chocolate chip cookies, clever song lyrics, the perfect romance movie, analyzing and talking about the perfect romance movie, playing card games, traveling with her family, and laughing with her husband.

If you'd like to learn about future books and get bonus chapters, sign up for my newsletter at www.kortneykeisel.com. Stay connected with me by following me on Instagram, Facebook, or Pinterest

Printed in Great Britain
by Amazon

32819017R00199